BEV PRESCOTT

Bywater BOOKS

Ann Arbor

Bywater Books

Copyright © 2018 Bev Prescott

Print ISBN: 978-1-61294-135-6

Bywater Books First Edition: September 2018

Printed in the United States of America on acid-free paper.

Cover designer: Ann McMan, TreeHouse Studio

Bywater Books
PO Box 3671
Ann Arbor MI 48106-3671
www.bywaterbooks.com

This novel is a work of fiction. All characters and events
described by the author are fictitious. No resemblance
to real persons, dead or alive, is intended.

For Dirty Bird, a most pugnacious penguin.

METRIC CONVERSION GUIDE

1 Centimeter = 0.39 Inches
1 Meter = 3.28 Feet
1 Kilometer = .62 Miles
1 Liter = 1.06 Quarts

AN INCREASE OF 2^0C IS EQUIVALENT TO AN INCREASE OF 3.6^0F

Scientists estimate that if the Earth's average temperature increases by 2^0C that life on our planet will forever change as we know it. Rising seas, mass extinctions, super droughts, increased wildfires, intense hurricanes, decreased crops, scarcity of fresh water, and the melting of the Arctic are expected. The impact on human health would be profound. Rising temperatures and shifts in weather would lead to reduced air quality, food and water contamination, and an explosion of infections carried by mosquitoes and ticks.

TO CONVERT TEMPERATURES FROM CELSIUS TO FAHRENHEIT, MULTIPLY BY 1.8 AND ADD 32

Temperature Celsius	Temperature Fahrenheit
0^0	32^0
2^0	35.6^0
10^0	50^0
20^0	68^0
30^0	86^0
40^0	104^0
50^0	122^0
100^0	212^0

The boiling point of water at 1 atmosphere of pressure is 100^0C and 212^0F

Chapter 1

"There are too many of us." Eve slipped the silk remnant from her pocket and looked up at Sharon. "We have to find another way. I don't have the strength to fight through the crowd." She wrapped the fabric adorned with the blues, reds, purples, and yellows of long-extinct flowers around her neck.

Sharon pulled her spouse into her arms and kissed her forehead. "I know, my love." She glanced from the ravenous human mass milling in the street to the building towering over them. Blood-red words and numbers scrolled across its solar wall panels, spelling out: *Friday, September 4, 2092, 9:37 a.m., 20⁰C. The City of Boston, Regional Capital of the National Order of North America.*

Eyeing the digital screen, Sharon considered the irony of such a benign description for a place that ate the weakest alive. "I'll find a different road."

Eve's hands shook as she tried to tie the scarf. The ashen pallor of her skin made the presence of cancer in her body obvious. "I'll have more energy once I get a dose of chemotherapy from Dr. Ryan."

"Let me." Sharon curled her fingers over Eve's to still her trembling. "There's a shortcut not too far." She tied the ends of the scarf into a loose knot. "We have to get past the edge of this crowd first. I'll hold you close." She slipped an arm around her and struggled to move them forward against the arrhythmic

1

cadence of Boston's desperate inhabitants. Every cell in her body tuned in to the frequency of sheltering Eve from ugliness and keeping her safe.

A clutch of masked street cleaners pitched another stiff corpse into the back of a lorry-hydro.

"You're going too fast," Eve protested quietly, as Sharon maneuvered them through a tangle of jostling people, each ravenous for space along State Street, near the region's only food distribution center. "I can't keep up."

"I'm sorry, sweetheart." The essence of the dead in the foul stench of the city clawed at Sharon. The reek reminded her that death wanted Eve, too. "We can't slow down, though. It isn't safe here."

To protect Eve, she cloaked her emotions and kept moving. The symbiosis between pain and life dictated that one didn't exist without the other. No matter how much it hurt to see Eve suffer, Sharon kept them running from the dreadful alternative that freedom from pain offered.

A derelict, wide-eyed and stumbling, veered into them, his filthy hands pawing at Eve's body to keep from falling. Eve grunted and struggled to free herself.

Sharon grabbed the frayed collar of his shirt and yanked him from Eve. "Don't touch her," she snapped.

One of his hands curled around the strap to Sharon's satchel. "What is that?" He sniffed the air, and tugged. "Give it to me," he growled. "That smell. It's good. Give it to me, stupid woman."

Panic pulsed through Sharon. One man she could handle. But she didn't stand a chance against a crowd of starving people keyed in to the notion that food might be in her satchel. "I don't have anything." She lifted him to eye level. "Let go—or I'll hurt you."

"Give it to me." Spit bubbled at the corners of his mouth. The pointed end of a shiv tipped from the open pocket of his coat.

Sharon stared into his milky eyes, searching for a reason not to harm him. "I said let go. If you don't, you'll regret it." She mourned the little piece of her soul that would be lost with all the other little pieces if he forced her to make her point. But like water, food and shelter, violence kept her and Eve alive in an unforgiving world. She'd pay whatever the price to keep Eve safe.

"Fuck you," he snarled, and slapped her face.

Sharon put a hand to her stinging cheek as he reached for the shiv.

"No!" Eve cried.

"I warned you," Sharon said through gritted teeth. She rammed the heel of her boot hard into the side of his knee. Bone crunched as his leg snapped into a grotesque angle.

Clutching the hem of Sharon's jacket in his dirty hands, he shrieked and crumpled at her feet.

She shut his agonizing screams out of the fragile part of her heart, and pushed his hands away. An urgency to get Eve to safety and the medicine that kept her leukemia contained drove Sharon past the disgust at what she'd done.

"Wait." Eve reached for the man writhing and moaning on the ground. "You broke his leg. We can't leave him."

"He didn't give me a choice. We have to keep going." Sharon took Eve's hand. "You're my worry. Not him, nor anyone else."

Eve glanced over her shoulder. "He needs help."

"We don't have any to give." Sharon searched for a way through the twisted tangle of people unfazed by the bawling man. "Just a little farther. Please, let's keep moving." To support more of Eve's weight, Sharon pulled her close and wove through the throng.

Graffiti-covered buildings battered by war and storms flanked them. Jagged fingers of broken glass jutted from rotting window sills, all of it reminders of the time before relentless storms, disease, and human conflict ripped the world apart. The couple stepped over and around trash picked clean of calories by starving people and animals alike.

Soldiers prowled the streets in pairs, fingers poised above the triggers of their spectralettos. The sleek and steely laser weapons hung from thick braids of parachute cord over their shoulders.

The feeling that she was being watched skittered up Sharon's back. Had the soldiers witnessed her skirmish with the derelict? She scanned for a way through the street heaving with the hungry.

A lanky soldier eyed them from a doorway across the street. The letters *NONA* spread out in gold across a black helmet that sat low on his head. Sharon looked at the ground. Adrenaline surged through her blood. "We can't stop here." She pressed her cheek to Eve's and pushed through the crowd with her shoulder. "If the soldiers notice us, they might want to search my satchel."

The stink of the dying city hitched a ride on each breath, guaranteeing that even after Sharon left this place behind for the sweet earthen scent of her fallow farm, the funk would persist inside of her like a parasite.

Eve's shallow breaths against her neck made Sharon's pulse quicken. She tamped down the urge to scream and shove her way out of the pitiable herd. But going unnoticed by the soldiers or anyone in the swarm of people kept them free to move. Her resolve to protect Eve by delivering her to Dr. Ryan at the gated community on Beacon Hill helped Sharon to maintain her wits.

"Let's rest. Just for a second." Eve tugged Sharon to a stop in front of a stone bench. Taking Sharon's hand, she sat and pulled Sharon down with her. "No one cares about two ragged women. There are thousands of us in the crowd. Besides, I'm worried about you. That man back there. He'll surely die with a broken leg." She put a hand to Sharon's cheek. "Where is the kind farmer who gave me food and a place to rest all those years ago? Where is the woman I fell in love with?"

Eve's questions burned into Sharon like a hot branding iron. "I'm still here." She covered Eve's hand with hers. "Always." Guilt and strength that came from indifference to everyone but Eve warred inside her. "No matter what, I can't lose you. The man back there was already going to die. I only prevented him from taking us with him." The words tasted like shards of glass. She craved the long-lost days when the idea of death existed as a far-off certainty that came for most only after a full life. Now, no one was safe. Ugly and regrettable things had to be done in order to stay alive. "You're all I have left. I love you with my whole heart."

"My sweet farmer. You used to be so kind and trusting." Eve turned Sharon's hand over and kissed her palm. "Don't lose you in order to keep me."

"Please don't think less of me. It's just—kindness and trust killed my parents. Carelessness murdered my brother Mark. And war took my other brother, Jon. I can't let my guard down. You're all I have." Sharon caressed Eve's cheek. "I love you so much."

"And I love you." Eve leaned into her.

Sudden shouting nearby flustered Sharon. She dared to look back at the soldier in the doorway. Relief pricked the bubble of disgust brought by the sight. Someone else occupied the soldier's sadistic notice.

He lifted a cigarette to his lips while the soldier next to him held a spectraletto to the head of a bare-chested man kneeling before them. Blood oozed from the scarlet, ragged hole burned into the man's jaw by the weapon's laser. The soldier's thumb rested on the dial that adjusted the gun's strength. Laughing at their new captive, one of them shot a finger of fire into the other side of their victim's face.

Fear pressed the air from Sharon's chest. "We've got to go. I'll carry you if I have to."

Eve nodded. "I know." The acquiescent turn of her lips into a smile suggested that she'd do the thing she always did for Sharon: draw from her dwindling reserves of strength and keep going.

Toxic guilt bubbled in Sharon's veins. It paled in comparison to grief, though. She tried to escape her simmering emotions by focusing on the present. "Something doesn't seem right today. There are more NONA soldiers than usual. Let's get your medicine and go home." She stood and helped Eve to her feet.

Eve whispered into the side of Sharon's neck. "We'll be okay."

We'll be okay. Sharon turned the words over in her head and clung to the strength that protecting Eve cultivated inside of her. "My Eve, you are my strength." Slipping her hand into Eve's, she made a path forward.

The cacophony of the hungry mob drowned out the shouting

soldiers trying to keep order. Soon the food distribution building's doors would open and rations would be passed out to the thousands of people incapable of feeding themselves. Each person would receive a six-ounce freeze-dried patty of beetle larvae, potato, and kale.

Sharon glanced around for a way through. Behind them, abandoned structures long ago drowned by the rising sea thrust up from the water like trees drowned by a wetland. Their decay, combined with the human waste clogging the Charles River and the stink of the refugee camp on Boston Common left the city washed in filth and disease.

Ahead, the gold dome atop the State House glinted in a ray of morning sun peeking through the overcast sky. NONA soldiers stood along the length of the top of the concrete wall surrounding Boston's only remaining government building, now the regional seat of NONA. Their spectralettos pointed at the voracious crowd. Famine pervaded all the nooks and crannies of the city. Everyone knew hunger and thirst.

"There." Sharon pointed to a narrow empty street leading to Beacon Hill. "The shortcut. We'll have to keep an eye out for Banditti. They don't wait in line for food. They steal it."

"I've got your back." Grabbing the hem of Sharon's jacket, Eve shadowed her into the dimly lit corridor.

Sharon whispered, "It's all I need," and then slipped into the passageway.

Nothing moved in the deserted, garbage-strewn street. A sinister energy oozed through the space. Instinctive reflex had a mind of its own; Sharon put a hand to the flap of her satchel. Closed, but she knew that already. She ignored her analytical inner voice, letting instinct drive. Her gut never let her down.

She unbuttoned her jacket and unsnapped the clasp to the baldric that concealed her claw hammer. With her jacket open, she shivered in the dampness of the dank street. She'd never gotten used to the persistent cool, wet weather that settled over Boston when the melting of Greenland's massive ice sheet shut down the ocean current that brought warmth from the Gulf Stream to the

North Atlantic. When was that? She tried to remember. Five years? Ten?

Sharon felt Eve tremble against her. The cancer that ravaged Eve's body made it hard for her to stay warm. "Beacon is at the end. Dr. Ryan's house will give us a chance to get out of the cold."

The stony structures along the narrow street blotted out the day's indifferent light. Tension vibrated through Sharon as she let her eyes adjust to the relative darkness. A deep breath steadied her jangling nerves. Sight, hearing, smell, touch, and intuition kicked in like an army circling the wagons.

A clicking sound, regular and metallic, stilled her momentum. She studied the space for the source. Her attention stopped on a rusted gutter that slunk over the top of a building and down its flank before curving upward a few centmeters from the ground.

Water dripped in regular succession from its rusted mouth onto a piece of metal refuse. *Tick, tick, tick* like the antique clock that used to hang in her grandmother's kitchen. A dumpster that likely hadn't been emptied for years spilled over with trash. Sharon watched it for signs of movement as they continued past it to the end of the street.

Muted light brightened their route. Just a few more meters to the relative safety of Beacon Hill. Iron fencing that walled off the brownstone buildings of their destination punctuated the end of the alleyway.

Someone small and wrapped ghost-like in a blanket lunged around the corner, blocking their path. Sharon's senses tripped into alarm. "Who's there?" Her hand went to her hammer.

The ghost person let go of the blanket. It fell to the ground, revealing a frail, dirty little boy. He wore frayed cotton pants and an unzipped leather jacket too large for him. Ragged embroidery of a long-extinct United States of America flag dotted the upper right breast pocket. He cupped his hands and said, "Please."

The last person Sharon had seen wearing a United States of America flag had been hanging dead from a broken light-post during the War of Earth's Rebellion, the fourth world war. The United Kingdom of Asia had destroyed what was left of America's electrical grid during the fighting and hanged those who tried to repair it. "Where'd you get that jacket?" Sharon asked. "You know it's considered treason to wear that flag? If NONA soldiers catch you, they'll throw you in jail. Or worse."

"What's your name?" Eve inched toward the boy.

Sharon grabbed Eve's elbow. "Don't trust him." She looked from Eve to the boy and back, wishing she could let her guard down, if only for a second. Let concern for a child smooth out the edges. "Eve, please, be careful."

"It's fine." Eve brushed the boy's black shaggy hair from his eyes. "He can't be more than ten." She crouched to his level and touched the wooden carving hanging from his neck. "Is that a polar bear?"

He scratched his cheek with dirt-caked fingernails and nodded. Grime covered his dark skin and black hair. But his wide brown eyes shone clear and bright.

"He's probably an Inuit refugee." Eve let go of the carving. "Boston's been taking them in for as long as I can remember. Once the permafrost melted and the polar bears and seals went extinct, they had nowhere else to go."

"These days, we're all refugees," Sharon said. "Let's leave him be."

Eve put her hands to her knees and struggled to rise from the boy. "We should give him something to eat."

Sharon slipped an arm under Eve's. "I've got you."

"*Por favor.*" The boy picked up his blanket in one hand while holding the other out. "*S'il vous plaît.*"

Two bright red socks knitted into the weave of the dirty blanket whispered to Sharon of a long time ago. "My grandfather took me to see the Red Sox play when I was your age. You should go find your family. We don't have anything to give you." Taking up Eve's elbow she tried to maneuver past him.

"*Bitte.*" The boy kept pace. "*Asseblief. Anugraha.*" He raced ahead, blocking Sharon and Eve's path. "*Sila.*" He reached for the strap of Sharon's satchel. "*Qing.*"

She caught his wrist, but avoided looking into his eyes. "No."

8

He whimpered and pulled away. "Please."

"I'm sorry," she said. "But no."

Eve put a hand to Sharon's shoulder. "Dr. Ryan won't mind one less apple. Let's give the boy one."

"We can't risk it." Sharon faced Eve, hoping to connect them to the same purpose of moving on without looking back. "The deal with Dr. Ryan is our apples for your cancer treatments. Plus, one boy isn't worth losing our apple tree over."

"He can't be more than ten," Eve repeated. She put a finger beneath Sharon's chin and lifted her head. "There's no way he's ever seen an apple. He won't know what it is. Just one."

"*Silahkan.*" The boy put his hands together as if to pray. "Please."

Eve tilted her head. "What are we if we don't?"

"Alive," Sharon sighed.

Eve caressed the boy's head like a protective mother. "There has to be more to us than alive."

Sharon searched Eve's expression for a way to deny her the act of kindness. But kindness *was* Eve. The line between protecting her and not becoming the weed that choked the compassion from Eve was one Sharon stumbled around, trying not to cross. "I hope we don't end up regretting this." She reached for her bag's clasp. "Just one apple."

Angry voices echoed through the dimly lit street. Sharon wheeled around.

Two men stormed toward them. The taller of the two pulled a long knife from a sheath on his hip. "There's the little fuck that stole my jacket."

Sharon slid in front of Eve.

The one carrying the knife grabbed the boy and shook him. "I'm going to cut your fingers off." The man jostled the boy hard. "You won't ever steal a goddamned thing from me again."

"Please." The boy tried to wriggle from his grasp. "Please." He started to cry.

The man put the knife to the boy's neck. "You're dead, little mutant."

"Leave him alone," Eve ordered.

The two men turned their attention to Sharon, Eve behind her.

Sharon stood straight. Making herself taller, she warned, "Touch him, and I'll take your head off."

"Who the fuck do you think you are?" The shorter of the two men took a step toward Sharon. A crocodile with a gaping saw-toothed mouth was tattooed in the center of his forehead.

To Eve Sharon said, "Go to Dr. Ryan's for help."

The tall man with the knife shoved the boy to the ground and faced Eve. "You just fucked up. You bitch." He pointed the knife at her. "Get that Chinese dumpling before she runs away."

Crocodile-man laughed and went after Eve, who had already stumbled.

"No." Sharon lunged at him. Her claw hammer was concealed in its baldric beneath her jacket.

The tall man sheathed his knife, gripped Sharon by the shoulders with his thick arms and slammed her into the dumpster. The blow stole her breath. She shook her head and got to her feet.

Eve's screams echoed in the enclosed space as Crocodile-man grasped the scarf at her neck. He yanked her to him, and laughed as she kicked and flailed.

"A feisty Chinese dumpling." The tall man with the knife grinned. "Let's have us some fun." He nodded at the man who held Eve against her will. "What do you think?"

"I'm always hungry for a good time." Crocodile-man chomped his teeth at Eve.

The voices and screams around Sharon receded as her anger bloomed. She welcomed the way rage focused her while it bubbled like lava in her belly before exploding without warning. It helped quell the fear that threatened to suck the air from her lungs. She felt its heat snake in through the soles of her feet, up her legs, and down her arm into her hammer at her side.

Her eyes locked on the eyes of the man with the knife.

"Get on your knees," he ordered.

She winced at Eve's cries and complied. The cold, crumbling

concrete cut into the thin cloth of her threadbare dungarees. Submission gave her the edge. The icy steel of her hammer against her gave her confidence.

The man with the knife grabbed a handful of her hair and tilted her head up. "What are you?" He ran the dull side of the knife blade from her chin down to her neck. "You're not quite white, brown, or yellow. I like to know who I'm fucking before I fuck her."

"Do what you want to me, but let her go." Sharon kept her voice steady.

The man slapped her hard in the face. "You answer me."

The sting made her eyes water. "I'm no one." Through the blurriness she noticed the boy curled in a little ball behind the man. The expression on his face matched the familiar one that Eve was wearing. *Empathy.*

The boy mouthed the word, *please.* Then he dove into the back of the man's legs, cutting his knees out from under him.

"Fuck!" The man landed on all fours as the knife bounced from his hand.

In that split-second, Sharon pulled her hammer from its baldric and said, "Hey, asshole."

As the man raised his head, she swung her hammer into his jaw. Bone crackled and blood exploded from the jagged cuts in his flesh. She yanked the tool from his face as he grunted and stumbled back.

She turned to the man holding Eve. "I fucking said let her go."

"I don't think so." Crocodile-man squeezed Eve's neck in the crook of his elbow. Eve gasped and struggled against him, but he was cutting off her oxygen.

"Then I'll kill you." Sharon bumped the clawed end of her hammer against her thigh.

Crocodile-man shoved Eve to the ground. "Come get me, rodent."

The zap of a spectraletto sliced through the commotion just as Crocodile-man lunged at Sharon. She sidestepped fast, and his body collapsed at her feet. A dark red stain spread over the back of his shredded shirt. The shirt itself was blackened and still smoking from the white-hot heat of a laser strike.

Eve caught her breath, then screamed. Sharon's eyes followed her. Three heavily armed soldiers advanced on them, blocking their escape. One of them kicked the body of Crocodile-man as he holstered his handheld spectraletto. A second soldier hoisted Eve to her feet.

"No." Sharon charged the soldier holding Eve. The soldier who'd holstered his weapon slipped a black bag over Eve's head.

"Stop!" A third soldier with a sergeant's insignia on his helmet pointed his weapon at Sharon's chest. His stark white skin contrasted with black hair and a large birthmark on his left cheek. "Drop that hammer and don't move."

The hammer fell from Sharon's hand. The sharp ping of it hitting concrete reverberated around the stone walls. "She's done nothing wrong," she protested, and put her hands up in surrender. "Please, she's done nothing wrong."

Eve slumped against the soldier gripping her.

"I'm begging you, let her go." Sharon eased closer to the sergeant, who kept the barrel of his weapon pointed at her chest. "What could you possibly want with an innocent person?" Words tumbled out of her without any strategy, all in the vague hope that something would resonate with him. "She's very sick. Please, take me instead of her."

A flash of remorse or something like it flickered in the sergeant's eyes before he narrowed them. He squared his shoulders and raised the barrel toward Sharon's head. "We're under orders to take all Chinese enemies off the streets of NONA." He seemed to look through Sharon rather than at her. "By order of the president."

"But she's not Chinese." Sharon held up her wrist making sure that he could see the scar that marked where the government had embedded her identity chip. "Check her status. Check mine. We're both citizens of NONA."

The soldier, now standing next to the sergeant, flipped the safety off of his weapon. "We don't give a shit what the stupid chip in her wrist says. She looks like a goddamned Asian. That's all I need." He put his face close to Sharon's. "So by god, we're taking her. Someone above our pay grade can sort her citizenship out later."

"Sharon," Eve cried, her voice muffled by the bag over her head. "I love you."

"Quiet," the soldier holding Eve said as he squatted and hoisted her over his shoulder like a sack.

Sharon dropped to her knees. Tears rushed past her defenses. "Please." She clasped her hands. "Don't take her. She's my wife. She's sick. She's done nothing wrong."

The soldier next to the sergeant raised the butt of his weapon.

"Don't!" the sergeant yelled too late as hard metal slammed into Sharon's temple. The blunt sting caused her eyes to roll back. Nausea swam in her stomach as her legs went limp. She fell to her side and fought to remain conscious. She tried to make sense of Eve's words as the soldiers stole her away. A hot wave rushed up her neck. Her eyes closed. *Eve.* Blackness.

Chapter 2

Sharon reached through the dank darkness for the woman who tethered her to the living. Her fingers curled around soft fabric. She put it to her face and breathed in. One by one, the scent of Eve flipped her senses to on. Recollection crept into the delusion of her subconscious. Her heart raced. *Eve.*

Instead of lying together in their warm bed, Sharon was alone. Half of her face was pressed against musty concrete, the other half into the scarf. She shivered and curled into a fetal position, hugging the silk. It must've been torn from Eve's neck in the chaos. The memory of her being dragged away by the soldiers sucked the air from Sharon's lungs. *I'll find you, my love.*

She lay still, taking stock of her physical condition. Sharp pain throbbed in her head and upper back. She touched the place where her hair clung sticky and wet to her head. A searing ache repulsed her hand. She struggled to sit but something impeded her. Lying motionless, she let her vision recover. The Inuit boy's blanket wrapped around the lower half of her body came into focus. She kicked it away to avoid becoming host to whatever might be living in the pathetic scrap of wool.

Nausea bubbled in her belly until it boiled over into a gag. Sharon slid her satchel out of the way and lifted herself into a sitting position. With her back against a wall, she leaned to her right side and retched out the meager contents of her stomach. A rustling snapped her into awareness that she wasn't alone. "Who's there?" She wiped her mouth with her sleeve and panted.

"Please." The boy slunk from behind the dumpster. Her hammer lay across his outstretched hands in an offering gesture. "*Bitte.*" Not taking his eyes off the human body heaped near Sharon, he took halting steps toward her.

The body of Crocodile-man lay face down. The fist-sized hole burned into his back by the spectraletto exposed blackened bone and muscle. To make sure he wasn't still a threat, Sharon kicked at him. The corpse rocked slightly and went still. Frothy pink drool hung at the corners of its mouth. Death owned Crocodile-man.

Sharon brushed Eve's scarf against her cheek before tucking it into the pocket of her jacket. "Thank you, boy." She lifted her hammer from his hands and surveyed the alleyway in both directions. A trail of blood meandered in the opposite direction from where the soldiers had stolen Eve. She assumed it belonged to the man whose face she had smashed with her hammer. The thought that he might be nearby, shoring up more Banditti members to seek revenge on the boy, and now her, ratcheted up an anxiety she couldn't afford.

The boy pointed at the crumpled blanket.

"Did you cover me with that?" she asked, trying to direct her mind from another swell of nausea.

He nodded.

"So you do understand." Sharon shakily got to her feet. "Can you say something other than please?" Pain and dizziness menaced her system.

His head moved from side to side in a resounding wordless *no.* He pointed again at the blanket. "*Por favor.*"

"Of course." She picked it up and handed it to him. "We all have that something, or someone, we need to hold onto. And I want my someone back." She leaned against the wall to keep upright.

He clutched the blanket and watched her.

An image of the brightly colored coverlet that lay over the bed she shared with Eve crept into her mind. Her mother, an

Abenaki Indian, had woven it for Sharon when she wasn't much older than the boy. The recollection hurt more than the pain in her head and threatened to obstruct her voice. A hot wave raced up the back of her neck, threatening to stifle her gathering consciousness. She cleared her throat and said, "Thank you for keeping me warm with your blanket. I'm Sharon. What's your name?" She focused on the boy to give her body time to recover.

He shook his head, eyes down.

"Eve said you might be Inuit. If you won't tell me your name, I'll call you Inu for short." One careful move at a time, she wiped blood from the claw of the hammer against her pant leg. "I have to find Eve. Did you see which way the soldiers went?" She secured her hammer in its baldric.

The boy put his fingers to his mouth then pointed at her midsection. "Please."

Sharon's satchel hung heavy at her side. "You could've taken my bag and left me. Why didn't you?" *And why didn't the soldiers who took my Eve?* Pain shot through her shoulder blade as she shifted the satchel. Wary of the throbbing, she slowed her arm and lifted the flap. She put her hand inside and counted. She'd started the day with ten. Ten remained. "My Eve, she's always right. You're just a boy. I thought you were a thief. Maybe you are. But you didn't steal from me when you could've. That means something."

"*Por favor?*" Inu tapped his fingers to his lips. "*Sila.*"

Instinct and better judgment aligned against her new desire to give him something, but gratitude prevailed. "It's what Eve would do," she said as she plucked a small, round apple from the bag. "Thank you for helping me." Her mouth was dry, and moisture might beat back the nausea. "It's not poison like the others." To prove it, she took a bite and handed him the fruit. "Don't tell. Okay?"

Inu took the offered apple and turned it over in his tiny hands. A bruise in the skin caught his attention. He picked at it with the tip of a dirty fingernail. No doubt he would've preferred a gold dimelet, the only tradable NONA currency.

"I promise, you'll be fine." Sharon grabbed the apple from him and took another bite. "If you don't eat it, I will. Because it's better than money." She held it out for him to take. "Be quick, boy, before I change my mind."

One thing Eve had been wrong about was that somewhere along the line the boy must've seen what an apple could do to a human being. Not so much the apple, but the parasite that left behind a lethal toxin similar to cyanide. The common knowledge that one bite came with a death sentence played across his gaunt face. He pursed his lips together as if waiting for the outcome of a battle raging in his head.

"Look, kid. I just swallowed a bite." Sharon put a hand to her hip. "I'm still standing. Either eat it, or give it back. I can't risk leaving you with it if you're not going to finish it. Besides, I don't have time for this. I need to find Eve."

Cupping the fruit in both hands, he put it to his mouth. He opened wide, pierced the apple with his teeth and stood stone still. An enormous grin spread across his face as juice dribbled down his chin. Grunting between swallows, he took ravenous bites until even the core was gone. Only the stem remained between his forefinger and thumb. He flicked it away.

"See? I told you." Sharon let herself relax into the boy's contentment. "My apples are special."

He nodded and pointed at her bag. "Please."

Sharon ran a hand through her unruly mop of hair, tugging it at the end. The prick of pain blunted her sudden impulse to give him all of the apples. The boy's vulnerability heaped a weight onto her too heavy to carry. He should be someone's responsibility. Just not hers. "No more. I'm sorry." She held his expression for as long as she dared. "I have to go. Take care of yourself, and stay away from bad guys."

The smile washed out of his face. "Please." He held out a hand sticky with apple juice.

"No more." Looking at the boy reminded her of a story from the Bible that her grandfather used to read every night. He had always kept the tattered leather-bound volume on his nightstand.

The tale was about a man named Lot whose wife turned into a pillar of salt because she ignored the warning not to look back at the destruction of Sodom.

Sharon felt her body hardening from the inside out. Not because she tarried in the alleyway with the boy, but because she intended to leave him. "I don't have anything else to give you." She looked away and hurried into the gray light of Beacon Street.

The eternally cloudy skies washed the days in melancholy. Eve's absence and the boy's desperation amplified the gloom. Remembering the scarf in her jacket, she retrieved and wrapped it around her neck. Sharon shut out her desire to crumble into a million pieces. Instead, she walked as fast as her battered body would allow toward the tall iron fencing that surrounded Dr. and Mrs. Ryan's home.

With the majority of Boston's inhabitants still occupied at the food distribution center, she moved easily along Beacon Street. When she reached the gated entrance to her destination, she curled the fingers of one hand around an iron post and jammed the forefinger of her other at the intercom button. "Dr. Ryan. It's me, Sharon. I need your help, please." She rested the palm of her hand over a flower design carved into the cool copper plate that decorated the intercom call box.

Eve had identified it as a bird-of-paradise the first time they visited the Ryan home. Sharon, longing to hear Eve's voice, ran a fingertip over its edges. Again she pressed the button. "Dr. Ryan, hurry. Eve's been taken."

Behind the wall of iron bars, the front door to the historic, tidy brownstone flew open. Dr. Ryan, a fair-skinned man, rushed from the house that had miraculously survived decades of storms and war. "Oh, dear," he exclaimed as his long-limbed frame scrambled toward the gate. "I'm coming." He pawed at the key-pad. "Damn NONA for confiscating all of our computers. I should be able to open this thing from inside. We're living in the dark ages while NONA basks in the hallucination that it's saving us from ourselves and terrorists."

On his third attempt, the lock popped open. "Good thing they're too inept to find all of my hidden gadgets. Come in, quickly," he said as he scanned the desolate street.

"They took Eve." Sharon slid inside the protection of the Ryan property as he locked the gate behind them. "NONA soldiers dragged her away."

"Shush." He glanced over his shoulder. "Not out here." He put an arm around her and pulled her close. "Rest your weight on me. You're hurt."

She collapsed against him, letting the strength of his friendship fill in the holes punched into her resilience by the events of the day.

Areva, his wife, appeared in the doorway. "Oh no. We're too late," she said. The slight Taiwanese woman took Sharon's elbow and helped hustle her inside their home dotted with artificial flora tucked into colorful clay pots. It had the feel of a lush rainforest, with plastic reincarnations of long-extinct Asian plants. A Buddha statue embossed in gold sat cross-legged against the far wall. Above him hung an oversized, framed tintype portrait of an ancient Taiwanese King. "I'll get your medical bag, dear." The woman with perfect skin and ebony hair swirled into a tight bun shut the door behind them. As she went to the closet, she moved like fluid in a silk gown adorned in pastels.

"What do you mean too late?" Sharon asked.

"Speaking of my clandestine technology, I sent a drone with a message to your farm this morning." Dr. Ryan eased Sharon into a chair. "You must not have received it in time."

"No." Boosted by a surge of adrenaline and worry, Sharon got up. "Tell me what's going on." A jagged bolt of pain stabbed into her brain, wobbling her. "Dammit." She pinched the bridge of her nose.

"I will. But first tell me what happened to Eve." Dr. Ryan tilted Sharon's head, scrutinizing her injury.

"The NONA thought she was Chinese. They cornered us in the alley off Walnut Street." She looked from Dr. Ryan to Areva. "You have to hide. They're rounding up people of Asian descent without checking identity chips." Fear sharpened her voice. "Eve is sick, and they simply took her. They wouldn't listen."

"We'd heard. That's the message we tried to get to you this morning—that they're rounding up any Asians they spot." Dr. Ryan gestured for her to sit on the sofa situated at a right angle to the chair and table made of chestnut, a long-extinct wood. The well-cared-for antique that had been used for elaborate meals before the world's food supply collapsed was now a makeshift medical table. "Either lie down or sit, please. You look terrible. You have to let me do something about that gash in your head."

"No," Sharon protested. "There's no time. I have to find Eve. Why would they take her?" Her words tumbled out in a stream of consciousness, marking the chaos of the circumstance without her having any idea of what direction to move in order to get Eve back.

Dr. Ryan motioned to the chair. "At least sit for a minute. You don't want to run the risk of infection. Please, let me check your wound. You won't be any good to Eve if you're sick."

Sharon lowered herself into the chair. A sharp sting shot through her upper back when she leaned against it. "Ah," she groaned.

"Do you have pain someplace other than your head?" He asked.

"My back." She leaned forward. "Upper right shoulder. I must've landed on it when I fell."

Areva set the medical bag on the table near her husband. "This can't be happening." She fumbled with its buckles.

Dr. Ryan took one of Areva's hands and kissed the back of it. "It's going to be okay, dear. I promise."

"Tell me what's going on," Sharon interrupted. "You know something more, right?"

"I have an idea. It's just a hunch, but please, let me take a look at you before we get into my theory. I'm worried about you. How'd you get the bang to your head?" Dr. Ryan plucked a pair of gloves from the medical bag and slipped them on.

"One of the soldiers hit me with his weapon," Sharon answered. "It must've knocked me out."

"From the looks of it, he hit you hard." The doctor retrieved a penlight from his bag and clicked it on. Shining the thin thread of light into her right eye, then the left, he said, "Your left pupil is slightly dilated. Can you tell me who the president of NONA is?"

"Of course, it's Miguel Lorenz."

"Good. That suggests the concussion you likely have isn't too bad." He brushed a strand of blood-soaked hair from her forehead. "Now, how long ago would you guess you were knocked out?"

"I don't know." Sharon tamped down her building exasperation. "Your street out front is empty, which means that people are still waiting for food distribution. Maybe I lost twenty minutes or so."

"Where were you when she was taken?" he asked.

"Close. Like I said, they cornered us on Walnut." Instinctively, Sharon tried to stand. "I know you're trying to help. But Eve doesn't have time for this. Tell me why they took her."

Dr. Ryan placed his hands on her shoulders. "I'll tell you everything we know." He maneuvered her back into the chair. "You have my word. But right now, we need to clean and close that cut. There's a lot of nasty stuff out there waiting to infiltrate an open wound." He touched her cheek kindly. "Please."

"It's happening sooner than you thought it would. Isn't it?" Areva said, more as a declaration than question. Her expression was grave as she stared out the window before turning her attention to Sharon. "Let me get you some water."

Sharon writhed in the chair trying to escape the pain. "Please tell me what's going on."

"Very well," Dr. Ryan sighed. "All hell is about to break loose." He moistened a piece of gauze with betadine. "It's the news of the Thwaites." He dabbed at Sharon's cut.

She winced. In spite of the pain, her head felt clearer and clearer. "What about it?"

21

Areva poured water from a filtering-jar into a glass. "You need to hydrate." She handed the glass to Sharon. "From the look of your skin, I'm guessing you haven't had any water to drink today."

Sharon took the offered glass in Pavlovian response. "Not since yesterday afternoon." Ignoring the subtle metallic odor, she gulped the cloudy water, trusting that the filtering-jar had done the job of removing the things most likely to make her sick. "What does the Thwaites have to do with Eve?"

"The collapse of the Thwaites is imminent." He tossed the bloodied gauze into a container. "Military personnel living on Antarctica are being evacuated now. They think that what's left of the Thwaites glacier will go anytime. Most definitely by the time the southern summer solstice arrives. When the Thwaites goes, the entire West Antarctic Ice Sheet will slide into the ocean."

"They've been threatening that for years," Sharon said. "What difference does it make now? With the collapse of the North Atlantic Oscillation, how much worse could things get?"

"Catastrophically worse." Dr. Ryan cut the top off of a tube filled with synthetic bio-glue. "It may be the last nail in the coffin for humanity." Sharon felt his gloved finger spread the material along her torn skin. "We received notice about it from NONA last night."

"Orders," Areva corrected him bitterly. "Orders in the form of notice."

"What does all of this have to do with Eve?" Sharon closed her eyes as the doctor pinched her cut closed and held it until the glue dried.

"So much of Boston, like the world's other cities, has been slowly drowning in the rising seas. When that ice sheet slides into the ocean, it will create what's known as the Extinction Wave. It will obliterate all remaining life in this city. Other coastal cities will drown as well. It will be the kind of flood not seen since old Noah built his ark. The deluge will usher in the world's fifth world war. Nation will destroy nation over what paltry resources will remain. I worry it will be called the End of Times War, quite literally." He let go of her cut, dabbed at it, and stepped back. "The sea will instantly rise at least another three meters. Humanity has always had a little time to adjust by getting to high ground. Not with this one. To make matters even worse, it will not recede in our lifetimes."

"Or that of our grandchildren's grandchildren," Areva added as she repacked Dr. Ryan's medical bag. "Assuming, of course, any of us will be left to bear children."

"Why the hell is NONA not telling us?" Sharon pressed a hand to her throbbing head. "So that we could get out of the way before it happens?"

"Because," Areva said, "it will mean fewer mouths to feed."

"So you're saying NONA is sentencing us to death. Why would they bother taking Eve then?" Sharon asked.

"They aren't taking any chances that anyone who might be an enemy survives the deluge that's coming." He pulled off the gloves and stepped on the foot pedal on the aluminum can. The can's lid snapped open with a clang, and he tossed them inside. "Like my darling wife."

"I don't understand." Sharon shook her head. "Areva is no more an enemy than Eve. They're both citizens."

"I suspect that NONA isn't taking any chances since the new prime minister of the United Kingdom of Asia has had his army drop propaganda pamphlets from drones all across NONA, urging people of Asian descent to rise up for the motherland. NONA must assume anyone of Asian descent is capable of being seduced by Prime Minister Tang. He's a very charismatic demagogue, hell-bent on convincing Asian people to betray NONA for what's left of its dwindling resources." With his thumb, he spun his wedding ring around and around his finger. "We received orders yesterday that we are to report to the Asian internment camp in Chicago."

"I've been ordered to register there in person," Areva said. She squeezed her husband's hand. "You always fidget with your ring when you're nervous. You're making me worry." She turned to Sharon. "The only reason NONA didn't yank me from the streets like they did Eve is because my husband is a doctor."

"Eve is sick. I have to get to her now." Sharon jumped to her feet. "I'm going to Chicago to get my wife back before it's too late." The quick movement brought a wave of dizziness. She gripped the edge of the table to steady herself.

"Listen to me," Dr. Ryan said. "I'm confident that once NONA checks Eve's identification and learns that she's a well-respected botanist, they'll take care of her."

"Why would they?" Sharon asked. "You just told me they think she's an enemy."

"Because," Dr. Ryan said, "she's a scientist. That makes her an asset. As for you, you have to go back to your farm in Maine where you'll be on high ground. Wait things out. Give yourself plenty of rest in order to heal that concussion. Believe me, you don't want it to worsen. You'll be safe at home. Let Areva and me find Eve."

"No." Sharon rubbed her temples, trying to clear the wisps of fog from her head. "I'm going with you. I can't just sit back and wait."

"We'll find her," Areva said. "We will."

"And when we do, we'll bring her home," Dr. Ryan added. He rapped his knuckles on the table. "We have contacts within the government who will help us."

"Then bring me with you."

"No. We don't want to arouse suspicion. The authorities are expecting just Areva and me." Dr. Ryan reached underneath the table and retrieved a silvery metal case the size of a small over-night bag. "Besides, now is not the time to leave your farm." He placed the case on the table in front of her. "When that glacier goes and the ice sheet behind it slides into the ocean, chaos and anarchy will reign. And the United Kingdom of Asia will use its military to take over what's left of the Manitoba grasslands. It'll be one of the last places left on earth suitable to grow food for thousands of people. You need to protect your apple tree and whatever else you have there that keeps you and Eve fed."

Sharon felt the urge to tell him what she'd never told anyone. To come clean about the secret that she and Eve kept from the world. But the secret was also a pact between her and Eve. "When do you expect to come back?"

"As soon as I register, and we find Eve," Areva said.

"What if they won't let you leave?" Sharon asked.

"All they want is for us to register Areva in person. As long as I pledge to be responsible for her loyalty to NONA, they'll let her stay with me." Dr. Ryan opened the case. "While we're away, I need your help."

Sharon put a hand to her unsettled stomach. "What do you need me to do?" Her gut begged her not to put Eve's safety in the hands of anyone other than herself. Dr. Ryan had never let her down, though. His contacts within NONA might be her only hope of getting Eve home safe and sound. It was all so complicated.

"You trade apples for medicine." He turned the open case to face her. "I trade medicine for supplies for Areva and me. This little titanium case is all that I have left, including the synthetic molecule that I use to make Eve's cancer treatments. I can't bring it to Chicago with me. NONA will surely confiscate it. Maybe even put me in jail for having it."

"But what about your contacts?" Sharon asked. "Won't they protect you?"

"Their protection only goes so far." He explained the contents of the case: an SComCat phone; six 30-milliliter syringes filled with Eve's medicine, Sprucanidone; a vial of the synthetic molecule to make it; and a wide assortment of other medications in small glass vials and dark brown pill bottles. "That medication is every bit as dangerous to be walking around with as your apples," he concluded. "I can't take the risk of having it with me."

"We can't leave it here, either," Areva added. "As soon as we're gone, NONA will search our home."

"Take it." Dr. Ryan snapped the case shut and pushed it over to Sharon. "You have your apple tree that needs to be kept safe. I need you to keep this supply of medicine safe as well. Hide it on your farm. Try to rest so that you heal quickly. We're all going to need our strength and health to survive what's coming. Wait for us to find Eve."

Sharon studied the shiny, hard case. The Sprucanidone-filled syringes inside of it kept Eve alive. So did the apple tree. But the idea of leaving the work of finding her spouse to someone else pressed in on her. "I don't think I can."

"You must," Dr. Ryan cut her off. "If you leave your farm unattended, it will most certainly be overrun by Banditti."

"They're opportunistic criminals." Areva paused as if remembering something terrible. "They'll tear your farm apart."

"And if the Banditti don't get in, the Yěxìng will." Dr. Ryan's eyes narrowed. "You and I both know what those feral humans are capable of. You need to protect your farm so that you can provide for Eve when she's returned to you. What good would it be to find her, only to see her starve because you've lost your farm and that precious tree?"

"And the medicine." Areva touched Sharon's arm. "We love you. You've been like daughters to us. Now more than ever, we need to help each other to survive."

"Let us find Eve. You keep our medicine and your food supply safe in the meantime. Is that a deal?" He reached into his vest pocket. "Here's a contact number. If you need to reach me, use it. But only if it's an emergency. As for the SComCat inside the box, turn it on every day at six in the evening for exactly thirty minutes. Even when it's off you can still tell the time by running your finger over the clock icon. The satellite that it communicates with scrambles signals every day at six ET. If I need to call you, that's when I'll do it so that our conversation can't be intercepted. Otherwise, keep it off and hidden."

Sharon took the small square of fragile, yellowed note paper. She hadn't touched paper in years. It felt brittle between her fingers.

"Hide it on your person where it won't be lost." Dr. Ryan resumed twisting his ring around his finger with his thumb. "It's the only way you'll be able to reach me."

Sharon folded the note and tucked it in between her leg and boot. The heavy leather boots on her feet had belonged to her mother. They were as rare now as paper, which had become obsolete in the wake of technology that replaced books in the years before Sharon was born. She touched the scarf at her neck for strength. "I'm scared."

"We are too," Areva said.

"Please bring Eve home." Sharon swallowed a rush of gloom and worry. "She's everything to me."

"I promise you." Dr. Ryan took her hands in his own. His eyes were kind and reassuring. "We will all be together again soon. For now, you should go. We haven't much time. Anyone left in the city when that glacier gives way will die."

"Do you have your solar-bike?" Areva asked.

"I do. It's hidden in some brush on the outskirts of the city so the Banditti don't see it." Sharon calculated time in her head. If she cut through the alleyway, she could shave off several minutes getting out of the city. Something other than time dictated her route, though. Without a second thought, she planned to take the Inuit boy to safety. If, that is, he was still in that alley, and she could find him.

"Thank you." Sharon lifted the flap of her satchel and felt around inside for two of the largest apples. "Take these for the road." She set the perfect red fruit on the table. "Please, bring my Eve home. If you do, I'll make sure neither of you ever go hungry."

Chapter 3

Sharon's right knee bounced. Anticipation of hearing from Dr. Ryan gradually replaced the headache she'd been nursing since leaving the city. Turning her eyes to the boy, she said, "You must have someone somewhere." She pressed the button on the sleeve of her shirt. The tiny clock imbedded in the cuff lit up with LEDs marking the time at 5:35 p.m. *Twenty-five more minutes.*

Inu sat mute in a chair facing hers. With his hands clasped together in his lap, he looked everywhere but at Sharon.

"I can't take care of you. But I'll help you get home, wherever that is." The titanium box rested on the floor at her feet. "I have to go wait for a private call in a few minutes. So start talking."

The boy's petite bare feet dangled a couple of inches from the scuffed faux-wood floor. Outside, near the barn's outdoor shower, the ragged nylon shoes, shorts, and contraband jacket he'd arrived in lay in a clump. The canvas pants and shirt she'd directed him to dress in after he showered fit loosely, but well enough with the hems rolled up several inches. Strands of freshly washed hair stuck to the sides of his face.

She laid the baldric and hammer on the kitchen table. The chair she sat in, weakened by decades of cradling members of Sharon's family, creaked under her weight. The sound of it wound around them, filling in the void. "I want to help you, but you're not making it easy." The snug fifty-five-square-meter house she'd cobbled together with scraps of building materials loomed, cavernous without Eve.

The boy picked at a loose thread on his sleeve.

Impatience fanned the flames of her growing frustration with his stubborn silence. "I don't take in strays. There isn't enough room." She cringed at the irony of the deception and truthfulness of her words. She could make space for a lonely kid in her house, sure. It was something she and Eve had always planned. But over the years, grief and loss had cemented over any gap left in her heart to love someone other than Eve. "But I also don't want anything bad to happen to you. So talk to me. Come on. You have to."

Glancing up, his dark brows furrowed. He seemed to be looking at something on the wall behind her. She knew what was there: an old photograph of a group of people standing in front of a two-story clapboard farmhouse. "That's my family." She turned and lifted its copper frame from the wall. "Well, it *was* my family. They're all gone now, except for me." She placed it on the table. "Eve is my only family now."

Inu put his forefinger on the image of Sharon as a baby swaddled in the arms of her mother, a dark-skinned woman with a long black braid that hung over her shoulder. Baby Sharon clutched her mother's braid. They and the rest of the family huddled happily together on the porch of that big, beautiful home, all of them unaware of the horror to come when Earth's backlash against humanity would plunge the world into chaos.

"That's me with my mom." She touched the glass. It held the auras of those she'd loved with every cell of her body. "The two boys were my brothers, Jon and Mark. The guy with the red beard and freckles was my dad, and him, well . . ." She pointed at the striking black-skinned man with a beautiful smile standing by her father. "That's Elliot. He was our beekeeper and my dad's best friend—until he wasn't. He betrayed my family and got my parents killed. It's too long a story to tell here." She swallowed the bad taste of Elliot's memory. After all these years, thinking of him still tasted like drinking poison. "These were my grandparents. My great-great-grandfather built the farmhouse they're standing in front of in 1986."

Inu pointed at the two-story clapboard building in the photograph, then up to the ceiling over their heads.

"The old farmhouse?"

He nodded.

"It used to be right where we're sitting. I had to burn it down during the War of Earth's Rebellion." She shrugged. "I built this shack in its place. You weren't even born yet. It was the war that came after the third world war called the Second Crusade. While people were fighting over whose religion was best, Earth was gearing up to have the last say. Unfortunately, she's not done with us."

He pointed at the woodstove near the far wall.

"Ever seen one of these?" Sharon asked. "It's an antique Jotul that's been in my family for one hundred and twelve years. My parents used it to keep warm during snowy winters. But then winter stopped coming. Eve and I use it to boil water and heat food."

A shadow of sadness moved across her companion's face before his expression hardened. He pushed the framed photograph away.

"What is it, boy?" Sharon lifted the frame from the table and returned it to its place on the wall. "Why did that hit a nerve?"

White-knuckled, he gripped the arms of the chair and scrutinized the floor.

A splinter of empathy pierced her frustration. "I'll do what I can to help you. But you need to help yourself. We're not getting anywhere with you not talking."

His eyes filmed over with tears and his lips quivered.

Sharon put her hands to his. "It's okay." Her throat tightened. "You're not alone. Terrible things have happened to all of us. If you tell me what happened to your family . . ." She gathered her courage. "I'll tell you what happened to mine."

He shot up and bolted from the chair. Slipping behind the ladder to the loft, he cowered.

Sharon recognized the tearless mask of anguish that covered

his face. It matched the one she often wore to conceal her own sorrow and fears. Like the shells of the walnuts that used to drop from the now-dead tree out back, her hard exterior protected the soft vulnerabilities inside. "I'm sorry, Inu."

His watery eyes closed, and he pressed his head to a rung. A fat tear splashed to the floor.

"I don't know what to do to help you." The clock alarm in the cuff of her sleeve vibrated. "I can't do this right now." His grief tugged at her like a deadly undertow. Fear of being swallowed by it blunted her desire to pull him into her arms.

Behind the ladder, Inu's body slid down the wall coming to a sitting position. He wrapped his arms around bent legs, hugging himself tight.

"I'm going to the barn." She briefly considered bringing him with her. But if he discovered her secrets, he'd be hers to keep. Instead, she got up and opened the blanket chest near the sofa in the middle of the room. It had been one of the many items she'd pulled from the farmhouse before she set it ablaze. "But I'll be right back."

She rifled through the contents of the chest until she found her mother's sketchbook and colored gel pencils. Made of a composite wax and silicone paper, the resilient pages of the book had stood the test of decades. She flipped through the pages until she came to one she thought he might like. It was her favorite. She held up the drawing of a black-eyed Susan. "You can't not smile when you look at this, don't you agree?"

Inu peered at her from behind the ladder. Subtly, he nodded.

She unclipped a couple of blank pages from the back of the book and picked up the box of pencils. "My mom drew pictures when she was sad. It reminded her of things that made her happy." She laid the pages and pencils on the couch. "Why don't you draw me a picture while I'm gone?" She grabbed the baldric and hammer from the table and slipped the strap over her shoulder. "Anything you want. Whatever comes to mind."

Curiosity replaced the sadness on his face. He crawled from behind the ladder.

"Good boy. I'll be back in a little while. You stay put." She picked up the titanium box and slipped out the back door toward the barn.

Sharon took in the bright orange glow of the setting sun at the horizon. But for the looming red structure of the leaning barn and bedraggled ancient apple orchard behind it, there was no evidence that the place had once been one of the most profitable farms in southern Maine. Up on the hill where her grandfather's favorite black walnut tree had used to reign over the orchard below, a knotty overgrown pine forest elbowed out anything else trying to grow.

In the distance, black specks flitted in and out of the hollow trunk of the walnut tree. Any living thing that got close enough realized before dying that the black specks were Africanized honeybees. Elliot was the only person who'd ever been able to survive their stings, or charm them.

She preferred the fallow, destitute look of the two hundred-plus acres that had been owned by her family since the mid-1900s. Neither a drone flying overhead nor a feral Yěxìng foraging for food, nor an opportunistic Banditti would have a clue that a luscious farm existed underfoot. Nor would they know that the forest camouflaged tens of thousands of electricity-generating solar panels shaped like pine needles on branches. Sprayed with a chemical containing a molecule isolated in 2043 from honeybee propolis, the trunks stood forever preserved in time.

Sharon slipped a hand into the pocket of her canvas dungarees and pressed the button on the palm-sized transmitter tucked inside. Her brother, Jon, had designed and built it to remotely control the farm's technology. The day he finished it, he declared the transmitter to be the Queenbee. The name stuck. On cue, the lifelike fiberglass owl in the cupola at the top of the barn came to life. Its head moved almost imperceptibly, as if taking in the view of the landscape. Sharon removed Queenbee from her pocket to make sure the image seen by the owl also displayed on Queenbee's viewport.

Through the viewport, she studied the expanse of the pine forest that hid the solar arrays. As the owl swiveled its head, the view changed to the trees in the bedraggled orchard bent under the weight of inedible apples, except for that one special tree only she and Eve could identify. Beyond forest and orchard lay an impenetrable tangle of Japanese knotweed and kudzu, two invasive species that had thrived in the decades of intense warming brought on by the change in Maine's climate.

Even though the owl's lenses revealed no one within miles of the farm, she looked over her shoulder to be sure. Her scrutiny landed on her small home constructed out of scavenged materials. Perched on cinder blocks, the space underneath protected the home from rodents, snakes, insects, and flooding. Through the window, she observed Inu with his head bowed in concentration, hopefully drawing a revealing picture that spoke to the whereabouts of his family. The likelihood that the boy was alone in the world nagged at her.

She turned, tucked Queenbee into her pocket, and slid the barn door open. Except for a few pieces of rusted farm equipment and her solar-bike, the musty interior was empty. She crept inside and shut the door. Three durable pine trunks stripped of bark held up the sagging ceiling along the center of the roof. On balance, she preferred the risk of the ceiling caving in on her hidden solar-bike to a Banditti easily discovering its existence. Given that her fingerprint started the bike's ignition, they'd take the bike and her hand as well.

She went to the southwest corner of the barn and stood in front of a rubber rug. With the toe of her boot, she pushed the rug aside. Underneath, three polycarbonate tiles indistinguishable from the slate tiles that surrounded them each had a thumb-sized circle etched into them. Hers was the one on the far left, then Eve's and Jon's. She bent at the knees and pressed her forefinger to her circle. The tiles whirred to life and slid open. Before climbing down, she looked again over her shoulder. Nothing moved.

Carrying the titanium box in one hand, she scrambled down the six iron rungs that led to the clandestine underground farm. Reaching into the space above her head, she slid the rubber rug

33

over the opening and pressed her thumb to the underside of the tile below her circle. All three tiles slid closed, shutting out the light. She reached into her pocket and pressed a second button on Queenbee. A small array of white LEDs lining the corridor came to bright life.

Before letting the rank blue-cheese smell of the grout that lined the walls and tunnels assault her nostrils, she took several big breaths through her mouth. Two things had come out of the War of the Second Crusade: the total destruction of American agriculture and transportation systems, and the discovery of the micoriden molecule.

In order to completely destroy the United States, the United Kingdom of Asia targeted U.S. agriculture and transportation infrastructure with bombs. In response, the U.S. government discovered that when mixed with salt water, micoriden formed a grout that hardened enough to withstand extreme weight and prevent energy transfer; that is, the material was a great insulator. Although too late to save the country, the discovery was used by its successor, NONA, to build high-speed transportation tunnels underground that were undetectable by heat-seeking drones. In the chaos from the aftermath of the war, Sharon and her brothers had easily stolen enough micoriden and other supplies to construct the underground farm.

She dropped Queenbee into her pocket and checked the clock on her cuff. In another seven minutes, Dr. Ryan would be expecting her to power up the SComCat. She hoped, anyway. The one thing she wanted to hear more than Dr. Ryan saying that he'd found Eve safe and sound was to hear Eve's voice.

The sixty-one-meter-long tunnel in front of her sloped upward to a tangle of kudzu at the top of the hill. To her right, the second of the two tunnels led to the underground farm. Choosing the latter, she took long fast strides through the fifteen-meter-long tunnel that sloped steeply downhill nine meters lower than its entrance underneath the barn. Humidity and warmth spilled from the opening of the growing room.

Sharon turned the corner into the thirty-square-meter room.

She was met by the soft purple glow from the blue and red lights used to grow the plants stacked in trays five meters high. She breathed in the heady scent of flourishing vegetables and fruits: tomatoes, kale, spinach, potatoes, squash, onions, eggplant, beans, pumpkins, and strawberries. A large food dehydrator rested in the corner next to a tall ladder. Next to it sat a desiccator-storage bin containing dried produce.

Hidden in the hollow of the dead walnut tree, an airtight container pressurized with argon contained their collection of heirloom seeds and genetic material extracted by Eve from the apple tree. The colony of Africanized honeybees lived in the tree, too. Nothing that breathed got past the resilient bees that guarded home and queen with their lives.

The thriving plant life filled Sharon with strength. While she longed for the days when she could plunge her hands into rich soil kissed by sun and rain, she felt grateful for these lush green beauties that sustained her and Eve. As a farmer's granddaughter, daughter, and farmer herself, Sharon always paid attention to the needs of trees and plants. When the rest of the human population had come apart during the War of Earth's Rebellion, Sharon, her brothers, and Eve kept paying attention.

In the tradition of her mother's Abenaki ancestry, Sharon believed the apple tree had been Earth's gift in response to her family's devotion to nature. By paying attention, they managed to find what they needed to build the underground oasis that included the plants, lights, and reclamation system that continuously recycled moisture, carbon dioxide, oxygen and other nutrients.

Sharon went to Eve's lab bench, laid the titanium box down, and snapped it open. She pressed the clock button on her cuff. Lifting the SComCat from the box she counted down the minutes toward 6 p.m., the time Dr. Ryan had instructed her to turn it on so they could—with any luck—communicate.

Inu's shouts of alarm, however, came at 5:59.

She yanked Queenbee from her pocket and scanned its viewport while flipping the SComCat switch to "on." Rotating the

35

thumbwheel below the screen to turn the owl's head, she perceived a beat-up black hydro-van approaching the house. She turned up the volume on Queenbee in order to hear better what the owl was hearing. Again, Inu screamed.

"Dammit," she muttered.

Two Banditti, a woman and a man, burst from the van as Inu ran out the front door of Sharon's house. The woman grabbed him by his hair. "Tell me where your people are."

Inu shook his head side to side.

"Check the barn," the woman ordered her companion.

"This can't be happening," Sharon whispered. "Not now." She continued to watch the Banditti while listening for the SCom-Cat to come to life with Dr. Ryan's voice.

The man, with spiked hair and a fraying vest, stormed into the barn. Beneath the open vest he wore a T-shirt with the letter S across the chest like some ghoulish mutant superman.

The woman stood outside and shook Inu hard. "And if you continue to refuse to answer my questions, I'll cut your tongue out." The tall blonde, in a trench coat that unsuccessfully concealed a baldric, jostled Inu like a rag doll.

Struggling against her, the boy whimpered. The remote microphone picked up everything. A solidarity with Inu bloomed in Sharon at his refusal to answer.

Super-ghoul-man blustered from the barn. "Hey Mags, there's a solar-bike inside. Nothing else, though, except some bullshit junk."

"I want that bike." Mags' words oozed out nasty and hard. "I'm guessing the sneaking asshole who can start it isn't far." She unsheathed a long knife from the baldric. "Wherever you are, asshole," she yelled, "you got ten minutes to show yourself." She shook Inu. "If you don't, I'm going to cut off your little shit's hand."

Inu tried to wriggle from her grip.

Mags drew the point of the knife across the back of his wrist. A stream of red blood oozed from the slice.

Brave Inu held still.

The kid needed Sharon's help as much as she needed to hear from Dr. Ryan that Eve was safe. *Fuck.*

"One way or the other, I'm going to get a hand today." Mags waved the knife.

"Goddammit! Ring already." Sharon picked up the silent SComCat and held it to her chest before shoving it into the outside pocket of her jacket.

Inu's scream blew from Queenbee's speaker, followed by Mags' voice reminding her that time ticked down.

Sharon turned the volume down and dropped Queenbee into her pocket, then bolted uphill through the tunnel to the space beneath the barn. Footsteps and rustling overhead prevented her from exiting where she'd entered. Instead, she raced through the second tunnel to the exit in the kudzu at the edge of the forest.

She scrambled up the exit's iron rungs and pressed her finger over the etched circle that matched her print. Again, tiles slid open. Above lay a knot of green that concealed the opening. Sharon checked Queenbee's viewport. Mags stood outside the barn. Inu lay on the ground at her feet, cradling his cut hand. Super-ghoul-man must still be inside.

Before climbing through the snarl of thick branches and leaves, Sharon peeked at the SComCat. Still no call, but there were another seventeen minutes in which a call might come. She pocketed it, and climbed through the snarled brush. The sun had slipped below the horizon, casting a bare haze of light. Darkness, along with her hammer, suggested themselves as reliable weapons. She pressed the tiles closed.

Crouching low, she moved fast, weaving from one tree to the next. Hiding behind a large apple tree about seven meters from the back of the barn, she watched her enemies. Then a third weapon revealed itself: the rope ladder she used to play on as a child! It hung down from the barn's second-story loft window. With Mags in front of the barn and Super-ghoul-man inside, a plan coalesced in her mind. It should work—providing she could get to her fourth weapon, hidden behind a trapdoor in the barn loft.

Slowly and deliberately, she pulled her hammer from its baldric. Holding it ready to strike, she sprinted to the back of the barn and scrambled up the ladder as quietly as she could. She peered inside before climbing through the window. Concentrating on sustaining her stealth, she crawled to the trapdoor in the corner and listened.

"Wait 'til you see this bike, Mags," Super-ghoul-man said in a loud voice.

Sharon turned the brass ring on the trapdoor and opened it. Inside, her father's bolt-action hunting rifle stood propped against the wall of the hidden space. After the war of the Second Crusade, no businesses remained that manufactured cartridges. People hoarded the ones that were left until they were all gone. For posterity, her father had saved two cartridges. He'd loaded one in the chamber and the other in the magazine. Chance and a little luck, not bullets, dictated whether the rifle would still fire after all these years. Would the ammo still be good? Would the firing mechanism work? Silently, Sharon laid her hammer down and picked up the rifle. The safety was on; she silently flicked the lever to off. She set the stock against her shoulder and sighted down the barrel from the loft.

Super-ghoul-man pawed at her solar-bike, pressing his forefinger to the ignition button. "We're going to need a fingerprint to get her started."

"Thanks for the info, Einstein. I'll check out back," Mags's voice came through the open space. "Come on."

Inu's pleading voice followed. "Please."

Sharon waited a beat for the woman to step away. "Hey, asshole," she whispered and raised the rifle.

Super-ghoul-man's head snapped up. His eyes widened, and he opened his mouth.

"Make a sound, and I'll put you down." She took a quick glance to locate her hammer. Poised on the floor at her knee, it was her backup should the rifle fail.

He squinted at the open door and started to say something.

"You heard what I said." Sharon moved her finger to the trigger. "You're going to get the hell out of my barn and off of my property."

"You think?" His lips turned up into a sneer. "I'm pretty sure I can take you, and your goddamned rusty gun. Mags can have what's left." He started toward the ladder.

Sharon backed away from the edge, tucking her hammer under some moldy straw.

As he reached the top of the ladder, Super-ghoul-man exploded into the space of the loft. His expression wrapped his face in a mask of cavalier indifference to the gun barrel pointed at his chest. "That fucking thing's empty. Who do you think you're kidding?"

"You and Mags are going to leave this place—and stay away." Sharon noticed a tremor of hesitation in Super-ghoul-man. "If you don't, I'll kill you both."

Standing at the edge of the loft about a couple of meters from the barrel, he cocked his head to the side. "Do I look stupid?"

"Do you want an answer? I'm the one holding the gun."

"Maybe the laugh's on you." He puffed out his chest to look bigger. "You don't have any bullets in that piece of shit."

"You could bet on that." Sharon smiled. "I wouldn't."

Super-ghoul-man's eyes narrowed. "I'm done fucking with you." He lunged at her.

She squeezed the trigger.

A tremendous bang reverberated around the walls as his body flew back over the edge of the loft. Sulfur mingled with the barn's musty scent. Her ears rang in the wake of the shot.

"You forgot your Superman cape, pal." Sharon turned as Mags appeared in the loft's window.

"What have you done?" she screamed, enraged and terrified as she advanced on Sharon with her knife drawn.

Sharon pulled the bolt back and then shoved it forward, shucking the spent brass cartridge and loading the last from the magazine. She raised the rifle. Click.

Mags cackled.

Sharon gripped the stock to swing the gun at her.

Mags kicked it from Sharon's hands. "You stupid bitch."

Sharon fumbled for her hammer.

Mags swung the knife. Sharon recoiled, but got a nick to her chin.

She aimed a kick at Mags' knee.

As Mags stumbled, Sharon grabbed for her hammer. Just as her fingertips touched its smooth handle, Mags' heavy boot slammed down on her hand. Recoiling in pain, she rolled out of the way of the knife and clambered out of the window.

Screeching like an angry animal, Mags followed.

With no hammer or rifle to defend herself, Sharon ran hard for the drainage pond that was filled with decades of contaminated runoff. It presented itself as a fifth weapon.

"You're going to suffer," Mags rasped heavily, too close behind her.

The SComCat in Sharon's jacket rang and vibrated against her. "No." She ran harder. "No, no, no."

Mags got closer with each footfall.

Not now, Dr. Ryan. Sharon raced through pain and fear. *Just give me a few more minutes? Please.* She stumbled when Mags jabbed the knife into the bottom of her jacket. Twisting around, she grabbed Mags's arm.

Mags reared her head and slammed it into Sharon's forehead.

"Ugh . . ." Sharon grunted at the sharp sting of skull on skull. Ignoring the pain, she returned the head-butt.

The knife dropped from Mags's hand and she stumbled.

Sharon bolted toward the pond, hidden just below a small cliff of granite boulders. Its funky, poisonous water killed anything desperate enough to touch it.

Mags followed.

Agonizing ringing from the SComCat drowned the ringing in her ears from the gunshot.

In the dusky light, Sharon could barely see the rope she used to swing from as a kid, into the pond before it got contaminated. Still running, she reached for the rope and launched herself over the toxic water. The rope held, but the SComCat slipped from her pocket. A splash enveloped it.

40

It sank.

Sharon slammed onto the bank at the far edge of the pond, which splashed deadly liquid over her boots. She scrambled up the bank and kicked them off. A gust of wind swept away the yellowed paper with Dr. Ryan's contact number she'd tucked into her boot earlier, then dropped it into the murk with the SCom-Cat. "No!" Helpless to reach it, she watched it dissolve into slime.

Mags tumbled over the cliff and into the water. A blood-curdling scream exploded from her as she thrashed to free herself from the lethal brew. "He knows you're here, you bitch." A gurgling came from her throat. She splashed onto her back, clawing at her face. "He—knows." Her arms and legs twitched before her body slipped below the gloomy surface.

Chapter 4

"Bastard weighs a ton." Sitting at the water's edge with her legs bent and feet planted at the back of the corpse, Sharon summoned her dwindling energy and kicked. The body of Super-ghoul-man rolled and plopped with a splash into the pond's noxious water. As she scrambled to her feet, she put her sleeve over her mouth and nose to avoid breathing in the unearthly sweet scent of the vaporous splatter.

Oblique light from Inu's flashlight illuminated the gloomy scene.

"There won't be anything left but bones in a few days." She broke off a long knotweed cane, and pushed the floating mass toward the deeper middle. It would sink as soon as water displaced the air in its lungs. "It's been a terrible day." She tossed the bamboo-like cane into the water.

From his perch at the top of the rocky ledge, Inu drew a line of light from the watery gore to Sharon.

She squinted up at him. "You're blinding me with that." The light in her eyes amplified her persistent headache.

He dropped his hand to his side. Moonlight over his shoulder betrayed a veneer of curious disgust on his face.

"I didn't ask for this." She gestured at the lifeless man beginning to slip below the surface of her pond. "I know it's awful, but it's not safe to bury a body. I'm sure as hell not going to burn it. I might as well send invitations to all the Banditti within a hundred kilometers. Plus, he's a murderous thief. He doesn't get to be buried with my family."

His eyes darted from hers as if trying to hide something he didn't want to reveal at the mention of thieves.

"Banditti, I mean. I won't bury Banditti next to my family." She thoughtfully adjusted her hammer, tucked in its baldric . The irony was that so much of what she and her brothers had used to build the underground farm came from supplies they stole from the government. "I know a lot of good people who had to steal in order to stay alive. Banditti hurt people for the sake of hurting. And for greed. There's a difference."

The boy stood rigid in his cocoon of silence. It spoke volumes she wished she could decipher.

"I would've preferred they just left." A sudden urge to explain her actions pushed against her own secrets, better left untold. "They asked for what they got." She clambered to her feet and brushed dirt from her backside. "I had no choice. I warned them, but they wouldn't listen. They'd have cut off both our hands to steal my bike. A print is all they need, even if it's from a severed hand."

The damned jacket with the flag of the United States patch he refused to part with was draped down the length of his skinny torso. Cloaked in the failings of grownups, Inu likely had been chased into adulthood before ever getting to be a child. She had noticed the highs and lows of his untold story in the glint of his dark eyes.

"You okay?"

"Bitte." Inu wiped at blood still oozing from the cut on his wrist.

"We'll clean and bandage that when we get back to my house. I can give you a week's worth of food and water. Then I'm afraid we're going to have to part ways." Sharon picked up the makeshift litter she'd used to drag Super-ghoul-man's body from the barn and started up the rocky slope. "Without the SComCat, Dr. Ryan can't call me. And without his number, I can't call him." She reached the top of the bank. "So—I'm going to Chicago to find Eve myself."

Inu stretched out his small hand.

"Dammit, kid, I'm going alone."

Inu's outstretched fingers trembled, but the determination on his face did not waver. He gripped her upper arm.

She regarded the stoic boy who had nowhere to go. A week's worth of food and water was only a week's worth of food and water. He'd run out. Then what? Maybe he was hers to keep until she found someone else, better suited to care for a child. "You think you can help me?"

Very slowly, very slightly, the boy nodded once.

"All right. You better keep pulling your weight."

The trace of a smile passed over Inu's face.

"If we hurry, we'll make it to Pennsylvania by morning." With the litter in one hand, she wrapped the other around his. Her thumb brushed over the crusty dried blood from where Mags had cut him. Well, they were united in blood now. "Once I find Eve, we'll find your family." She scrambled to the top of the ledge with the litter banging over the rocks. "You'll have to keep up, because Eve is my first objective." She let go of his hand and stepped around him, setting a pace too fast for his short legs.

He tugged at the back of her jacket. "Please."

She wheeled around. "And stop saying please. Not in English or any other language. Just stop. No more. Okay?"

The spirited boy stood his ground with her towering over him. His eyes locked with hers. Not in the way of David taking on Goliath, but more like a valiant warrior extending an olive branch. Literally, the leafy top of a branch that drooped from his hand.

"I see. You were falling behind because you were covering up the tracks of the litter with the branch." An impulse to wrap him up in her arms rattled her. She blinked and closed the distance between them. Placing her fingertips beneath his chin and lifting his eyes to hers, she said, "Good thinking, kid. I'm sorry I yelled at you. I'll try to slow down. But not much. We've got a lot of ground to cover by morning."

He pressed a fist to his lips.

44

In the dull light Sharon couldn't tell whether he was stifling a cry or his propensity to speak the only word he either knew or was willing to share. She pulled his fist from his face. "Don't cry. You can say whatever you want to say. Or go ahead and cry. Whatever. Do what you've got to do. Just keep up." Gripping the litter in her other hand, she pivoted and went on. The moon glow was enough to see by, and she followed the litter's drag marks back to the farmyard.

Inu clomped close behind, brushing away their tracks.

As Sharon topped the rise, silhouettes of her small home, the barn, and the Banditti van came into view. Without a fingerprint to start its engine, the van wasn't going anywhere. Based on Mags's last words, she suspected someone would be coming for it, and her. Desperation to find Eve wasn't the only good reason to set off before daybreak.

Sharon took the flashlight from Inu and flipped the beam around the van's dark interior. Clutter she couldn't identify was heaped in the space behind the two bucket seats and operating controls. "While I get my bike, you see if there's anything of value we should take with us. Things like food, tools, or electronics." She handed him the flashlight. "Be quick. My bike is packed, and we need to get out of here before more Banditti come."

Not wasting time, he yanked the van door open and disappeared into its messy interior. His beam of light bounced around in a thorough search for things to scavenge.

Sharon strode to the open barn.

Its familiar musty scent triggered a chain of memories of her family and what they'd built together. The last time she'd been away from the farm overnight her parents were still alive. While the world came apart at the seams, the sanctuary of the farm protected her and Eve. She ached at the thought of leaving it. But that ache didn't compare to the searing hole cut through the middle of her gut when the soldiers had taken Eve.

The Banditti would likely trash the place while she was gone. But they wouldn't be able to touch her underground paradise of food and water. Thanks to Jon's brilliance in designing the farm's technology, the place could run all on its own, undetectable, for months. The farm, like Eve, tethered Sharon to existence. Every speck of soil, the trees, and the plants—they all formed the building blocks of her identity. She lived because the farm lived. Her family was buried here. Every single one. Wherever her travels took her, the farm's tether would keep her. "I'll be home soon," she said into the stillness of the barn.

Her midnight-blue bike sat poised, ready. In the frenzied aftermath of her battle with Mags, she'd packed a large backpack and secured it in the sidecar. The pack's contents included several weeks' worth of dried food, her satchel containing the seven remaining apples, a survival kit, an emergency supply of Eve's medicine, and her mother's treasured sketchbook. Stored in the grow room underground, Dr. Ryan's titanium box and its life-saving medicines would be safe until she could return it to him. Sharon popped open the fully charged solar dome that enclosed the bike's two seats and sidecar.

She slipped on the weightless black Kevlene helmet decorated with a sunflower, and adjusted the flexible protective material snug to her head. Given the elasticity of Kevlene, the second helmet secured to the passenger seat that Eve always wore would work for Inu. The ride would be long. If he got fidgety, she'd let him draw on blank pages in her mother's sketchbook. Maybe he'd even reveal something about himself in the things he left on the pages.

To feel her wife's presence, Sharon caressed the softness of Eve's scarf tied around her neck. She slid onto the driver's seat, snapped the helmet strap closed, and pressed her forefinger over the ignition button. The bike's quiet motor purred to life. Inside the tight space of the barn, she opted to use the bike's manual rather than voice controls. Pulling back the hover-throttle, she coaxed the bike from the ground. Dust and old hay that had set-tled on the floor boards blew out from underneath the rotating blades at the bottom of the bike. She eased the bike forward through the dusty storm and out of the barn.

Inu stood waiting with a bulging duffel bag slung over his shoulder.

"Nice haul," she said. "Put your bag in the sidecar with my pack. Then go shut the barn door and hop onto the seat behind me."

Inu plopped the duffel into the sidecar. He ran to the door, heaved it closed, and scrambled on behind her.

Sharon tapped her head. "Seat belt and helmet." She pulled the dome over them and latched it shut, watching him fumble with the helmet. Even though Inu created more worry for her, it did feel good not to be alone. Plus, she liked the clever and tough kid.

He snapped the strap closed and smiled.

"Good man." She moved the hover-throttle to the maximum height position. The bike rose thirty meters above the ground. Sharon swiveled the bike's search beams downward and gave her farm a last look. The trees cast shadows that reminded her of an army at the ready to protect her home. Below, in the tangle of dark woody profiles, stood her remarkable life-giving apple tree. "Keep standing, my friend," she said under her breath. "We'll be home soon." She glanced in the rearview mirror at Inu. "Ready?"

The boy gripped the arms of his seat and nodded. His helmeted head swiveled from side to side, taking in the view as the bike rose still higher.

"Settle in. We have about nine hundred and twenty kilometers to go. We'll stop for the day somewhere around State College." She switched from the search beams to infrared, then activated the global positioning system and the cabin environmental sensors. "We should be able to make it in a little less than six hours." Her eyes went to the solar battery gauge. "The bike can fly seven in the dark before we need to recharge." She tipped the steering grips in the direction of the dirt road and throttled up the engine to full speed at one hundred and sixty kilometers per hour. According to the bike's instruments and force of acceleration against their bodies, it took a mere eight seconds for the engine to comply. Using the object-sensors, she could fly without lights and not worry about crashing into things she couldn't see.

o   o   o

Following the remnants of obsolete roads destroyed during the last two world wars, they sped south and then east along what had been Interstate 80. Crumbling pavement pocked by bombs or swallowed in large sections by ravenous weedy vegetation marked the route. Like stone walls built by European settlers centuries ago, the ramshackle roads left traces of a long-dead civilization.

Instead of sleeping during the more than five hours of travel, Inu scribbled on a page of the sketchbook. He'd tucked the other pages into the satchel.

A ribbon of fiery orange nicked the eastern horizon behind them. The clock on the dash read 6:10 a.m. Even though the bike's controls kept the temperature inside the dome a comfortable 20°C, outside the heat already measured thirty-two and climbing. Much of the Great Plains, and everything west of the Rockies, had morphed with climate change into desert. The land between the Great Lakes and the Gulf of Mexico, meanwhile, turned hot and tropical. Violent storms, orders of magnitude more powerful than had ever been recorded in history, lashed the region in all seasons. People nicknamed the place Gaia's Wrath. Dark heavy clouds loomed in the distant western horizon. There was no other way to get from NONA's east coast to its capital city, Chicago, but through Gaia's Wrath.

"Inu, we're just east of State College by a few kilometers. Help me look for a spot to land. Someplace we can hide the bike and find cover." Sharon pointed at the sky. "Storm's coming. And we'll run out of power if we don't stop soon."

The boy folded the sketch he was working on and tucked it into his duffel of scavenged loot. He turned his attention to the landscape below.

"Be on the lookout for people, too. There aren't many around here anymore. The storms are too unpredictable. But there's water, which means they'll travel for it. We can't risk running into anyone."

"Por favor." He pointed.

Her eyes followed his direction to a clearing in the brush.

"Good eye." She veered right and hovered over a barren patch of pavement with clumps of vegetation growing through cracks here and there. She thought it must have once been a parking lot. The remnants of a lopsided building almost obliterated by vines and thick brush stood its ground at the edge of the smattering of concrete. Impenetrable vegetation surrounded the ruin as far as the eye could see.

"Looks like an old highway rest area. Let's check it out. As long as no one's down there, that's where we'll sleep." A thicket of brush made it impossible to land close to the building, or the parking lot. "We'll have to find a clear spot to land and then make our way on foot through the brush." Sharon pressed a button on the bike's GPS to store the coordinates for the rest area.

She turned her craft away from the building, dropped in elevation, and spotted what might have been an old building foundation. Her GPS indicated they were ninety-one meters from the rest area structure. "There, probably the foundation of an old shed or storage building. That's a good spot."

Easing the steering grips into the down position, she hovered the bike lower until it touched ground with a soft bump. Before shutting down the engine, Sharon watched the bike's infrared sensors for any signs of humans in the area. Since large mammals had been hunted to extinction during the War of Earth's Rebellion, humans were the only predators of concern.

Little dots of red light flitted to and fro across the screen. "No signs of humans," she said. "But lots of rodents. We'll catch one for breakfast." Speaking into the voice command module she said, "Power down and store coordinates." The rotors, protected by the rotor guard beneath the bike, slowed to a stop. She removed the bike's GPS chip.

Assessing their surroundings, she took in the green that ensconced them. Except for a clump of soft moss growing over a patch of concrete not far from the bike, the vegetation looked mean and angry. Thorns protruded from scabrous branches everywhere. "The good news is that anyone trying to make their way through this stuff to get us would have to go through a meat grinder. The bad news is that we have to." She pointed at the tangle of thorny brush. "Stay close behind me so you don't get shredded."

Inu held up a finger.

"What?"

He reached into his duffel and retrieved a sheath less than half a meter long. A black handle protruded from it. Inu gripped the handle and slid a machete from it.

Sharon nodded and smiled. "I had a feeling you could be trusted to know which stuff to take from that Banditti van. What else you got in there?"

Turning the machete around without touching its blade, he handed the grip end to Sharon. Then he fumbled in the duffel and retrieved a NONA-issued extreme weather blanket sealed in its original packaging.

She recognized it because it was the same blanket her brother, Jon, had been issued when he was a soldier.

Inu smiled back at her.

"Nice work." Sharon flipped the switch to the canopy. When it popped open, a rush of soupy hot air snuffed out the comfort of the bike's interior. She sucked in a breath thick with humidity. "Holy hell, it's hot." A bolt of lightning flashed a distant jagged line in the sky. "We better hurry."

Sharon placed the machete at her feet, and tucked the GPS into her pocket. She removed her helmet, unclasped her seat belt, and stepped from the bike. "Let me help you." She freed Inu from his helmet and seat belt and lifted him down.

Inu shoved the blanket back into the duffel and lifted its shoulder strap over his head. In the few minutes it was exposed to the outside temperature, his hair matted into clumpy wet strands.

"We have to drink some water soon." Sharon hoisted the backpack onto her back, picked up the machete, and shut the canopy. "I have an air moisture extractor in my pack. There's plenty of water we can pull from this humid air. As long as we can find food and make water, we won't touch the reserves I packed." A bead of sweat slid down the middle of her back. Her clothing got damper by the second.

Another jagged crack of light flashed in the sky followed by a tremendous boom that shook the ground. She could smell the sweet, sharp scent of ozone stirred up by the winds. "The storm's getting closer." Sharon raised the machete and slashed through the wall of bullying vegetation. A gusty wind blew against her wet clothes, cooling her skin. She swung the heavy knife harder through the brush, looking back frequently to check on the boy.

Inu kept close as the western sky filled in around them, turning to an ominous greenish-black.

The storm's pressure pushed in on Sharon's chest. But for the cracks and booms that got closer and louder, an eerie quiet began to replace the rattle of the wind through the brush. Sharon debated whether to go back to the bike or keep going toward the shelter of the rest area building. On balance, the storm would be a factor regardless of her choice. At least the shelter option didn't involve the possibility of crashing if the bike didn't have enough power to outrace the storm. She pushed on faster through the brush as it nicked and sliced her exposed skin, hoping that by breaking a trail for Inu, he'd be safe from the unforgiving thorns.

Mercifully, the brush gave way to the small clearing at the decrepit rest area building. The destination looked a lot less inviting up close. Only three walls and part of the roof remained. The crush of vines and brush that seemed to be swallowing it whole were actually keeping it propped up. Sharon shuddered at the reality that Earth, when angered, could be a monster that easily chewed and devoured the things made by humans.

Before taking a step closer, she froze at the sight of the approaching blackness. Strands of rain twisted down from the base of a long, horrible anvil-shaped cloud that was clearly on its way to becoming a tornado. It had them in its sights. Sharon opened Inu's duffel, returned the machete to its sheath, and zipped the bag shut. She'd take her chances with the thorns over running from a wind storm with a machete in hand. Even though the building had managed to stay on its feet through years of storms, she had no confidence they could hold onto its thorny tangle of walls and not be sucked up into the center of the tornado that bore down on them. "We can't stay here. Run." She tugged him in the opposite direction.

Rain caught up to them as they slashed and tumbled through the brush toward the bike. The ground quaked as the storm roared at their heels. A gust of wind ripped Inu's hand from her grasp. Sharon spun around and grabbed him up in her arms. "Tuck your head against my shoulder!" she yelled over the wind and rain, as she shielded him as best she could from being sliced by thorns or hit by debris.

Lightning slammed into the ground ten meters to their right. The thicket exploded into fire. Sharon risked a look over her shoulder. The monster tornado stretched across the sky behind them as far as she could see. "Hold onto me, Inu!" She ran harder, her heart pounding almost as loud as the storm.

The bike's profile through the tumult of rain came into view. "Just a little farther." She labored under the combined weight of the pack on her back and the boy with his duffel in her arms. Her chest ached and seemed to constrict under the exertion. Panting through the pain, she hugged him closer and kept moving to stay ahead of the storm.

"Holy hell?" Sharon stopped in her tracks as the patch of moss she'd noticed earlier popped open. "It's a trapdoor over a shelter!"

A rain-soaked woman beckoned to her from the opening in the ground. Another crack of lightning, way too close.

Inu clung tighter to Sharon.

She looked from the woman to her bike. The bike shook and shuddered sideways. Her ears ached with the roar of the storm. *Fuck. No choice.*

The woman's mouth moved in a shout she couldn't hear through the chaos. Sharon raced toward her.

Her features came into view as she reached for Inu. The thin brown-skinned woman with snow-white hair took Inu from her and descended.

Sharon followed her down the steps to safety. As she gripped the handle of the moss-covered trapdoor to close it over them, the monster yanked her bike up into its fury. She screamed almost as loud as the storm, but no scream, no curse, no prayer was going to get the tornado to release her bike. Panting, she shut the door over herself, Inu, and the stranger. *How the hell do I get to Chicago now?*

Chapter 5

Sharon gripped the handle on the inside of the trapdoor. The tornado screaming overhead rattled it back, mocking her. *Even if I have to crawl, I'll get to you, Eve.* She slammed a fist against the door in defiance of the storm.

A slurry of blood, rain, and sweat smeared her hands and drenched her clothing. On top of the throbbing from injuries inflicted by the NONA soldier and Mags, a searing pain shot up through ribbons of bare flesh sliced by thorns. Her waterlogged clothing threatened to drag her down the steps into the space below. She ached to collapse.

A woman's voice, strong but gravel-edged by age, ordered, "Come down the stairs. And keep your hands where I can see them."

Sharon turned in the narrow portal and carefully stepped down each rusty rung into the musty chamber. A problem more immediate than the loss of her bike demanded her full attention. The storm had deposited her and Inu into an odd lair that lifted the hairs at the back of her neck. She could feel Inu's eyes on her, but kept hers locked with their captor's.

A rusty, mangled yellow door that looked like it belonged to an old school bus was propped against the wall. Remnants of children's clothing were draped over the door. It begged the question, where were the kids that used to wear them?

"We're not going to hurt you," Sharon said. "When the storm passes, we'll leave."

Their rain-drenched savior stood behind a heavy wooden desk streaked by a fading walnut stain. Spheres of mold dotted the creases in the wood. A scuffed plastic apple perched on the front left corner of the desk. On the right, a small bouquet of wilting yellow wildflowers was stuffed into a glass of cloudy water.

The woman, finger poised on the trigger of a loaded crossbow, said, "Slowly take a seat." She wore a frayed cotton T-shirt with the sleeves cut off. The words *Property of Clearwater Middle School* were spelled out over the chest. Scars zigzagged over her bare arms. A rope cinched baggy dungarees at her bony waist.

Sharon held up her hands. "Okay." Her eyes scanned the room. Twenty school desks in various stages of disrepair occupied the greater part of the old woman's underground den. Spaced into five rows of four, the hodgepodge of desks appeared to be relics from various eras. Sharon recognized the stand-up type workspace with built-in computers she had used as a young girl. There were also some vintage wood laminate-topped desks with attached seats from the late 20th century. Inu sat at a workstation with a cracked computer screen. Use, time, flooding, and battering marred the desks.

In the back of the room, a cot rested next to an enormous book-case filled with mildewed volumes published before electronic books replaced paper. Geology, math, classic stories, biology, history, the books ran the gamut. Stuffed mammals and birds cluttered the top of the case. Tacked with pushpins, yellowed and frayed drawings decorated the walls. A photograph of smiling kids mugging for the camera hung above the cot. Wrapped over the small bed was a NONA-issued blanket, the same as the one Inu had pilfered from the Banditti van.

A single fluorescent lightbulb plugged into a solar battery lit the room. A large digital whiteboard hung from the wall behind the old woman. On the small table near the cot, steam wafted from a pot over a hot plate, also plugged into the battery. Next to the table was a hard plastic cabinet with double doors.

Sharon shot a glance at Inu sitting motionless. *Good boy.* She dropped her pack from her shoulders, and wedged into the tight space between the seat and nearest desk. "We won't hurt you. We're just passing through. Once the storm is gone, we'll be on our way."

"Both of you, put your bags atop a desk where I can see them," the woman ordered.

"Please." Sharon displayed her empty hands. "I lost my bike and still have a long way to go. We can't make it without the little bit of food and supplies in our bags."

"I'm not interested in your tchotchkes. Anyone desperate enough to go through Gaia's Wrath can't be trusted. So that means you." Keeping the crossbow's arrow trained on Sharon, she dropped into the high-backed chair behind the desk. "And stop looking at me like I'm a crazy person."

"I'm sorry. I just lost my bike. If I look a certain way, it's because of the shock of it," Sharon lied. "I'm curious, though. What is this place? Are there others around, and did this used to be the school?"

Sorrow flickered in the woman's eyes. "Some days, it's my comfort. Other days, my punishment." The woman tipped her head toward a desk. "Mostly, it's me stuck at a lonely moment. Bags on the table. Now."

Inu glanced up at Sharon. His skin was pale and his teeth chattered.

Sharon turned her eyes from the cold, wet boy to the woman.

Her bony finger stayed poised next to her weapon's trigger guard. She shot a sympathetic glance at Inu and then resumed the showdown with Sharon.

Taking a chance on the woman's spark of empathy for Inu, Sharon reached for his hand. "He's cold. Please don't take our things."

A breath of frustration blew from the woman's lips. "Do I look like a person not able to make hard decisions?"

"You look like a survivor to me. I don't know what your story is, but you're no Banditti. You'll hurt us if you have to. But I don't think you want to."

"I'll tell you what." The woman moved her finger to the trigger. "You're trying my patience, petulant woman."

56

"Please!" Inu shot from his seat and put an arm in front of Sharon.

The woman flinched as if Inu's act of selflessness inflicted pain on her.

"Please," he said, more quietly.

"No, no, no." The woman lowered the weapon. "No, honey, I won't hurt your mom. Not ever. I just don't want her to hurt me."

Inu slipped a hand into Sharon's and turned to face her. "Please," he said as he paused before reaching into her open jacket. "Please."

Sharon touched the top of his head. "It's okay."

Inu removed her hammer from its baldric and placed it on the desk.

"I'm sorry for scaring your son," the woman said. "Just can't be too careful these days. I truly don't want your things."

Sharon thought it best to let the old woman think Inu was hers. She squeezed his hand. "Who are you? And why did you help us?"

"My name is Annie Wade. Who are you?"

"I'm Sharon. And this is Inu."

The woman flipped on the crossbow's safety and let the weapon dangle from the strap over her chest. "I don't want anything from you. I just couldn't watch another child die in a storm." A faraway look flashed across her face as if she'd remembered something awful. "I've watched too many humans ripped apart in Gaia's Wrath. Protecting children is my life's work." She reached for Inu. "May I?"

Sharon got up and put her arms around Inu to shield him.

"I know what it looks like." Annie rose and gestured around the room. "But I'm really not crazy. If I was crazy, I wouldn't know it one way or the other. Crazy makes one oblivious. Unfortunately, I'm not oblivious." She sighed. "I have a salve that I made of witch hazel and chokeberry root. You really need to put some on those cuts. The thorns up there"—she tipped her head up toward the ceiling, above which the storm raged and roared—"transmit sporotrichosis. Nasty, nasty stuff."

57

Given how much the cuts on Sharon's hands and face burned, Inu had to be in agony from the big one on his cheek. Plus, the kid was shivering violently, ramming his chest against her. "Thank you for helping us. I need to get the boy his blanket." She reached for his duffel.

"Don't you dare." Annie lifted the crossbow.

"But he's cold. You must care."

"Of course I do." Annie's voice smoldered with anger. "Let him get his own blanket. Him I trust, you I don't. You keep your hands where I can see them."

"Bitte," Inu said.

"You're salt of the earth, boy. I can tell these things." Annie lowered the crossbow again. To Sharon she asked, "Do we understand each other?"

"Yes," Sharon answered with strained patience as Inu went for his blanket.

"Good." Annie lifted the weapon's strap over her head and laid the crossbow on the desk. "Now, let's clean up those cuts and get some good salve on them. I've got enough bottled water that's been boiled. You'll feel better right away." She went to the cabinet and unlatched the doors. She jutted her chin at the steaming pot on the hotplate. "I also have something special for . . ."

A deafening rumble blotted out Annie's words and shook the room. The cabinet shimmied as its doors swung open. Annie slammed the door and held her back against it.

Sharon put a hand on a desk to steady herself. With the other, she held onto Inu to keep him from falling. The jostling of the room continued for several seconds until it slowed to a faint vibration. "What the hell was that?"

"The MagLev." Annie reopened the cabinet. "It passes right under this room four times a day. I should've warned you. Guess I lost track of time."

Inu, eyes wide, hung tight to Sharon's hand.

"Do you know what the MagLev is, Inu?" Annie asked.

He shook his head.

"It's a high-speed magnetic train," Annie explained. "Its opposing electromagnetic fields make the train hover while hydrogen thrusters move it forward."

The boy pursed his lips and nodded as if electromagnetic fields and hydrogen thrusters made sense.

"You're a smart kid." Sharon smiled, and noticed the scratch on Inu's cheek continued to redden and swell. She tipped his chin and touched it. Heat radiated from it.

"The president of the United States at the time ordered that the MagLev track system be built one hundred feet below ground to keep the Chinese from destroying it," Annie added. "President Bowman managed to save the train, but not her country. Now NONA uses it to move supplies and personnel." From the cabinet, she retrieved a small wooden bowl and a purple box. "Let's clean those cuts. A mild case of sporotrichosis will give you a painful nasty welt. A bad case will put you on your back for days."

"That we can't afford." Sharon guided Inu by the shoulders to Annie.

Inu lifted his nose in the direction of the pot on Annie's stove. His stomach gurgled loud enough to hear.

Inu's hunger reminded Sharon of her own. She breathed in the earthy, salty scent. *Wild greens in broth?* She would've guessed artichoke, but artichokes, like most of the world's vegetable crops, no longer grew anywhere on Earth. "Smells like artichokes. But that can't be, since the last of them were lost when the seed banks were destroyed."

"Ah, you noticed my lunch." Annie picked up the wooden spoon next to the pot. "You two must be hungry. You can each have a bowl of my soup while you tell me why it is you thought you could travel through Gaia's Wrath without getting your asses handed to you. Not a smart move." She lifted the lid on the pot and stirred its contents. "Milk-thistle soup."

"Thistle?" Sharon asked. "Around here?"

"Oh no. I had to forage for it many kilometers from here. Where it's drier and a lot less stormy."

Inu opened his duffel and extracted the neatly packaged NONA blanket.

Sharon grabbed the collar of his prized U.S. jacket. "Let's take this wet coat off of you." She slipped it from his shoulders.

Annie took the jacket and hung it on a hook near the cabinet. She pointed at an old machine with louvers and a switch. "Flip that on," she ordered Sharon. "It's a vintage water extractor. They called them dehumidifiers in the olden days. It'll have your clothes, with you in them, dry in an hour. We'll have some more water then, too."

Inu unfolded the blanket and laid it on the floor by the cot. He sat and curled one end over his body, leaving the other half spread out on the floor. He looked up at Sharon and said, "Please."

"Sit." Annie handed a bottle of water and the bowl of witch-hazel salve to Sharon. "Spread this over your and the boy's cuts while I pour you some soup. Use the cloth in the bowl to dab the cuts with water first. It's clean."

"Thank you for this. And thank you for taking us in." Sharon wondered what the story was behind the tough-as-nails, kind old woman. "You saved our lives today." She took the bowl and water bottle, and eased onto the floor next to Inu. "Do you live here alone?" She carefully cleaned and then spread the salve over the slices in the boy's skin, then hers. It felt blessedly cool.

"I might tell you my secrets." Annie placed three wooden bowls with matching spoons on the table next to the pot. "If you tell me yours. Where are you headed, to be so careless to come this way?" She lifted the pot of thistle soup and poured it evenly into the three bowls. "There's not much, because I wasn't expecting company. I can make more later. But here." She set the pot down, opened a green box from the cabinet, and turned it so that Inu could see its contents.

His eyes widened and a smile spread across his face.

"Ha! I thought you'd like these." Annie tousled Inu's hair. "Fried beetles. I traded a basket of cut thistle for them. They're really good with soup. Cup your hands."

Inu complied.

Annie shook out a serving of the dried bugs. "You're a fine and sweet boy."

"There are people around here to trade with?" Sharon hungrily eyed the bowls.

"No." Annie's brow furrowed. "Well, sort of."

"What do you mean, sort of?" Sharon gingerly pressed her back against the wall. Her shoulder still ached from the soldier's blow. She leaned into the pain, straightening and strengthening her spine.

"No one above our heads." Annie pointed at a closed doorway where the room sloped downward. "That leads to a passage of tunnels that'll bring you to where the MagLev stops for fuel. It's also where the government-sanctioned costermongers are allowed to trade with the soldiers, passengers, and hydros."

"What's a hydro?" Sharon's mouth watered when Annie handed one of the steaming bowls to Inu, who was crunching on the last of the beetles.

Using both hands, he lifted the bowl to his face. "Please." He put it to his lips, blew on it, and took a sip. He closed his eyes and smiled.

"Thank you." Sharon took the second bowl offered by Annie.

"Hydros are the people who refuel the MagLev with hydrogen. It's a hard job to get and even harder to endure. Hydros sign a contract to live underground for two years without ever seeing the light of day. Can you even imagine going two years without seeing the sun?"

"It would be the end of me." Sharon blew on the hot soup. "Why two years?"

"You see," Annie answered, "every two years, NONA changes the places for fueling the train so that the United Kingdom of Asia can't easily figure out where it's located. If they did, they'd blow it up."

Sharon put the bowl to her lips and sipped. She wanted to guzzle it, but it was too hot. Her body would better absorb the nutrition if she ate slowly anyway. "Ah, destroy the train and you bring NONA to its knees."

"That's right." Annie seated herself on the floor across from them. "They'd be sunk without a way to move supplies and soldiers. NONA calculated that it takes about two years for the Chinese to figure out where the fuel is, so they keep moving it." She put both hands to a bowl of soup. "Not for all the food and water in the world could you pay me to be a hydro. You can tell the new ones from the old ones. Their skin goes pale and their eyes dim. Like they lost a part of their humanity that only the sun can cultivate in humans. They're given supplements, but it's not enough." Annie put the bowl to her lips and slurped. "They scare me."

"More than NONA?" Sharon sipped another mouthful of the hot soup. It warmed her insides. What a pleasure after the trials she'd been through.

"No." Annie shook her head. "Hydros aren't evil. Just desperately sad, and desperate for the money NONA pays them. That's why NONA lets the costermongers sell to them. It's a way to keep them from losing their minds while being trapped underground for two years. We trade them everything from foraged food to water, tools, weapons, and sex." Annie put up a hand as if to stop the next question. "I don't trade sex. But others do."

"You're a costermonger?"

"Not exactly. You know, you'd be surprised what you'll find when you're looking for something else." The old woman nodded at a chartreuse coat hanging on a hook near the door to the tunnels. "I cut the identity chip out of a dead costermonger who made the unfortunate mistake of being in the open during one of Gaia's wraths. Wasn't much left of her when I found her. But the chip looked to be in good shape. So I sewed it into the sleeve of my coat."

"That gets you in?"

"NONA wands me every time. I keep my other arm down with my hand in a pocket so my real chip isn't triggered. The soldiers don't have much enthusiasm for checking the details. They're not evil, either. They're just trying to get by like the rest of us."

"On that, we'll have to agree to disagree."

Annie paused, seeming to scrutinize the comment. "NONA's

predictable. Stay out of its way and follow the rules. That's doable. It's the Banditti who keep me looking over my shoulder." She set her bowl down. "What's your beef with NONA?"

Sharon leaned forward and placed her empty bowl next to Annie's. "They kidnapped my wife for no reason other than she has Chinese blood. NONA's rounding up people of Asian descent and herding them into an internment camp in Chicago. Eve is very sick. I have to find her. That's why we came through Gaia's Wrath from Maine."

Inu lifted his empty bowl to Annie with a respectful nod of thanks.

She took it from him. "You poor child. To have a parent stolen. I know what it's like to keep looking for someone you love."

Inu curled into a ball and rested his head on Sharon's thigh.

She hesitated before pulling a corner of the blanket over him. As her hand brushed the hair from his forehead, she considered her options. Every move she made was for Eve, yet the thing she contemplated doing was the last thing Eve would do. "I told you my story." Her voice flattened under the heaviness of guilt. "What's yours?"

Annie folded her hands together in her lap. "I guess a deal's a deal. What do you want to know first?"

Pointing at hash marks etched into the wall, Sharon asked, "How long have you lived here?"

"Thirty-seven years."

"Alone?"

"Yes, except for my demons." Annie's strong voice waivered. She swallowed and cleared her throat. "I was a schoolteacher."

"Yeah? What grades?" Sharon moved her hand to Inu's shoulder and laid her palm on him. He trusted her, and now she was about to break that trust. It felt like the worst thing she'd ever done, and she hadn't even done it yet. *It's the only way. I hope he'll forgive me. I hope Annie will forgive me, too.*

Annie closed her eyes and breathed in. "The most beautiful, brilliant, lovely seven- and eight-year-olds," she breathed out the words. "Thirty-seven years ago I was thirty-seven. It's the year I stopped having birthdays, because my life ended, and this"—she lifted her hands to the room—"this limbo began."

"Tell me what happened." Sharon watched as Annie's guard came down with the telling of her story.

"I was teaching school, here in State College." Annie's hands shook with a subtle tremor. "The War of the Second Crusade had ended, and the War of Earth's Rebellion had begun. But we were all trying to maintain a sense of normalcy by keeping kids in school." Annie wrapped her arms over her chest. "It was also around the time that the tornadoes and storms were becoming more and more frequent. Lots of parents wanted to take their kids out of school. Didn't want to entrust their children to someone else for protection during the day when the storms were most violent. But we teachers convinced them that keeping their kids in school would be best for society going forward. That it was a must for all of our survival."

"Obviously you had shelters like this one?"

"Oh, yes." Annie's eyes glassed over. "We had storm drills too. We did them routinely."

Sharon suspected that no amount of preparation could've been enough. "A storm came, didn't it? A bad one?"

Annie wiped the corners of her eyes. "One of the worst I've ever seen. And by far the fastest." She lifted her legs to her chest and hugged her knees. "I'd brought my kids out into the country to teach them how to forage for mushrooms and berries. All I had to protect them was a bus. We were too far from the shelters." She turned her eyes to the floor. "That was my fault. Once I realized the storm was coming, I rounded them all up into the bus and tried to outrace the tornado."

Sharon noticed Annie's body go rigid with the memory. "It's okay if you don't want to tell me anymore. I don't want to upset you."

"It's okay, dear. Like I said, a deal's a deal. I've never told anyone this story. Maybe if I tell it, the demons in my head will go quiet for a while."

"I'm listening," Sharon said quietly.

"In my rush to get the kids to safety, I didn't bother to put my own seat belt on. But I'd trained all of them to instinctively put theirs on. I floored the bus down the dirt road. Just when I thought we'd make it, a second tornado dropped from the sky in front of us. I had nowhere to go. The storm sucked the bus into oblivion. I was thrown out and dropped in a field six kilometers away. I was naked." She touched her left elbow. "And this arm was bent sideways, but I was alive. The scars on my body mark that terrible day."

"And the kids?"

"I've been here for thirty-seven years, searching. I scrounged for all the stuff you see in this room, so that if they ever came back I could be their teacher again. Everything from the bus door to the clothes ripped from their precious bodies, I collected and dragged here." Annie laid her head on her knees. "But they never came back. I miss them so." Her shoulders shook and she gave way to sobs.

The woman's grief sat heavy in the room.

"I'm so sorry. You really don't have to go on." Sharon put a hand to Annie's shoulder. "It's okay."

"No, I do. Maybe the universe will finally redeem me for speaking the truth." She lifted her head. Tears streaked her face. "I'd promised the kids I'd never leave them. Ever. So, every day I get up and search. I search for any sign that even one of them survived. I know that after all of this time it's a futile endeavor. But, now, it's all I know. When I close my eyes at night, I see them being torn apart by that monster storm."

"I do understand." Sharon wanted to move her bent leg. It tingled from lack of blood flow. If she moved, she might wake the now sleeping Inu, his head still resting on her thigh. "I'll search every day for the rest of my life to find Eve. There's nothing I wouldn't do to bring her home." Sharon hoped her words carried no hint of the terrible thing she planned to do. Suddenly, her stomach churned with nausea.

"Then find her you must," Annie said.

"Would you mind if we sleep a little before we're on our way?"

Sharon resisted the urge to hug Inu goodbye. But this *was* good-bye. Part of her, a big part, wanted to bring both Inu and Annie on her journey to find Eve. But it was too dangerous, and they'd slow her down. Annie shouldn't have let her guard down. Sharon was as desperate to find Eve as Annie was for redemption. "We'll have a long way to go, all on foot now."

"Of course." Annie got up. "I'll leave you both to sleep. I'm going out to forage now that the storm is past. I need some time alone with my thoughts anyway. When I get back, I'll pack you some food and draw you a map for safely making your way through Gaia's Wrath."

"Thank you." Sharon closed her eyes, wanting to sleep and wishing there was some other way. Inu had proven to be a brave and loyal boy. But the dangers ahead were likely going to get much worse. And she had to move fast; there just wasn't time for a camping trip. As for Annie, she wasn't crazy, only lonely like Inu. Why did the idea hurt so much if it was the right thing to do?

Chapter 6

Sharon pressed the pen to the sketch paper. It felt awkward between her fingers. The last time she had written by hand was when her mother had taught her how to draw her name. Electronic communication had replaced handwriting decades ago. Only artists wrote by hand. Sharon was no artist. In halting strokes, she drew large block letters.

> Dear Inu, I am sorry to leave you. But it is better this way. I have to find Eve. I brought you as far as I could to a safe place. You are a good boy. Take care of Annie. I hope you find your family someday. Your friend, Sharon.

She lifted the pen to inspect the message. The slanted letters looked chaotic but legible. Inu probably couldn't read anyway; Annie would have to read it to him.

Taking extra care, she pressed the pen to a second page.

> Dear Annie, please forgive me for taking your coat. I know it does not make up for my bad deeds, but I am leaving all of my supplies for you. I should have asked first, but I could not take the chance that you would say no. Eve will die if I do not find her soon. Inu is a special boy. He deserves to be with someone who can take better care of him than I can. With humble thanks, Sharon.

A knot of guilt lodged in her chest. She laid the pen on the paper and watched Inu. His eyes flitted back and forth beneath his eyelids as his chest rose and fell with each deep breath of sleep. Sharon lifted the blanket to cover his shoulders and hoped he was dreaming of only good things. The medicine of sleep, the witch-hazel salve, and Annie's soup seemed to be shrinking the welts on his face. Even though Sharon's body begged for sleep, the soup had helped to revive her too. The need to find Eve drove her forward.

She opened her backpack and laid its contents on a nearby desk. Going without the water-extractor, handheld solar panel, knife, bivouac shelter, fire starter, water filter, copper pot, shock of rope, synthetic sweater and two weeks' supply of dried vegetables, beans, and beetles would be tough. But trying to make it to Chicago on foot posed an insurmountable challenge. Seven apples remained in her satchel. She set five of them in the pile for Annie and Inu.

Leaving everything but two apples, Eve's medicine, the small box of insect drones and microbots, and a water flask didn't make up for stealing Annie's coat and leaving Inu. Plus the risk that Annie might try to trade Sharon's clandestine apples and food was huge. On balance, though, Sharon bet that she wouldn't. Every NONA soldier and Banditti in the area would descend on Annie's private lair. Maybe even take Inu. Anyone savvy enough to survive three decades alone in Gaia's Wrath knew that being under the microscope of NONA never ended well.

She laid the empty pack next to the things she was leaving. "Goodbye, brave boy," she murmured. She raised the satchel strap over her head. After giving Inu one last look, she buttoned her jacket to conceal her hammer. She hesitated before taking Annie's chartreuse costermonger coat from its hook.

Pushing through remorse, she descended the steep grade into the darkened tunnel. Musty damp air tickled her lungs, causing her to cough. Not wanting to wake Inu, she suppressed the urge and moved deeper into the darkness. Navigating by touch, she kept a hand to the wall. In the *off* mode, the voice-activated micro-flashlight sewn into her sleeve would charge with the movement of her body. Not using illumination helped her stay in the shadows. She'd use light only if necessary.

As she hiked farther into the tunnel, something snagged her right cuff. Holding her breath, she froze. When nothing moved, she brushed the fingertips of her free hand down her arm to a hard, cold and gritty rod. It stuck out from the wall just enough to hook her sleeve. She freed herself and whispered, "Flashlight on." Its beam of light illuminated a piece of rusted rebar protruding from a patch of crumbling concrete. Sharon exhaled, grateful that it hadn't sliced her skin. Ever since the antitoxin for tetanus had stopped being made, the deadly infection had become commonplace.

Aiming the light at the length of wall, she resumed walking, taking care not to touch the occasional exposed rebar. She traveled lower into the underground bowels of Gaia's Wrath until the tunnel stopped abruptly at a T-shaped intersection. Her heart raced. Which way to go? She shone the light left, then right, exposing drawings on the walls. She lifted her light to see better. Images in bright reflective colors lined the adjacent tunnels.

Turning into the passageway to her right, she studied the figures and shapes. Her hand flew to her mouth to stifle a gasp. The things of her nightmares played out in crude pictures. Earth, drawn in the form of a woman being gutted by two swords labeled *gluttony* and *violence,* pointed her bony finger to the next image. Dead trees, dried riverbeds, and denuded mountains knelt before the image of their matriarch dying by a thousand cuts. Children struck down by famine, drought, disease, and war were heaped lifeless at Mother Earth's feet. One lay on its side, blood pouring from its eyes, nose, ears, and mouth.

Sharon stumbled backward into the left tunnel, away from the awful depictions. Her body trembled at the flashes of memory they conjured. She remembered her beloved farmhouse blazing with her parents' bodies inside. The plague that had killed them played by the rule of kill or be killed. Since the disease succumbed only to fire, she had torched her home with their corpses inside in order to save herself and her brothers, Jon and Mark. Sharon, nineteen at the time and the oldest, had kept tears at bay as she and her brothers dug through the ashes for the charred bones of their parents. They buried them next to their grandparents on a hill overlooking the farm. Standing on the rise that day in front of their graves, her heart formed its first protective callus.

She touched the scarf at her neck and longed to be safe in the arms of Eve. Instinct always made her reach for her when the world got too heavy. Squeezing her eyes shut, she breathed in, catching a whiff of fried beetles and human sweat. She followed her nose and turned back into the tunnel at the right. Faint ribbons of light sliced the tunnel floor in the distance.

With her arm at her side, the sleeve-beam of light fell on her boots, her most scuffed and tough possessions. Sharon willed them to take her past the ghastly scenes and toward the light. The tunnel narrowed the farther she traveled. The occasional glance at the murals, which went on and on, lifted the hair at the back of her neck. Wiping at perspiration forming at her temples, she hoped whoever painted them was long gone.

Up ahead, the muddy light slicing the passageway grew brighter. She stopped to listen. A hum blending both human and mechanical sound drew her on. Something rustled in the bits of trash that lined the tunnel. She pointed her sleeve toward the floor. The glistening black eyes of a well-fed rat stared back at her. *Where there are rats, there are people.*

She pressed the light on her sleeve off and took deliberate, quiet steps. A square opening in the lower part of the right wall covered by a grate let light and noise waft into the tunnel. Sharon got to her knees. Taking care to be silent, and hoping not to be noticed, she peered into the openings of the grate.

A darkened corridor opened into a larger space where the sound and light came from. But she couldn't see around its bend. Sharon sat and leaned against the wall with the grate in front her. She rummaged through her satchel for the box of insect drones and microbots.

Inside the box lay a collection of bugs constructed by her brother, Jon. She chose the cockroach over the housefly. The roach would go unnoticed skittering at the edges of walls in the dank place, which smelled of musky, unwashed humans milling about. She'd noticed her own odor while moving through the tight passage. The funk assaulting her nose here was that of countless men and women enclosed in tight quarters without a means to wash themselves.

Carefully, she activated the roach-bot, reached through the grate, and released it. Leaving the controller nestled in the box, she touched the icon for the cockroach and watched as it flexed its six skinny legs. Its antennae probed the dirty concrete. Sharon powered up its eyes and the microphone embedded in its abdomen. Watching the screen, she maneuvered it toward the space filled with people.

Keeping close to the edge of the wall, the bug scuttled along the floor of the first room, which remained dark. Its antennae brushed something solid opposite the wall. Sharon paused its movement and let the nocturnal eyes focus. Boxes stacked high and labeled *NONA Surplus Food* were piled all around the room. Sharon guessed it must be a storage area for things to be moved on the MagLev. After doing a quick visual scan, she directed the roach-bot toward the room's doorway.

She watched costermongers hawking their wares to passersby from carts set up on the platform of the MagLev. The shoppers, wearing bright orange jumpsuits, milled from cart to cart, looking for a buy. Their eyes were milky: hydros. The few clean-clothed people hunched over carts looking at the wares were likely the rare passengers who could afford a train ticket. NONA soldiers carrying weapons randomly moved among them. Sharon directed the roach-bot onto the MagLev platform, careful to keep it safely near the wall.

"What the?" Something pinched at her calf through her dungarees. Sharon kicked out and whispered, "Light on." The beam on her sleeve glowed into the eyes of a hungry rat taking advantage of her prone position. Through gritted teeth, she said, "Get away," and rammed the heel of a boot into its long body. It darted into the dark.

She shook off the encounter and resumed her inspection of the platform through the eyes of the bug. It jostled forward. With a swipe of her forefinger, the roach-bot turned one hundred eighty degrees. A live cockroach flapped its wings and lunged at the roach-bot. Stopping short, it turned and backed into the electronic bug. *You've got to be kidding me.* Again, the cockroach circled the roach-bot and backed into its aft section. *You're barking up the wrong tree. She's not interested.* Sharon pressed the battery icon on the controller just as the cockroach made his next attempt to mate with the roach-bot. A jolt of electricity flipped it onto its back. Its legs wiggled and went limp. *Should've asked her first.*

Sharon depressed the power button to check the unit's battery pack. The defensive use of electric current to ward off the sexual advances of the cockroach had drained the roach-bot's power down to 50 percent. She swiped the forward icon on the controller. A quick look around was all the roach-bot could afford. It skittered along the wall, stopping to survey the expanse of the enormous platform.

The MagLev, ten cars long, sat flat on the powered-down electromagnetic tracks. Large fuel tanks labeled H_2 were connected to the MagLev by hoses large enough for a human to crawl through. *Geeze.* If they blew, they'd take out everything and everyone for kilometers. No wonder NONA went to great lengths to hide the locations of the fuel.

Using the controller's homing device, Sharon summoned the roach-bot to return. The bug scurried back through the storage room, coming to a stop at the toe of her boot. She shut down the system and returned the roach-bot to its spot in the box next to the dragonfly. Not wanting to be surprised by the harassing rat, she kept the sleeve light on as she removed her jacket and replaced it with Annie's. She stuffed her jacket and the small box of insect drones and microbots into her satchel. After prying the grate open with the claw of her hammer, she slipped the hammer into its baldric and zipped the costermonger coat closed.

She squeezed through the opening into the storage room and

replaced the grate. Getting to her feet, she gingerly wedged between the stacked boxes. Stopping short of the doorway, she waited for a moment when no one was looking, and slipped into the station.

Keeping her head down, she joined the underground bargain hunters. A variety of foraged foods were spread out on carts along the station platform. The mishmash of barely edible and not entirely nutritious plants had been dried, or made into salves or steaming soups that scented the air.

A man with a beard down to his skinny belly tossed and shook a pan of sizzling beetles. "Best damn beetles around," he said to a passerby. "I got a secret recipe. Get 'em here." He shook the sputtering pan.

Jars of cloudy liquid lined the cart of a tiny, ancient woman. With knobby fingers she twirled the jars. "Get your drinking water here," she croaked. A ragged yellow shawl draped over her bony shoulders. She smiled as Sharon passed, showing a mouthful of decaying teeth. "Wet your whistle, honey?"

"No, thanks." Sharon returned the smile and kept walking.

A soldier stepped into her path.

Sharon kept her head bowed at the floor, her eyes fixed on his heavy black combat boots. "Excuse me." She tried to step around him, hoping he wouldn't recognize Annie's coat, and that the woman wearing it wasn't Annie.

"Why aren't you selling?" He sidestepped left, keeping her blocked. "Look at me."

Sharon lifted her head. Keeping her breathing even, she answered, "Just looking for a good spot."

"Show me your ID," he ordered.

She slipped one hand into her pocket and lifted the other. "I have beetle larvae to sell," she lied. "Would you like some?" Her gamble that well-fed people turned down the food of the poor, she hoped, would pay off.

The soldier flashed an indifferent expression. "No." He pressed a handheld chip-reader to her raised forearm. After noting the readout, he clipped the reader to his belt. "Put your arm down and start selling. The MagLev leaves shortly."

73

"Yes, sir." She squeezed past him before letting out her breath and heading toward the back car of the MagLev.

Reaching into a pocket of her dungarees, she fished around for stray coins. Her fingers closed over a gritty pollo, a NONA coin minted out of sand from the Nebraska Desert. Not enough to buy a bottle of water, but maybe enough to buy something hot, fried, and salty. Annie's soup had helped to take the edge off of her hunger, but only the edge. She needed to keep up her strength. Moving past cart after cart containing goods she didn't have enough money to buy, she stopped in front of one operated by a skinny, hunched-over woman with a glass eye.

With one live eye and one dead eye, she stared at Sharon. "Goddammit, I don't have all day." She lowered her chin. "Three fried beetles for a pollo. Make up your mind or move along."

Sharon laid the pollo on the cart.

"I don't remember seeing you here before." The one-eyed woman put three crunchy bugs into a scuffed wooden bowl and passed it to Sharon. "Coat looks familiar, though."

"Thank you." Sharon took the beetles from the bowl. "You must be mistaken."

"You think I can't see clearly with one fucking eye?" She pounded her fist on the cart, nearly upsetting the pan of beetles. "Get the fuck away from my cart."

Sharon shoved the bugs into her pocket and hightailed it away from the cranky one-eyed woman.

Someone who smelled of cut sweet fern crashed a shoulder into hers. "Watch it," a man growled.

She stopped to look back.

He looked at her over his shoulder. Wearing a neatly trimmed beard and unsoiled clothing, he had the air of a passenger. "Watch where you're going, costermonger." He flicked his fingers at his shoulder as if to brush off any of her residue left on him when they'd touched. But instead of returning his head forward, he studied her.

His scrutiny seemed excessive. As if he, like the one-eyed woman, was trying to place her, but couldn't.

74

"I'm sorry." She turned and hurried away from his gaze.

A tall, thin man sitting cross-legged playing a guitar smiled as she neared him. His light brown eyes matched the color of his hair and skin. He had a thin mustache that curved around his mouth into a goatee at his chin. An aura of kindness surrounded him. *"Mujer."* He strummed again and sang a song she recognized.

The lovely sound made her stop. It soothed her clattering nerves and made her think of Eve. Plus, maybe by interacting she'd look more like she fit in. "Is that the song 'Amigo'?" she asked.

He laughed. "Ah, you know it." Continuing to strum, he said, "Not many people know the names of songs anymore. It's such an old one. How do you know it?"

"My father was a farmer. A man named Elliot who worked for him used to sing it."

"Was the man Latin, like me?"

"No." Sharon glided closer, drawn by his gentle demeanor. "His parents were South African. But he loved music. That song in particular."

"The South Africa that no longer exists?" He smiled. The twinkle of his eyes suggested that laughter rather than age had etched the fine wrinkles into his face.

"That's the one." With the beetles held loosely in her fist, she removed her hand from her pocket. "I don't have any money." She turned her hand palm up and opened it. "Will these do for another song?"

"Money buys food." He stopped strumming and pointed at the open instrument case next to him. "Food is what I'm after. Yes, it'll do. More of 'Amigo'? Or something else?"

"Do you know anything from 'Madame Butterfly'? It's my wife's favorite opera." His manner calmed her. Eve liked to say that some people carried their hearts on their sleeves. This man seemed like one of them, and with a good heart. It felt safe to be honest with this stranger. She dropped the bugs into his case. "I'm trying to find my way back to her. I miss her more than I can describe. Maybe hearing it will help me feel closer to her."

"As you wish." He set the guitar in the case and got to his feet. "In honor of love, I shall give you my best." Waving his arms in a flourish, he sucked in a deep breath, then let it out on the most beautiful singing her ears had ever experienced. His voice was like a river that flowed clean and pure from snowcapped mountains, down, over and around boulders.

It paralyzed her as it moved in and over her with its soothing sweetness. She closed her eyes so that only her ears took in the experience, which somehow helped to block out the noise of people and machines. She thought of Eve and their farm and their beautiful, life-giving apple tree. Her arms felt empty without her wife to hold and touch. Listening to the man's voice was like reaching through space and time to Eve. Sharon listened until this subterranean troubadour's voice slowed like a river reaching its destination in a cool, fresh pool of blue water.

He sighed at the end. "I hope it was worth the beetles."

She opened her eyes. "I only wish I had more to give."

"I'm Federico." His expression turned serious. "What's your name?"

Sharon turned to follow what had caught his attention and tried to remember the name of the dead costermonger. *Dammit.* She couldn't remember whether Annie had even mentioned it. Before she could make something up, a bald man dressed in an orange jumpsuit tried to rip her satchel from her. She shoved him away.

"What are you selling?" The bald man yanked at the satchel strap. "Bitch, what are you selling?" His milky eyes bored into hers.

Federico touched the man's shoulder. "Let me play you a song, friend."

"I don't want a fucking song." The bald man put an open hand to Federico's chest and shoved him.

A soldier looked up from his conversation with a nearby costermonger.

Sharon glanced from the soldier to the man in orange. His bald head reflected the light beaming down from the ceiling. The absence of ultraviolet radiation in the synthetic light left his skin chalky pale. He shook her satchel strap. "Sell me something."

"Get your fucking hands off me," she spat. "I have nothing to sell."

"Oh, I get it." He grinned. "Even better." The bald man grabbed her elbow and yanked her behind him toward another room off of the platform.

"Let her go." Federico's voice, even with an order spilling from his mouth, sounded calm and fluid. "She's not selling sex."

"No!" Sharon shoved out of the bald man's grasp. "I'm definitely not."

In a quiet voice, Federico said to Sharon, "If you don't find something in your pack to sell him, he's going to drag you into the brothel room and take whatever he wants."

"Do I need to call a soldier over?" The well-dressed passenger she'd bumped shoulders with emerged from the crowd. To the bald man he said, "You like this job, don't you?"

"Of course." The man glowered.

"Well then, you're going to leave the woman alone. Or I'm going to ask a soldier to quiet this skirmish. You know they don't tolerate things like this down here." The passenger, who smelled of sweet fern, tipped his hat. "They, like the rest of us, prefer tranquility around so much explosive fuel."

The platform shook as a horn sounded.

Federico snapped his guitar case closed and picked it up. "Saved by the bell." He curtsied to the passenger. "Thank you."

The bald man clad in orange puffed out his chest and stormed off toward the fuel tanks.

"Shall we?" Federico said to Sharon.

"What?" she asked.

"You're a costermonger, aren't you?" He winked. "Who's looking for her wife."

She nodded.

"Well, let's go. The train is boarding. Which means costermongers either get on the train or are left behind. There's lots to sell in Chicago."

She ran a hand through her hair. "Chicago's where I'm going." Her heart raced with joy. Unscathed so far! In a couple of hours she'd be where Eve was. Somewhere in that city, Sharon would find her. She touched the scarf at her neck and trailed Federico onto the train.

Chapter 7

The soldier tore Eve from Sharon's grasp. "*No!*" Sharon strained to hear the words her wife mouthed: *I love you*. Her own inner voice, tinny and distant, cautioned that Eve existed only in dreams. She held tight to sleep. "*Eve!*"

Curling his finger around the trigger of his spectraletto, a second soldier pressed the muzzle to Eve's temple.

"*Let her go.*" A burst of terror let loose in Sharon's belly. She rode it to her throat where it wedged. Mustering her voice, she managed to beg, "*Please.*"

"Sharon."

A nudge to her boot prodded her further from sleep.

"Wake up."

"Leave us alone." She lifted a knee and slammed her boot onto the floor. The sting to her heel hoisted her out of slumber.

"You were dreaming something bad." The fluid voice of Federico filled in the blanks of consciousness.

Her leaden limbs reminded her that it had been almost two days with no sleep and no Eve. The inside of her mouth begged for water, her belly for food, and her eyes for rest.

"*Lo siento.* I had to wake you." He smiled. "Before you busted my head in."

Sharon followed his eyes to her hand curled tightly around the handle of her hammer tucked into its baldric. She let go and shook out the tingling in her fingers. Pulling the chartreuse costermonger coat over the hammer, she said, "It was a very bad dream."

"Looked like you were tangling with a nasty phantasm. Didn't want to be in the middle of it."

"Where are we?" She rubbed the residue of the nightmare from her eyes.

"Maybe ten minutes or so from Chicago." Federico twisted the cap off of a filtering flask. "*Agua?*"

The risk of getting sick from a stranger's flask outweighed the discomfort of dehydration. "No, thank you."

"*Bueno.* Suit yourself." Federico gulped from his flask. A tattoo resembling a snowflake stretched over the inside of his wrist. The snowflake had a circle at its middle bisected by two perpendicular lines creating four quarters. Pointing from the circle were six short crystals alternating between six long ones. He wiped his mouth with his sleeve and replaced the cap. "You were calling the name Eve in your sleep. Is she your wife?"

"Yes."

"Why did she leave you?"

"She didn't." Sharon cleared her dry throat. "NONA took her from me."

"Ah, I see." He slipped the flask into his coat pocket. "I'm very sorry. What virus is she suffering from, then? Or do they claim she committed a crime?"

"Neither. She's not sick from a virus. She's Chinese. And . . ." She blinked, trying to erase the gauzy image of the nightmare from her mind.

"And, what?" Federico asked.

"She has a blood cancer she'll die from without treatment. NONA took her to the Asian internment camp in Chicago. Haven't you heard? NONA's rounding up people of Asian descent."

He shook his head. "I'm surprised I haven't. Although I did hear that Prime Minister Tang is ratcheting up his tired threat to occupy the Manitoba Grasslands."

"Because the Thwaites glacier is going to collapse," she added.

"They've been saying that for years. For as long as Tang has been threatening to take over NONA's only food basket." Federico stretched his long limbs, which had been scrunched into the small jump seat. "It won't be long before NONA starts drafting young men to fight Tang if it's already plucking people of Asian descent off of the streets." He snorted. "It's ridiculous. Really. Given the number of people who have Asian blood, who would be left to fight Tang? How does one even measure who's Asian and who isn't?"

"I don't know. And I don't care." Her headache grew more intense. She rubbed her temples to tamp it down. "I just want to find my wife. When I do, we'll disappear someplace safe until the world goes back to simmer from a boil. Like we always do."

He touched her arm, his eyes soft with compassion. "It's very difficult to get into the camp now. A new virus has sprung up. NONA closed it to visitors yesterday."

Needles of panic pricked her skin. "Why the hell would they bring new people there? Eve's body can't handle fighting a virus."

Almost whispering, he said, "You don't want me to answer that."

"A cleansing?"

"Yes. Put a bunch of sick people NONA doesn't want around in a place they can't escape. Well . . ." Federico paused. "I'm sorry."

"I have to get her out of there." Sharon tore her eyes from his. Staying in the moment buttressed her from the parade of horribles trying to march through her mind. She fixated on the cloudy Plexiglas containers in front of her that secured supply crates and costermonger carts to the floor. A thread of red light ran the length of the narrow walkway between the containers and the line of jump seats. The MagLev bucked, then decelerated.

Costermongers slept, chatted, or watched the news screens that dropped down from the ceiling of the MagLev supply car. The programs were exclusively NONA propaganda acted out by government-paid journalists in silent skits annotated in English, Chinese, Spanish, and French subtitles. A line of flashing red words interrupted the program: PREPARE FOR ARRIVAL IN FIVE MINUTES AT CHICAGO, THE CAPITAL CITY OF NONA.

Federico leaned into her and whispered, "There's no time to explain. As soon as we stop, you have to come with me if you are to have any hope of finding your wife."

"Who are you, really?" Reflexively, she reached for her hammer.

"Easy." He lifted his hands. "I'm only trying to help. I know a way to sneak out. He won't be able to see you."

"Who won't be able to see me?" Sharon studied Federico's face for a lie or setup. Decades-old advice from her grandfather had taught her how to size up people and their motives. *Always measure a person by what their eyes tell you,* he'd say. But the only thing gleaned from the man next to her seemed to be genuine concern.

"Listen to me." Federico gripped her elbow. "If the passenger who helped you back at the station finds you, you won't live to find your wife." He pointed to her face. "He'll do a whole lot worse to you than those bruises and that cut."

She touched where the NONA soldier's weapon had slammed into her. Annie's magic salve had gone a long way toward healing the gash. But the bruises from the soldier's strike and Mags's head-butt were still tender. And the persistent ache in her shoulder blade was maddening. Federico was talking about the nice-looking man who smelled of sweet fern. That didn't make sense.

The MagLev heaved left, then right. The g-force pushing Sharon against the seat slackened as the train decelerated. The red letters on the screen scrolled, PREPARE TO STOP IN 45 SECONDS. "Why should I be afraid of him?" She pressed her thumb to the latch of the jump seat restraint. The strapping retracted, freeing her from the seat.

Federico stood, pulling Sharon with him. "I've been watching him watch for someone. For days he's been waiting. Finally, that someone came along. And it was you. I don't know why. You have to get out of here because he works for the Strelitzia. Come with me. We'll help you find Eve."

"I've never heard of the Strelitzia. You both must've mistaken me for someone else." Dread wormed into her belly. Getting

82

caught up in a case of mistaken identity would slow her quest to find Eve. "I'm just a poor farmer from Maine looking for my wife. That's all."

"Maybe so. But just in case you need help." He reached into his pocket and retrieved an acupalmtell. With his forefinger, he scrolled through several photographs on the small handheld computer. "Here, take a good look. If you run into trouble, come to this building. You won't be able to get in. But we'll know you're there." He stowed the device. "To find us, stand south of the Cloud Gate sculpture in Millennium Park. It looks like a big silver bean. In fact, that's what people call it. Once you find the Bean, look to your left. You'll see the building."

"I really appreciate your help. But I've got to go." She tried to push past him.

Federico blocked her path. "I'm trying to help you."

"If you want to help me, tell me how to get to the internment camp." Sharon glanced at the line of costermongers marching forward out of the train. "My wife needs me. I have to find her now."

Federico sighed. "Very well." He bent to her ear and spoke quickly. "The MagLev surfaced where the old interstates 90 and 290 intersected. The only way to go when we exit is east on West Harrison toward the lake. There aren't many streets left open by NONA. Only two go north toward your destination. The camp is just north of the Jardine Water Purification Plant."

Shouting erupted at the front of the line as NONA soldiers ordered the cargo operators onto the train to unload the Plexiglas boxes.

"Harrison ends at the entry to Millennium Park," Federico continued. "Go north through the park. Most people will go south to skirt it and then north again on Lake Shore Drive. That's the way the passenger will expect you to go."

"What makes you think that?" Sharon asked.

"Because no one goes through Millennium Park. Not even NONA. Banditti gangs rule there. If I were you, I'd take my chances with the Banditti before the Strelitzia. Go fast and careful."

Alarm drummed an ominous beat through her veins. Sharon turned away and got moving.

"Please, Sharon," Federico called after her. "Stay safe."

She rushed past men and women dressed like homogenous robots in stark black uniforms. They worked in silence, unlatching the containers. Sharon stumbled on the last step up into hot, humid air hanging over Chicago. Stopping briefly, she wrestled out of Annie's warm coat and stuffed it into her satchel. To conceal her hammer, she slipped on her old jacket. Falling into the current of costermongers and passengers surging east toward their mundane machinations, she felt inconspicuous.

Battered by war and storms, the infamous Willis Tower loomed over the city like a defiant ogre. To the east, a three-story brick barrier walled off Lake Michigan from the thirsty. It ran north and south as far as she could see. Graffiti decorated the barrier in an incomprehensible jumble of exaggerated letters, symbols, and pictures. She'd read that NONA built the wall using bricks from the one that had separated its predecessors, the U.S. and Mexico, at their former border. Erasing the tangible boundary, NONA tore the wall down and rebuilt it around the precious water of Lake Michigan.

A dreary miasma of gray sky and gray smog framed the gray buildings. The smokestacks of the long-dead steel mills to the east jabbed at the distant horizon. Her late grandparents had honeymooned in the city more than half a century ago. Sharon imagined the sickening sulfur smell of quenched coke as her grandmother had described it. On reflex, she lifted the scarf at her neck over her nose and mouth. Eve's scent reached deep into Sharon and tugged at her worst fear, of losing the woman she loved. Jostled by a sea of people shoulder to shoulder hurrying along, a hollow loneliness settled over her.

Ever since she and Eve had gotten together, Sharon had always felt her wife's presence even when they were apart. The thread that tied them thrummed with Eve's energy, somehow, always. Sharon put a hand to her heart, confident that it would lead her to Eve.

Someone bumped her from behind. She looked back only to see faces masked in indifference. Satisfied that the passenger Federico warned her about wasn't following, she kept pace until the street ended. Stepping aside to let the herd move south, she entered Millennium Park.

A vast shantytown built of scavenged materials made from old vehicles, dilapidated buildings, and hunks of random plastic, metal and wood extended the length of the makeshift settlement. The cornucopia of ethnicities, including Asian, surprised her, given that NONA was plucking them off the streets.

Young, old and middle-aged, everyone shared the common characteristics of being rail thin and unwashed. Even though Sharon was relatively healthy, the densely populated park and her filthy clothing helped her blend in.

Conjuring her brother Jon's last words to her before NONA shipped him off to fight and die in the War of Earth's Rebellion, Sharon squared her shoulders and set her face in a hard expression. *Especially when you're scared, carry yourself like a madwoman who kicks ass. I love you, sis.* "I love you too, Jon," she said under her breath.

She continued north until a line of people blocked the way. Carrying a variety of containers, they shuffled toward an odd marble structure. At its center the marble formed what looked like a layer cake. Surrounding the cake were four pairs of weathered bronze seahorses in various states of disrepair. One had no head while another lay in pieces.

A teenaged girl with stringy hair carrying a five-liter bucket shuffled next to her.

"Where's everyone going?" Sharon asked.

"The Buckingham Fountain." The girl lifted the bucket. "NONA turns it on once a day. Got to get a good spot since they only leave it on for about five minutes. Everybody knows that." The girl looked at her curiously, then rushed ahead.

Sharon salivated at the mention of water. If she hoped to keep her strength, she needed to drink. She opened the satchel flap, fished out her empty water flask and followed the teenager.

People shoved and jostled for space around the empty pool that surrounded the fountain. In front of her stood a tall, gangly man holding a bucket and large plastic bag. A small boy held to one of his legs; a little girl clung to the other like human weights keeping him tethered to life. He caught Sharon's eye when he tried to move closer with the children in tow. After wedging in near one of the seahorses, he motioned for Sharon to move closer.

"Thank you." She squeezed into the offered space.

Staring straight ahead, he nodded.

The mouths of the seahorses and top of the cake sputtered, blew mists of water, and hissed before spewing jets of clear liquid. The crowd shook as thirsty people buzzed in a frenzy to fill their containers.

Sharon submerged her flask into the pool. When the bubbles stopped, she gulped the water until it was gone. She savored the cool liquid deep inside her body as it hydrated and revived her. She filled it again, then moved back to let someone else take her place. She found a quiet spot near a large tent with a bent pole. It leaned heavily to one side like a sailboat in a brisk wind.

Lifting the flask to her lips she drank again, slowly, in spite of the heavy chlorine smell. The water soothed her mouth, while the chlorine stung her dry, cracked lips. When she lowered the flask, she noticed two young men standing near a lorry with no wheels. *Banditti.*

She tucked the flask into the satchel as the jets of water at the fountain went dry. The crowd groaned. Like zombies, they turned and began to lumber away. The man with the two children emerged from the others carrying his full bucket and bulbous plastic bag. Instead of hanging at his legs, the little boy and girl held tight to the back of his shirttail.

The two Banditti in stealthy unison locked onto the man like predators to prey. One of them, his face pocked with acne, grinned at the other. Sharon guessed he was barely out of his teens. The stick-skinny thieves followed the man. Sharon followed them.

"Hey, you, with the water," one of them said.

The man with the two kids stopped and turned.

"Leave our daddy alone." The little girl glared.

"We will," said the acne-faced Banditti. "As long as he gives us his water."

Sharon debated whether to intervene. On the one hand, time kept ticking down for Eve. On the other, the man with the two little kids had shown her kindness. Plus, he looked no match for the two Banditti men. And the brave little girl tugged at Sharon's conscience. She slid her hammer from its baldric. "Leave them alone."

Acne-man turned and pulled a knife from his back pocket. He sneered and flicked it open.

The father set his water down, shielding his kids with his arms. "Take it."

"We intend to." Acne-man lunged at Sharon, who had interposed herself between the thieves and the water.

She dodged the guy's blade and swung her hammer, making solid contact with his jaw.

He howled and dropped to his knees, cupping his mouth. "My . . ." He moved his bloodied hands from his face, and two teeth clinked onto the concrete.

She stepped toward him with her hammer raised.

He cowered as his formerly brave accomplice ran off.

Sharon returned her hammer to its baldric and realized she was panting. Her body ached with exhaustion.

"Let us share some of our water with you." The father put a hand to her shoulder. "To repay you. We have some food as well."

"No, thank you," her voice quivered. "I still have some left."

"Are you all right?"

"No, but I have to keep going."

"I understand." He lowered his hand from her shoulder. "May Earth keep you in her good graces."

"It's been a long time since I heard someone use that saying." Sharon managed a faint smile. "You as well."

"Earth and the people we love carry us through." He laid his hands on the heads of the boy and girl. "I remind myself every morning so that I have the strength to keep going. You keep going too, stranger."

"I will." Sharon turned and walked north away from the man and two children. Death in a place like Millennium Park, she suspected, came quickly and often. She hoped that he'd live long enough to raise his kids. They reminded her of Inu. She missed him.

As she went on, her legs grew more tired. She needed food, water, and rest. A man yelled something in the near distance. He spoke like a preacher and grew louder the closer she got. A flash of light like the sun hitting metal and bouncing off burned her eye. She turned her head to see a giant glistening object shaped like a kidney bean. *The Cloud Gate sculpture Federico described.*

The preacher stood on a bench nearby with his hands held toward the sky. "Oh, the end of times is upon us. Repent now." He shook a fist. "No one believes anymore. This"—he spread his arms wide—"is how we die."

Ignoring the preacher's superstitious yammering, Sharon stood in front of the glassy bean and studied her reflection. Her face sagged under the weight of despair and exhaustion. Bags circled her eyes, and the color of her skin had gone ashen. Her thick, dark wavy hair curled in haphazard directions. A yellowed bruise marked the middle of her forehead where she'd head-butted Mags. Crusty dark blood discolored the glue Dr. Ryan had used to close the gash at the side of her head. "Whatever happens, keep going," she said to herself. She closed, then opened her eyes as if somehow that would help.

The scent of sweet fern wafted over her shoulder as a familiar reflection joined hers in the bean. *The passenger from the MagLev platform.*

He smiled. "Hello, Sharon. Please come with me. I want to help you."

How the hell does he know my name? She wheeled around and reached for her hammer just as Federico jabbed the muzzle of a short-barreled spectraletto at the passenger's torso.

"Not likely," Federico said.

A young, well-built man a head shorter than Federico flanked the passenger's other side. With bright green eyes, bushy beard, high, freckled cheekbones and red hair, he looked like a human oddity. "No, not likely at all." He tightened his arm around the passenger's.

"Get your filthy hands off of me." The passenger tried to yank free of the red-haired man.

"No." Federico leaned toward the man's ear. "You do not speak until we ask you to speak." He turned his eyes to meet Sharon's. "Now do you believe me?"

"You are a . . ." The passenger's eyes rolled up into his head and his mouth froze around an empty attempt to finish his sentence. The fingers of his hand, at the end of the arm held by the red-haired man, splayed out like a claw.

The red-haired man's thumb pressed into the pressure point at the passenger's wrist. "I'm a Buddhist. It goes against my grain to hurt people." He let go. "But it also goes against my grain to let someone hurt my friends. That's where I make an exception to not inflicting violence. So shut the hell up—so I don't have to hurt you."

"Thank you, JJ." Federico smiled at the red-haired man. "This is Sharon. Sharon, meet JJ, which is short for Jujitsu Jack. As you can see, he knows a thing or two about the martial arts."

"I'd be a fool not to believe you now." Sharon kept hold of her hammer. "Tell me what's going on?" She locked eyes with the passenger. "How do you know my name?"

"Not here." Federico held her gaze as if trying to lay open his motives for her to see. "The Strelitzia doesn't play by the same set of rules as we do. Come with us." He reached into the coat pocket of the passenger and retrieved an acupalmtell. "The Strelitzia has something that belongs to us. We want it back. Given the passenger's interest in you—you're somehow connected. You help us, and we'll help you."

Sharon studied the three men for clues. The young freckled and red-haired man, and tall, slender, distinguished Federico seemed more earnest than the clean-cut passenger, who now seemed sinister. "How?"

"We have ways of getting inside the internment camp." Federico's soft voice left no hint of anything resembling a lie. "We can have Eve out by this afternoon. But first, we need to have some questions answered by the Strelitzia." He tilted his head left. "We go to our building, ask the questions, and then sneak into the camp to rescue your wife. You have my word."

"I've known Federico a long time," JJ interrupted. "He never lies."

"Everyone lies," Sharon said.

"Give us a chance to prove our word is good." Federico cocked his head. "Take a walk with us to the building I showed you in the picture. We'll have you inside the camp before sundown."

Sharon squinted skyward. The sun hung around one o'clock. If Federico kept his word, she would have her arms around Eve within five hours. "If I go with you, I want the spectraletto."

Federico laughed. "We saw you back there with your hammer. You really need our weapon too?"

"Yes. There are three of you."

"All right then." Federico slapped the passenger on the back and spoke into his ear. "You don't want to know what JJ will do to your pressure points if you misbehave." He thumbed his weapon's safety switch to on. He turned it butt end toward Sharon. "Here you go. Now will you come with me?"

Sharon checked the weapon's energy gauge. The needle pointed into the green at 80 percent full. "For now, yes." She stuffed the spectraletto into the waistband of her dungarees.

The passenger's top lip twitched. "You're making a mistake."

"No talking." JJ put a hand to the back of the passenger's neck pressing his thumb and forefinger into pressure points there. "I don't need a spectraletto to shut you up. And hey, there are pressure points you don't even know you have. Think about that."

Federico fished around in the passenger's pockets. He retrieved an SComCat and a knife. "A trade." After slipping the items into his own pocket, he pulled out a flexible mask. "You won't be able to see, talk, or hear with this on. Not to worry, you'll be able to breathe just fine." He slipped the mask over the passenger's head. "Shall we?" Federico pointed toward the building west of the glistening Cloud Gate sculpture. "Let's get our questions answered, and then find your Eve."

Chapter 8

Picked-clean bones of what looked like a rat littered the floor of the dimly lit room. "What is this place?" Sharon covered her mouth with Eve's scarf to stifle the clammy smell of the filthy, shabby building.

"The entrance to our underground safe haven." Federico swiped the tiny screen on a micro-acupalmtell embedded in his sleeve. Soft light flooded a staircase that sloped downward. "These take us to an abandoned underground parking lot. Only things down there are rusted and burned-out hydro-cars and trucks." He motioned for Sharon and JJ to follow.

JJ tugged the masked passenger with him.

Once the four of them were on the staircase, Federico locked the heavy steel door behind them. He pecked and swiped at the screen of the micro-acupalmtell. "Just need to check for any intruders." He pointed at the top of the wall where it met the ceiling. "We have cameras and heat sensors all around." He studied the screen.

"We good?" JJ asked.

"Yeah." Federico swiped the screen off. "Come." He led them across the parking lot to another door. When he touched all five fingers of his right hand to a key pad, the door slid open, revealing a small room that looked like the cockpit of some kind of vehicle. "This is an amphibious travel pod built in the 2040s. The city used to use it to inspect the sewer pipes.

It was a brilliant idea. The pod can move through the tunnels whether they're full or empty." He climbed into the pod. "Unfortunately, there are only two left. On the upside, we control them both."

JJ maneuvered the passenger inside and into a jump seat. "We can travel to wherever we want beneath the city." He lowered the seat's torso-restraint over the passenger's chest, clicking it locked.

With his hands tied at the wrists and the mask over his face, the passenger sat motionless and silent.

Wondering what he was thinking and why he was after her lifted the hairs on the back of Sharon's neck.

Federico gestured for her to follow. "I know it seems gross, but the pod is sealed. It's equipped with air scrubbers and an O^2 generator, just like the mud subs that helped win all those Continental Shelf Wars. As you can see, she seats five, originally for a pilot, two technicians, a mechanic, and a diver." He pointed at a gasket surrounding the entryway. "When the pod lands in a room off of the tunnel, it's sealed at the doorway. You'd never know we're about to travel through a river of shit unless I told you so."

"Thanks for the visual." Sharon eased into the pod's tight space and lowered the scarf. Lights, levers, and buttons took up the real estate on the dash. She guessed the pilot's seat was the one with a classic-style throttle and steering wheel. "Who are the 'we' that you refer to?"

JJ lifted his wrist and pulled back the sleeve of his jacket. "We're the Qaunik people. I'm guessing you've never heard of us." The tattoo on his wrist matched the one on Federico's.

"No," she confirmed.

"When we have more time, I'll fill you in. For now, please, sit." Federico pointed at an empty jump seat. "We must go." He slid the pod door closed, settled himself into the pilot's seat at the control panel and flipped a switch. The pod's systems whirred to life. A series of clear panels and exterior lights gave a three-hundred-and-sixty-degree view of the ick in the tunnel.

Sharon shook her head in disbelief as she sat and secured the torso-restraint of her jump seat. "So, where are we going that requires traveling through a river of shit?"

"To the Goldfinch jazz bar, as we call it." JJ settled into the jump seat next to Federico. "Not the nicest view to get there, but one doesn't typically run into anyone else while traveling through a river of sewage." He flashed a smile. "You know your true friends by the ones willing to go through shit with you."

"Does this make me a friend?" Sharon asked.

JJ gave her a wink. "Time will tell."

"NONA must be backed up cleaning water at the Jardine Water Treatment Plant; the tunnel is full." Federico slid his finger across the command-screen and pressed a button several times, ramping up the engines. "That's the propeller you hear. We'll be there very shortly."

Sharon glanced at the subdued passenger. The Caucasian-skin-colored mask fit snug over his face. It covered his eyes, mouth, and ears, exposing only his nose. With his hands folded in his lap he seemed relaxed, almost as if he might be meditating. His unnatural calmness under the circumstances and the fact that he knew her name unnerved her.

After traveling about twenty minutes, Federico unlatched a transceiver from the console. "Coming in to dock. Please prepare the hatch."

"Roger," a voice replied. "Preparing hatch. Over."

Federico slowed the engines and maneuvered the pod from the tunnel into a large room.

"See the gasket?" JJ pointed at its outline, which glowed reflective yellow in the beam of the pod's forward lights.

Federico lined the pod up with the gasket. "Docking now," he said into the transceiver.

"Roger," the voice acknowledged. "Hatch ready."

Federico returned the transceiver to the console. He pressed the pod against the wall and flipped a switch. A whoosh blew from the pod as it suctioned to the wall. "Here we are." He got up and opened the pod door.

JJ freed the passenger from the restraint and lifted him to his feet by his armpits. They followed Federico from the pod.

Sharon unlatched her torso-restraint and got to her feet. Music played somewhere in the distance, a brassy sound she didn't recognize. She liked it. Peppered in the quiet space of the music was the sound of human laughter. She couldn't remember the last time she'd heard music and laughter.

"We'll stop in the communication room first. The boss wants us to do a deep interview on this guy, if we can." Federico led them down the hallway. "Then we'll report in."

JJ tugged the passenger along by his elbow.

Federico motioned for them to join him in a room, bare except for a large video screen and various types of electronic equipment. "Let's find out why the Strelitzia is after you, Sharon." He set the SComCat he'd taken from the passenger's pocket on the table in front of the screen. He jutted his chin at the passenger. "You can take that off of him."

JJ released the restraints on the passenger's wrists and pulled the mask from his face.

The passenger rolled his head back, gulping in big mouthfuls of air. His wiped his splotchy and sweaty face with his hands.

"Hope you enjoyed your quiet time." Federico pointed at the SComCat. "Because now it's talking time."

"Fuck you." The passenger crossed his arms over his chest, though he looked afraid. "I'm not going to tell you anything."

Sliding the SComCat in front of him, Federico said, "Lucky for you, it's the Strelitzia we want to talk to. You're going to call him."

"Like hell I am," the passenger snorted. "It'll be the last call I ever make."

JJ put his hand to the back of the passenger's neck. "Press in the code."

"Are you hard of hearing?" Lacing his fingers together, the passenger laid his hands in his lap. "I said I'm not doing it."

"What is that smell?" Federico lifted his nose and sniffed the air around the passenger. "You recognize that, JJ?"

Sharon wondered if Federico referred to the scent of sweet fern she'd noticed on the passenger at the MagLev platform.

JJ pressed his fingers into the soft spots of the passenger's neck. "Smells like someone who has the luxury of three square meals, plenty of water, and a shower every day."

The passenger winced. "You filthy idiots won't make me talk. In fact, your two-bit torture routine is starting to bore me. If you had it in you to make me bleed, you'd have done it already."

"We don't need to make you bleed." Federico bent and put his lips close to the passenger's left ear. "I know what kind of person you are. Which means I know your worst fear. You're not afraid to bleed—you're afraid of the dark. Just like everyone else."

The passenger's lip twitched.

Federico straightened and nodded at JJ.

JJ pressed hard into a pressure point at the passenger's neck.

He kicked and struggled against JJ, unable to speak.

"That's enough," Federico said.

JJ let go.

The passenger bent over the desk and panted. "You fucker," he growled.

"A fucker who doesn't have time to waste. Which is why I'll spell out with specificity the only two options you have." Federico held up a finger. "One, you punch in the code and call the Strelitzia."

"And then he kills me," the passenger added.

"Or two." Federico held up two fingers. "We take you to one of our holding cells. There, your skin will not feel the sun. Your eyes will not see light. You'll be fed just enough water and dried insects to keep you alive. No one will talk to you. You will hear no sound. Your life will be spent in perpetual darkness, hunger, thirst, and isolation. And you most definitely will not smell nice, like sweet fern. You'll wish you were dead."

Holy shit. Sharon made a mental note not to end up on the wrong side of the Qaunik. For such outwardly kind people, they had a brutal streak.

The passenger glared at Federico.

"See?" Federico slapped a hand to the table. "I told you we don't need to make you bleed."

"Personally," JJ added, "I'd rather die a horrible death than live hungry, thirsty, and lonely in the dark."

"Will you let me go if I do it?" the passenger asked. "I'll take my chances running from the Strelitzia."

"We'll do better than that." JJ clamped a hand to his shoulder. "We can drop you off someplace far away."

"I'll make the goddamned call." The passenger reached for the SComCat.

"Good man." Federico sighed. "I'm sorry, Sharon, you had to witness such harshness. We must do what we must do, though."

"I plan to stay on your good side."

Federico smiled his empathetic smile. "This from the woman who knocked a man's teeth out for trying to steal water from a father and his children." His smile evaporated when he looked at the passenger. Laying his palms on the table, he leaned to within inches of the passenger's face. "Call him. Now."

Flinching, the passenger put his hand to the SComCat and pressed a sequence of numbers on its keypad.

A crackling preceded an electronically altered voice that spoke from it. "I trust that you've found her."

"Do tell the truth," Federico said to the passenger.

"Yes." The passenger kept his eyes to Federico's. "Unfortunately, I've been found, too."

Several seconds of silence passed. "Qaunik," the voice said in a tone of resignation.

"Let's talk face to face, shall we?" Federico waved his hand over what looked like a bowl suspended over an electronic stem. "I've activated our satellite video. Turn yours on, Strelitzia."

The screen flashed a gauzy green before the pixels settled into an image. A person wrapped in a colorful coat decorated with red, yellow, pink, and purple flowers sprawled in a high-backed chair. The black mask he wore over his face made him look birdlike except for his exposed mouth. Two soldiers wearing masks like his, only white, stood armed behind him.

"Aaron," the Strelitzia said to the passenger. "How did someone of your caliber not only get captured by the Qaunik," he leaned toward the screen, "but be convinced to disturb me?"

"It's not been one of my better days." Aaron's Adam's apple slid down his throat. "I'm sorry."

"Shut up." The Strelitzia glared. "The world is wild and you're a coward." To Federico he said, "I trust you'll return my coward to me when you finish with him."

"He won't be staying with us," Federico answered. "We have enough mouths to feed and water."

"Ah." The Strelitzia hooked the heel of his boot on the top rung of his throne-like chair. "Food and water. Our common denominator. There's just so little of either. We humans were warned for decades. What did we do? We destroyed our seed banks, poisoned our water, and made so much of the world a desert. Now we survive on a diet of kale, potato, and cockroaches washed down with dirty water when we can scrounge it. Fools, the collective *we* are."

"Don't forget thievery." The words dripped with disgust from Federico's lips. "Where is our ship?"

"A man who cuts to the chase." The Strelitzia put his elbow on his knee and rested his chin in his palm. "Tell me, sir Qaunik, what is your name and that of your red-bearded associate?"

"I'm Federico and this is JJ. You stole our ship and we want it back."

"Lighten up." The Strelitzia sat up straight. "I have no doubt that you do. But I can't allow that to happen. Your boss, Woody, and I just don't mix. We're like oil and water." He flicked a wrist. "I'd have to kill such a worthy adversary."

Federico froze as if the flippant comment bit into him and crawled beneath his skin.

Aaron grinned.

"Why were you following me?" Sharon's patience grew thin for the eccentric man.

Reaching into his pocket, the Strelitzia smiled. "We finally meet, Sharon. I've so been looking forward to it." He drew out his hand, hiding something in his palm. "You have something that I want." He turned his hand over, revealing an apple. "Lovely, isn't it?"

Heat shot up Sharon's back. The apple, looking plump and fresh in shades of pale green to red, filled up the room like an elephant. Her apple tree produced the Pink Lady variety, like the one now screaming that this strange man must somehow know her secret. Keeping her voice even and calm, she asked, "How do you know me?" She hoped the slight quiver to her voice went unnoticed.

"It's not so much that I know you, but rather your prototype." The Strelitzia lifted the apple to his lips, took a bite, and balanced the fruit on his knee. He chewed slowly, swallowed, and smiled. "Unbelievably good. You must share your secret with us. Don't you agree, Federico and JJ?"

"Holy hell." JJ's eyes cut to Sharon's.

"An apple that's not poison?" Federico studied the Strelitzia as if waiting to see the beginning of his tainted end, which didn't come.

"Where did you get the apple?" Sharon asked, terrified of the answer.

"A friend of yours." The Strelitzia took another bite. "Dr. Ryan, I think his name was. It was hard to tell with all of his blubbering about sparing his wife." Using his sleeve, he wiped juice from his chin. "This is the last of the two he had on him. I'm betting there are more."

Sharon could almost taste it. "Where are the Ryans?" Panic spread out of her like blood from the cut of a knife. "You work for NONA, don't you?"

"Heavens, no," the Strelitzia chuckled. "They're like ants running all over themselves. Except that ants at least have a plan. NONA's running scared of what's to come when the Thwaites lets go. The fools will either drown or starve. I, on the other hand, have a plan. And it involves you telling me what I want to know."

"It was you," she gasped, as the pieces of the puzzle fell into place. "You took my Eve. Where is she?"

"Now you're catching on." In dramatic fashion, the Strelitzia slowly finished the apple.

Sharon struggled to keep a lid on her searing anger.

"You know, I miscalculated you and Eve." He held the core by the stem between two fingers. "I could've taken you both at the same time. But after studying your prototypes, I expected that if I took you together, you'd close ranks and never reveal your secret to me. Some romantic pact you'd never break. So I decided to separate you."

"For the love of all things good!" JJ exclaimed. "I hardly believe my eyes. You ate an apple and you're still talking."

"Remarkable, isn't it?" The Strelitzia grinned.

A rising panic chipped away at Sharon's wall of composure. "I'll bring you more apples. Please, just let my wife go."

"That's not going to work for me." He dangled the apple core. "You see, I assume that Eve, because she's the botanist in the family, is also the brains behind your special apple tree. I'm not wrong about that, am I?"

Sharon didn't answer.

"I tried growing the seeds of the other apple. They're not viable. You two have a secret. I don't know what it is, but I want it. Let's be clear, your Eve is worth a whole lot more than a bushel of apples." He popped the core into his mouth and flicked the stem over his shoulder.

"She's not well. You have to let her go." Sharon gripped the edges of the table. "If she dies, so does the secret. Because if something happens to her, I'll never tell you."

The Strelitzia swallowed the chewed core. "Not to worry." He wagged a forefinger. "She's being well cared for. Plenty of food, water, and medicine for her cancer. With me, she has the promise of a very long life. As for your apples, you keep them. What I want is the secret that makes them perfect. Eve knows the secret, and so do you."

"If you know so much about us," Sharon said, "why didn't you just steal it?"

"Don't think I didn't try," he snickered. "I had a plan to do just that. I took Eve and then sent some of my Banditti friends to pay you a visit. The plan was to make Eve watch them rough you up until she couldn't take it anymore. In exchange for ending your misery, she'd tell me where on that ratty patch of dirt you call a farm the secret I want is hidden. I already know it's not in the seeds. It's far more subtle than that. The Banditti would've killed you and brought me your delicious mysteries." He shrugged. "And I would've kept Eve all to myself."

Sharon's hands clenched to fists. "You son of a bitch!"

Federico grasped her shoulder.

"Yeah, things didn't turn out how I'd hoped." The Strelitzia smirked. "I overestimated old Mags and her boy-toy's ability to get the job done. You and Eve, on the other hand, I totally *underestimated*." The Strelitzia leaned against the chair back. "Now I'm at plan B."

"Which is?" Sharon's jaw clenched.

"Since I can't trust the hired help, I want you to personally deliver your secret to me." He pointed at her. "You. No one else. You do that, and I will free your wife."

"Don't listen to him. He already told you he planned to kill you. He's a thief." Federico spit out the words. "We made a deal with him and he screwed us. We kept our side of the bargain. Instead of keeping his, he stole our ship and relegated us to eking out a living in the bowels of Chicago."

"Oh, Federico," the Strelitzia interrupted. "Woody just doesn't get that sometimes a leader has to make really tough choices. Your predicament is Woody's fault, not mine."

"Who's Woody?" Sharon asked.

"Besides your stubborn wife who refuses to cooperate, Woody is the most maddening human on the planet." The Strelitzia rolled his eyes. "And the so-called leader of the Qaunik."

"Don't listen to him, Sharon," JJ said. "He can't be trusted."

Sharon stared into the screen at the masked man. Her choices were both bad. If Federico and JJ were right, she'd give up her secret and risk never seeing Eve again. If they were wrong, she'd get Eve back only to watch her starve to death without medicine and food. Her whole body ached with the weight of her decision. "Tell me where to meet you."

The Strelitzia got up. The hem of his flamboyant coat brushed the floor as he walked to the screen. His bird face grew as he neared. Dark eyes and slightly pink lips divulged the human beneath the mask. He smiled. "You've made the right choice. But, before we get to the details, I'm afraid I need to—drive home how serious I am about Plan B."

With the grip of a python, the horror that he might hurt Eve wrapped around Sharon. "Please, don't," she said. "There's no need to drive home your point. You've already made it by taking my wife."

"My insurance that all goes well is the cost of taking the time for you to fully understand what I'm capable of." He turned and took gliding steps toward the back of the room. Coming to stand behind the soldiers he said, "Bring her in."

The soldier to his left spoke into a microphone on his collar. His voice was too low to decipher his words.

The door swung open.

The python of fear squeezed harder as Sharon watched the soldier drag Areva, Dr. Ryan's wife, into the room. Her hair stuck out unkempt, and her face was blemished with tears of grief. "They killed him, Sharon." Areva wrapped her arms around her trembling body.

"No." Sharon touched the screen, wanting to comfort Areva. "Please, no."

"Let her go," the Strelitzia ordered.

Free of the soldier's grasp, Areva fell to her knees and crawled to the screen. She scrambled to her feet and put her hands to where Sharon's were.

"They found the apples you gave us," Areva chattered through tears. "They tried to get him to say where they came from. But he wouldn't." A howl spilled out of her. "They tortured him until he gave in. Then they killed him." She held her head in her hands and wept.

"Areva," Sharon whispered. "I'm so sorry."

"Not as sorry as I am. Bring her to me," the Strelitzia sighed. One of the soldiers dragged Areva, kicking and flailing, to him. "Kneel, woman," he said barely above a whisper.

The soldier pushed Areva to her knees. She clasped her hands together and wept as she prayed.

"You will come to understand, Sharon, that I am not a bad man." The Strelitzia looked from Areva to the screen. "I am a man who does what must be done. That makes me a brave man. It's because of me that the human race will go on. It is a terrible burden. But one I will not shirk."

"You're not brave. You're a monster." Sharon clenched her hands into fists. "Don't do this. Please. Don't hurt her."

"Some of us must go so that others may thrive." The Strelitzia held his head high.

"Who are you to decide?" Federico punched the air. "Who?"

"Who am I not?" The Strelitzia touched Areva's shoulder. "I'm taking her pain away." Keeping his grip on her shoulder, he said to Sharon, "And I'm showing you that I do, in fact, have all of the leverage."

"I'll do anything." Sharon sank to her knees. "Please don't hurt Areva. I'll get you what you want. Just let her and Eve go. I'm begging you. I don't need for you to show me that you're capable of killing." She held her hands out. "Don't do this."

"It's too late for this woman." The Strelitzia's electronic voice revealed no emotion. "But not for Eve."

"No!" Areva howled. "Sharon, help me."

"I must show you that I will not flinch." The Strelitzia put his hands to his waist. "You will bring me what I want."

"Where? Tell me." Touching the screen at the place where Areva knelt, the words tumbled out of Sharon. "You don't have to do this. You can trust me."

"I trust no one." He nodded at the soldier to his left.

The soldier sidled up to Areva.

To Sharon, the Strelitzia said, "You have two weeks to bring me the secret of the apple. My people will be waiting for you at the place of the highest tides in the world."

"Highest tides?" JJ asked. "You must mean the Bay of Fundy? I've been there. Great place to hide a very large ship."

"A man who knows his geography. But if you think you can trick me into giving up its location, you still underestimate me." The Strelitzia brushed a strand of hair from Areva's watery eyes. "Some things, even awful things, must be. Forgive me, sweet woman." To the soldier he said, "Set your weapon to its highest strength. The woman must not suffer." He strolled out of the room.

The soldier next to Areva thumbed the gauge on his spectraletto clockwise. He aimed the muzzle at Areva's heart.

"No." Sharon pressed her head to the screen, wanting to connect with Areva, but afraid to watch her die.

Areva screamed.

The *pft* of a spectraletto silenced her. Her body tumbled backward onto the floor.

Stunned, Sharon's mind refused to accept what was happening. But her eyes couldn't deny Areva's gruesome end.

A fist-sized hole punched through Areva's chest. Fine strands of smoke wafted from the singed fabric of her dress. Her head rested on an arm as if she were only sleeping. But the blood pooling around her like a halo and matting her silky black hair left no doubt that she was dead. Her dainty left hand lay outstretched toward Sharon as if begging for her to take hold. The silver wedding ring on her finger contrasted against the stark white of a body draining its blood.

"No," Sharon breathed and got to her feet. Hot tears burned down her cheeks. Her knees wobbled and queasiness filled her belly. Strong arms kept her from falling. She looked into Federico's eyes.

"We'll help you," Federico said in a soft voice.

JJ put a strong arm around her shoulders. "Let us help you."

"I have to get to"—Sharon tried to pull away. *Two weeks.*

"Don't talk." Federico brushed his hand over the bowl. The

satellite screen went black. "We'll finish this conversation when prying eyes and ears can't see or hear us." He slipped the mask over Aaron's head and yanked him to his feet. "Come on."

"I have to get to California to find a man named Elliot." Sharon let JJ support her. "Help me get there."

Keeping a strong arm around Sharon's shoulders, JJ said, "Woody will help you, and so will we."

Chapter 9

Sharon's hands shook slightly as she lifted the cup to her lips. A musky steam rushed up her nose to the back of her throat. "What is this?"

"Stinging nettle tea." Sitting across from her at a small table, Federico blew over the cup in his hand. "Spiked with dandelion wine." He took a sip. "It'll help settle your nerves. I'm so very sorry about your friend."

The Strelitzia's mask and the image of Areva begging for her life played over and over whenever Sharon closed her eyes. "Only a monster would kill someone like Areva. She never hurt anyone." She took a sip big enough to burn. It helped cover the pain of the woman's death knotted in her gut. "Who is he?"

"The Strelitzia." Federico leaned forward. "Besides operating under the delusion that he's some kind of god, he is the worst kind of person. He exploits people's vulnerabilities to get what he wants. It's how a mediocre scientist managed to steal our ship, kidnap your wife, and kill your friends."

"A scientist, that has to be it." She ran a finger over a chip in the rim of the cup. "I've been wracking my brain trying to think of how he knows Eve and me. They must've crossed paths when she was at Harvard."

"Tell me about Eve." Federico took another sip. "Was she a well-known botanist before the universities were disbanded?"

"I didn't know her when she was at Harvard." Sharon managed

a slight smile. "Eve is the best kind of person. She's modest and kind. If she was well known, she never talked about it. I wouldn't be surprised if she had been, though. My wife is brilliant. She's the smartest person I know."

"Is she the reason you have an apple tree that's not poison?" Federico lifted his cup to his lips, watching her over its rim.

Sharon surveyed the bizarre underground room that resembled an old bar. It had taken Federico just ten minutes to get them there. A note of caution played in her head. The secret of the apple tree belonged to her and Eve alone. "I really have to get to California as soon as possible. I have to—get things done there. My bike blew away in a storm over Gaia's Wrath. I have no transportation. When can I see Woody?"

"I'll take that as a decision not to answer. I respect that. You don't know me well. And I don't know you." Federico set his cup down and touched a clock icon at the corner of the table. Red LEDs flashed *6:45 P.M.* "Woody will see you in another fifteen minutes. How about I tell you a little about us? Ask me anything. Although, like you, I reserve my right not to answer on certain subjects."

Sharon studied the dimly lit room. Couples occupied a smattering of tables nestled at the base of a stage. A voluptuous dark-skinned woman crooned sultry music from her perch at the center of the dais. "How in the world do you have time for music and a bar? And what does Qaunik mean?"

Federico pulled back the cuff of his sleeve, revealing the tattoo that matched JJ's. "Qaunik means snow. It represents the sacred place we intend to get to someday where we won't have to live underground anymore. We took our name, and these tattoos to honor it."

"How is winter a place? It marks time. Not a spot on a map."

"Because time is what's important. We get so little of it." He let go of his sleeve and smiled. "Which is why we make time for music, and art, and laughter. They're among the great pleasures of our fleeting lifetimes."

"Does NONA know you're down here?"

"We don't think so. But we're pretty sure NONA suspects something might be going on beneath its nose. It just doesn't know how far beneath." Federico finished his drink. "Much like the abolitionists in the early 1800s had their Underground Railroad to save people from slavery, we have the underground sewer system of greater Chicago. Funny how history likes to repeat itself."

"Who are you trying to save?" Sharon looked from Federico to the diversity of faces around them. From black to white and all shades in between, there didn't seem to be a common denominator to their ethnicities or class standing.

"Anyone who wants to be saved." Federico folded his hands on the table. "And is willing to live by our code."

"Since everyone wants to be saved, I'm guessing your code is the deal breaker. What is it?" She drank the last of her tea.

Federico laughed. "You have good instincts." He twisted in the direction of the crooner belting out a schmaltzy song. "You see that woman? That's Ruth. Her great-grandfather, Troy LeRoy, was one of the best jazz singers in all of Chicago. And right above our heads used to sit one of the most famous jazz bars, the Goldfinch."

Sharon set down the empty cup. "That must've been before the Church of Revelations took over the government during the War of the Second Crusade and banned music?"

"*Sí, amiga.*" He turned back to Sharon. "Instead of disbanding, the Goldfinch bar went underground. Troy was more than a jazzman. He was a gifted leader who understood that while music feeds the soul, it doesn't feed the belly or keep you safe. Troy encouraged a wide variety of people with lots of different skills to join them. Everybody got to do what they did best as long as they also took on the mundane stuff no one wanted to do. From Troy on down, everybody cleaned toilets and took out the trash. For decades, we've thrived by carrying Troy's way of doing things forward."

"You said Woody is your leader. What happened to Troy?"

"He died of old age years ago, in 2084. Just went to sleep and never woke up. Woody was the chief scientist at the time, working on a ship that would be our new home. We've been living underground for far too long. The Qaunik elected Woody to succeed Troy as our prime minister." Federico looked past her and grinned. "Ah, here comes JJ."

JJ sidled up next to the table. "How you doing?" He placed a work-worn hand on Sharon's shoulder. "Can we get you something to eat? There's plenty of fried beetles in the kitchen."

"I'd love some later, after I meet with Woody." Even though her brain begged for sustenance, her stomach still roiled with stress. "If you don't mind."

"Not at all." JJ folded his muscled arms over his chest. "You just let me know."

"Where did you leave Aaron, the Strelitzia's soldier?" Federico asked.

"Let's just say it'll take him a very long time to walk from anywhere to anywhere." JJ winked. "It's a good thing he had a sunhat stuffed inside his jacket."

"The Nebraska Desert?" Federico asked.

"The one and only."

"You leave him with water?"

"Enough."

"Good work." Federico swiped the table clock. "It's time to meet Woody. A couple of things first." He got up. "I'll need my spectraletto back and any other weapons you might have."

"Why?" Sharon asked. "I need Woody to help me. You think I'm going to bite the hand that feeds me?"

"It's more for your protection than Woody's." JJ held out a hand. "I once saw Woody take out five armed NONA soldiers before they even knew what hit them. Questions were asked later. Your weapons, please."

"The spectraletto you're carrying is mine anyway." Federico smiled. "We'll take it, the hammer, and whatever else you've got." He pointed at her shoulder. "And the satchel."

"What is this?" Sharon handed the spectraletto butt-end to JJ. "I hope you're not setting me up."

"You have no choice but to trust us." Federico held out a hand. "Your hammer, please."

Sharon took it from the baldric and laid it in his hand. "That's all I've got." Then she slipped the satchel strap over her head.

"Good." Federico tucked the hammer into his waistband and took the satchel. "One last thing. You're going to exit this room through the red door behind you. It leads to Woody's quarters. Take off your boots before going through that door. You can leave them on the rack."

"You know." JJ made a sour face. "Boot funk. We don't wear shoes or boots in our quarters."

"Me neither." Sharon straightened her jacket. "Anything else I should know before meeting Woody?"

JJ put a finger to his lips. "You should probably know our way of greeting."

"Yes, you should." Federico motioned for JJ. "Let's show her."

JJ ducked around Sharon to Federico.

Standing face to face with JJ, Federico said, "As you know, shaking hands went out with the Great Plague of 2067. But we still value a proper greeting." He grabbed JJ's upper arm with his right hand.

JJ did the same to Federico. "That's our formal greeting. For friends we have an informal greeting which adds a gentle head butt." He bumped his forehead to Federico's.

"If Woody decides to greet you, it will be formal," Federico added.

JJ beamed. "You're lucky to meet our one-of-a-kind Woody."

"Woody defies definition." Federico clamped a hand to JJ's shoulder. "Engineer, boat builder, sailor, adventurer, ukulele player, teacher, leader. You name it." He held a hand out toward the door. "Let's not keep the boss waiting."

Sharon and Federico removed their boots before exiting through the red door. He led her down a long hallway before stopping at a door with a complicated schematic drawing framed in glass hanging over it. He rapped four times. "Our guest is here."

"Enter." A woman's soft but firm voice came through the door.

Federico turned the old-fashioned knob and pushed the door open for Sharon. "We'll see you in a little while. When we do, we'll get you something to eat and drink." He turned and walked away.

Cautiously, Sharon went in. The room was filled with dusky light. A fragrant smoke wafted up from some smoldering sticks propped in a metal container. On a colorful rug, a woman with long chestnut-colored hair and olive skin knelt, her hands pressed together.

"Come." The compact, middle-aged woman rose up onto her knees and motioned for Sharon. "Would you like to pray with me?"

"I don't believe in a God." Sharon made her way to the woman kneeling on the ornate red rug. At its center was a rectangular box with two lines coming together that pointed toward a stick figure, building what looked to symbolize a house of worship.

"Neither do I." The woman got to her feet and lifted the back end of the rug.

"If that's the case, why are you praying over a Muslim prayer rug?" Sharon asked.

"For many reasons." The woman rolled the rug into a tight, neat tube and tucked it onto a shelf. "To meditate. To connect with the people and history that I came from. To connect with the people I'm with now. To connect with myself. To connect with our dying planet." She turned to face Sharon. "To seek its forgiveness. Tell me, how does someone as young as you know what a Muslim is, let alone recognize a prayer rug?"

"My mother was an Abenaki Indian and rug weaver." Sharon could feel the woman's presence. It filled up every nook and cranny of the room with its life and power. "She taught me about the spirituality of rugs of many religions." Sharon glanced around for any sign of Woody.

"And yet, you don't believe in a God?" The woman pulled a second rolled rug from the shelf.

"I said that I don't believe in a God." Sharon hesitated to consider her words. If this woman was another gatekeeper to Woody, she didn't want to risk being offensive. "But I do believe in things I can't see, like the spirits of my family."

The woman snapped the rug open and spread it on the floor. She smiled. "Ah, then. Sit with me, please. This rug is for communing rather than praying."

"I'm sorry. But may I see Woody now?"

"Not what you expected?" The woman laughed. "I'm Wilhelmina Woodhouse." She patted a spot on the rug next to her. "My friends call me Woody."

"They told me you defy definition," Sharon managed to say. While Woody's demeanor made her feel safe, the sheer power oozing from the smaller woman intimidated and humbled Sharon. "And I could tell that your friends love and respect you very much."

"The feeling is mutual. Please. Sit." She scooted to the edge of the rug and faced its middle.

Sharon sat across from her and folded her legs. "Thank you for meeting with me." She fully expected that the subject of the apple would surface, but she wouldn't be the one to bring it up. "I hope I didn't offend you."

"Of course not. Who would expect a Muslim woman called Woody?"

"If you don't mind my asking, where are you from that a Muslim woman is named Wilhelmina Woodhouse?"

"Not at all do I mind." Woody leaned back on her palms. "My grandmother was a Syrian refugee during the War of the Second Crusade. Their overcrowded boat capsized. Everyone drowned but her. She was only ten years old. A Norwegian family adopted her and brought her to Great Britain. I'm named after the former Norwegian Queen Wilhelmina. My father was of British descent." She closed her eyes for a moment, revealing long lashes. "There you have it. Now tell me about you."

"I'm a farmer." Sharon waved her hands as if trying to erase the words. "I mean, I was a farmer. My family owned a farm in Maine for more than a century. My wife, Eve, and I eke out a living there.

Well, we did, until she was taken from me. Which is why I hope you will consider helping me get to California."

"How would that be helpful?"

Sharon felt her hands figuratively being tied behind her back. She and Eve had sworn to each other they'd always keep their secret. No matter what. But keeping the promise might mean losing Eve. "There's a person there whose help I need. Please, all I'm asking is that you get me to northern California. I don't have . . ."

"Stop," Woody interrupted. "We can get you there."

"What's the price? There's always a price."

"Well, I agree, most of the time there is. But not always." Woody locked eyes with Sharon. "This time, however, there is most definitely a price."

"I don't have any resources. I'm just really good at getting by with what I can find."

"Let's make a deal." Woody held up an open hand. "Don't ever insult my intelligence with a lie. Of course you have something of value. Otherwise, the Strelitzia would not have taken your wife. And you would not be so desperate to get to California to bring him whatever it is he thinks you have that he wants."

"I'm sorry." The slap of Woody's retort stung. Sharon had no leverage. This powerful woman had all of it. "What will it cost?"

"The Strelitzia stole the one person in the world you live for. Am I right?"

"Yes." Sharon laced her fingers together and rested her hands in her lap.

"You and I are in the same boat." Woody straightened and exhaled. "He stole from me the one thing in this world that I need to keep myself and all of the people who rely on me alive. You want your wife back. And I want my ship back."

"How can I help you do that?"

"You're going to lead me to him. Whatever you have has brought him out of the shadows. I need for you to keep him in the light of day until I can get to him."

113

"So you're going to use me and Eve as bait somehow?"

"I asked you not to lie. And neither will I to you." Woody spread her hands. "That's exactly my plan."

"I don't have a choice. Do I?" Sharon asked.

"Not if you want to get to California any time soon. There's desert that's standing in your way. Not to mention the mountains."

"Okay," Sharon conceded. "If you're willing to help me, I have to be willing to help you. When do we go?"

"In the morning, after you steal a shipment of water from NONA."

"I hope you have a good plan for that too." Sharon's heart rate ticked up. "Seems pretty risky, bordering on a death wish."

"Tomorrow morning NONA will be loading water-transporters for delivery to one of their bases in Atlanta. You and Federico will pose as water-walkers in order to divert one of the transporters. From there, you'll be with a crew assigned to deliver the water to California for trade. There's a black market there that has supplies we need. We give them the water. They give us the supplies."

"How are we going to pull off the identities of water-walkers?"

"The same way that we're going to hide you from the Strelitzia. I have no doubt he'll be tracking you. In the morning, your own chip will be surgically removed. It'll be replaced with the chip of a dead water-walker. We'll also implant a countermeasures device inside your jaw that can jam facial recognition software. And for good measure, we'll cut your hair and set you up with a pair of contact lenses that'll change the color of your eyes from green to brown. And last but not least, the lenses will project a holograph onto your retina. You'll be unrecognizable."

"You've got to be kidding."

"I don't kid. After you get to California, we'll help you find whomever or whatever it is you're looking for."

"I don't want your help for anything other than getting to California. I'll get where I need to go after that."

"You asked what the catch is." Woody held Sharon's gaze. "There you have it. I told you that you will lead me to the Strelitzia. We get you what you want. Then we go together to the Bay of Fundy to catch up with the Strelitzia. That's what I'm offering. And it's not negotiable."

"Then we part ways, and I keep everything that's mine, including what the Strelitzia is after."

"You have my word."

"I don't know you well enough yet, but something about you makes me believe you." Sharon considered the incongruous feeling. "Maybe it's your commitment to not telling each other lies."

"That's certainly a good way for us to begin." Woody got up and motioned for Sharon to do the same. Then she reached out with her right hand and squeezed Sharon's upper arm.

Sharon returned the greeting, grateful for Federico and JJ's earlier demonstration. "Thank you."

"I'll call Federico to retrieve you. Get some food, water, and a good sleep. We have much to do. First thing in the morning, Dale, our physician, will replace your identity chip with a new one." Woody walked Sharon to the doorway. "Wait outside. Federico will be along."

Chapter 10

"You ready?" Dale pressed the stainless-steel chip-injector to the hinge of Sharon's right jaw. "The chip has an anesthetic coating, but the needle is a bitch. Sorry about that." The imposing woman was painted in swirls of black ink that bloomed up her arms to her neck where a thick scar traced her jawline. She had bright blue eyes, high cheek bones, and wore her salt-and-pepper hair in a buzz-cut. Dale looked more warrior than healer in a vest, white synthetic shirt, canvas dungarees, and heavy boots.

Sharon readied herself. "Do it." She gripped the chair's armrests and stared at the opposite wall of the well-lit medical supply room.

"I like you." Dale supported Sharon's head with her other hand. "You've got grit." She pulled the instrument's trigger. It clicked, then whooshed as the hydraulic mechanism recoiled.

"Holy hell." Sharon winced, rubbing her jaw. "I'd hate to see what you do to someone you don't like."

"Well, you didn't flinch."

"Long years of self-discipline." A merciful tingling chased after the piercing ache. "At least the anesthetic works fast."

"You might get a bit of a headache once it wears off." Dale held the injector over an open glass carboy and pressed a button at its side. The needle clinked into the carboy. "Let me know if it persists, though. I've got stuff I can give you for it."

Sharon ran a hand over the soft stubble on her head. "You weren't kidding when you said you'd cut my hair. Not that I'm complaining. It feels—freeing."

"Yeah, well . . ." Dale returned the injector to a case with a foam insert molded to its shape. She pointed at her own head. "I can stitch up the nastiest of gashes, but I've only got one hairstyle in my repertoire. Now, let's take a look at the incision on your wrist." She sat on a stool and turned Sharon's hand over.

"How does all this stuff work, anyway?" Sharon massaged her tingling jaw.

"The chip distorts photographs taken of you so that facial recognition software can't determine your identity." Holding Sharon's forearm, she lifted the bandage and examined the incision, snugged closed with four tight stitches. "We gave you brown eyes with the new contact lenses. More important, they've erased your retinal scan identity. As for the chip in your wrist, you're no longer Sharon Clausen."

"Who am I? And I hope you've kept the real me someplace safe. All I want to be when this is over is Sharon Clausen, wife of Eve. They live happily ever after on a patch of green in Maine."

"Not to worry. Your chip is in secure storage. We'll replace it when the mission's finished." Dale closed the bandage over the wound. "This looks good. Keep it covered and clean. You let me know right away if it gets infected." She wheeled the stool to a desk in the corner with a digital screen. She slid her finger across the screen and pressed the icon for a dark-haired woman who looked to be in her thirties. "You're Midge Riendeau, water-walker."

"I'm afraid to ask." Sharon rolled her sleeve down. "What happened to the real Midge?"

"By now, she's a pile of ash."

"You didn't."

"Of course not." Dale wheeled back to Sharon. "She died about six months ago from a cardiac virus. All dead bodies within

117

five hundred miles of Chicago are brought to Wrigley Field, the regional crematorium. As you know, it's a criminal offense to bury a body. Fortunately for us, NONA doesn't put resources into identifying all of the corpses that show up there. They barely pay their pompiers a living wage. One of our own is a pompier." She winked. "Unlike NONA, we pay him well."

"A pompier?"

"Funeral directors stopped being funeral directors once people started dropping like flies from disease. Now we have people who run the crematoriums. That's what we call them here in the Midwest, pompiers. What do they call them where you're from?"

"People who run the crematoriums," Sharon answered. "I guess."

"What do you mean you guess?" Dale asked.

"I never had the occasion to deal with one. I had two brothers. One was a soldier who died overseas. He never came home. I buried my other brother myself on our farm after he was killed by Banditti. As for my parents—" she ran her palms from her forehead to her chin—"they contracted the Siberia Permafrost Plague. My father died within hours of my mother. I burned our farmhouse to the ground with their bodies inside. After I found their ashes, I buried them."

"I'm so sorry. I think everyone knows someone who died of that plague. No one would've guessed that it would be orders of magnitude worse than the Great Plague. It scared people senseless. Nobody thought twice about making the law permanent that bodies had to be burned instead of buried."

"I didn't want my brothers to get sick too. But I couldn't send my parents to a crematorium to be burned with a pile of other bodies."

"You did what you had to do."

"You mind if we talk about something else?" Sharon cleared her throat. Part of her wanted to keep talking. Something about Dale made it okay to rehash the memories she worked hard to contain. But leaving them near the surface might get in the way of keeping her head.

"You bet." Dale smiled. "What else do you want to know?"

"How do you get the chips out of bodies before they're burned?"

"Like I said, our guy on the inside is one of the pompiers. He excises them when the bodies come in. We sterilize them and use those identities when the need arises."

"Doesn't NONA know they're dead? They must deactivate the chip when the body's picked up. That wouldn't cost them anything."

"Our hackers get into NONA's database and switch a person's status from dead to alive. Plus, that's how we know the deceased's identity and credentials. We chose Midge for you because she was a water-walker." Dale's head snapped toward a rap at the door. "Who is it?"

"It's me, *amiga*," Federico answered.

"Come in." Dale got up.

The door swung open. Federico breezed in, with JJ at his heels. Both wore blue coveralls with name tags not their own. *Water-walker* was stitched over the left breast pocket of both pairs. JJ carried a bag slung over his shoulder.

"*Hola*." Federico whistled. "Good work, Dale. Sharon looks totally different."

"Yeah, she does," JJ agreed. "Is there anything you can't do, Dale?"

"Dance." Dale lifted her arms and snapped her fingers. "Want to see?"

In unison, JJ and Federico answered, "No!"

The smile that spread across Sharon's face felt good. Even if only for a moment, the surrender of her muscles into levity boosted her optimism about the Qaunik. They were serious and unnerving at times, yet warm and funny.

"Not that you're not good at it," Federico added. "We don't have time for a dance party."

"Right." Dale smirked. "You're a terrible liar."

"Honesty is one of the codes we live by. That's why my brother looks guilty when he tries to fib." JJ elbowed Federico. "Right?"

"*Sí.*" Federico smiled. "We must go."

JJ unslung the bag and tossed it to Sharon's feet. "Put these on, my fellow water-walker. Your hammer is in there too."

"What about my satchel?" Sharon asked.

"It's secured. You'll get it back after we finish this job. You can hide the hammer beneath your clothing. The satchel will draw attention." Federico swiped the clock on his sleeve. "Actually, we're running late. You can put the water-walker uniform on en route to the Jardine Water Purification Plant. We'll blow our cover if we're not there on time."

"What's your plan?" Dale asked.

Sharon picked up the bag at her feet. She worried that they'd searched her satchel and found the apples. Federico was right, though. She had no choice but to trust him, and hope he kept his word.

"We'll come above ground about two blocks from the Jardine, then walk the rest of the way. There should be plenty of other water-walkers we can fall in line with."

"What does a water-walker do?" Sharon asked. "More to the point, what are we—posing as them—going to do?"

JJ said, "Once we get past the NONA checkpoint at the Jardine, we'll be allowed on the water side of the wall." He pointed to the number seven on his shoulder. "Our job will be to deliver water containers to the seventh transporter. Once it's filled, we'll stow away onboard. After the pilot takes off, we hijack the transporter."

"Let's head out," Federico said. "We'll fill you in on the rest of the plan along the way. Plus, you're going to need to learn a few fighting techniques for use once we're in the cramped confines of the transporter. That hammer of yours is no doubt effective. But we'll need something not quite so—messy. JJ's going to teach you some jujitsu."

"Joints and pressure points." JJ put the heel of his hand to his

120

jawbone. "Do it right, and no adversary is too big to take down."

"Let's see." Sharon crossed her arms. "You're going to teach me jujitsu, then we sneak onto the other side of the wall, posing as water-walkers, to steal a transporter. You make it sound so simple."

"All in a day's work, *amiga*." Federico made toward the door.

After traveling almost an hour through the sewer, they exited and climbed toward pinpricks of light coming through an iron manhole cover. With a soft grunt, Federico lifted the cover by a crack. "Coast is clear." He pushed it aside. "Hurry."

Sharon and JJ scrambled out of the tunnel onto the dark street. The sun rested below the horizon, and no stars or moon lit the muddy early morning.

Federico pushed the cover back over the hole. "We move."

They marched shoulder to shoulder in their blue coveralls as other sleepy water-walkers spilled out of doorways and around corners.

Keeping her voice low, Sharon asked, "Wouldn't it be less of a threat to NONA to use robots instead of people to move the water? I can't imagine all of these thirsty people can be trusted."

"Thirsty people are cheaper to maintain than robots," JJ answered.

Federico drew a forefinger across his throat. "And the punishment for stealing water is execution on the spot. It's a pretty good deterrent."

"You guys are just now telling me that?" Sharon easily kept pace with Federico's lead. The wall loomed larger as they neared. Even though she couldn't see the lake, she could smell its damp, sweet fragrance. It made her think of eating pan-fried trout her grandfather used to catch out of the cold water of Moosehead Lake. They'd wash it down with iced lemonade.

"No need to tell you, because we don't intend to get caught." Federico slowed as they neared the checkpoint. "Be sure to keep your sleeve over the bandage at your wrist and your head down. If they ask to see your eyes, don't blink. I'll go first."

He lifted his wrist as he neared the NONA soldier keeping guard at the entry.

The guard waved a chip reader down Federico's arm to his hand. He glanced at the readout on the wand and said, "Enter."

It went the same for JJ.

Sharon lifted her wrist to the soldier. A smidge of white from the bandage edged from her sleeve cuff. She lowered her wrist just enough for it to disappear. *Did he notice?*

"Show me your eyes," the soldier ordered indifferently.

Sharon looked into his, and did not blink.

He moved the wand in front of her face and then studied the readout. "Go."

Sharon lowered her head and walked through to the other side. When she lifted her eyes, the sight stunned the fear out of her. A vast ocean of fresh water shimmered in the dim light of the rising sun. It was hard to wrap her head around the enormity of it. The steady rhythm of the lake's lapping at the shore soothed her as early mornings did on her farm. The gorgeous gray-blue vastness left her feeling awed and small. A reminder that the planet was so much larger, more beautiful, and more powerful than the pestilence of what humanity had become. She wished Eve could see it, too.

"You okay?" JJ asked.

"Yeah, sorry." Sharon tore her eyes from the humbling lake to the water-walkers scuttling from building to shore and back. "All of this expanse reminded me of my farm."

"You're a rare bird," Federico said. "One doesn't meet too many farmers these days."

"My family's been for generations. Now there's nothing left to grow. But I still think of myself as a farmer."

"Yeah, that was the genius of humanity." JJ yanked a blue cloth cap that matched his overalls from a pocket and put it on. "Humans fucked up the food supply. Sort of, if I'm going to starve to death, so will everyone else on the planet."

"Now all we have are a few genetically modified seeds." Federico shook his head. "Of potatoes and kale, of all things. You'd think we could've at least saved a few cayenne pepper seeds to jazz things up."

Sharon held her breath, hoping he wouldn't ask about the apple that the Strelitzia had eaten without dying. Surely they must be intensely curious. Maybe they'd searched her satchel and found the apples. Maybe they were baiting her for information. She gestured to the large building that loomed in front of them. "Tell me what's next for us to do."

The Jardine Water Purification Plant sat on a square platform that stretched into the water. Navy Pier, with a derelict Ferris wheel rusted in place, bordered it to the south. A concrete breakwater carved a barrier between the Jardine and the massive expanse of gray-blue Lake Michigan.

"Ever seen so much drinking water?" JJ asked. "Beautiful, isn't it?"

"I want to throw myself into it and drink until I can't fit another drop," Sharon murmured.

"Well, that'll get you shot." Federico motioned for them to follow. "Transporter number seven is at the far end." He pointed to a line of bulbous silver transporters floating in the sliver of water between the Jardine and Navy Pier. Their round fuselages sacrificed aerodynamics for cargo space. Lashed to the dock, their gangplanks stuck out like tongues from their wide-open mouths, making them look gluttonous. "See the other water-walkers? We get the water from the number seven bay and load it onto the transporter. There'll be two other number seven water-walkers. Don't converse with them unless you have to. And if you do, grunt your answer."

"What happens after we've loaded all of the water?" Sharon asked.

"We wait for the guard to exit the transporter," JJ answered. "That's when the pilot will close the hatch for takeoff. There'll be six of us on board. The pilot, two water-walkers, and the three of us."

123

"You and I," Federico pointed to Sharon, "when I give you the signal by taking my hat off, we're going to subdue and mask the other two water-walkers. Use strikes to the pressure points, just like JJ showed you. He'll mask the pilot like we did the Strelitzia's hit man. After we take off and get someplace safe, we'll let them go."

"We'll be long gone before they make it back from wherever we leave them," JJ added. "Like Aaron, that guy who works for the Strelitzia who tried to grab you. I'm pretty sure he's still out there. Somewhere."

"Hopefully rethinking the side he's on." Federico veered toward an open bay. "Here we go. Lucky number seven." He led them inside.

Thousands upon thousands of glass one-liter bottles filled polycarbonate crates.

Sharon leaned into Federico and whispered, "I've never seen this much glass in one place. I'm surprised they use something so heavy to hold water."

"The trouble with Lake Michigan is the brain-eating amoeba known as Otto's Demise that lives in it. North Korea dropped it into the lake via a long-range ballistic missile seven decades ago. The only way to kill it is by boiling the water. After it's filtered, NONA puts the water in glass bottles and autoclaves them."

"Damn." Sharon sighed. "I drank from the fountain in Millennium Park. Just like all those other poor thirsty people."

"Not to worry. You're healthy. It's only the sick and weak who are generally susceptible to the amoeba." JJ gave her shoulder a squeeze. "Our doc, Dale, has an anti-parasitic drug we can give you. Just in case."

"That's a relief. A parasite making a home in my brain is on my top ten list of things *not* to die from."

"I'm with you on that, sister," JJ said.

Two NONA soldiers stood guard on either side of the warehouse as water-walkers shuttled crates to transporters. Each crate contained fifteen bottles. The larger and stronger water-walkers carried a crate at a time. The smaller ones schlepped them in pairs. In silence, Sharon, JJ and Federico joined in, grabbing a crate apiece.

Following JJ, Sharon lugged her crate into the transporter. A long hallway flanked on each side by stacked crates led toward a cockpit. The pilot sat with his back to them, studying a command screen that showed the weight distribution in the vessel. In fluid motion, his fingers pressed buttons and slid over silky touch-sensitive surfaces.

Over and over, Sharon retrieved water from the bay and loaded it onto the transporter. Her arms felt like rubber; her thighs burned from squatting and lifting. Mercifully, it wasn't long before the hallway couldn't hold any more crates, and Sharon joined JJ, Federico, and the other two number seven water-walkers in securing straps to hold the crates.

"Transporter's full," the guard yelled to the pilot. "All clear?"

The pilot turned in his jump seat. "All clear."

"See you when you get back. Have a good flight, sir." The guard tipped his hat and jogged out of the transporter and down the gangplank.

"Stay clear of the bay door!" The pilot yelled and flipped a switch. The claws on the end of the gangplank holding it to the pier snapped open. Bobbing free in the water, the transporter backed away as the gangplank rose and the bay door slid closed over it. "Finish securing the crates and prepare to take off."

Sharon grabbed a safety-yellow webbed strap and snapped the j-hook at its end into the recessed bar on the wall. As she cinched it tight, Federico coughed. She turned her head and caught him lifting his cap. She recited JJ's words of training in her head, *one two three, just like dancing.*

Federico shoved the cap into his pocket while the two water-walkers continued to place straps around the crates. He pulled two masks from his other pocket and tossed one to Sharon.

She snatched it as the movements of the water-walkers shifted from rote to surprise. Out of the corner of her eye, she saw JJ dashing into the cockpit.

"Hey!" The water-walker nearest Sharon grabbed her left wrist. "What are you doing?"

She planted her feet firmly, flexed her knees, and struck him with a right knife-hand between his elbow and wrist. As his arm swung back, she took a step forward, made a hammer fist with her right hand and swung up into his ribs. A grunt of air puffed from the water-walker's mouth as he slumped forward. She rammed the heel of her open left hand into his jaw.

The water-walker crumpled to the floor. No blood, no sound.

She pinned his limp arms against his sides with her knees and slid the hooded mask over his face. Scrambling off of the unconscious water-walker, she slipped her arms under his armpits and wrestled his flaccid body into a sitting position against a stack of crates. With one of the loose straps, she latched him to the wall. "Wow, that actually worked."

"Good job, *amiga*." Federico shoved the other water-walker against the crates and secured him next to his comrade. "We predicted you'd be a quick study."

JJ led the quiet and compliant masked pilot from the cockpit. His fingertips dug into the pressure points at the pilot's neck as he lowered him next to the other captives. "You're one badass farmer." He grinned and tied the pilot to the crates.

Sharon flexed her left hand. "Didn't even hurt. One, two, three and he was out cold at my feet. Just like you said. Maybe you could teach me some more moves?"

"I'd be happy to." JJ straightened. "Pressure points. Takes the biggest and baddest guys down every time."

"We better hurry." Federico got up. "No one's the wiser and the other pilots are firing up their engines."

Sharon followed the two men into the cockpit.

JJ sat in the pilot's seat and stretched a Kevlene helmet with communicator over his head. He flipped a switch and the thrusters turned over with a smooth hiss.

Federico motioned to one of four passenger seats.

Sharon sat next to him and closed the torso-restraint over her chest.

JJ pressed and held a button on the helmet. "Seven, ready for takeoff."

A woman's voice responded through a speaker on the dash. "Cleared to fly."

Keeping his hand on the button, JJ counted, "In three, two, and one." He moved his finger from the button and slid it over the command-screen. The transporter's forward camera showed them backing away from the dock and turning toward open water. JJ gripped the throttle and pushed it forward, revving the thrusters. Frothy water swirled in front of and below them as the transporter lifted into the air and burst forward.

The acceleration pressed Sharon against the seat. Her shoulder still ached from her scuffles with the Banditti and NONA. Hauling seventy crates of water hadn't helped. She fidgeted in an effort to get comfortable. "Now what?"

"The tricky part." Sunlight streamed in through the window onto Federico's face. His accent, dark skin, long slender nose, and brown eyes hinted at an ancient South American heritage. His hair flecked with gray at the temples made him look resilient in a chaotic world. He laughed easily, and she liked that about him.

"What part of this *hasn't* been tricky?" Sharon asked.

JJ smiled. "We have," he glanced over his shoulder, "about fifteen minutes to find our ship, the Belostomatid, before NONA realizes we're going the wrong way. We're tracking toward the Belostomatid's signal now. She's close."

"I've never heard of such a ship." Sharon looked out the window with Federico. "What does it look like?"

"A big water bug," Federico answered. "She can fly, swim, and walk on land. Woody built her. She's a thing of beauty. Like the woman who conceived of her." Admiration and warmth seemed to twinkle in his dark eyes.

"How long have you known Woody?" Sharon asked.

He resumed his looking. "Since I was seventeen. Woody vouched for me." The affection in his eyes was discernible in his voice too. "That subject is for another day, though. Let's not be distracted from the task at hand."

Sharon wanted to know what he meant by Woody having vouched for him. He said it with such gravity that she wondered whether it held special significance to the Qaunik. She'd ask him again later. "So your Belostomatid looks like Bugzilla?"

Federico laughed. "*Sí*, and there she is." He tilted his head to the window. "At the horizon, two o'clock."

JJ maneuvered left, and Sharon saw the ship's globular black body bobbing on six pontoon legs. The two in front curved up like crushing weapons.

"That might be the ugliest ship I've ever seen," Sharon said.

"Ha!" JJ exclaimed. "Ugly and effective. Now's the moment. I'm turning off the transporter's tracking. As soon as I do, NONA will know that its transporter has gone rogue."

Federico reached for a microphone on the dash. "As soon as you turn off the tracking, I'll communicate with the Belostomatid. Then land us inside of her."

"Won't they still find us?" Sharon asked. "A giant water bug's bound to draw attention."

"Not a chance. The Belostomatid is covered in a material similar to that of a chameleon. Once we're inside, we'll activate her invisible shield. The material she's covered in will blend in so well with the surroundings that she can't be seen or tracked." Federico curled his bottom lip under his top teeth giving him a look of sharp focus.

"It'll even hide the ship's mass?" Sharon asked.

"Don't ask me how it works; that's above my pay grade." JJ held his finger over a button. "Now?"

Federico readied the microphone at his lips. "Yes."

JJ pressed the button. "Here's where it gets tricky."

Federico spoke into the microphone, "Phillip, open the hatch. We're coming in."

"Is there anything you need me to do?" Sharon asked.

"Be ready." Federico held the mic in his lap.

Sharon touched her hammer at her side, and watched out the window as the hatch on the back of the Belostomatid lifted open. Something raced past her peripheral vision. "There's another ship out there."

"Fucking NONA mosquitoes." Federico hit the mic button. "We've got company. The instant we land, get the hatch closed and make us disappear."

"I'm on it," a man's voice confirmed through the speaker.

JJ flew the transporter into the ship through the opening. It bobbled, bounced hard, and stopped. He flipped a switch and the engine quieted.

A loud boom preceded a splash against the ship.

In synchronized movement, JJ and Federico clicked out of their torso-restraints.

"They're shooting at us." Federico dashed from the seat toward the cockpit.

"How the fuck did they find us so quickly?" JJ followed him.

Sharon unlocked her restraint and kept pace with the men as they raced out of the transporter.

Another boom, followed by a splash, rocked the Belostomatid left, then right. Sharon reached for a wall to keep upright.

"Dammit, Phillip, shut the hatch!" Federico kept moving toward a blond man who was stabbing ineffectually at a set of controls on a podium.

A second, older man fumbled with a manual. Thin skin dotted with age spots fit tight over his shaking hands. He wore a tweed jacket frayed at the elbows. It was hard to tell which was older, the jacket or the man.

"The hatch isn't responding," the blond man said in a panic.

"We've got to unlock the S-bolts on the outside to shut it manually then." Federico spun on a heel. "Give me a hand, JJ."

"Right behind you."

As soon as they disappeared outside, the blond man calmly pulled a short-barreled spectraletto from his coat pocket.

"Phillip!" The old man stared in disbelief. "What are you doing?"

"Saving myself, Dr. Elan." He slid his finger over the screen in front of him and pressed his finger to a hatch icon. It closed, leaving Federico and JJ exposed on the Belostomatid's outside deck. "Someone made me an offer to betray Woody that I couldn't refuse. And I will not be banished."

"They'll kill us all," the old man said. "JJ and Federico will be first. You can't leave them out there with no cover!" He tossed the manual aside and pointed a bony forefinger. "Open that hatch."

"No." Phillip shook his head. "I'll turn on the invisibility shield. Yes, JJ and Federico will die. But we'll be fine. We're still going to California. Just not with them."

"But why?" Dr. Elan asked.

Federico's face appeared at the starboard window. He banged on the hard plexi, screaming, his voice muffled.

Sharon started to rise.

"Sit down," Phillip ordered.

Another boom and splash knocked her off balance. She fell into the seat.

"Woody's idea is insane. If she manages to get her ship back, we'll all die with her. I'm not going, because she's not willing to make the kind of decisions that'll keep us alive." Phillip rattled out his words. His cheeks flushed red and beads of sweat dotted his forehead. "Listen, we can trade all of this water on the black market. I've already arranged for a buy. We'll split the money three ways. With mine, I'm going to buy supplies and hunker down someplace safe."

"You fool!" Dr. Elan bellowed. "How dare you?"

Phillip wiped a bead of sweat from his temple. "You know as well as I do Woody can't feed us all. Yet she keeps taking people in like some modern-day Noah. I don't intend to starve on a ship in the middle of nowhere."

Dr. Elan's thick gray eyebrows furrowed. "You'll never make it to California, and NONA will kill us all."

Phillip seemed to waver.

Sharon reached for her hammer. "And I don't intend to die today. My wife is waiting for me. Open that fucking hatch and let Federico and JJ in."

"Sit down." Phillip raised the weapon to her chest. "I'm going to California to trade this water. If I have to die trying, so be it."

Sharon weighed the situation. NONA had them in the crosshairs. In the time it'd take to open the hatch, go invisible and take off, they could all be dead. Eve would die alone. Sharon glanced at Federico and JJ trapped outside. Laser shots bounced all around like the conflict in her head. Their fate was sealed in whatever decision she made. In one swift movement, she shoved the butt of her left hand into Phillip's nose as her right hand grasped her hammer.

He grunted, dropped the weapon, and put his hands to his bloodied nose.

Dr. Elan flipped a switch and the hatch opened. "Let's go invisible." He pressed a square icon on the dash screen.

Sharon yanked Phillip's slumped body upward, slamming him into a wall.

He slid down and into the fetal position. "You don't know what you've done," he whimpered.

Federico and JJ stormed into the Belostomatid.

"*Amiga!*" Federico gripped Sharon's shoulders. "You saved us today. *Gracias.*" He bent and retrieved Phillip's weapon. "When you neutralize a threat, you neutralize a threat." To JJ, he said, "Tie and mask Phillip."

Sharon stood mute. Her limbs felt as if she'd been immersed in concrete. Her instinct to save Federico and JJ had been about more than finding Eve. How did things get so complicated in such a short amount of time? "I don't know what I'm doing."

"Following your heart." Federico said from one of the passenger seats. "The thing we need more than food, water, or shelter is love. Just keep following your heart."

"Sharon, this is Dr. Elan. Dr. Elan, meet our new friend, Sharon." JJ lowered himself into the pilot seat. "You okay, Doc?"

"It's especially nice to meet you under such dire circumstances." Dr. Elan took a deep breath and blew it out. "Well, that just proved my old ticker's still got some juice." He patted his chest. "Get us the hell out of here before I use it all up. I'm not ready to keel over."

"You got it, Doc." JJ turned to Sharon. "Meet STELA, the brain of this mighty ship." He waved his hand over the complicated flight dash cluttered with buttons, levers, switches, handles, a keypad of simple icons, and a flat-screen monitor. "She's our Systems Technology and Electronics Launch Applicator. All these buttons and switches are for manual control. The screen, however, is an interactive computer that makes it possible for a layperson to fly her. All you have to do is sketch a command, and the computer does the rest. Once it understands the sketch, the sketch fades, making space for a new one."

Federico aimed his thumb at the wall-sized screen on the portside. "And that's OVA, the Overhead Video Amplifier. She lets us see and talk to Woody wherever we are in the world. OVA and STELA are on all of the ships and aircraft designed by Woody."

"Yeah." Sharon sat in a seat next to Dr. Elan. "Maybe you'll let me try to do the flying at some point."

"You got it, sister." JJ sketched on STELA. "Watch the OVA; we can see everything she sees or does. We'll be invisible within seconds."

Sharon turned her eyes to the OVA and watched the ship's legs swivel back and disappear into the landscape along with the rest of the ship. The NONA aircraft flew in futile circles looking for the Belostomatid hiding beneath their noses.

"We're safe for now." JJ leaned back.

"Have at it, NONA bastards." Federico rested his head against the headrest. "We're here, but then again we're not." He sighed, closed his eyes and started to hum a soft, lilting tune.

Something from an ancient opera, Sharon guessed. Whatever it was, it soothed her.

Chapter 11

In the hour since leaving the NONA pilot and the two water-walkers on the western outskirts of Wisconsin, a blanket of rusty sand had spread out below them. The dry expanse crawled over Earth, bullying life into submission. Only a few stubborn tufts of greenish-brown vegetation dotted the desert. The scene reminded Sharon of a flash flood. Except, instead of rushing water drowning the living, the Nebraska Desert snuffed it out by its relentless creeping.

Building remains covered in sand gave the otherwise flat landscape a hummocky look. The desiccated environment doomed the zombie structures to a purgatory of fading and reemerging in the shifting sands. Their forlorn shadows grew as the sun made its retreat below the horizon.

The quiet drone of the Belostomatid's engines enveloped Sharon and her companions. Lights on the cockpit dash filled the cozy space with a soft green glow. Through the open cockpit door, Sharon could see into the Belostomatid's cavernous cargo bay. Lashed down in the center of the bay, the transporter rested on its belly with its pontoon legs tucked at its sides.

Fatigue, hunger, thirst, and not having washed in days weighed heavy on Sharon. "I'd really like to wash my face. I assume there's a sanitation room aboard?"

"*Sí*," Federico answered. "The green door next to the OVA."

"Thanks." Sharon released her torso-restraint and got up. Her knees felt stiff from dehydration as she lifted her feet over the threshold of the sanitation room. Motion-activated lights lit up the tiny compartment as she shut the door. A flush handle hung over a small squatting stall. The handle connected to the same fresh-water holding tank as the sink. The tank was half full. She guessed the waste holding tank was just under the floor where the dirty water drained. Leaning over the sink, she waved a hand over the faucet and cupped her hands. Water flowed until she moved her cupped hands to her face.

Overlooking the chemical smell, she savored the feel of cool water splashed onto her skin. Lowering her hands from her face, she studied the woman in the mirror who she no longer recognized. She cinched her belt tighter, and wondered how much weight she'd lost over the past several days. *You look like hell.* Not knowing whether Eve was okay *felt* like hell. She filled her cupped hands again and drank the water. The little bit of it helped to revive her. She pressed the antiseptic dispenser, dropping a few dollops of the clear gel onto her palm. She slathered it over her hands and face. The alcohol in the antiseptic dried the water on her skin. She slipped out of the sanitation room and shut the door.

"You okay, *amiga?*" Federico asked.

"I feel better. Thanks." She nestled back into a flight-seat and gazed out the window. "How far are we over the desert?"

"Ah, a good question," Dr. Elan answered. "Our hefty Belostomatid may have the gift of invisibility, but she tends to dawdle." He examined the satellite image displayed on the OVA. "Let's see. We are over western Iowa. Not too far from Omaha."

"I read that the Nebraska Desert grows every year. How big is it now?" Sharon asked.

"You want to talk hefty? She's one big sand pit," JJ answered. "Iowa, South Dakota, Wyoming, Colorado, Arizona, New Mexico, Oklahoma, Missouri, and Kansas. It's a beast."

"Don't forget Texas," Federico added. "It's swallowing Texas too."

"Anyone still manage to live down there?" Sharon reached into her satchel for her flask. "Just looking at it makes me thirsty."

Federico waved a hand. "Save your water." He released his torso-restraint. "We have an entire ship of the sweetest *agua* left on Earth. You, *amiga*, deserve a taste of the good stuff." He got up. "*Un minuto, por favor.*"

"The doc here," JJ aimed his thumb at Dr. Elan, "can tell you all about who lives down there. I don't even like to think about, let alone talk about, them. It's why we bring him whenever we travel over the desert. He's a former anthropology professor. An expert in the study of the feral."

"The feral?" Sharon asked. "You mean the Yěxìng?"

"Yes. Yěxìng is the Chinese word for untamed." Dr. Elan swiped a finger over STELA. The OVA displayed an image of a group of naked, wild-eyed, and unkempt people.

Dr. Elan steepled his fingertips. "You've heard of them?"

"Oh, yeah." Sharon nodded. "Fortunately, I've never had a run-in with them. Aren't they supposed to be more dangerous than Banditti?"

"You could say that again. I'd rather tangle with fifty Banditti than one Yěxìng." JJ pressed a button on STELA. "Huh?" Concern spread across his face as he fumbled with the controls.

"Is everything all right?" Dr. Elan asked.

"I'm not sure." JJ flipped a switch, and then another. "No, no, no! Federico, you better get up here."

Federico rushed in, handing Sharon and Dr. Elan each a glass bottle of crystal-clear water. "What is it?" He sat next to JJ.

"The cryo-converter storage tank." JJ scrutinized the numbers scrolling across STELA. "It must've been hit when NONA was shooting at us. The tank's been leaking fuel since. I don't know why the gauge isn't working, but we're losing power. Fast. We're running on fumes." He sketched a command. "I've got to find a place to land. We have about ten minutes before the Belostomatid takes matters into her own."

"There." Federico pointed to a large canyon. "Head toward the Platte River bed. We'll land inside it." He snapped his torso-restraint into the locked position. "Brace yourselves, everybody."

Sharon stuffed the water bottle into her satchel and kicked it beneath her seat. Through the windshield, she studied the fast-approaching deep, dry scar in Earth that used to flow with water. Wind had deposited sand in haphazard hills and gullies along its snaking reach. As the Belostomatid dropped in altitude, its whirring engines kicked up a sandstorm.

JJ swiped his fingers in quick motion over the command-screen that conveyed the ship's altitude, angle, and speed. He moved the red-handled throttle forward while holding the yellow one steady. The ship bounced once, hard, and then settled onto the sand.

Everyone let out their held breath.

"Okay, boss. Now what?" JJ asked.

Flipping through map images, Federico said, "We go dumpster diving."

"I suggest you shut the lights down before the Yěxíng find us." Dr. Elan rubbed his temples. "I sincerely hope they haven't already."

"Just what are we dumpster diving for?" JJ flipped several switches. The exterior lights on the ship went black as the window shades slid closed. "Should I power up her invisibility skin?"

"Yeah, just until we're ready to go." Federico glanced at JJ. "Then we'll have to turn it off and hope she goes unnoticed. We'll need battery power to get the engines started once the cryo-converter refills the fuel tank."

"What good is that going to do if there's a hole in it?" Dr. Elan asked.

"You up for a walk, Doc?" Federico asked.

"Of course." Dr. Elan smiled. "A lovely full moon is in the forecast. You know I'm always up for an adventure, especially with Yěxíng milling about."

"It's why you're one of us, *amigo*. Always up for an adventure."

"Hm." Dr. Elan nodded. "Indeed."

Federico squeezed his shoulder. "I'm going to need JJ to patch the cryo-converter tank. He's the only one of us with the know-how. I have to stay with the ship to ensure it isn't overcome by the Yěxíng. That leaves you and Sharon to find us some conversion materials. You'll keep Sharon safe because you know the Yěxìng. And Sharon will keep you safe because she knows how to use a weapon."

"I'm up for it," Sharon said. "Anything to get us on our way. But what conversion materials could be out there? I'd think any sources of energy would have been picked clean long ago."

"No, *amiga*." Federico opened a large cabinet revealing a stash of spectraletto pistols and bulky turbo-vests. "You'll be looking for something that lasts forever and that no one wants. Plastic."

"Ah." Sharon nodded as the realization dawned on her. "The cryo-converter can superheat plastic into its hydrocarbon components. The hydrocarbon gets stored in the tank and burned as fuel. My brother, Jon, explained it to me years ago. But I thought the technology was lost after the War of Earth's Rebellion."

"It's when science went by the wayside," Dr. Elan added. "Research came to a screeching halt."

"It's when my wife, Eve, lost her job at Harvard."

"Yeah, well, governments may have stopped doing science," JJ said. "But not scientists like Woody and Dr. Elan."

Federico passed an acupalmtell to Sharon. "There's an ancient recycling plant in what used to be Boys Town, just outside of Omaha. The acupalmtell has the coordinates for the plant and our location programmed in." He held the palm-sized computer in front of her. "See? Here. That's where you're going."

Sharon tucked it into her pocket. "What do we carry the plastic in?"

Federico lifted a turbo-vest from a hook in the cabinet. "In the left pocket of each vest is a mesh cargo bag. You can clip the bags onto the back of the vest once they're filled. If you stuff both, that'll make enough fuel to get us to California. You ever flown one of these?" He handed her the turbo-vest.

"Nope." She slipped it over her shoulders and pushed her satchel aside in order to buckle the vest closed. The heavy red vest fit snug against her body like a second skin. Her satchel fit tight against her back beneath the vest. Sharon double-checked that each of the four buckles were locked.

"May I?" JJ reached for her right pocket.

"Go ahead."

JJ removed a black box with a touchpad. "The controls on this are like your run-of-the-mill drone. If you can fly a drone, you can fly one of these. Just go easy on the thrust." He dropped it back into her pocket. "You've only got enough secondary thruster fuel to return to the Belostomatid. Use it as a last resort."

Federico handed Sharon a spectraletto pistol while JJ helped Dr. Elan into a vest. "If you do run into the Yěxìng, do whatever the doc tells you to do."

"Good advice." JJ pressed a spectraletto into the palm of Dr. Elan's hand. "They're scary."

"Only if you don't understand them." Dr. Elan secured the pistol in the vest's weapon slot.

"We can track the whereabouts of the vests, which means we can track you." Federico lifted his arm and pressed the time button on his cuff. "Try to be back here in less than three hours. Call if you get into a bind. We'll notify Woody of the delay and get the ship patched while you're out."

"A full moon is good fortune and good light." Dr. Elan slipped a pair of night-vision goggles over his eyes. "But these old eyes are going to need some help."

"You ready?" Sharon asked.

"Good to go." Dr. Elan stood shoulder to shoulder with Sharon as Federico opened the door. JJ kept a spectraletto trained at the opening as it grew large enough for them to step through. Nothing moved outside; everything looked safe.

"Walk along the riverbed until the sand rises enough for you to climb up to level ground." Federico faced Dr. Elan and put his hands on his shoulders. Dr. Elan touched his forehead to Federico's. "Be careful, *amigo*." He turned and put his hands to Sharon's shoulders. "*Amiga*."

Eve, as well as Dr. Ryan's and Areva's friendship, had been Sharon's only source of human connection for so long that Federico's gesture of friendship made her feel awkward. Yet, the camaraderie sparked a hope she thought had long been extinguished. Hope that she'd find Eve and avenge Areva's and Dr. Ryan's deaths. Hope that she had more room left in her heart to love. She bumped her head to his. The herbal scent from his hair reminded her of her brothers. How long had it been since she'd last hugged them? She kept her forehead pressed to Federico's a moment longer, savoring the human touch. "We'll be quick. I need to get to my wife." She backed away.

"And you will." Federico peered both ways into the darkness. "Go now. See you both soon." To JJ, he said, "Shut the door once they exit."

With Dr. Elan at her heels, Sharon moved quickly east along the shallow canyon formed by the riverbed. After several moments of silence, she could hear his breathing grow labored. She slowed their pace. "What's the likelihood that we'll run into a Yěxìng?"

"Not along the riverbed, but I suspect once we enter Boys Town, the likelihood will rise dramatically. They have plenty of shelter there."

"How do they manage to survive with no water?"

"Well, they get moisture from cactus plants, and collect rainwater during the brief rainy season." His breathing slowed with the pace. "They're really quite resourceful for such superstitious creatures."

"I can't imagine it ever raining here." Sharon gestured to the cracked walls of the arid riverbed.

"For all intents and purposes, it doesn't. Except for that brief window of time when the Pacific Ocean currents throw moisture hard enough at the Rockies that some of it manages to land in the Nebraska Desert before evaporating. They catch every drop."

"I'm afraid to ask, but what do the Yěxìng eat?" Sharon came to a stop to let him rest.

He removed the night-vision glasses, put his hands to his hips and drank in a couple of deep breaths. Even in the dark, his grave expression showed. "Ah, mostly rodents, unlucky birds stopping along their way from point A to point B." He shrugged. "Basically, any living creature unlucky enough to be herded into one of their prey lairs."

"A prey lair?" Sharon asked.

"It's a hole in the ground where they trap living things the old way—camouflage a pit along a game trail. Obviously, since they don't have a way to store meat, they keep it alive until they're hungry. As I said, they're quite resourceful."

"That bit of information makes walking through Yĕxìng territory seem even more ominous." Sharon studied their way forward, straining her eyes for any signs of a disguised hole in the ground.

"Well, my dear, the good news for us is that for all of their resourcefulness, they're a deeply superstitious people. If one knows how to manipulate them, they're quite prone to fright. Fear, as you know, is a powerful weapon." He stuffed the night-vision glasses into his vest pocket.

"And is that your specialty? Knowing how to scare the living daylights out of the Yĕxìng?"

"Indeed." He chuckled. "Knowing what gets beneath their skin makes them more fascinating than frightening."

"I'll take your word for it." She held her hand palm up toward an incline. "You ready? Looks like we can climb out here." Her hand moved to the spectraletto at her side.

"My advice is to use that only if absolutely necessary," Dr. Elan said. "The sound will bring an army of them."

"Good to know. I've got something better, then." She tapped the handle of her hammer tucked in its baldric. "What's that old saying? Never bring a knife to a gunfight."

"Rest assured, the Yĕxìng do not have guns. And knives do not run out of bullets."

"And, in the case of my hammer, it never runs out of spectral juice, or the gas needed to fire it."

"Then I am in very good hands. Shall we check the map?"

She retrieved the acupalmtell and handed it to him.

He studied its map and passed it back. "We're right where we should be."

She dropped it into her pocket. "Let's do this."

They carefully climbed out of the canyon and began walking on the soft sand surface toward Boys Town. When they crossed to hard-packed sections where loose sand had blown away, they picked up the pace. Sharon welcomed getting to stretch her legs and burn off nervous energy. The abrupt rise of a hummocky surface—the buried buildings and vehicles of the late town—along with occasional jagged fragments protruding from the sand, told them they were on track.

Something bright on the ground caught Sharon's eye. Moonlight hit the object just enough to make it glow a rich yellow. She stopped to study it: a tiny delicate flower that reached toward the light in rebellion against the desert. She lowered herself to a knee and touched it.

Softly, as if not to disturb the yellow miracle, Dr. Elan said, "The Desert Golden Primrose. Also known as Desert Gold. A rare sight. It's lovely."

Sharon touched the flower and resisted her grief. "Eve," she whispered. "It reminds me of my wife, Eve."

"Are you all right?"

"Yeah." She got to her feet and brushed sand from her knee. "Eve used to . . . I mean, Eve says that the one thing she loves almost as much as me are flowers. Seeing it kind of punched me in the gut." She shook her head and laughed in spite of her misery. "I'm lucky my wife is like a flower in the desert. The whole world could be falling down around her, but she remains. I miss her with every cell in my body."

"What a beautiful way to think about your wife." His voice was soft and empathetic. "Hang on to believing that she will endure." He touched her arm. "In the meantime, we'll help you find her."

"Thank you." She searched the shadows ahead. "We're not far. Maybe four hundred meters."

"I'll follow you. We should avoid talking as we approach."

"Okay." She tugged the cuff of his sleeve. "Stay close, Doc."

"I'll keep you safe," he whispered, "and you keep me safe."

"You got a deal."

They continued walking in silence until they came to crumbling pavement. Sharon retrieved the acupalmtell and scrutinized the map. "This has to be the road to the recycling plant, based on our GPS location. We go left here."

"Careful as you do," Dr. Elan reminded her.

After walking another four hundred meters or so, the shadow of a metal hangar rose in front of them. Half of it, including the bottom section of its double doors, was buried. Sharon returned the acupalmtell to her pocket and started to push sand away with her hands. "I'll dig. It's not very deep. You keep watch."

"Good plan." Dr. Elan squinted into the dark.

Sharon dug until she was able to brush the last of the sand from the bottom of one of the doors. She got up and yanked it open. Lifting her arm, she shined the light on her sleeve into the void. Mounds of cans and plastic debris filled the hangar. "This is it." She waved him in.

They shut the door and scurried to dig through the heaps of plastic.

"I assume we want the thicker stuff, right?" She held up a dented laundry detergent bottle and a scuffed skateboard.

On his hands and knees, Dr. Elan rifled through the refuse. A strand of gray hair fell over one eye. "Yes, the denser the better. It'll burn longer." From the pile he pulled a thick, green object that looked like a doughnut. "Like this." Holding it up, he explained, "It's an old O-ring from the hover-tracks the U.S. government built during the War of the Second Crusade." He opened his sack and tossed it in. "These things will burn for hours."

"Got another one." Sharon dropped a burgundy-colored O-ring into her sack. "There's a bunch here." She tossed aside several Diet Coke bottles to reach another O-ring. "I would've guessed that it would smell in here, but it doesn't."

"It's too dry for microorganisms to break down the plastic. That's why it doesn't smell." Dr. Elan tossed a plastic doll's head over his shoulder. He plucked a black O-ring from the pile. "Oh dear, this is a great find. Let's gather as many O-rings as we can. They'll do the trick."

"I do feel like my lungs are being desiccated down here." Sharon flung a vase with a hot-pink plastic flower in it.

"We'll both need a couple of liters of water when we get back to the Belostomatid." Dr. Elan held up an orange shoe with a spiky heel. "This could *not* have been comfortable." He dropped it and continued digging.

"I'd rather poke my eyes out than put those on my feet." Sharon smiled.

"I wonder if that was the purpose of that dreadful heel." Dr. Elan shook his head. "People are interesting creatures."

"If you say so, Doc." Sharon stuffed her sack with another O-ring.

They continued to dig. The volume and quality of the discarded O-rings made it easy to fill both sacks within minutes. Sharon cinched hers closed and helped Dr. Elan finish filling his.

"Will this be too heavy for you?" she asked.

"No, I can do it."

She helped him lift his bag, and shrugged hers over a shoulder.

"That was easier than I thought it'd be." Sharon pushed the door open. When she crossed the threshold into open air something whacked her on the side of the head. The sting forced her eyes shut. "What the hell was that?" She opened them and noticed a small rock at her feet.

A clicking sound not unlike crickets, although definitely human, replaced the quiet. She touched her head and felt a swelling bump.

Dr. Elan emerged from the hangar. "Well, this is an unfortunate circumstance."

Sharon reached for her spectraletto.

"Wait." Dr. Elan grabbed her elbow. "Don't. Remember what I said. Make a loud enough noise and you'll conjure them all."

"Why are they making that weird chatter?"

"They're trying to frighten us. It harks back to a form of prayer. The method is twofold. They're asking whatever gods they believe in to help them, and they know it scares the hell out of their adversaries."

"I hope you have a plan B, Doc." Sharon shuffled back as human figures emerged from the shadows. "They don't look friendly."

Men and women who no longer bathed or cut their hair gathered into a small, pungent crowd. They wore remnants of clothing over their genitals, mouths, and noses. Sharon lifted her sleeve, shining the light onto wild faces. Bloodshot eyes framed by scruffy hair stared back at her. Dark, leathery skin sagged in wrinkles. Even the children were shriveled by the sun. A variety of painted religious symbols covered their skin. The clicking from their mouths grew furiously loud. They carried sticks, rocks, and an assortment of repurposed household items as weapons. One held a hubcap at his side like a shield.

"I count twenty-three," Sharon said. "And those are just the ones I can see. What do we do?"

"First, don't panic." Dr. Elan lowered his bag of plastic to the ground. "Follow my lead."

"All right." Sharon set her bag next to Dr. Elan's. Her fingers itched to grab her hammer in one hand and the spectraletto in the other. "Just so you know. I'm pretty good with a hammer."

"I have no doubt." Dr. Elan tugged the hem of her shirt. "The thing is, if you show them that you're powerful, they'll keep you around for a while. You'd be viewed by the ones who'd eventually overpower us as breeding stock. They'd mate with you before they ate you."

"Okay, then." Sharon relaxed her hands. "Let's take the hammer off the table for the time being. But let's be clear, Doc, I don't intend to be eaten. And I sure as hell am not going to be mated."

"Again, I have no doubt. Confidence is healthy. Usually." He scrunched the hem of her shirt again, but did not let go. "They're herding us."

"What does that mean?" Sharon asked.

"They expect us to run. They've left a path for us to go." He pointed. "There. That's where they want us to go. It'll most likely lead to a prey pit. This is actually a good thing for us."

"I don't mean to be dense, Doc. But how is that a good thing?"

He let go of her hem and slipped his arm around hers. "Follow me."

"To the prey pit?" Sharon asked. "I mean, never mind."

"Not to worry. They no longer understand language beyond grunts and hand signals." He marched forward with Sharon in tow. "As for our plan, the Yěxìng began their transformation to feral during the War of the Second Crusade. They're stuck in a purgatory of religious beliefs. Universal among them is the superstition that food must not be eaten in the dark."

"So that means we've got about six hours to figure out how to escape." Sharon glanced over her shoulder. The ominous clicking followed.

"Precisely. If they don't sense that we're dangerous, they'll let their guard down." Dr. Elan patted her wrist. "That's why, for now, we don't challenge them."

"And because they have us outnumbered by at least ten to one, right?"

He laughed quietly.

Sharon felt Dr. Elan shiver next to her. "The desert gets cold at night," she said.

"Yes, it does." He huddled closer to her. "We'll have each other to keep warm."

They continued walking until a large hole in the ground gaped before them. A rusty ladder dipped into it.

Grunting preceded a harsh shove at Sharon's back. Dr. Elan stumbled and she caught him by the waist.

The crowd of Yěxìng started yelling and waving weapons.

"They want us to go into the pit," Dr. Elan said.

"Maybe we can outrun them. I really don't want to go into that pit." Sharon tugged him to a stop. "There's got to be a plan B. What about the turbo-vests? We could just fly out of here."

"Trust me when I tell you that where there are twenty-three Yěxìng, there are at least a hundred more hiding close by. We can't risk them following us to the ship. The turbo-vests are a last resort." He put a foot on the top rung of the ladder. His harried expression did not match his calm words.

"You look scared," she said.

"I am." Dr. Elan glanced down into the dark tomb and back. "I'm scared that the Yěxìng won't act as I predict. But as long as they do, I have a plan that will work. The good news is that I'm betting they'll take the predictable approach to dealing with us. Humans, even the feral ones, are usually unsurprising."

"You're the expert." Sharon inhaled a breath that wasn't as calming as she'd hoped.

With his foot on the top rung and the Yěxìng moving closer, Dr. Elan looked into the black void. "Would you mind shining your light? I'd like to know what I'm stepping into."

Sharon lifted her sleeve. A mangy, frail dog cowered below. Bones lay scattered around the periphery. Disgust and fear rattled Sharon's resolve. "As hard as it's going to be to make myself climb down there, I'm right behind you, Doc. I trust you."

"I'm glad to have you at my back." Dr. Elan smiled up at her. "Looks like it's just us and an unfortunate dog." As he climbed down he said, "While I'm not a fan of NONA, I like that they revere dogs. Now that we've found it, we can't leave it."

Sharon didn't need any more to know that she liked Dr. Elan. Deciding in the instant to save the dog was her instinct too. When she got to the bottom of the pit, she looked up at the ominous deranged faces gathering at its rim.

A tall, thin man with a gray beard that brushed his belly set a box on a wooden platform near the fourth rung down. Using a long pipe with a hook at its end, he lifted one side off the box. A dark gray snake lay coiled inside. Its diamond-shaped head darted at the retreating pipe and lid, but missed.

"Ha." Dr. Elan clapped. "It's just like in the books. A black mamba. They used to be one of South Africa's most deadly snakes. But they've learned to survive quite well in the Nebraska Desert. Its venom kills within minutes. The ancients called the bite of a mamba the kiss of death. This one appears to be guarding the ladder."

Sharon struggled to keep track of the snake above and the dog at the bottom of the pit with them. "I have to admit," she said, "it worries me that you find pleasure in being in close quarters with a killer snake."

"That snake, my dear, is our predictable ticket out of here." He wheeled around and regarded the dog. "Poor beast. Let's earn his trust with some food."

"What about the snake? How the hell do we get us and the dog past it?" Sharon unfastened her turbo-vest and slipped her satchel from her shoulders.

"I have a plan that will work and doesn't involve interrupting JJ and Federico from repairing and guarding the ship." He crouched down with his back to the wall. "They're leaving us. That's why the snake is there. They think it'll keep us from escaping. It's universal, the innate human fear of snakes. I suppose religion has planted its own seeds of snake hate. They expect it of us."

"Snake hate?"

"They *are* the most underappreciated reptile." The expression on his face suggested he meant it. Sincerely.

"No offense, Doc, but I hope your plan involves us killing the underappreciated reptile." Sharon stared up at the snake. "I'm thinking we can probably find something to knock it off the ledge. Then maybe throw a jacket over it. Once it's trapped, I'd kill it with my hammer."

Dr. Elan curved a finger through the eye-socket of a human skull near his foot. "This poor bastard," he lifted it, "likely tried to get past a mamba." He set the skull down. "We have to keep in mind the characteristics of the snake in order to get the better of it."

"Okay, what are they?" Sharon asked.

"The bad news is that the mamba is one of the fastest and most agile snakes on the planet." Dr. Elan scooped sand from the floor into his hand. "The good news is that they're clumsy on soft sand." He opened his hand, letting the fine grains sift through his fingers. "I think you're right. We have to knock it down. But clumsy as it may be on sand, if it gets close enough to strike, it will strike again and again. They're relentless when threatened."

Sharon had been trying to avoid looking at the human remains scattered in the pit. "You mean these people were killed by the snake instead of being eaten by the Yĕxìng?"

"That's right." Dr. Elan got to his feet and unbuckled his vest. "The Yĕxìng won't touch a body that's been contaminated with snake venom. These people were left to decompose. How this is supposed to work is that the snake keeps prey from exiting. The snake stays in the box because the walls are too smooth for it to climb. The prey stays in the pit because it's too afraid of the snake. At sunrise, the snake handler replaces the wall of the snake's container. Then the Yĕxìng come down to retrieve their prey. The tricky part for us will be figuring out how to kill the snake before it kills us."

Sharon eased the turbo-vest from his shoulders and set it on the ground. "I have an idea." She lifted the flap of her satchel and plucked out a container of fried beetles and her flask. "I'll use my bag as a shield. It's made of Kantolean, a laser-proof fabric. Maybe get the snake to strike the bag enough times to tire it out. Then I'll get close enough to kill it." She opened the container and offered a beetle on her open palm to the dog.

The dog sniffed and snapped it up.

"Good boy." She cupped her hand and poured water into it. "How about some water too?"

Dr. Elan smiled and showed her the tattoo on his wrist. "These points on the snowflake hexagon are significant to the Qaunik. They represent the six virtues, the six great professions, and the six essential human needs. Two of the virtues, kindness and bravery—you have those in spades, Sharon." He reached into his pocket. "See if he'll eat this too." He held out his palm. "It's rat jerky. It'll give him strength for our journey out of here."

Remorse over stealing Annie's coat and leaving Inu hung over Sharon like a black cloud. "I'm not kind. And not even all that brave." She touched the turbo-vest. "You sure we can't just fly out of here? We can make a sling to carry the dog. Why not call Federico for help?" She scratched the dog's neck, feeling sure that it was smart enough to know the difference between being saved versus eaten. Plus, it was too weak to be a threat. It barely mustered the energy to wag its tail.

"We still need to retrieve our bags full of plastic. It's too risky to fly. If we land in a nest of Yěxìng, they'd kill us then and there. Plus, we don't want them following us back to the Belostomatid. They need to be too terrified to come after us. Killing the snake is the best way. And your idea to use your satchel as a shield is a good one. Federico needs to stay with the ship while JJ makes the necessary repairs."

"All right. Killing the snake it is. Then we walk out of here, get our bags, and fly back to the ship. The Yěxìng will be too freaked out about the dead snake to follow us?"

"Precisely." Dr. Elan reached into his jacket and retrieved an aluminum flask. He untwisted the cap. "How about some liquid courage? Enough to make us brave, but not enough to make us stupid. You ever taste bourbon?"

"Yeah," Sharon answered. "It was my grandfather's favorite. After he died, I found a couple of old bottles that he'd stashed. I saved them for special occasions. My wife and I shared the last bit of it the day we got married." She caressed the dog's nose. With a wiry reddish coat and long legs, he looked like a cross between a husky and a German shepherd.

Again, the dog's tail wagged feebly.

"You should call him Erik." Dr. Elan took a sip and handed the bottle to Sharon. "Erik the Red. Our new comrade in adventure."

"I like it. Erik it is." Sharon put the bottle to her lips and tipped it back. The smoky amber liquid warmed her throat and nose. "That's good." Its calming effect bled into her veins. "Thank you." She handed the bottle back to him. "Just enough to take the edge off. Let's get this over with, Doc. Before I lose my nerve."

Dr. Elan took off his jacket. "Here's the plan." He wadded his jacket into a ball. "I'm going to throw this so that the snake's box falls to the left. You be ready with your shield and hammer. Hit it hard before it gets its bearings."

"Got it—in theory."

Dr. Elan chuckled.

She gripped her hammer in her right hand and held the satchel in her left. Her pulse raced. "I'm ready."

"Here goes." Dr. Elan heaved his jacket at the snake box. It tipped off the shelf and landed in soft sand with the open side up.

The snake's head popped from the opening. It hissed and spread its neck flap like a cobra.

Sharon shone her light at the snake. It opened its mouth wide and flicked its tongue. Its fangs glinted in the beam of light. Holding the bag in front of her, Sharon moved closer. The snake struck the bag in quick violent succession, five or six times. The force of the last strike pushed Sharon off balance. Her foot landed on something, maybe a bone. She stumbled onto her back.

The snake lunged from the box.

Keeping the satchel in front of her, Sharon scuttled away from it.

Erik barked and stomped his front paws.

Instantly, the snake turned on the dog.

Sharon flung her hammer. The clean shot sank the claw into the snake's neck.

Dr. Elan threw his vest over its writhing body.

As the snake's head edged from the vest, Sharon drove the heel of her boot onto it. Its meaty flesh squished and bone crunched. She pulled her hammer free and lifted her foot. Blood oozed from the snake's open mouth. She bent over and exhaled.

"Good work." Dr. Elan nudged the snake with his boot. "Looks pretty dead. I hate having to kill it. But it was the only way." He picked up his jacket and put it on.

"I know." She wiped her hammer on her dungarees and returned it to the baldric. "Let's get out of here."

They retrieved their gear and helped each other put their turbo-vests back on. Sharon lifted the frail dog onto her shoulders. Dr. Elan threw the snake's tail over his shoulder and curled the remainder of its body into a bundle he could carry.

Then he climbed to the top of the pit and scouted for Yĕxìng.

Sharon followed, carrying the skin-and-bones dog like a sack.

"Oh, dear." Dr. Elan turned. In the soft glow of the light from Sharon's sleeve, he looked ashen.

"What is it?" She set the dog down. "What's wrong?"

Dr. Elan dropped the snake and tried to say something. Beads of sweat bubbled at his temples. "My arm, it hurts."

Sharon kicked the snake body away. Panic fluttered through her. "Let's rest."

He shook his head, and put his hands to his chest. "Heart ..." He dropped to his knees and fell over onto his back.

"No!" Sharon got down beside him and fumbled to open the heavy vest. She put her ear to his chest, willing his heart to beat. Nothing.

"Dr. Elan!" She heard the weird chattering of Yĕxìng in the distance.

Erik leaned against her and growled at the darkness.

Sharon put two fingers to the old man's neck and felt no pulse. "Stay with me, Doc." She put her stacked hands to his chest and counted compressions. *Goddammit.* She couldn't remember how many she was supposed to do. Ten, before giving a breath? Fifteen? She covered his mouth with hers and blew.

His chest rose.

She repeated the compressions and breaths in several cycles before checking again for a pulse. Still nothing.

"No, no, no, no." Sharon tried to lift him by his jacket collar.

The dog whimpered.

"Sharon!"

She looked in the direction of the familiar voice. "JJ!"

"We've been tracking you. When we saw you move farther east of the recycling plant, we thought something might be wrong." JJ dropped to his knees and put two fingers to Dr. Elan's neck for several long seconds. "What happened?"

"Heart attack," Sharon whispered. "I think."

"How long ago?"

"Five, ten minutes." She shook her head. "I can't be sure."

"I think he's gone." JJ's voice sagged with grief.

"No." Tears escaped past Sharon's defenses. "Let's keep trying."

The clicking sound grew louder.

"We got to go." JJ took her by the elbow and helped her to her feet. "The Yěxìng are coming."

Sharon listened to the ominous clicking creeping toward them.

Erik stood his ground at Sharon's side and continued to growl. She put a hand to his head. "We won't leave you."

A mask of sad determination replaced JJ's usual lighthearted demeanor. "You can introduce me to your new friend when we get back to the ship. For now, we have to hurry. A massive sandstorm is coming as well."

Sharon glanced at Dr. Elan's body. "We can't let them eat him."

"They won't." JJ lifted the dead snake onto Dr. Elan's chest. "They'll think his body is contaminated by snake venom."

"We still can't leave him," Sharon pleaded. "Not here."

"Listen to me." JJ shook her slightly. "He was my friend, and I'll miss him forever. But what I know is that he'd rather be reclaimed by Earth than dragged off to be burned in a crematorium. The Yěxìng will leave him alone and the sand will cover him." JJ knelt and touched his forehead to Dr. Elan's. "May Earth reclaim you, as she will all of us. Goodbye, my friend."

Sharon knelt and did the same. "I knew you less than a day, but I miss you already. Goodbye, Dr. Elan. Safe travels."

Chapter 12

"Thanks to Sharon and Dr. Elan, we have enough fuel to get to California." JJ's voice was somber as he pushed away from the control panel. "For now, the Belostomatid is buttoned up against the storm. Her systems are sealed and secured. Maybe we can take a few seconds to remember Dr. Elan?"

"Yes, we should." Federico lifted his head. "Wherever we go, we go with you, Dr. Elan. Your energy is part of us."

They sat in silence for several moments.

"You're a good man." Federico cupped the back of JJ's neck. "Dr. Elan loved you. I know you're tired. It's been a tough couple of days. We'll all rest soon. For now, we need to prepare for Phillip's trial for the murder of Dr. Elan. Woody's assembling a quorum by video transmission. We'll put this time hunkered down to good use."

The storm had continued, for more than six hours now, to roar outside. Wind-driven sand lashed at the ship. The bulky Belostomatid shuddered with occasional violent gusts.

"I'll prepare a last meal for Phillip." JJ seemed sluggish, his movements bogged down by more than fatigue. Without waiting for a response, he left the cockpit.

"Murder?" Sharon asked. "Dr. Elan died of a heart attack."

"You doubt his guilt?" Federico asked.

"No. I was there. He intended to steal the ship and leave you and JJ to die." Sharon pressed her foot closer to the sleeping dog at her feet. Erik's presence was as much a comfort to her as she suspected hers was to him. "I hope he gets what's coming to him. But how is it murder?"

"Phillip set the events in motion that led to Dr. Elan's death. He'll very likely die for what he's done, but not at the hands of the Qaunik. I assure you, our way is more than fair." He plucked a bottle of water from a crate near where he sat and passed it to Sharon. "Please, you need to drink more."

When she reached for it, she noticed the tattoo. "All of you wear that snowflake. What does it mean?"

"It's our symbol." He pushed his sleeve up.

"Dr. Elan told me that the points represent six human virtues, six great professions, and . . ." She paused, trying to remember the last one.

"The six essential human needs," Federico filled in the blank. "Inspiration, purpose, connection, freedom, identity." He counted them off on five fingers, and held up his thumb on the other hand. "And love."

"And the others?" Sharon flipped the top open on the bottle.

"The six human virtues we all strive for are loyalty, kindness, bravery, humility, curiosity, and honesty." He pointed at the circle from which the three hexagons anchored. Each hexagon had a unique length and shape at its ends, like a snowflake in nature. "The circle cut into quarters is an ancient symbol for Earth. All of life, including humanity, is born from Earth. Nothing living exists without her." He moved his finger to the first hexagon. "These are the six great professions: scientists, artists, teachers, healers, builders, and leaders."

"What about farmers?" A note of disappointment tinged her voice. "The world is starving."

"Not everyone has to aspire to engage in one of these professions. We all do lots of different things. Those just happen to be the ones we revere. Being a farmer, on the other hand, is like being able to breathe. It's not a profession, but something we must all aspire to do. We're all would-be farmers."

"Would-be?" Sharon put the bottle to her lips and let the cool liquid soothe her dry mouth. "You don't grow anything?"

"We have nothing to grow." He reached for a plate on the pull-out desk beneath STELA. "A long-term food supply is our greatest vulnerability and why the water on this ship is so important." He passed the plate to her. "There are only so many of these disgusting reconstituted, freeze-dried potato-kale-beetle larvae patties we can trade for or steal. We need to be able to grow our own potato and kale. Please, you eat the last one. I've had enough."

"I thought retaking the ship the Strelitzia stole from you was Woody's biggest concern." Sharon broke the patty into two pieces, and offered one to Erik.

Tail wagging, he nibbled up the food.

"Good, gentle Erik." She scratched the dog behind an ear and bit into the remaining half. A salty, earthy tang coated her tongue as she swallowed the starchy patty. "These things are pretty disgusting."

"Indeed, *amiga*." Federico smoothed Erik's fur. "Woody intends to trade the water for seed potatoes and kale seeds. That's all that's available on the black market. Of course, we forage for other things when we can. But foraging isn't as reliable as a bank of potato and kale seeds our would-be farmers can grow. The black-market seeds and getting our ship back are both essential to our survival when the Thwaites collapses."

Sharon recalled the looks on Federico and JJ's faces when they saw the Strelitzia eat the apple he attributed to her. The thing that most unsettled her about the Qaunik is that they hadn't, at least yet, interrogated her about it. As far as she knew, they hadn't even searched her satchel. Maybe they had, but intended to manipulate her with silence. "Why haven't you asked me about the apple the Strelitzia ate?"

"Probably for the same reason you haven't told us about it." Federico leaned against his seat. "Whatever you have is not ours to take."

"You took this water." She displayed the empty bottle.

"Yes, we did. Because it didn't belong to NONA. It belongs to Earth. Whatever you've cultivated on your own is yours." He brushed his sleeve up his arm again. "These things on the snowflake are not just talk. The Qaunik believe in them the way the old world believed in its religions. We won't steal from you. And we'll tell you the truth. We don't live by a set of laws only when it's convenient. We live by a code of humanity. When that code is broken, it's not a crime to be punished. It's a breach of faith that results in banishment."

"Phillip used that word. He said he didn't want to be banished."

"Then he shouldn't have broken the covenants he made with the Qaunik." Federico clipped each word short as his voice rose.

Erik lifted his head and whimpered.

Federico bent and scratched the dog under his chin. "It's okay, *amigo*," he said in a softer tone. "A little food, water, a bath, and rest have given you strength. That's a good thing, loyal dog. You're a fighter. A dog would never break the covenants."

Erik lowered his head to his paws and resumed his convalescence.

"What are your covenants?" Sharon asked.

"To become a citizen of Qaunik, one must be vouched for by another citizen who recognizes one of the six virtues in the candidate. Even babies born to Qaunik parents must be vouched for once they become adults."

"I don't mean to offend you. But that seems a little elitist. Like some cliquish cult."

"I get why you'd say that." Federico continued to scratch the back of Erik's ear. "You'd be surprised. There's usually someone willing to vouch for another person. Getting in is the easy part. The hard part is staying true." He gave Erik another pat and leaned against the seat back. "JJ vouched for Phillip. He didn't just lose Dr. Elan, he lost faith in someone he trusted."

"I don't know how you find people with all of those virtues. Seems unrealistic to me." Sharon touched the scarf at her neck. Eve was the only person she'd ever known who fit that description. Over the years, Sharon had betrayed those virtues time and again in order to keep Eve safe. Like Phillip, she'd probably mess up too. "Doesn't life get in the way of being virtuous all of the time?"

"Yes, it does. Which is why our covenants are straightforward—with that in mind. Every person must first promise to strive for the six virtues, respect the six great professions, and not keep anyone from the six human needs. People get to choose their professions, whatever it is that they want to do. The only promise is that people must work by carrying the weight they are capable of carrying. We're all in this together. Therefore, everyone must contribute something of value. Whatever that is."

Sharon thought of Annie and Inu. Her heart still hurt at leaving him. She had abandoned a little boy, left him with an old lady. Her disgust at herself simmered over. She'd never forgive herself for doing it. But she had made the choice to save Eve. The Qaunik ideal sounded virtuous, but they abandoned people too. "Sounds like you're exclusive to those who aren't imperfect, sick, old, or young—the same as me."

"Oh, Sharon." Federico shook his head. "You're coming to all of the wrong conclusions. A person's contribution isn't always measured in brute strength, or perfection. To the contrary, the old, sick, and young satisfy some of our greatest needs as an imperfect people. The old give us wisdom, the young give us hope, and the sick, a strength of purpose to survive. All we ask is that people carry the weight they're able to."

"Aren't you also asking for people to be perfect?" She looked him in the eye. "We're all human. What happens when someone makes the inevitable mistake—or when they get greedy, or lazy?"

"Greedy and lazy aren't tolerated. But we're all imperfect. Every one of us makes a bad or tough choice from time to time. That's why everyone gets three strikes," Federico said. "This is Phillip's third. It's why he'll be banished."

"What's the trial for, then? If his banishment is a foregone conclusion?" A ferocious gust made the ship quiver, whistling through its seams. Erik moved his head from his paws to the top of Sharon's boot.

"We know the facts of what Phillip did. Even without you as a witness, or his confession, the neuron-incident-scanner does not lie about the facts. He's already been connected to it and read. The scanner reads a person's memory of a particular incident. We see, through the scanner, everything that happened. What the scanner can't read is a person's heart. It tells us what happened, but not why."

"So the trial is to learn the why of something?" Sharon asked.

"Yes. The accused gets three strikes before being banished. On the third strike, he is given the opportunity to plead his case as to why he did what he did. If the jury concludes that the motive fits within the confines of the six human virtues, then the accused will not be banished. For some breaches, such as the deliberate murder of another Qaunik, it may not matter how many strikes a person has against them. If the jury believes that the motive of the accused was contrary to every virtue, banishment will be automatic."

"So the best sob story wins?"

"I like your cynicism, Sharon. I'm not saying this is a perfect system. It's the best we've come up with."

"What does it mean to be banished?"

"The convicted is ejected from our society. He'll learn very quickly just how difficult it is to survive alone. In the ire of Earth, I'm certain, most people don't make it. And if they do, I'm guessing it's a very desolate existence."

The OVA flashed white; then a red light in the upper right corner blinked.

"That must be Woody." Federico brushed his finger over STELA and said, "Video connect."

The OVA came to life with the image of Woody, flanked by six people all dressed in what looked like the clothes of ancient cultures. Their ages and skin color were as varied as their clothing. Woody looked regal in a dark robe and royal-blue silk hijab.

Erik laboriously got to his feet and woofed.

"Ah, so happy to finally make your acquaintance, Erik the

Red." Woody smiled. "Thank you all for saving the Belostomatid. We're behind schedule, but thanks to your diligence we're still able to move forward with our plan to trade water for food. Is the accused ready for his trial?"

"Yes." Federico reached for a microphone. "I'll have JJ bring him in."

Woody held up a hand. "First, I must ask Sharon some questions. Tell me a little more about this person you seek in California. How can we most efficiently find him given that we've already missed our appointment to trade the water?"

"The man's name is Elliot Addington. He used to work for my father. What I know is that he works in a labor camp in San Francisco. I'm certain he's there now."

"How can you be certain he's alive, let alone where you say he is?" Woody asked.

Erik was leaning against Sharon's knees. She reached down and sank her fingers into Erik's fur reassuringly. "When Elliot left, he gave me a Sat-tracker. I checked it about four months ago. He was there then."

Woody put her hands on the arms of the high-backed chair in which she sat. "Are you aware that the camp is divided into male workers and female workers?"

"No."

"We'll need to implant JJ with a chip from a deceased man from the camp. There's no way they'll let a woman waltz in there to find this Elliot you seek. We're going to need to split up. We're already a day and a half behind schedule. JJ will find and kidnap Elliot. I ask that you, Sharon, accompany Federico to meet our underground operator to help facilitate the water trade. He could use someone like you to help."

"I'd rather be useful than not." Sharon left out the part about not being certain Elliot would be happy to see her anyway. Maybe he'd put up less of a fight being confronted by strangers than by her.

"Thank you." Woody nodded at Federico. "Please, bring in Phillip."

Federico spoke into STELA's audio-comm. "JJ, the quorum is ready."

Several seconds passed in silence. The people surrounding Woody were three men and three women. Their expressions suggested they understood the gravity of their power to decide the fate of a human being.

JJ entered the room with Phillip, struggling against him. Phillip's broken nose was bandaged. JJ helped him into a seat in front of the OVA.

"Phillip Guster, formerly of the State of North Carolina." Woody's voice was smooth and deliberate. "You violated the virtues of honesty, loyalty, kindness, and bravery. Therefore, you broke your covenant with the Qaunik. Your purposeful actions put the lives of your fellow Qaunik people in jeopardy. In fact, because of those actions Dr. Elan is dead. How do you defend yourself?"

Phillip's battered body shivered. He lifted his head and stared into the stoic faces looking back at him. "Because I don't wish to be trapped on a ship in the middle of nowhere waiting to die. You all surely will die of starvation, eventually. I choose to take my chances on land."

"Perhaps," Woody said. "But we will not die alone, should your prophecy come to fruition. We will die with our integrity and surrounded by love."

"You're fools," Phillip snapped. "We're all dead anyway. Some sooner than others, but dead is dead. I did it to be free. Isn't that one of the essential human needs?"

"Freedom doesn't come without sacrifice. Freedom isn't free." Woody sighed. "All things exist in balance. Without balance, it all falls apart." She held up her wrist; the snowflake tattoo was like an indictment. "All of this must exist in balance. We need each other as much as we need freedom. One doesn't come without the other. No human, like a snowflake, is exactly like another. Each has a unique value. But we survive as one. Have you anything else to say?"

"No." Phillip's jaw clenched. "I know what's coming."

"Then I ask the quorum to vote," Woody said. "By a show of hands, who votes for banishment?"

Six hands rose. Each bare wrist bore the snowflake of the Qaunik. Woody lifted hers, making the vote unanimous.

"It shall be done immediately," Woody declared. "Have you packed a last meal and water for Phillip?"

"Yes," JJ answered.

The Belostomatid shook in a gust as blown sand clawed its windows.

"Can you at least wait for the storm to end?" Phillip pleaded. "Give me a fighting chance to survive my banishment."

"As difficult as it is to banish another human being, it must be done. We have few resources. We are gracious in our openness to vouch people in. But we must be firm when our covenants are broken. Your choices are not our problem." Woody turned her attention to JJ. "Give him his pack, and escort him off the ship at once."

JJ hesitated before gripping Phillip's elbow. "Come," he said. "This is your own doing."

Woody motioned for the members of the quorum to leave. They filed out one by one. "As soon as the storm allows, go to our meeting spot in the Nevada Desert. That's where you'll split up." Like the members of the quorum, Woody seemed weighted by a cloud of sadness over their decision. "We will soon be together. Be safe, my friends." The OVA went black.

Federico flipped on STELA. A jet of wind-lashed sand blew in as the hatch opened.

Sharon shielded her eyes.

Phillip raised a fist to the dark squall. He turned to those banishing him. "I wish the Qaunik death by a thousand cuts." He disappeared into the fury.

The hatch closed him out.

"No one can survive out there," Sharon said.

"You'd be surprised what people are able to survive. If he manages to stay alive, he'll be alone." Federico brushed his dark hair back with his hands as if trying to brush away Phillip's banishment. "Me, I'd rather die out there than live alone."

"Me too, brother." JJ joined them, all of them staring mutely at the hatch.

Sharon thought of Eve, and her parents, grandparents, friends, and brothers. They had been her people. She felt so alone without them. Except, she wasn't alone in this moment. In a hushed tone, Sharon said, "You remind me of my brothers. I miss them more than I could ever describe."

She reached into her pack for one of the two remaining apples, and polished the fruit against her jacket.

A look of caution spread over JJ's face.

"It's okay. Trust me." Sharon smiled and held up the apple. "To brothers, and to Dr. Elan. I'm glad I got to know him, and you." She bit into the apple. The texture, the sweet, the sour, the juice, it all marked life. It felt good to share. She handed the apple to JJ.

Chapter 13

"Welcome to the Nevada Desert." JJ sketched a stop symbol on STELA, and tapped it. In sync with the fading drawing, the Belostomatid lowered to the ground. "The hottest and most fucked-up place in North America." He pressed the water-bug-at-rest icon. The ship's engines hissed and went quiet.

"Let's have a look around." Federico powered and rotated the camera controller. The OVA flashed green and split into two images. The Belostomatid's left antennae relayed a panoramic view, and the right a selfie of the ship. Nestled among an army of thirsty solar panels anchored in hardpan, the conspicuous insect-like vessel broadcast its presence. "Better put her in defense mode."

"Scary bug, coming up." JJ drew a sword. The Belostomatid's four back legs deployed, lifting the fuselage about five meters. With pincers open, the two front legs swiveled forward. "She's ready to crush or shoot on command."

"You're right, JJ," Sharon said. "It does look pretty fucked up. It must be at least fifty-two degrees."

Erik dozed at her feet.

JJ tapped the thermometer icon. "Fifty-four point four, to be exact. That won't boil water, but it'll cook a brain fast."

"So why are we in defense mode?" Through the port window, Sharon watched heat undulate off the arrays gulping the sun.

"As a precaution. This is one of NONA's military power grids.

Even though it's a dead zone for hundreds of kilometers, they still send out inspection drones." Federico brushed his palm over the ship's invisibility icon. "Out here, the Belostomatid will generate more power than she uses. In invisibility mode, we could hide out indefinitely."

"Except that we'd starve." JJ drew a circle and tapped it twice. A supply list emerged onto the OVA. "Not counting the water for trade, we've only got enough to drink and eat for two weeks."

"That'll be remedied once we get the seeds," Federico said.

"I have an idea." JJ made a series of sketches. A satellite image popped up, showing several collapsed buildings near a deep depression. "This is the old Lake Tahoe basin. I'll pass over it on my way to meet Woody. I could touch down and do a little foraging."

"Absolutely not. We've already lost Dr. Elan. I don't want to lose you too." Federico pressed the release on his torso-restraint. "It's too risky."

JJ looked defeated. "All right."

Federico pushed the torso-restraint away and got up. "We're not deviating from the plan. You take the ship and rendezvous with Woody outside of San Francisco. Sharon and I will take the high road into the city." He gave JJ a hard stare. "Okay?"

"I guess it has to be."

"Someday you'll thank me for not letting youthful bravery get you killed before learning your most important lesson."

"Which is?" JJ asked.

"That you matter." Federico beckoned to Sharon. "Please, come with me."

Sharon released her restraint and attempted to stand. But the sleeping dog anchored her. "Hey, pup. I got to go."

Erik lifted his head.

"It's okay." She stroked the dog's snout until he resumed his half-sleeping, half-guarding responsibilities. "And what exactly is the high road?" With effort, she maneuvered over Erik.

"Ever heard of El Capitan?"

"Yeah, the big rock face in what used to be Yosemite National Park. In the Sierra Nevada, right?"

"*Sí*, the one and only. Actually, it's a rock face in Yosemite Valley, not a mountain. The park boundaries are gone, but El Cap still stands. No one goes there anymore. Which is why it's the way we're going." Federico looked to JJ. "Keep watch on the radar for drones and storms. We're easy targets in turbo-vests. We'll need a quiet sky to lift off."

Erik struggled to his feet. His malnourished body still fragile, he leaned against Sharon.

"A turbo-vest?" Sharon scratched the scruff of his neck. "I didn't think they could fly that high."

"The average vest can't," Federico answered. "But Icarus can."

"Icarus?"

"A winged turbo-vest integrated with a biothermal survival suit powered by solar and thermoelectric energy." He pointed at the ceiling. "We'll just be sure not to fly too close to the sun."

"Another Woody invention, I assume." Sharon smoothed Erik's head before stretching the kinks in her back from sitting. "Where does the thermoelectric energy come from?"

"Heat from your body while you're flying. And no, Woody didn't invent it." Federico smiled. "But she perfected it." Affection and awe seeped through his voice. To JJ, he said, "Once we're suited, I'll signal you to open the launch bay." He gripped the younger man's shoulders. "We're in the last days that will define our future. If something bad happens to me, I just want you to know how proud I am of you."

Like a voyeur looking in on a pact to which she didn't belong, Sharon watched the moment play out between the two men. Even though she didn't know the stories that made them, it was obvious they'd become like father and son. She craved the camaraderie of family.

"I won't let you down." JJ unlocked his restraint and rose. "We'll all be together again soon." He turned and bumped heads with Federico. "I promise you. These are the beginning days, not the last."

"Ah, the optimism of the young. Hold tight to it. Just don't let it kill you." Federico patted JJ's cheeks. "Come, Sharon. The skies are quiet and clear. Perfect for flying."

"I'll hold enough for both of us." JJ crouched and slapped a thigh. "Erik, you have to stay with me, boy."

The dog whimpered at Sharon's side.

She got to a knee and cupped his head. Erik exuded the measure of loyalty and resolve to protect her that she carried for Eve. "We're kindred souls, you and I." She smoothed his fur. "I can't wait for Eve to meet you, and you her. I'll be back. You keep JJ out of trouble."

"A tall order." Federico laughed and lifted a foot over the portal threshold. "See you two soon," he said to JJ and Erik.

Sharon trailed him out of the cramped cockpit into the Belostomatid's cavernous cargo bay. They moved past the stolen water-transporter. The number seven prominently etched onto its side gave it the forlorn look of being out of place.

At the end of the cargo bay, Federico climbed a set of four stairs into a cramped storage space. Bulky turbo-vests, jumpsuits, and footlockers jam-packed the room. He put a finger to his lips and scrutinized Sharon. "You must be a little less than two meters tall?"

"About one point eight," she answered.

He pointed at one of the suits. "You're thin, so Icarus-nine might be a tad loose, but should fit your height. That's most important." Lifting it from its hook, he said, "Slip it over your clothing, including your boots."

Sharon grasped it. "It's heavy." Lowering it to her feet, she tugged it up over her boots to her shoulders. She slid her hammer's baldric more left, to under her arm, and zipped the suit.

"Even heavier with the vest. But, you won't notice once you're airborne." Federico lifted a vest from the hook. Two silver wings integral to the vest hung tucked closed at its back. "Turn around. I'll put it on you." He held it open. "The skin on the wings generates solar power. The two cylinders circulate a bio-thermal plasma through the suit that regulates body temperature."

She lifted her arms to help him place the vest onto her back.

He clicked the chest buckles closed and handed her a pair of gloves. "The controls are in the palms of these."

She pulled the gloves on and flexed her fingers. Thick black pads bulked up the palms. "How do they work?"

He turned her left hand over, and tapped her palm. "It's a touch screen. But it powers on as soon as it comes in contact with skin. See?" He pointed at the digital numbers. "The suit's already calculating external and internal body temperatures. It's calibrated to keep you at twenty degrees Celsius. You can bump it down or up, as you like. The controls are similar to a hydro-bike. They're pretty straightforward."

"I can fly a hydro-bike in my sleep." She rolled her shoulders. A stab of pain shot through her upper back. "Damn."

"You okay?" Federico asked as he handed her a helmet.

"Yeah, I just moved the wrong way." She molded the flexible helmet over her head. "My shoulder's still bothering me."

"You could have a bone fragment loose in there or something. We'll have Dale take a look once we get back to Belosto-One."

"A different ship?"

"A predecessor of the Belostomatid. Belosto-One isn't nearly as maneuverable, and a lot harder to hide. But Woody built her big enough to transport all of the Qaunik at one time." He lifted a suit labeled Icarus-eleven from a hook. "You okay to fly?"

"Yeah. No problem."

"Let me know if things change. We'll stop to rest if necessary." He shimmied into Icarus-eleven, a vest, helmet, and gloves. "Let's go fly."

Sharon followed Federico into the open bay. The vest's wings brushed the backs of her calves. "Speaking of bugs. I kind of feel like a housefly."

"That's about to change. With those wings spread at your back, you'll feel like a raptor." He paused at the hatch door and reached in his pocket. "This is a GPS memory-drive." Holding the thimble-sized device between his forefinger and thumb, he snapped it into a port on her left vest pocket. "The GPS is programmed to bring you over El Capitan, the High Sierras, and down to our landing near the city. You can override the system and fly manually should the need arise, so take a few minutes to get used to the controls. My advice is to settle in and let the vest do all the work. It's a once in a lifetime trip where we're going. Enjoy it."

He plugged a second memory-drive into his own vest. "There's a button on your right chin strap. Press it to talk to me." He closed the space between them. "Before we go, I have to say thanks again for sharing your apples with JJ and me. It was kind of you." He bumped his head to hers. "I'm glad we got to cross paths in this life."

With their heads pressed together, she realized she had never expected to feel warmth again for anyone other than Eve or Dr. and Mrs. Ryan. Her well of caring had gone dry—or so she thought—with the death of her family. But Inu, Annie, Erik, Federico, and JJ had tugged her into the fragility of caring. Part of her wanted to let go and be pulled into their deep current of friendship. The other part resisted that vulnerability. "You're welcome," she said, pulling away.

"Shall we?" he asked.

"Yeah, let's fly." Sharon smiled.

Federico pressed the audio-comm button on the wall next to the hatch. "If the sky is quiet, JJ, please open the hatch. We're ready to fly."

"Looks like you'll have a brilliant sky all to yourselves." JJ's voice emanated from the audio-comm in the ceiling. "I'm envious. Hope you see a rare bird or two."

"Not likely," Federico responded, "but it sure would be nice."

"May you fly like snow," JJ said as the hatch door hissed and slid open.

Federico pressed the audio-comm. "Exceptional as one. Inexorable together."

Sharon squinted at the sharp sunlight and dry heat. A twinge of sad irony plucked at her. How could a people pledge to fly like snow and expect to survive in such a hot world? She lowered the helmet's face shield, and hoped they could.

With her thumb, she flicked the wing icon on her palm. The titanium extensions at her back snapped open. Catching her shadow where the Belostomatid blocked the sun's rays, she glanced over her shoulder at Federico. "You were right."

He hopped down and said, "Definitely not an insect. You look like an eagle. Ready?"

"Can't wait." She pressed the flight button that powered the booster at her back, lifting her into the sky. She held her finger to the screen to hover, then swiped right. Icarus-nine moved horizontally toward the east. She swiped left and her direction changed to the west. "Very responsive."

"*Sí.*" Federico swooped past her.

She pressed the autopilot icon and watched the altimeter in her palm rise to six hundred meters before Icarus-nine leveled off.

Federico rose until he hovered about twenty meters away. His smooth, calm voice wafted into her helmet. "You ready to see El Capitan?"

A flutter of excitement moved in her. She pressed her finger to the chin strap. "I wish Eve were here too."

"Someday, *amiga*, you will show her El Cap. Now, press the 'D' on your right ring finger. Icarus-nine will do the rest." He zoomed off ahead of her.

Following the programmed flight card, Icarus-nine gathered speed, gliding Sharon west toward the dark, craggy mountains looming at the horizon.

The Nevada Solar Farm and human graffiti in the form of deserted roads and ramshackle buildings receded into the east. Wind buffeted her suit where the fabric was loose. Yet, inside her helmet, the only sound was her breathing. Soaring over hills and troughs covered in a blanket of dust-brown flecked with occasional avocado green, she settled into the solitude. The stunning craggy mountains to the west seemed to have their own gravity, pulling her to them. Snow capped only the highest of them. From her perspective in the sky, the enormity of Earth revealed itself. *God, it's beautiful.* She stumbled over the word *god* in her head.

"You okay back there?" Federico's voice sliced through the silence.

She pressed her chin strap. "Thinking about *God* of all things."

"Not many believers left in the world. I wouldn't have guessed you're one of them."

"I'm not. I don't believe in things I can't see." She kept a finger to the strap.

"What about love?" Federico asked. "You can feel it, and act on it. But can't see it."

"Touché," Sharon said. "How about you?"

"Being Catholic is a hard habit to break. Although I do wish believers before us had spent more time appreciating the things they could see. Maybe they would've noticed the world coming apart while they planned for the afterlife."

The wings at her back lifted her higher with the rise of earth toward the Sierra. A distinctive round depression swathed in crusty yellow lay below the eastern slope of the mountains. Sharon turned her wrist to view the GPS map.

"That's what's left of Mono Lake," Federico said. "When the snow stopped falling decades ago over the Sierra, the lake died of thirst. We'll be seeing El Cap soon. You'll know it when you see it. Then we'll head northwest over the Sierra and down toward San Francisco. Our touchdown location is just outside the reach of NONA radar."

"How do we get into the city?"

"By way of much more inconspicuous transportation." He sounded amused. "I guarantee it will not be as luxurious as Icarus-nine."

"With you guys, I've stopped trying to predict modes of transportation."

"Wise woman. Until then, enjoy the scenery." Federico's mic squawked off.

The flaps on her wings slid back, lifting her higher. Nude rocky peaks reached upward too, as if grasping for her. A deep gouge in the mountains yawned below as her altitude leveled off. Yosemite Valley bent into a slight smirk. She felt her face melt into one that mimicked it. She believed in the universe. With or without humans, Earth would keep spinning among other celestial things. The notion was comforting.

A smooth, gray, rounded mountain with half its face sloughed off jutted from the valley to her left. *Half Dome. Ha.* She pressed the mic button. "I feel like a kid up here seeing this stuff for the first time."

"Imagine the days," Federico said, "when waterfalls spilled into cool blue lakes, and shades of green shrouded the valley. I've never seen it, but I can picture it. Reminds me of opera. Grand, nuanced, fast, slow, dramatic, complicated, lovely, and—ultimately tragic."

"I'll hold onto hope that I get to share this with Eve here someday." Letting her body fully relax into flight, she imagined being an eagle gliding on thermals.

"I didn't take you for being an optimist, either."

"I'm not." The granite profile of a broad-shouldered sentinel standing guard filled her vision. "El Capitan!"

"Indeed." Federico laughed. "A sometime optimist with a little kid still inside."

Sharon twisted her head to follow the majestic rock formation with her eyes. "Just a little."

"*Sí, amiga.* Take it all in."

When she could no longer see El Capitan, she looked forward. Icarus-nine brought her higher as they flew over enormous craggy peaks. The humbling enormity of it made it hard to breathe. "If I live to be an old woman, I'll always remember this view." Dissolving into the moment, she exhaled.

"I wish you a long and peaceful life," Federico said.

They topped the highest peaks and dipped into the clouds hugging the western flank of the Sierras. A plane of blue-green ocean butted against the length of California. A distinct line of

171

chaotic rock and broken buildings sliced the land from north to south.

Pulling herself from the silence, Sharon pressed her chin strap. "Is that the fault line?"

"*Sí*," Federico answered. "The damage along the San Andreas after the Quake of 2067 was so bad, people just left everything where it fell. With the wars, NONA couldn't afford repairs anyway."

"It looks like a horror show."

"Won't get any better as we head into San Francisco. Not much left standing except for the Golden Gate Bridge." Federico veered right, pushing north along the fault line. "Couldn't kill that beast."

Scorched, blackened earth lay dormant under buildings that had toppled and burned. It reminded Sharon of an unkempt graveyard. "In a single day, I've witnessed some of the most beautiful and ugly things I've ever seen. Why the hell are people still down there?"

"Because down *there*, you can get away with anything. Assuming you manage to stay alive. Can't eat the fish from the ocean after Hawaii got nuked. No one's going to build anything only to have it knocked down." The flaps on Federico's wings lifted and he slowed. "The thing is, 80 percent of the world's black-market goods flow through San Francisco. If you can avoid getting killed, there's plenty to steal and sell."

"Not worth it," Sharon said as Icarus-nine brought her to where Federico hovered.

"Depends on how much you value your life." He dove lower toward a small clearing, pointing his feet toward ground. "We're just outside of San Fran. These hills are called the Marin Headlands. Get ready to land. Icarus-nine will put you down slowly, but you'll have to run a few steps before you come to a stop. Remember to flex your knees."

"Got it." The ground rushed up and scraggly vegetation ran by in Sharon's peripheral vision. Her feet touched ground. She jogged and slowed to a stop. The suit's wings swiveled closed.

Suddenly the contraption felt heavy again. She bent at the waist to catch her breath.

Federico removed his helmet and vest. "Nice job." He wriggled out of his suit.

Sharon slipped her helmet off. Hot, humid air slammed into her. "It's hotter than hell out here." She tore the vest from her shoulders and wrestled out of the suit.

A not-so-rare raven circled overhead as if annoyed by their presence. The low hillside surrounded by dry brush concealed them from anyone on the ground. The scent of the ocean wafted in from the west. It was thick with the aroma of decay.

"Let's get some water." Federico pulled branches away from a pile of debris, revealing a polycarbonate box. He flipped it open and retrieved two flasks. "Here you go."

Sharon fumbled with the top and guzzled. The water tasted flat and slightly rank. "Thanks."

Federico tore more branches from the heap. "We'll leave the vests and suits here." He tossed another prickly branch aside, revealing an old solar-bike. "Like I said, we need to be inconspicuous in the city. You think you can fly this thing, right? I'll navigate and keep a lookout." He laid his suit, then Sharon's, inside the box and stacked the vests on top.

"This must be a 2033 Skyhawk? My grandfather had one. Does it even start?"

He leaned over and pushed the ignition cartridge in place. "Doesn't need a fingerprint, and she does fly. Sort of."

"Sort of?" Sharon threw a leg over the bike and revved the engine. Its raucous rattle vibrated her insides. "I thought you said we needed to be inconspicuous. Bad guys will be able to hear this beater coming from kilometers away."

Federico shut the box and covered it with branches. "Trust me." He hopped onto the back of the bike. "We'll fit in fine."

"If you say so."

"*Sí.*" He patted her shoulder. "Head south toward the Golden Gate Bridge. That's how we'll enter the city. If this thing cuts out, I'd rather be over the bridge than water."

"Right." Sharon rolled her eyes and moved the lift throttle forward. The loud clatter necessitated looking over her shoulder so that Federico could yell commands into her ear.

He cupped his mouth and shouted, "When you get over the bridge, hang left over the only street!"

"How high can this thing fly?"

He cocked his head and shouted, "Maybe three meters. Five, tops! Don't worry. You've got this!"

"And you're an optimist, always." She eased the throttle forward.

As they neared the bridge, Sharon searched for a path through the rubble and squatters' camps. The grand rust-colored bridge tying the land together seemed more haphazard living space than thoroughfare. Shanties, broken vehicles, and broken people spread along its expanse in both directions.

Thick fog crept in from the ocean, seeming to grope at them. Sharon checked the altimeter and dared to lift the bike a meter higher. It shook, coughed, and clanked. The fog thickened. "Holy hell." To keep on course, she gripped the steer bar with both hands.

A hunched woman rummaged through a pile of trash near the north tower. A little boy tethered to her by a long rope played with a palm-sized rock. He tossed it up, caught it, and tossed it again. Neither of them seemed the least interested in Sharon and Federico. The boy was dark-haired and skinny like Inu. Sharon struggled to tear her eyes from him.

Federico's hand pointed ahead. "Up here, there's a path!" he shouted. "When you clear the bridge, hover!"

Refocusing, she left her thoughts of Inu behind with the woman and boy on the bridge. The bike complied when she pressed the throttle forward. She brought it to a hover barely above ground once they cleared the bridge. The rattle mercifully quieted. "That is one awesome bridge. I can't believe it's standing."

"A miracle of human ingenuity." Federico pointed in the direction of a badly rusted cable. Beyond it, an ominous concrete building perched on a craggy island. "She may have survived the earthquake, but the salt mist is slowly eating her away. No one paints her anymore. And that's Alcatraz Island. The prison still stands. Probably too haunted with the souls of evil men to fall." His pointing finger moved from the cable and island toward the left of the bridge. "Go four blocks and bang a right," Federico said. "At the end is Fisherman's Wharf. That's where we meet the facilitator of our exchange. Keep your hammer handy. The place is crawling with Banditti. And since we're late, we're likely to get a rash of shit. Hold your ground."

Sharon nodded and unbuttoned her jacket's two middle buttons. She reached inside and adjusted the baldric. "Hold tight."

"*Sí*."

Keeping watch for anyone making a threatening move, Sharon lifted the bike a meter high. She followed the contour of road toward the wharf. An old-style ship's wheel with the words FISH-ERMAN'S WHARF OF SAN FRANCISCO, hanging on a leaning pillar, marked the entrance. More ramshackle shelters occupied the wharf. Banditti squatters had taken up residence in a broken-down green trolley car. The wharf ran a length of shore to a long pier that curved out into the ocean like a bent finger. "Is that Pier 45?"

"*Sí*, it is. Here." Federico squeezed her shoulder. "Set down here."

Sharon landed the bike and switched off the engine. The people on the street peered at them from the shadows. Several seconds passed.

A man stepped from a rotted building reinforced with concrete at its weak points. The whites of his eyes accented a dark face covered in a thick black beard and moustache. A fedora adorned the top of his head, and he wore a black military-style uniform with no insignia. With a hand to the spectraletto at his hip, he pressed closer.

Federico got off the bike. "Stay ready to get this thing in the air," he whispered. "We didn't get here when we were supposed to. The facilitator is a stickler for punctuality. He's also an asshole."

"You're late," the facilitator growled. "By more than a day." He pulled a flat tin from his pocket. Eyeing Sharon, he opened and offered it to Federico. Six hand-rolled cigarettes lay in a neat row inside the tin. "You got my water?"

"We do." Federico took one of the smokes. "You got our seeds?" He fished a sulfur-flint from his pocket and clicked it into a flame.

Holding the tin open to Sharon, the facilitator asked, "For you?"

The last thing Sharon wanted to do was smoke old tobacco. But there were times one did not turn down an offering. This was one of them. "Thank you." She plucked a cigarette from the tin.

The facilitator snapped the tin closed and dropped it into his pocket. Leaning toward Federico, he accepted the light and sucked in a lungful of stale tobacco smoke. He exhaled and said, "Thanks. Aren't many of these left in the world. I'll savor 'em, even if they kill me."

Federico lit Sharon's, then his own. He dragged in, then blew smoke from his mouth and nose. "You didn't answer my question." Squinting, he asked, "You got my seeds?"

Sharon put the cigarette to her lips, took a small drag, and blew out. The tobacco tasted ancient, but the nicotine almost instantly smoothed the edges of her nerves.

"Do you know how many people are left in the world?" the facilitator asked. Without waiting for an answer, he said, "In 2025, there were eight billion of us. Can you imagine that? Eight billion fucking mouths to feed?" He dragged on his cigarette. Tilting his head back, he streamed the smoke out sideways. "Three wars later, sprinkled with some very ugly diseases, and humanity's shitting on its ability to farm, hunt and fish, we've pretty much fucked ourselves." He held up two fingers. "Two billion. That's all that's left."

"I appreciate the dissertation on recent human history, but do you have our seeds?" Federico stubbed out his cigarette and dropped the butt into his pocket. "I'll save this for a rainy day. Now, about our trade."

"On the positive side, humans, cockroaches that we are, are hanging on by a thread," the facilitator continued. "The trouble is, we took everything good with us. Food, clean water, good air to breathe. Fuck, you know what people will do for a little food and clean water?"

"All I'm interested in is trading water for seed potatoes and kale seeds." Federico locked eyes with the facilitator. "No more pontificating."

"The lesson isn't over, my friend." He poked Federico's chest with a forefinger. "If you want to deal with us, you meet the terms we set. You were late. You want seeds, you get us more water."

"I told you. We have the water. You get it when we get the seeds."

"That's not how it's going to work." The facilitator snapped his fingers.

A hulking tattooed man with a spectraletto rifle slung over his shoulder sauntered out of the building toward them.

"You were late. We already traded your fucking seeds." The facilitator motioned for his armed comrade. "You'll give us the water you have now, and a second shipment. Then"—he popped a single thick smoke ring from his lips—"you get your seeds."

Sharon's heart raced, and her fingers itched to reach for her hammer. She took a deep drag off the cigarette. This asshole and his goon were another hurdle to climb to get to Eve.

"That wasn't our deal." Federico shot a glance at Sharon. His fists were clenched. "We want those seeds now, or you don't get the water."

"What's that old saying?" The facilitator paused. "Shit in one hand, and want in the other." He tipped his hat to his goon. "We'll keep you two as collateral until we get not one . . ." he held up two fingers, "but two shipments. If that doesn't work, we have effective ways of making you give us that goddamned water."

The goon moved toward Sharon. She didn't flinch, waiting for him to get close enough. In a swift movement, she flicked the cigarette into his eyes, seized her hammer, and swung its claw into the side of his head.

He grunted and fell back.

"Hey!" the facilitator yelled.

177

Sharon smashed the ignition card into place and the bike rattled to life.

"Let's go, Sharon!" Federico brandished a spectraletto from under his shirt and leaped onto the back of the bike. "Go! Go! Go!"

Sharon gunned the engine as laser shots zipped past them. Glancing over her shoulder, she saw the goon she had hit still lying on the ground. Three other goons spilled out of the building and climbed into a hydro-lorry with the facilitator at the wheel. She jammed the throttle forward, maxing out the bike's altitude and speed. At least the hydro-lorry couldn't fly.

A shot grazed the side of the bike, causing it to buck left. "Dammit." She glanced back. The hydro-lorry on its heavy tracks bore down on them with surprising speed, flattening everything and everyone in its path. The Golden Gate loomed ahead.

Sharon swerved to miss a shanty, looked back and then forward. "No! Get out of the way!" Adrenaline surged through her veins as they tore past the woman and the tethered boy. Sharon waved an arm and yelled, "Get out of the way!" She glanced back once more after narrowly avoiding them.

The woman lifted the boy into her arms and tried to climb to safety. But the hydro-lorry slammed into her with the child clutched to her chest. Its impact tore them apart like rag dolls and flung them over the guardrail. The horror was splayed out in crimson gore on the front of the hydro-lorry. The vehicle kept going, into her makeshift shelter of stacked concrete blocks covered in a ratty blue tarp. The hydro-lorry skidded and rolled several times before stopping.

"No!" Sharon screamed. "No!" Her hands, sweaty and tired from gripping the controls, shook. She slammed her eyes closed a moment, begging her brain to shut off the image of the brutal deaths she'd just witnessed. "We can't leave them!" she yelled, and turned the bike toward where they had fallen into the water.

"No. They're gone." Federico grasped her waist firmly. "Keep going, Sharon. You have to keep going. Don't look back."

Chapter 14

A pillowy swell rolled toward the hulking ship known as Belosto-One, the predecessor to the Belostomatid. Five times the size of the Belostomatid, the ship's hull-skin soaked up enough solar radiation during one sunny day to power it for months under cloud cover. Standing low to the water on one of Belosto-One's pontoons, Sharon breathed in the pungent air blowing over the Pacific. She hoped the sharp, sweet scent might overwhelm the gruesome image in her mind of the deaths of the woman and boy on the bridge.

Seven kilometers offshore from San Francisco, Belosto-One was too far out to be reached by thieves, and in a sunny place to recharge her batteries. Sharon gripped the pontoon's retractable railing and watched the murky green water, clogged with algae.

The roller lifted the blanket of algae covering the Pacific, dipped beneath the ship's bow and past the stern. Another swell took its place. The predictable rhythm of the water helped to soothe Sharon only a little. Complicated and contradictory emotions roiled inside her gut. They'd failed to make the water exchange and gotten two people killed in the process. Would her actions lead to the deaths of Annie and Inu, too? What if she'd been killed? Did Eve still hold onto hope that Sharon would come for her? Was she even alive? *You have to keep your head.*

She plucked a dried beetle from her pocket. Holding it in her palm, queasiness swirled in her belly at the sight of the pathetic insect. With the horrific scene on the Golden Gate Bridge still fresh in her mind, she couldn't eat. "For any fish left in the ocean, it's your lucky day." She tossed the bug onto the watery green carpet.

Erik's eyes followed it from her palm to the water. He rested his snout on the low railing and kept watch on the carcass.

"I know. Should've given it to you instead." Sharon reached into her pocket for another and offered it to the dog.

He snapped it up.

"Good boy." She rested her elbows on the railing and touched Eve's scarf, tied at her neck. A warm breeze wafted in from the water, flooding her nose with the heady scent of decay and thriving algae. "When we get inside, I'll get you another beetle patty and more water from our allotment."

Erik's ears pricked back. "Woof."

Sharon turned to see what sparked him to bark.

Woody stepped down onto the pontoon. "May I join you?" She strolled forward, wearing a flight uniform and hijab. Her modest insignia included the Qaunik snowflake, an Earth symbol, and a patch bearing her name, Dr. Woodhouse. The color of the ocean brought out the green in her eyes.

On instinct, Sharon straightened. "I'd like that."

Woody's demeanor demanded respect. Not because of authority, but because she was extraordinary. She projected power, wisdom, intelligence, humility, and kindness.

Erik trotted toward the petite woman. "Woof." He wagged his tail.

Woody scratched his head. "Hello, Erik."

"I'm sorry we didn't get the potato and kale seed," Sharon said. "But I hope we're still going to the Bay of Fundy once you find Elliot. He's the only one who can get what it is that the Strelitzia wants. I have to save my wife."

"I'm sorry too. And, yes, we're still on schedule to head east. We certainly needed those seeds. But right now, that worry is secondary to getting my ship back. The Qaunik won't survive the Thwaites collapse without the Bird of Paradise."

"Your ship is called the Bird of Paradise?"

"Yes."

"Let me guess." Sharon smiled. "A ship engineered to resemble a bird of paradise flower?" Sharon tried to imagine such a vessel. "What's special about it?"

"She's a magnificent floating city. Besides being stunningly beautiful, she has everything we need to survive indefinitely, assuming I'm able to gather more seeds to grow. We can raise plenty of insects for food. But we need the nutrients from the kale, especially." Woody leaned on the railing and studied the sea. "She's a self-contained floating biosphere that makes her own air and power; desalinates seawater; filters pollutants; dives deep to avoid storms; and maintains temperature and humidity at set levels. She'll be our island sanctuary while Earth recovers from the fever we humans caused her."

Erik sniffed the wind as another large swell rolled toward them. The ship rose and fell slightly in its wake.

Sharon caressed the dog's soft ears. "A biosphere without things to grow doesn't seem much of a biosphere."

"True," Woody agreed. "Even if I had gotten those kale seeds and potatoes, they wouldn't provide enough nutrients to keep us alive indefinitely. Not to mention their susceptibility to any number of fungi wafting around Earth. We can get protein and fats from the insects, but there are things the body needs that only plants can provide. My plan after I get my ship back is to search for vegetation that I might be able to grow or synthesize more nutrients from. Unfortunately, Earth has slim pickings these days. And things will get worse when the ice sheet slides into the ocean after the Thwaites collapses."

"Which is why the Strelitzia wants the secret to my apple tree."

"Yes," Woody answered. "That's my assumption too."

"I've been wracking my brain trying to figure out how he knew about Eve's work. Maybe they crossed paths at Harvard before the university shut down. Or maybe he knew Dr. Ryan and Areva, and they inadvertently tipped him off about the apples."

"That would explain why he kidnapped them too," Woody

said. "When Dr. Ryan refused to reveal your secret, the Strelitzia murdered him. Then killed Areva to get to you. It certainly fits his profile."

Erik nudged between Sharon and Woody.

"What do you know about the Strelitzia?" Sharon scratched Erik's head.

"His real name is Thomas Randel. He worked with my father at the Massachusetts Institute of Technology, and then the Ministry of Scientific Advancement. They collaborated on designing biospheres that could keep people alive during the worst of climate change."

"Like your ship, the Bird of Paradise?"

A scavenging gull screeched overhead, circling the massive ship.

"That's right. But for a variety of reasons, they were never very successful together. When my father died, I continued his work on my own, and built the Bird of Paradise."

"Then the Strelitzia stole it from you." Sharon turned her head to look at Woody. "Why does he go by that name?"

"Thomas has always had a fascination with flowers." Woody pushed the cuffs of her sleeves up. "The bird of paradise flower belongs to the plant genus *Strelitzia*. I think he does it to be frightening. It's common in nature for animals to puff themselves up and act a little deranged in order to scare predators."

"It's certainly working on me. I'm terrified that he'll hurt Eve if I don't give him what he wants." Sharon glanced back at the rolling water. "He didn't flinch when he killed Areva. It's all I can do to keep my head on straight after seeing so many innocent people die in the past few days. Dr. Elan, Areva, and Dr. Ryan— the woman and boy on the bridge. I can't let Eve be next."

"About the woman and boy." Woody put a hand to the middle of Sharon's back. "Federico mentioned you took their deaths particularly hard. We can talk about it if you'd like."

Sharon nodded. "I think I need someone to talk to. Being alone with my thoughts certainly isn't helping."

"I'm all ears."

Sharon blinked and sighed. "After my family died, I got good at not letting myself care about the random awful things that happen to other people. Because it's easier not to care. I justify it by telling myself that caring is a weakness. That innocent people die all the time because they aren't fit enough to survive. Part of me says that the smart way to stay alive is to look the other way."

"Biology dictates that everyone dies, whether we care or not." Woody clasped her hands together. "And what does the other part of you have to say?"

Sharon studied the floating beetle corpse. A waterlogged leg dangled past the algae to below the surface. "I can't help thinking of the mangled bodies of the woman and the boy underwater. I wonder whether they'll be missed. Whether they meant something to someone. Were they happy to be alive? Because I know what it feels like to love and be loved. To be happy. I should care because I'd want *them* to care. And because I feel empty when I try not to."

"Ah well, love, happiness and caring, that's where biology gets complicated. How do we let go of what can't come back, or what we can't change?" Woody pointed. "You see that worm trying to bite into the dead beetle?"

Sharon strained to look more closely. An army of tiny green worms wriggling on the algae came into focus. "Now that you've pointed them out, I see a whole bunch."

"The simple biology of things. The climate changed and the oceans acidified, killing the large fish and creating an environment in which algae, fish too small to feed the world, and sea worms thrive. One thing dies, another takes its place. It's simple biology. Nothing complicated. But throw emotion into the mix and things get very complicated. Maybe there's nothing wrong with trying to figure out how to keep things simple."

Sharon imagined the beetle frolicking on a sunny day, unaware of its ultimate fate. *Just a bug. Just a stupid bug. Just a boy and an old woman. Just a stupid boy and an old woman.* "There's a price to pay for keeping things simple. I'm running out of currency."

The circling gull swooped down and snatched the beetle.

"I know what my costs are," Woody said. "I'm curious. What is it that you pay?"

Erik prodded Sharon's hand with his snout.

"My memories." She caressed his velvety ear.

Woody tilted her head. "Why your memories?"

"Because forgetting buries the pain of losing."

"We've all buried the ashes of loved ones. Buried never means forgotten. Tell me about the ones you can't forget."

Sharon conjured the memories of those who existed as scars on her heart. "I grew up on a farm my great-grandfather built."

"Farming runs in your blood. And his farm became your farm?"

"Yeah, after my parents got sick and died, my two brothers were drafted by NONA. The only reason the government didn't take me too was so I could keep the farm going."

Woody nodded. "The War of Earth's Rebellion, when NONA started taking 80 percent of everything a farmer could grow."

"By then the world's seed banks, water, and soil were destroyed. NONA couldn't care less about my farm. It was barely functioning anyway."

"Wasn't that also around the time that NONA took the Manitoba Grasslands?" Woody asked.

"Yeah. They realized there was only so much food and water to go around. The people they considered most important were the ones who got to eat."

"And the rest of us," Woody added, "had to fend for ourselves. NONA adopted the simple biology of cold practicality."

Erik leaned against Sharon.

"There's the cost." Sharon gave the dog the last two beetles in her pocket. "My grandparents and parents were dead. My brother Jon came home from the South China Sea in a box. Mark was murdered by three Banditti he was kind enough to share water and food with. They took his jacket and boots and left his body in a ditch. He'd only been home from war for twelve days. His refusal to kill anymore got him killed. To NONA, my brothers were nothing more than bodies that breathed, ate, drank, and fought. I realized that it was easier to go on if I tried to think of them in the same way. But I had to pay with my memories."

"Why did the deaths of the woman and the boy, two strangers, bother you so much, then?" Woody asked.

"Because I'm afraid I can't tell where the line between practicality and inhumanity is anymore." She swallowed the knot of repulsion in her throat. "No amount of practicality can ever make me forget seeing that poor woman and little boy torn apart on the bridge like they were nothing. For as long as I live, it will haunt me."

"Not everyone can be saved, Sharon." A breeze ruffled the end of Woody's hijab. "And none of us escapes having to sometimes choose practicality over humanity. I'm not even sure there's a difference. I may have to face the same choices sooner rather than later. If I can't find more things to grow, how will we decide who gets to eat?"

A voice crackled out of the SComCat clipped to Woody's jacket, "Woody, Woody, Woody."

Woody unclipped it and flipped it open. "Woody here."

"The expedition crew has returned with the man named Elliot. Shall we prepare the ship for departure?"

"Yes, but give me fifteen minutes. I'm down on the port-side pontoon. I need to finish a conversation and climb the stairs into the ship."

"Roger that," the voice responded.

Woody returned the SComCat to its clip, and studied the horizon. "There she is, the Belostomatid, maybe two kilometers out. Let's get inside. Are you anxious to see Elliot?"

"Not in the least."

"Sounds like another story for another time. For now, we must go." Woody made for the stairs.

"Wait."

"Yes?" Woody wheeled around.

Sharon hesitated, wondering what Woody's age was. She didn't look much older than Sharon, but she had the wisdom of someone who'd lived several lifetimes. Sharon suspected the Qaunik would walk through fire for Woody, and that she'd never leave a single person behind, practicality be damned. "Thank you for listening and caring. I have a deal I'd like to make with you." Sharon's heart raced at what she was about to reveal. She hoped it might fill some of the empty space inside her. "Eve and I. Besides the apples, we have some seeds in an underground growing area. More than kale and potato. There's lots. Plus some medications Dr. Ryan gave me to safeguard. I'll share them with you in exchange for something."

"Are these other seeds what the Strelitzia is after?"

"No." That the answer was the truth didn't make Sharon feel less guilty about not telling Woody everything. There was something about the woman that made Sharon revere and trust her. "There's a boy I left with a woman living in Gaia's Wrath. If you agree to bring them with you wherever it is you're going, I'll give you the seeds in my underground farm. All of them. And, except for what I need to make Eve's cancer treatment, you can have Dr. Ryan's medicines."

"Sounds like a deal I'd be a fool to pass up." Woody folded her arms. "As for the woman and the boy, the seeds will get them an opportunity to become Qaunik. But they'll have to earn being vouched in. I have no authority to wager away that essential requirement."

Sharon reached for Erik, a habit both she and the dog had developed since claiming each other. She curled her fingers into his fur. "I understand. Thank you for giving them a chance."

"I suspect it will turn out to be a good and practical decision." Woody lowered her arms to her sides. "One last question. Besides being your wife, who is Eve?"

"The person who saved me after I'd lost everyone I loved." Sharon looked to the sky and blinked at the sun. She lowered her eyes. "Eve is a botanist. She worked at Harvard before the universities were disbanded." Sharon smiled at the recollection. "She came to my farm looking for work. Imagine, a brilliant, beautiful scientist asking a grungy, barely functioning farmer for work." Inside, Sharon felt the growing pressure of emotion threatening to erupt out of her. "She was so beautiful and sweet and funny. Ha, I gave her an apple, and she gave me her heart. God, I miss her."

Woody put a hand to Sharon's shoulder. "Thank you for telling me. We're going to help you find her."

"Thank you."

"A deal is a deal." Woody grasped Sharon's shoulder. "Now, I can't risk flying Belosto-One into Gaia's Wrath. But, we have a small shuttle called the Albatross. It's designed to fly in ferocious winds. I'll have Federico go with you. After you retrieve the boy and the woman, you'll have to deal with Elliot."

"Of course," Sharon agreed. "The Albatross? How do you come up with this stuff?"

"It's easy, because we don't." Woody tilted her head toward the ocean. "Every problem can be solved by looking for the answer in nature. If we want a ship that flies in strong winds, we study how birds do it. Then we build something that mimics them. Mother Nature has all of the ideas."

"What's her answer for fixing the climate?"

Woody chuckled. "Well, Earth *is* fixing things, her way. We had our chance to have an optimal environment, and we messed it all up. Now we need to adjust to Earth's terms, if we have any hope of surviving. Let's get you to Gaia's Wrath. My engineers are getting hungry."

Sharon peered through the windshield of the Albatross. The reinforced glass curved over, around and under four sleek cockpit seats, giving the occupants a bird's-eye view. The cloud-heavy sky was empty of storms, for now. Secured to the floor by cargo straps, Erik lay sleeping at her feet. Using the wind to fly, the nimble aerodynamic shuttle barely made a sound as it swooped on thermal currents. Sharon had expected the craft to be shaped like a huge bird, but it was simply a wing—one beautifully sym-metrical, cambered wing, with a solar skin to supply power when needed. She felt the Albatross meld into the wind.

Sitting in the pilot's seat tilted slightly back, Federico swiped and sketched commands over STELA. Oxygen supply masks hung over their heads, at the ready for flying at Mach speed. A 3-D globe plotted out the Albatross' coordinates and altitude.

"Woody's inventions are incredible. How did you meet her?" Sharon asked.

"Her parents kidnapped me." He laughed. "I guess you can't kidnap the willing."

"Well now you have to tell me the story."

"It's the best story I know." He drew a *W*. As it faded, the Albatross' radar tracked their surroundings out to thirty kilometers. "There's some ugly stuff." He pointed to a splotch of green with yellow to red at its center. It edged into the lower left corner of the radar. "I'll tell you my story, but let's keep an eye on this storm. It's moving to meet us."

"Will do." Sharon smoothed Erik's fur. "As for your story, start from the beginning. Where are you from?"

"What used to be Ushuaia at the southern tip of South America. For some reason, God, or whatever higher power one believes in, gave me the gift of singing. I was considered a prodigy, and I could earn coin with my voice. It's what kept me from starving during the South American Famine. After my parents died, instead of going to an orphanage, I was sent to Chicago to study and sing at the Lyric Opera House."

"I remember hearing about the famine. Didn't it start after the glaciers in the Andes melted?"

"*Sí.* No more fresh water turned into no more farming."

"That's when things were getting really bad. I'm surprised anyone cared much about opera." Sharon pulled the shade a touch lower to block out a strong ray of sun beaming through a crevice in the clouds.

"Music never dies, *amiga*." Federico held up a finger. "Even now, just listen for it. Remember, I was singing when we met. You paid me to play you a song."

She recalled the fluidity and sweetness of his voice. "And I'd pay you again."

"Next time I sing for you, it'll be free." He glanced at the radar.

"Anyway, I continued to sing there until my fifteenth birthday. Of course, the only people who could come to the opera were those who could afford to spend money on something other than food or water. Woody and her parents were among them."

"Are you and Woody close in age?" she asked.

"I'm forty-nine. She's a couple of years older. Her father was an important scientist in the Ministry of Scientific Advancement before it was abolished. At age seventeen, Woody had already earned a Ph.D. in biomechanical engineering." A sheepish smile spread across his face. "I always knew when she was in the audience."

"Yeah, how's that?"

"Because she's the most beautiful woman I've ever seen." Federico's cheeks flushed. "I fell in love with her the second that I saw her."

"So, are you two together?"

"No." His smile faded. "Woody only thinks of me as a brother. You get the idea. Back to the kidnapping, as I like to call it. The night of my seventeenth birthday, Banditti carried out a terrorist attack against Chicago. They blew up several buildings, including the opera house. I was in the middle of my best ever Roberto Devereux performance."

"Didn't something like twenty thousand people die?" Sharon asked.

"Twenty-three thousand, one hundred and forty. When the building started to collapse, I had one single thought. Find Woody." He held up his hands. "I dug her and her parents out of the debris. The building fell less than a minute after we escaped."

"And they took you in after that?"

"Yeah. I've spent my life by Woody's side ever since."

"What happened to her parents?"

"Her father was falsely accused of colluding with the Kingdom of Asia nine years later and executed. Her mom, who was a Muslim, got deported to Syria. She died of cholera before Woody could bring her home."

"Woody is lucky to have you," she said.

Federico sighed. "And I'm lucky to have her." His attention went to the radar. "Speaking of luck, ours is running out. We need to get your friends on board and get the hell out of here. Remind me of their names."

"Inu and Annie."

"If we don't get Inu and Annie on board and above the clouds, that storm is going to chew us up." He drew an *X*. A pulsing red circle on the OVA marked the coordinates of the old rest stop. "We've got about twenty minutes."

Buffeted by gathering winds, the Albatross' wing swiveled back on its hinges, bringing her into a dive.

The acceleration pressed Sharon to her seat. Her ears popped.

Erik lifted his head and whimpered. His ears were probably popping too.

"It's okay, boy." She slid her foot closer to the dog to reassure him.

He laid his head on the toe of her boot.

A gust slammed the shuttle hard to the right.

"Easy does it." Federico switched off the autopilot and grabbed the steering rudder. "Almost there."

The Albatross maneuvered upright. Its landing skids dropped down, and the shuttle glided to a soft landing.

"We're down to eleven minutes before the storm is on top of us." Federico switched the engine to idle. "That's how much time you have to get back here. I'll stay with the bird so she's ready to take off. If something happens, and I have to get her in the air sooner, wait for me. I'll circle around and come back when it clears."

Undoing her restraint, then Erik's, she said, "I'll drag them if I have to." She hopped out of the shuttle. With Erik at her heels, she raced toward the rusty storm-shelter door.

"Stop!" Annie shouted from somewhere outside.

Sharon turned in a circle looking for the feisty old woman.

Erik woofed and held still, pointing.

She followed his direction and shouted back, "Annie, it's me, Sharon!"

"You mean the thief who stole my goddamned coat, and abandoned an innocent boy?"

"Yes! I'm that asshole. And you have no idea how sorry I am."

"Sorry doesn't cut it." Annie emerged from the bushes pointing a handmade bow and arrow at Sharon's chest. "I ought to shoot you right through your black heart."

Erik lowered his head and growled, showing his teeth.

"It's okay." Sharon smoothed the dog's head.

Federico opened his side of the shuttle.

Annie trained the arrow on him. "Get back inside. Or I'll land this arrow between your eyes."

"Nine minutes!" Federico yelled. "Before the storm chews us into a million pieces."

"Annie." Sharon pressed closer. "I have your coat and something better. You and Inu can come with us. There's decent food, water, music, art." She paused. "Kids who need a teacher." She held out her empty hands. "They're good people willing to take you in. You can have a life."

"This is my life." Annie shook her head. "Unlike you, I won't abandon my kids. You know I can't leave."

Time conspired against gentle persuasion. And Sharon bet that Annie's moral compass was stronger than her anger. She moved forward, shielding herself from the possible projectile with her forearm. "You have to face it. The kids you've been looking for are gone. I'm sorry you lost them. I'm sorry I took your coat. And I'm sorry I left you. I beg you to forgive me. Either way, I'm taking Inu. But I want you to come too. Please."

Annie glanced in the direction of the storm-shelter door.

It lifted a few centimeters before bursting open.

"Please!" Inu scrambled out and bolted, arms wide, to Sharon.

"Inu," Sharon whispered, ignoring the arrow pointed at her. "Inu." She scooped him into her arms and hugged him close. "I'm so happy to see you." The void in her heart felt a little less empty. "I missed you, brave boy."

He buried his face in her neck. "Please."

The western horizon grew black as streaks of lightening cleaved the sky. The Albatross bobbled in a gust. Erik moved protectively in front of Sharon and Inu.

She felt the storm's building pressure in her chest. "Annie, there's no more time to think. There's nothing for you here anymore! Come with us."

"Please, A ..." Inu's mouth formed a word he couldn't seem to get out. "A ... a ... Annie."

The old woman's eyes filled with tears as she lowered the bow.

"Please, Annie." Inu opened his hand to her. "Please."

"Oh, my darling boy." She hugged her shaking body.

Federico jumped from the Albatross and ran to her. Putting an arm around the old woman, he whisked her into the shuttle.

Erik hopped in behind them.

Sharon settled Inu into the back next to Annie and secured their torso-restraints.

Federico snapped his closed. "Two minutes." His fingers played over STELA, drawing out commands.

Sharon strapped Erik down and secured her torso-restraint. As the Albatross lifted into the air, she said to Federico. "I think I just kidnapped a kid and a teacher."

"That you did, *amiga*." He looked from the radar to over his shoulder and down at Erik. "A dog too." Federico pulled back on the steering rudder and sang.

His cheerful aria ushered them above the murderous storm.

Chapter 15

Standing with Sharon in the hallway outside the holding cells, Woody offered her the end of Erik's leash. "JJ fed and watered the dog about an hour ago. Annie and Inu are settling into rooms here on Belosto-One. Nice people. As for Elliot, the jury's out on that. He's sitting in the brig. You've told me nothing about him, and he refuses to speak to us. Granted, we did yank him out of the work camp against his will."

"Have you mentioned me?" Sharon took the leash.

Erik sat on his haunches staring up at the two women.

"No. I still don't know the nature of your relationship. I didn't want to jeopardize his cooperation." Woody unclipped a small canvas bag from her belt and offered it to Sharon. "You need to eat and drink too. There's a flask of water and dried rat jerky inside. Now, tell me, from your perspective: Is Elliot a good or a bad man?"

Sharon took the bag. "Thanks for this. I'm not sure I can give an unbiased answer."

"I didn't ask for an unbiased answer. I want to know what your gut says."

"If I had my way, I'd never have to see him again." Sharon clipped the bag to her own belt. "He betrayed my father, which led to the deaths of my parents."

"So you're put into a position of relying on an untrustworthy person to retrieve the thing you need to get wife your back?" Woody asked. "How can you be so sure he'll help you?"

"Because he's the only one who can. And he'd do anything for my forgiveness. That I know."

"What's the backstory?" Woody asked. "We'll be landing in Vermont soon. From there, I'll send JJ with you and Elliot on to Maine to retrieve the seeds, and whatever it is the Strelitzia is after. I won't have time for surprises. And I need to have an idea of what could go wrong."

"I understand." Sharon shoved her hands into her pockets. "Elliot used to work for my parents. He cared for our honeybees and helped with the farm. He had an affair with my mother. It was during the time of the reemergence of the Arctic Plague from bodies uncovered by the melting ice. When my father found out about the affair, he fired Elliot and hired a migrant worker. At the time, the worker wasn't showing symptoms, but he had the Arctic Plague. It killed him and my parents within weeks."

"Why is Elliot the only person who can retrieve what the Strelitzia is after?" Woody crossed her arms over her chest.

"The secret to my apple tree is contained in a fire- and weather-proof box filled with argon gas. It's hidden in the cavity of a dead oak trunk near the apple tree. A robust colony of Africanized honeybees also calls that cavity home. There are only two ways to get the box. One, burn the trunk, which would destroy the apple tree. Or, find someone with an immunity to Africanized honeybees who can retrieve it."

"And Elliot has the immunity? What happens to a person who doesn't?" Woody asked.

"The bees are a mutant strain. They make the originals seem like flying puppies. One sting brings death within two to three minutes."

"A beekeeping suit isn't enough protection?"

"No." Sharon shook her head. "They're capable of stinging through most materials. Even if you found one they couldn't sting through, they're relentless. They'll chase a person to the ends of the Earth. Once angered, they won't stop until they kill the source of what pissed them off. Elliot knows this particular colony. He's the only person who's ever been able to get near it. God knows how he developed his immunity."

"I'm guessing he won't be surprised to learn that it was you who had him summoned," Woody said.

"He's probably been expecting it for years. Dreading it." Sharon cleared her throat. "He knew the day would come when I'd need that box. He also knows I'd rather die than burn my apple tree."

"Okay." Woody exhaled, thinking. "So, mutant, weapons-grade Africanized honeybees, any other hazards I should be aware of?"

Sharon smiled ruefully. "Yeah, I killed two Banditti the day I left. Their crappy van is still parked next to my barn. Unless, of course, their friends have shown up and are now living in my house."

"Oh yeah, the thugs the Strelitzia sent your way. Good reminder." Woody turned to the door of the brig. "Anything else?"

"You've managed to drag everything out of me," Sharon said. "Even my dirty laundry."

"Yeah, well. You don't live properly without getting a little dirty." Woody pressed her fingertip to the print reader on the door to the brig. The lock clicked open. "You'll find Elliot in a cell down the hall to your right. I'd prefer to launch your shuttle and crew prior to landing Belosto-One in Vermont. There's a call box outside the cell. Once you've had your say with Elliot, let me know." With her hip, she shoved the heavy door open. "That's when you launch."

Sharon walked the length of the hall, stopping short of Elliot's cell. She glanced at Erik. "Thanks for doing this with me."

He wagged his tail, then composed himself, as if sensing the gravity of the moment.

"Elliot." She moved in front of the cell. "It's me, Sharon." The sight of him sucked the air from her lungs.

Sitting on a cot, the man lifted his head. A scar ran from his right ear to his chin. His steel-gray hair contrasted with skin black as night. Filthy torn clothing hung on his spindly body. "I know." His voice had graveled with age. Three bottom teeth were missing. "Unrecognizable," he whispered.

"What happened to you?" She gripped the bars of the cell. Seeing the once-robust man so diminished and frail knocked her off balance.

"It's what happens trying to survive a living hell. A hell of one's own making." He wiped spittle from the side of his mouth and stared at the floor.

"I'm . . ." Sharon couldn't finish expressing remorse. "You were like a second father to me. But you betrayed me." Rage and compassion battled in her belly.

He wagged a finger. "I can see it. You're tasting the past. Bitter and sweet have always been the most complicated of tastes. Remember that . . ."

"Don't," Sharon snapped. "You don't get to talk to me about the past. What's done can't be undone. I have no desire to relive it, either."

"All I do is relive it."

"Yeah. I see."

"Very well." Using his hands, he scooted back from the edge of the cot. "There's only one reason you're standing in front of me, then. It's why I kept on keeping on all these years. I knew you'd need the box."

Sharon closed her eyes and shook her head. "You look like you can barely walk. How the hell are you going to be able to get it?"

"Really, Sharon?" He pressed the back of his head to the wall. "I've been living every second of my miserable fucking life hoping you'd need me. Once I get that box, I get to let go. I'll crawl through fire, if I have to." His eyes met hers. "Maybe then you'll forgive me."

Remorse swelled as she struggled to see the man she used to know inside the man in front of her. "I can't."

"Fair enough. All I can do is ask. If we can't talk about the past, at least tell me about your life. I've never stopped loving you, or your family. Your family was my family. How are your brothers?"

"Mark and Jon are dead." Sharon swallowed back a bitter taste. "And you threw us away."

"I'm so sorry about the boys. But you must understand by now. I didn't throw you away. My only sin was to fall in love with your beautiful mother." He leaned forward. "Did you ever find someone to love?"

She bit her lip. "I never wanted to see you again." The irony of his question rattled her. Her love for Eve was why she needed him. "Yes."

"Tell me about him."

"Her. Her name is Eve."

"That's a lovely name." He beamed. "Could anything ever keep you from your Eve?"

"No." She rested her forehead on the bars. "Not even having to see you again."

Elliot laughed. "You were always the most stubborn Clausen. Such grit."

There was the Elliot she remembered. His smile always had made her feel better as a child. The gentle, sweet smile of the man who stole her mother from her father. She tore her eyes from his. "Will you help me get my box?"

Using his arms to boost himself from the cot, he struggled to his feet. Elliot reached through the bars and put a hand to her cheek. "If it's the last thing I do."

Sharon flinched, but couldn't pull away. His suffering tugged her close. She covered his hand with hers. Savoring the connection to the only living person linked to a past she still longed for. A frayed connection, but one she still, she realized, cherished. Maybe redemption would be possible for Elliot after all . . . and for her.

"Nothing." JJ lowered the strange-looking eyeglasses from his face and tapped a command onto the Albatross's STELA. Offering the glasses to Elliot, he said, "No one's in or around the house or barn. Want to have a look?"

"You were able to see inside a building from twelve kilometers away? Humans. Destroyers of Earth. Creators of extraordinary gadgets." Elliot took the burnished metal glasses and slipped them on.

"It's an OALI, short for Ocular Amplification Light Intensifier." JJ pushed the throttle forward. "Maximum amplification and light gathering all in one."

"Huh." Elliot leaned closer to the Albatross' window. "I haven't seen the farm in nearly two decades. What happened to the old house?" With a shaky hand, he offered the glasses to Sharon.

"After mom and dad died, I burned it down with them inside." Without making eye contact, she took the glasses. "I had to kill the plague bacterium."

Elliot remained silent.

She lifted the glasses to her eyes. "The Banditti van is still there." So was her orchard, farm, and home. It had only been seven days since she left, but it felt like seven years. Most of the trees had dropped their apples. Tucked in the midst of the poisonous trees stood her perfect mutant apple tree. The tree that had given Eve the answer.

"I'm going to hover the Albatross." JJ swiped a finger over STELA. "Wouldn't put it past the Strelitzia to be watching for us through the instruments on that van or some other contrivance. Any good ideas for getting down there undetected?"

Sharon handed the glasses to JJ. "See the overgrown area northeast of the barn, below the rise of the hill? If we go in low and land there, the hill should give us some cover. It's about a kilometer walk to the entrance of an underground passageway."

"Underground passage?" JJ peered through the glasses. "Cool. Let's do it. Only trouble is that if they can't see us, we can't see them."

"Oh yes we can." Rummaging through her satchel to retrieve Queenbee, she said, "I've got eyes on the farm. Look at the cupola."

"You mean the owl in the cupola?" JJ grinned. "Those are some big eyes."

"The better to see with." Sharon powered up Queenbee. The screen flashed and the owl woke. "She's got a three-hundred-and-sixty-degree view out to five kilometers."

"The kid actually did it." Elliot put his forearm to his mouth and coughed.

"You okay?" JJ asked.

The worn man blotted the corners of his mouth with a sleeve. "Don't worry. I'm not sick. Just older than dirt."

JJ shot Sharon a glance that suggested his lack of confidence in Elliot's physical stamina.

"You want some water, Elliot?" Sharon asked.

"Thank you, but save it for yourself." He blinked and rubbed his eyes. "I remember when Jon thought of the idea of building a place underground to hide from all the badness going around. Your dad was skeptical. But he scavenged for what your brother needed anyway. That boy was a wonder. Just like you and Mark."

"Jon was the smart one. Mark had the big heart." Sharon tried to picture their faces. But they'd faded long ago. Only the few pictures she had salvaged from the fire reminded her of their likenesses.

"And you were always the one who held everything and everyone together." Elliot paused. "The practical child."

"Maybe too much so, sometimes," she whispered.

A gust of wind slammed the Albatross, bucking the shuttle up and down.

JJ dropped the glasses and gripped the controls. "We need to fly. The Albatross is the kind of bird that likes to be on the move. What's the plan once we get to your underground passage?"

"We take the tunnel to my hidden growing area where the seeds and Dr. Ryan's box of medications are hidden."

"And the beehive?" JJ tapped STELA.

"Not far from the tunnel entrance," Sharon answered. "That should be our last stop."

JJ sketched two arrows. "We'll head due north, then west behind the hill." He glanced at Elliot. "Once we land, we have to move fast. You stay at the passage entrance and wait for us. No offense, but you don't seem in a condition to keep up."

"None taken," Elliot said. "My job's to get that box."

"Good man." JJ leaned into the Albatross' turn. "Here we go."

Sharon's stomach fluttered at being home. She clenched her fists, determined to get what she needed to bring Eve home too.

The Albatross' wing curved backward and her landing skids dropped.

"This could be bumpy." JJ gripped the controls. "She doesn't have much room to land in that thicket." He drew a bird talon. "Have to do a grip landing."

"Grip landing?" Sharon asked.

Branches scraped the shuttle's wings and the Albatross pitched forward. Debris kicked and bounced at the fuselage. The bird lurched backward, slowed, centered, and stopped.

"Instead of landing on the ground, it gripped the bushes with its titanium talons. A grip landing." JJ released his torso-restraint, popped the capsule open and hopped out. He helped Elliot down.

Sharon opened her restraint and then unbuckled the straps holding Erik. The dog shook himself and jumped out after Elliot. After Sharon climbed out, she checked the owl's view through Queenbee. "Nothing."

Erik relieved himself on a bush and followed her.

"Good, let's go." JJ started up the hill.

"Wait," Sharon jogged ahead of him. "Let me go first. I know the way and the best route through the brush. You help Elliot."

JJ nodded and held an elbow out to the older man. "I got you, friend."

As they approached the top of the hill, Sharon paused and rotated the view scope on Queenbee. The owl's head swiveled three hundred and sixty degrees. "All clear still." She pressed forward along a herd path that wound through a tangle of kudzu. A peek over her shoulder confirmed Erik at her heels and JJ helping Elliot stay close.

They crested the rise and picked their way down the steep slope. Sharon stopped to check Queenbee.

"I sure hope you know where you are." JJ wiped beads of sweat from his brow. "It's like a maze with no end. I can't see a damn thing through this brush."

"Queenbee's got our backs." Sharon waited for him to catch up and showed him the screen. "She sees all and knows all. The yellow dot indicates we're standing right over the entrance." She passed Queenbee to JJ. "Hold this." Squatting down, she tugged branches from the circle in the ground and pressed her fingerprint to it. The circle slid open. She brushed a palm inside the lip of the opening. Light flooded the passageway.

"How long will it take?" Elliot eased into a squat.

"Ten, fifteen minutes, tops." Sharon climbed down a couple of rungs. "You okay?"

He folded his legs tailor-style and waved off the question. "That hill about did me in. I'm glad to sit and catch my breath."

Sharon unclipped the water flask from her pack. "I insist." She reached over and set it on the ground next to Elliot.

JJ retrieved an acupalmtell from his shirt pocket. He unclasped the communicator attached to it and handed it to Elliot. "You call us if you see or hear anything. We need to close the passage in case someone comes along. Hide in the brush. We'll be able to find you so long as you have the communicator." He stuffed the acupalmtell back into his pocket. "It'll only vibrate against my chest. Not ring. So don't hesitate to call."

"All right." Elliot scooted into the cover of knotweed.

"Be careful," Sharon said and leaped to the passage floor.

Erik followed her.

JJ climbed down and slid the entrance lid closed. "What is that funky smell?"

"Micoriden."

"Really? How'd you get it? Black market?" JJ kept pace with her.

"A more direct way." Sharon jogged faster. "My brothers and I stole it from NONA."

"No shit? That was ballsy."

"They didn't seem to miss it." Sharon glanced at Queenbee. "What do you see?"

"Just that crappy van." She halted. "Except—"

He crashed into her. "Oops. Sorry. What is it?"

Pointing at a cracked floor light, she said, "I don't remember that being blown."

"Maybe it happened when you turned them on," JJ said. "Power surge will do it."

"Yeah. Except it'd be the first time since we built it." She tugged his arm. "Let's keep going." She jogged to the underground farm entrance. "This is it." She pressed the lock and the door popped open.

Humidity and the intoxicating scent of growing, healthy vegetation enveloped them. She inhaled luxuriously, filling her nose and lungs to capacity. She pushed the door open. The flowers on the hydroponic tomato plants had fruited. Ripened squash dangled from wilting vines. Leafy, dark green potato plants hinted at tubers below the surface. She lifted her hands to her plants. "Hello, lovelies."

"Holy cow." JJ caressed a tomato. "Are these . . ."

"Cherry tomatoes."

Erik trotted past them with his tail wagging. He sniffed every nook, cranny, and leaf before biting off a tomato.

"I thought we were getting potato and kale seed. I didn't think there were any tomato or squash seeds left to grow." With eyes wide he asked, "May I? I'm salivating!"

"Please do." She grinned. "Erik's already helped himself. I'm glad to share with you."

JJ plucked a tomato from its vine. He rolled it over in his palm and popped it into his mouth. His eyes gleamed. He closed his eyes and chewed with great concentration. "I'm pretty sure that's the best thing I've ever tasted in my entire life. These things were long gone by the time I was born. Thank you, Sharon."

"You're welcome." She picked two tomatoes and offered another to JJ and one to Erik.

Erik chomped and swallowed.

"Did you even taste it?" She patted the dog's head and took a tomato for herself.

"That's some good stuff, huh, boy?" JJ gave Erik a scratch. "Mind if I stuff my pockets with a few for Federico?"

"Not at all. But we should hurry. The seeds for all of these plants are stored in that tray." She pointed to a sealed green container. "You carry it, and I'll grab Dr. Ryan's box."

He popped the tomato into his mouth and filled his pockets with more. "What about you and Eve? We should leave some of the seeds for you."

"That wasn't the deal I made with Woody." She opened the cabinet. "Don't worry about me. I'll be able to grow more. I've got another stash." The cabinet was empty. She wheeled around.

"What's wrong?"

"I thought I'd left Dr. Ryan's box in the cabinet." Turning, she saw it beneath the lab bench. "Maybe I'm losing my mind."

"Do you think someone was in here?"

"There's no way. They would've taken everything." She shook her head. "I did leave in a rush. The Banditti were threatening Inu."

"You're right. No one could've come in here and left without eating this stuff." JJ's breast pocket buzzed. "Elliot," he said. He fished out the acupalmtell and pressed the call button. "That you, Elliot?"

"Banditti," Elliot whispered.

Sharon woke Queenbee's screen. "Fuck. There's at least ten Banditti and two more hydro-vans. They're headed to the barn. There's another entrance into here from there. Maybe someone *has* been in here."

"Let's go." JJ brought the acupalmtell to his lips. "Elliot, stay put. We're coming."

"There's no time to wait." Elliot's words rushed out. "I'm going now."

"Don't." JJ dropped the acupalmtell into his pocket and hoisted the seed tray onto a shoulder. "Stubborn old man."

Sharon yanked the titanium box from beneath the bench and ran with JJ and Erik through the corridor. She thought she heard someone clanging at the entrance in the barn floor. Daring to slow down, she checked Queenbee. "Oh, my god." She halted.

"What is it?"

"The Banditti see Elliot. They're going after him."

JJ set the tray on the floor and took the acupalmtell from his pocket. "Elliot. They're coming your way. You have to hide."

"I'm drawing them to me," Elliot panted.

Watching with JJ through the eyes of the owl, Sharon saw the blast of a spectraletto. The laser slashed across Elliot's upper torso.

He fell to his knees, got up, and kept going until he stopped at the base of the dead oak tree. He pounded on the trunk wildly, with both fists. A black cloud emerged from a low cavity. The Banditti kept coming as the cloud of bees engulfed Elliot, stinging him mercilessly.

"No!" Sharon yelled, sickened by the thought of the pain he must be experiencing. While Elliot was immune to the bee venom, he no doubt felt every stab of their sharp, barbed stingers.

"The killer bees?" JJ asked.

Before Sharon could muster an answer, a Banditti yanked Elliot from the tree. He reared a fist back before jerking several times as bees jabbed into him. Queenbee's speaker transmitted his blood-curdling screams. The Banditti wailed in agony and crumpled.

The cloud of bees flattened out and spread down the hill toward the other oncoming Banditti.

Elliot labored to his feet and thrust his arm inside the cavity. A second Banditti shoved him aside while a third pulled a black box out of it. His body jerked too, and he dropped hard. The third Banditti screamed, hitting himself over and over again before collapsing.

Sharon swiveled the owl's head. The remaining Banditti gaped at what was going on before bolting toward the safety of her house.

"Guess they got the message about the bees. They're going to wait it out." JJ rubbed his forehead. "When will the bees calm down? We have to get that box before the Banditti do. And we can't leave Elliot to die."

Elliot lay on his back with the box clutched to his chest. He lifted his knees and curled into the fetal position. His clothing was dotted with disemboweled and dying bees that still clung to him. Like Elliot, they had sacrificed themselves for their others. A sting by an Africanized honeybee was a death sentence for the bee too.

Speaking into the acupalmtell, JJ asked, "Elliot, how badly are you hurt?"

"Can't . . ." Elliot sucked in several shallow breaths. "Breathe. My chest."

"The laser might've hit a lung. How the hell do we get up there?" JJ asked.

"Fuck." Sharon slammed her back against the tunnel wall and slid down onto her butt. She pulled her knees to her chest, hugging herself. "Fuck."

Erik laid his snout on her knees and whimpered.

"We can figure this out." JJ crouched next to her. "Let's think of something I can wear to protect myself. I'll go after him."

"There's only one thing that will work." She put her hands to her face, trying to blot out the only option. "Fire and smoke."

"How?" JJ asked.

Sharon butted the back of her head against the wall and got to her feet. "By destroying the only home I've ever known." Her body vibrated with fury. She banged her fists at the tunnel wall. "What more will I have to lose!"

Erik barked excitedly.

"Tell me." JJ gripped her shoulders. "How to help you."

"Don't let me change my mind." She exhaled her reservations and put a hand to Erik. "We have to hurry. Follow me."

She bolted to the exit and stopped. "When my brothers and I built the underground farm, we devised a way to destroy the surface in case we ever needed to hide." Her voice sounded detached from her body. "We figured if nothing was above ground, no one would suspect we were under it. I'm going to blow my home to smithereens." Sharon looked through the eyes of the owl at her home and tried to sear the sight of it into her memory. In another ten minutes everything above ground would be gone.

"There's got to be another way."

"There isn't."

"I'm sorry it's come to this." JJ pulled her into a hug.

It felt foreign, yet comforting to be embraced by someone other than Eve. "I'm glad you're my friend."

"Me too." He held her tight.

"I told you not to try to talk me out of it." She pushed him away. "Don't make me feel all sentimental."

"Sorry." He smiled affectionately and picked up the box of seeds. "How do we get out of here?"

"I'll detonate the buried explosives. It'll make lots of smoke and fire. Hopefully, by the time the Banditti get their bearings, we'll be long gone."

"Should I tell Elliot the plan?" JJ asked.

"No. He'll try to talk us out of it." She tapped in the key combination to arm the bombs. "Let's hope it works." She pressed the detonation key.

Boom, boom, boom! The concussion tossed Sharon against the wall. She regained her footing, shoved the exit hatch aside and scrambled out.

JJ handed up the box before hoisting himself through the portal. Erik shadowed them.

Heavy gray smoke flooded the air. *Boom, boom!* The ground convulsed as if in an earthquake. *Boom!*

JJ coughed and pressed his forearm against his mouth and nose.

Sharon pulled Eve's scarf to her face to block out the smoke. Flames flicked from the house and barn. Sparks from several engulfed orchard trees spread the fire. Black smoke blotted out the sky. She squinted, hoping to get a glimpse of her apple tree. There it was, in the middle of her orchard, writhing in hideous flames. She'd swear she heard it scream. Remembering Federico's words, *Keep going, Sharon. You have to keep going,* she tore her eyes from the awful death of her extraordinary tree. The bees had lifted off to safer air.

Sharon and JJ ran toward Elliot, passing a bloated Banditti covered in vicious red welts. His face looked inhuman, with swollen lips that protruded past his nose and chin. The white of his right eye bulged out of its socket.

"Holy fuck!" JJ yelled.

When they reached Elliot, he lay limp, staring up at the sky. Blood pooled around him. Quick, shallow gasps puffed from his lips.

"Be careful of any live bees that might be stuck in his clothes."

"Okay." JJ tried to lift him.

"No." Elliot reached for Sharon. "Let me stay with your family. My family."

Overcome by warring emotions, she smoothed his hair. "I'm your family," she whispered.

"I love you." A tear slid from his eye. "Thank you for bringing me home. I'm home." His eyes fluttered before staring, vacant, into the blackening sky.

She bent down and touched her forehead to his. "I always loved you too. I still do." Her stomach clenched, trying to hold in the sorrow of so many memories, buried, but not gone. "Thank you for helping me." She brushed her hand over his eyes to close them. "Sleep well, Elliot."

Streaks of lasers whizzed past them. JJ put his arms under her and helped her to her feet. "We have to go."

Erik woofed.

Sharon untangled Elliot's fingers from the box's handle.

JJ hoisted the tray of seeds to a shoulder and took Dr. Ryan's box.

Sharon grabbed Erik's collar.

Together, they stumbled up, and down the hill to the waiting Albatross.

Erik leaped into the open capsule, followed by JJ and Sharon.

In silence, JJ tapped out launch commands.

Sharon tried in vain to see through the heavy smoke as they got airborne. Clutching the box to her chest, she rested her head against the port window. *Good-bye, for now.* With Eve, maybe she could rebuild.

Chapter 16

The altimeter on the wall of her assigned cabin aboard Belosto-One caught Sharon's eye. Displaying the layers of Earth's atmosphere, its arrow hovered at seventy-five kilometers within the mesosphere. She lifted the shade over the window. Cottony clouds blanketed Earth below. Sapphire colored the sky while orange burned at the subtle bend in the horizon.

Memories of her childhood surfaced. She imagined morning, her favorite time of day. In springtime, her family's orchard trees had bloomed with fragrant pink flowers. By summer, the farm's rich soil teemed with vegetables of all kinds. She'd sit in the orchard with her back against a tree watching Mark and Jon play hide-and-seek.

On her fourth birthday, her father had given her the honor of planting an apple tree seedling. It became the most special tree in the orchard. With the sun warming her skin, she'd watch thrushes and warblers building nests in its branches. They always seemed thrilled to live at the edge of the woods, as if they woke every morning ecstatic for another day. The world had dimmed forever when the majority of its birds died. With the loss of her apple tree, Sharon's world was darker too.

"I miss them." She rubbed Erik's ears. "My family. The birds and the trees. But most of all, I miss Eve." A vision of black smoke and raging fire elbowed out happier recollections. In spite of the bath she'd taken earlier to remove the dirt, sweat, and soot from her skin, the scent of the fire's destruction lingered in her nose. The box Elliot had retrieved sat safely against the wall. The solid gold lock she and Eve had made by melting down all of Sharon's family's jewelry still secured its contents.

The dog laid his head on her thigh. His brown eyes locked with hers. He sighed as if sensing her grief.

"Don't worry. I'll bring you with me wherever I go. JJ told me you went on a hunger strike when I went to California."

He blinked.

"You understand." She plucked a dried beetle from a bowl on the desk. "Starving yourself is one way to get what you want." She offered it to him. "I don't want you to ever be hungry again."

He sniffed and lapped it into his mouth. Tail wagging, he crunched once and swallowed.

Erik's head snapped toward a knock at the door.

"Come in," Sharon called.

The door opened. Clad in the clothes they'd arrived in and only socks with a snowflake pattern on their feet, Annie stood with her hands on Inu's shoulders. "May we talk with you?"

At the sight of Erik, Inu backed into Annie. Under his left armpit, he clutched the pages from Sharon's mother's sketchpad.

"It's okay." Annie crouched and held a hand to the dog. "Come, Erik."

"Go see Annie." Sharon kissed the dog's head. "She's a friend."

Erik trotted to the old woman and let her nuzzle him.

"I had a dog when I was little." Annie got to her feet. "Her name was Daisy. Best friend I ever had." She motioned for Inu. "Bring the sketches to me. Let me show you."

Keeping wary eyes on Erik, Inu handed the pages to Annie.

"The pencil too, boy."

Inu fished it from the pocket of his rolled-up pants. He still wore the clothes Sharon had given to him back at her farm.

Annie took it and scribbled on a page. "There." She displayed her work.

The drawing looked like a pile of stacked round rocks with a large flat one on top. It reminded Sharon of the cairns placed in the White Mountains to mark hiking routes over the bare tops of the Presidentials.

"Do you know what this is?" Annie asked.

Inu lowered and raised his chin. "Inuksuk."

"Ha!" Annie giggled. "Yes. Inuksuk. Among the many uses and meanings in Inuit culture, it symbolizes friendship and welcoming." She laid a hand on Erik's head. "The dog is our friend."

"F . . . fr . . ." Inu crouched, holding his hand to Erik. "Friend."

Erik wagged his tail as Inu rubbed and patted him.

"Annie!" Sharon exclaimed. "You got him to talk. That's amazing."

Annie put her hands to her knees pushing herself upright. "He's a brilliant boy." She tousled his hair. "And artist. He communicates through pictures. He does the drawing, and I translate. Then he copies my words. We've had lovely conversations."

"Did he tell you where he's from?" Sharon asked.

"He's from Greenland."

"Anything about his family?"

"Reluctantly." Annie's voice lowered. "It was very difficult for him. They died from the Arctic Plague. It was that trauma, I think, that took his voice away."

Sharon watched Inu hugging and kissing Erik. "Poor boy." She didn't share a bloodline with him, but their histories bound them. "Mine died the same way."

Annie clutched the sketchbook pages to her chest. "Two degrees." She sat on the end of the small bed. "If my parents' generation had only listened."

"About what?" Sharon asked.

"Scientists warned them not to let the Earth's temperature increase by more than two degrees Celsius. That it would be a tipping point for all kinds of bad things to happen. Back then, the permafrost in the Arctic was already melting. They'd opened Pandora's Box. Disease was only one of the awful things that escaped."

"I wonder why they didn't care about what would happen to us."

"I don't know that they didn't. Might've just been human

210

nature. We're a self-absorbed lot. It's why you stole my coat. Which, by the way, I'm still mad at you for." Annie gave Sharon's wrist a gentle squeeze. "But I know that you're a good person deep down. Your actions were motivated by the desire to save your wife, even if it meant sacrificing someone else. Most people would've done the exact same thing to save the ones they love."

"I really am sorry. I hope someday you'll forgive me."

"Now's not the time to hold grudges," Annie said. "We humans better evolve away from our bad selves, or die. I may still be mad at you, but I do forgive you."

Inu reached for the sketchbook pages. "Please."

"You have something to say?" Annie asked. "Speak your mind, boy." She handed him the pages and pencil.

He riffled through the stack. "E . . . Eve." Inu passed a page to Sharon.

"Oh my gosh." She stared in disbelief. Drawn on the page was a perfect likeness of Eve, down to what she'd been wearing the day she was taken. "You only saw her once."

"Inu has a photographic memory as well as being a talented artist."

"The only thing that could be more perfect would be Eve standing in front of me." Sharon lifted an arm to him. "It's amazing."

He wrapped his arms around her waist.

"Thank you." She kissed the top of his head.

Inu beamed. "Eve."

"Yeah." She squeezed him tight. "You gave me Eve."

"Sorry to interrupt." Woody stood in the open doorway. Her usual poise showed signs of fracture. "If you don't mind, Annie and Inu, I need to speak with Sharon."

"We understand." Annie took Inu's hand. "Thank you, Sharon, for coming back for us. Hopefully, we can talk more later."

"I'd like that, Annie." Sharon smoothed the top of Inu's head. "And thank you for the picture."

He reached up, took her face in both of his hands, and kissed her forehead.

211

"A kiss to the forehead is an expression of protection." Woody smiled. "You seem to be collecting protectors." She ran a hand along Erik's back.

"I guess I look as fragile as I feel," Sharon said.

"Worn and thin, yes. Fragile, no." Woody ushered Annie and Inu to the door.

Sharon waved to Annie. "Thank you for looking after Inu."

"He's looking after me as much as I'm looking after him."

Woody held the door and said to Annie, "Be sure to let us know if there's anything more you need for the reading class you agreed to teach."

"I will. I can't wait to get started. Teaching is all know."

"Wonderful," Woody replied. "It's our good fortune to have another educator among us."

Woody shut the door behind them. "I can't tell you how sorry I am about your farm and the apple tree, Sharon." She pressed farther into the room and rested a hip on the table. "Thank you for keeping your word, though. Never in my wildest dreams would I have expected seeds other than kale or potato. They'll go a long way toward feeding the Qaunik. Not to mention the boost in morale they'll give everyone."

The acupalmtell on Woody's belt crackled with a woman's urgent voice: "Woody, Woody, Woody."

"Excuse me." She slipped the device from her belt. "Woody here."

"You asked to be notified if the Strelitzia made contact." The muted tone of the woman's voice made her sound far away. "He's waiting on the line."

Woody got up. "Any sign of the Bird of Paradise?"

"Negative," the woman answered. "We've searched the entire Bay of Fundy and out to sea five hundred kilometers. There's no sign of the ship."

"Please keep looking. It can't be far. As long as she's not deeper than sixty-one hundred meters, the Belostomatid's radar will find her."

"We will," the woman said.

"Stay invisible while you're at it," Woody added. "The Belostomatid would be easy prey for the Bird of Paradise."

"I have to go with you to talk to the Strelitzia." Sharon stood. "I need to see Eve. I need to know she's alive."

"Agreed." Woody secured the acupalmtell and motioned for Sharon to follow.

Sharon held up a hand. "You stay, Erik. I'll be back."

He sat and lowered his head.

"You'll be okay." She topped off his bowl with the water from her flask, and shut the door.

In their sock feet, Sharon and Woody hurried down the hall to the command room. Neatly stacked boots filled a storage case outside the room. They grabbed their respective pairs and put them on.

When they entered the room, JJ, flanked by Dale and Federico, turned to them. "The Strelitzia is on the SatCom, line four."

Woody seated herself in the command seat. She motioned for Sharon to take the adjacent one. "Let the scoundrel do all the talking." Woody acknowledged Dale and Federico, then turned to Sharon, "Keep your head." She pressed the blinking blue light on the STELA.

The OVA flashed white. Pixels dotted its surface, then resolved into the image of the strange man dressed in a flowery robe and bird mask.

Standing on a small beach surrounded by enormous rocks twelve to twenty meters tall, the Strelitzia straightened the mask on his face, and outstretched his arms. His robe fluttered in the wind as water lapped the shore behind him. In his distorted electronic voice he said, "Is this lovely, or what?" His hands went to his hips. "Have you ever been here, Sharon?"

Keeping Woody's order to let him talk in mind, Sharon asked, "Where is here?"

"Pity. You lost everyone so young. Of course you've never been here. You're just a dirt-poor farm girl. Except for your recent forays with Dr. Woodhouse, you've never been anywhere." He pointed a finger skyward. "Not to worry. You too will soon visit Hopewell Rocks." He spread his hands. "Here in lovely New Brunswick. I, of course, prefer the more fun name, Flower Pot Rocks. I can see it. Can't you?"

"Cut the drama," Woody interrupted.

"You're a killjoy, Wilhelmina. You're always in here." He tapped his forehead. "You really should get out of your own head from time to time. Take a walk outside. You could always ask Sharon about the outdoors. Oh, wait." He put his hands to his cheeks elaborately. "I almost forgot. Sharon's outdoors is nothing but charred trees and buildings. Another terrible pity."

"Where's Eve?" Sharon gritted her teeth.

"Oh, Sharon. I have to give you credit. You outsmarted my band of Banditti not just once. But twice." He put a forefinger to his chin. "You always seem to be just a little bit ahead of me. But you know what? This is like a marathon. Eventually, you'll tire and wear yourself out. Me, I'll just keep coming until I get what I want. And if I don't get what I want, you don't get what you want."

"Let me see her." Sharon swallowed back rising anger. "Let me talk to Eve."

"Well." He put his arms behind his back and paced. "When I get the secret to the apple tree, you get your wife."

"How can we trust you?" Woody asked.

The Strelitzia threw his head back and laughed. "What is this *we* business? Do you have any idea what this woman is keeping from you, Wilhelmina? If you . . ." He wagged a finger. "Wait. Have you two made some kind of a deal? Yes. That would explain things."

His image on the OVA grew bigger as he moved forward. "I may look odd, but I'm certainly not stupid. Brilliant, actually. Shall I clear a few things up for Wilhelmina, Sharon? Bring her into the loop?"

Sharon glanced at Woody.

Keeping her eyes locked to the Strelitzia, Woody didn't flinch or speak.

"So you don't know." He stepped back. "Doesn't really surprise me. I don't even know myself, and I'm the one who's got her wife. Granted, I pulled many tricks out of my hat trying to get Eve to fess up."

Sharon bolted to her feet. "I'll kill you if you've hurt her."

"In the face of my efforts, Eve's silence confirmed the value of whatever it is that you're hiding." He sneered. "And I fucking want it."

"Tell me where to meet you," Sharon growled. "I'll give you the damn thing. Just please, don't hurt her." Sharon scanned every centimeter of the OVA for some sign of Eve. "Where is she? Why isn't she with you?"

He rubbed his hands over his upper arms as if to warm himself. "Do I have to remind you that your wife is a sick woman? What kind of person would I be if I brought her out onto this frigid windy beach?"

"Show us that she's alive," Woody demanded.

"Fine. I'll show you that she's safe, warm, and medicated. For now, anyway. I don't think I need to remind you of what happened to poor Areva and her husband." The Strelitzia pulled an acupalmtell from his robe and spoke. "Connect with our captive."

The OVA split into two images, the Strelitzia on the left and a stark room containing Eve on the right. She lay curled on a cot. Her hands and feet were bound. A beige jumpsuit replaced the dress she'd been wearing the day she was taken.

"Wake up, woman!" the Strelitzia ordered. "Your wife is here to see you."

Sharon fumbled around the command desk to get closer to the screen. "Eve." She laid her hands on the OVA's cold, flat screen, willing it to let her pass through.

Eve looked up. Her face looked splotchy, as if she'd been crying. She struggled into a sitting position. With her bound hands, she tucked a loose strand of hair behind an ear. The telltale signs of torture with a low-strength spectraletto manifested themselves in pinpricks of angry red burns dotting the backs of her hands and tops of her feet. Her complexion suggested, mercifully, that her cancer was being kept at bay. A tear streaked down her face. She struggled to lean forward to meet Sharon.

They pressed their foreheads together as if the OVA and the kilometers didn't separate them.

"Eve, I have what he wants. I'm going to get you out of there."

"Don't, Sharon," Eve whispered. "Don't give it to him. No matter what happens, you can never give him our secret. I'd rather die."

"Enough!" The Strelitzia spoke into the acupalmtell, "Disconnect." He stuffed the instrument into his pocket.

"No!" Sharon yelled.

"I love you. Always," Eve said before her image disappeared.

"I love you too!" Sharon clasped her hands over her heart.

"Now." The Strelitzia reached for the gaudy silver ring on his right middle finger. Twisting it round and round, he said, "You're already late. You've got forty-eight hours."

"Why so long?" Sharon asked. "We can be there in a few. I want her back now."

"Unless you want to deal with the category-five hurricane roaring up the coast, I wouldn't advise it. I don't intend to be in its path. Not to worry, though; Eve and I will be safely riding out the storm nearby. You do the same, and await my next instructions." He smirked at Woody. "Don't bother trying to take back the Bird of Paradise. If you do, I'll make you watch me behead every Qaunik we capture. One by one. After that, I'll have you disemboweled." He clapped his hands and the OVA went blank.

Sharon hugged her shaking body.

Woody got up and put an arm around her. "He's lying. Let's sit." She eased Sharon around the command desk and into a seat. "I think I know why your shoulder still hurts."

"I don't give a damn about my shoulder." Sharon studied Woody's expression for a reason it mattered. "It's the least of my worries."

"If I'm right, it's at the heart of our worries." Woody jutted her chin at Dale. "Do you mind if Dale takes a look?"

216

Sharon caught Federico's worried expression. "Go ahead."

"I'll need you to remove your jacket." Dale set a medical case on the command desk and retrieved a chip-wand.

Sharon slipped her jacket from her shoulders. Pain flared with the movement.

Using her fingers, Dale pressed Sharon's upper right back. Sharon winced.

"That's the spot." Dale hovered the chip-wand over the point where her finger pressed into Sharon. "You were right, Woody. She's wearing a tracking chip. It's the kind NONA sometimes slips into unsuspecting people they're interested in. The trouble is, if it's injected wrong, it can hurt like hell. That's why it's always placed out of reach and out of sight of the victim. People just assume a bug bite or some benign injury that'll go away. I suspect this one's rubbing on the scapula."

"Do you remember when you first noticed it?" Woody asked.

Sharon ticked through the past several days. She'd been in a lot of scuffles. "Early on, maybe when the soldiers took Eve. Can you cut it out of me now?"

"That fits with my theory." Woody put a hand to her hip. "We know the soldiers who took Eve worked for the Strelitzia. I'll bet one of them injected it—clumsily. Because the Strelitzia has known your every move since day one. Dammit, I wish I'd thought of this sooner."

"He knows about your underground farm too," JJ added. "He left a calling card in Dr. Ryan's box of medications."

Woody reached into her pocket. "He did send someone into your underground growing room. The reason they didn't steal your vegetables and fruits is that he didn't want you to know he'd been there." She opened her palm. "It's another tracking chip. I'm guessing he assumed you'd come back for the box because it has Eve's medication. It's a backup for being able to track you."

"Probably drives him crazy that he's been following you all over the planet," Federico added, "but you haven't led him to what he wants."

"What is it that Eve discovered about your tree that's so valuable?" Woody asked. "You've got to tell me everything. It's the only way for us to beat him at his game."

Sharon closed her eyes and hugged herself. Enough had happened to prove that Woody and the Qaunik were her only hope of getting Eve back alive. She was ready to tell Woody everything. Almost. "Eve isolated the genetic material that made the tree resistant to pests and drought. Then she spliced the material into our seeds in the underground growing room. The result is that everything grows lush even with little water. She did some controlled experiments with certain pests. Our squash became completely resistant to the squash beetle. We hid the material inside a box in the tree where the Africanized honeybees lived."

"How the hell did you get past the bees?" JJ asked.

"We waited for one of those rare cold snaps we'd occasionally get. Extreme cold makes the bees too sluggish to be agitated." Sharon rolled her sore shoulder. "The box had already been put inside the tree by Elliot to hide my family's valuables. Eve and I got it out and put the genetic material inside with argon from Eve's old lab to preserve the contents. Trouble is, it never got cold enough again for me to be able to get it back out."

"That's one way to hide the family heirlooms," Federico said.

"I have a plan." Woody motioned for Dale to sit. "And it doesn't involve going to the Bay of Fundy."

"We have to go." Sharon shook her head. "Or he'll kill Eve."

"We're not going to the Bay of Fundy," Woody insisted, "because the Strelitzia and Eve aren't anywhere near there."

"But we saw him." Sharon gestured to the blank OVA.

"No." Woody shook her head. "We saw a digital illusion—a green-screen, in effect. Twenty minutes ago, when we were talking with him, the tide was in, not out. If he really had been on that beach thirty minutes ago, he would've been underwater."

"And Eve? Where is she?"

"She's on the Bird of Paradise. I know every nook and cranny. The room that Eve was in had a slight crack in the wall exactly like the crack in holding cell 6B."

"Where do you think they are, then?" Dale asked.

"That's tougher. But I have a hunch, given that Belostomatid's radar can't find her. The Bird of Paradise's electronic systems require rare earths. Not much, but enough on hand for repairs or building new things. One of the last sites on the planet where you can find rare earths is in South Carolina." Woody swiped STELA, bringing up a satellite image of the Palmetto State on the OVA. "See these?" She pointed to several large containers. "This is the location of the Old Naval Weapons Station near Charleston. They weren't there a week ago."

"So you think he's near Charleston?" Federico asked.

"Not yet," Woody answered. "I'm guessing, because of the hurricane, the Bird of Paradise is hidden deep within the Milwaukee Depth of the Puerto Rico Trench. That's why we can't find her. He's riding out the storm there."

"But he told us we'd exchange the secret for Eve in New Brunswick," Sharon said. "I don't understand."

Woody swiped STELA again, bringing up an image of the entire North American coastline. The eye of the hurricane swirled near the former Washington, D.C. "He has no intention of letting Eve go."

"Everything you're saying is the opposite of what we were told." Sharon rubbed her temples. "What if you're wrong?"

"Listen to me." Woody gripped Sharon's shoulders. "Eve is too valuable. The Strelitzia still doesn't know the secret to the apple tree. He knows enough about you to know that Eve is the most likely person to understand it." Woody pointed at the screen. "This is what he's up to. His plan is to send us on a wild goose chase in the Bay of Fundy. Those containers, which as I mentioned weren't there a week ago, are filled with rare earths. That's what I'm betting. While we're chasing our tails, he'll transfer the containers to the Bird of Paradise. He'll send a crew to meet you. With that chip in your back, they'll find you, take your box with its secrets, and kill you. Then he slips away for good."

"What's your plan?" Federico asked.

"First thing we need to do is get that chip out of Sharon's back." Woody got up.

"There's a problem with that," Dale interjected. "It won't work outside a living human body. If we take it out, its temperature will drop and he'll know."

"That's why we need a decoy." Woody sketched on and tapped STELA. "We'll find a Qaunik willing to volunteer, and prep that person with an incision. The instant you remove that chip from Sharon, you'll implant it into the volunteer. That person will go to the Bay of Fundy, accompanied by someone who can extract them both using the Albatross, when the time is right."

"I'll do it alone." JJ stood. "It's safer that way."

"No." Federico shook his head. "It's too dangerous."

"Why does danger matter for me, and not someone else?" JJ asked. "I want to do this. For the Qaunik." He turned his head. "And Sharon, and Eve."

Federico opened his mouth to protest.

"You know our ethic," Woody cut him off. Her expression was worried and sad. "The honor of risking one's life for another person is sacred. The only way we could prevent JJ from this act of heroism is if we believed he wasn't capable."

"Are you willing to say I'm not capable?" JJ asked.

"No." Federico swallowed. "You're more than capable."

"Don't worry," JJ said. "I'll get away. Like I always do."

"Yes, you will. Because you'd better." Woody kissed his cheek. "Because we prefer the world with you in it."

JJ put a hand to where Woody's lips had touched his face. "I won't let you down."

Woody exhaled deeply, resigned to the plan. "Never in a million years could you let me down. No matter what happens." She looked at Sharon. "You and Federico are going with me to South Carolina. When the Strelitzia rears his head to take the rare earths, we'll be waiting."

"And what's my job?" Dale asked. "Because I'm all in, too."

"You're going to command Belosto-One in my absence. I want you to gather all of our people, including those left in Chicago. Get them and all of our equipment aboard Belosto-One. Stay invisible and head to the Puerto Rico Trench. Hover in the mesosphere above the Milwaukee Deep. Once we get the Bird of Paradise, I'll bring her to the surface. That's where we'll meet to bring everyone on board." Woody pressed STELA's Earth icon.

A satellite image of the planet from the Arctic to Antarctica popped up. Woody pointed at a stretch of broken pieces of jagged white. "This is what's left of the Thwaites. It collapsed eighteen hours ago. With Pine Island Glacier already gone, there's nothing left to hold the West Antarctic Ice Sheet. According to the transponders placed in the ice during the last century, the sheet slid three meters in the last seven hours."

"What happens after that?" Sharon asked.

"When the sheet finally goes, the Extinction Wave will swallow Earth's coastlines. Horrific storms will rage. The climate will change in ways our worst nightmares can't conceive." Woody leaned over the control desk. "Humanity will face its greatest test."

"We're almost out of time, then," Federico whispered.

Chapter 17

"Woody, Woody, Woody." JJ's voice crackled, barely audible above roaring wind and banging.

"Finally!" Woody pressed the audio-comm. "Woody here. We were starting to worry. I've got you on speaker. I'm here with Federico and Sharon. Are you in the storm shelter?"

"Safe and sound!" JJ answered.

"When the storm subsides, get moving. They'll be coming for you. Keep running until you hear from Dale." Woody studied the satellite image on the OVA showing the pinwheeled mass of clouds swirling along the length of North America from North Carolina up to Nova Scotia. "The hurricane has started to make its turn toward the east, out to sea. Looks like it'll batter the coast for a few more hours until it moves off shore. In the meantime, we'll slip south of it and take back the Bird of Paradise. Don't get risky."

"That's right." Federico rubbed his goatee. "Get out of there if the chase gets too hot."

"I'll be the cat that can't be caught! Count on seeing me soon!" JJ's voice crackled. "I signed up for Annie's reading class! And now that I've discovered Sharon's tomatoes, I want to live at least a few more decades."

Sharon leaned toward the audio-comm. "Come back, and I'll grow all you can eat."

"I'm in!" JJ replied. "Better sign off before my batteries die! With this storm, I don't know when . . ." The audio-comm crackled and hissed with static.

"JJ?" Woody said. "Do you hear me?"

Several seconds of crackling white noise passed.

"Storm must've knocked out the signal." Federico rapped his knuckles on the desk. "That's all. Right?"

"He'll be okay." Woody touched his arm. "Once the eye reaches New Jersey, we'll drop down in Water Skipper One to north of what used to be Charleston before Lolly."

"Lolly?" Sharon asked.

"The category-five hurricane that wiped the city off the map in 2071," Federico explained. "All that's left is a swamp."

Woody tapped in commands. An image of a strange, bug-like shuttle with long legs popped onto the OVA's split screen. "Which is why we'll land Water Skipper One on Lake Moultrie where it spills into the Cooper River."

"It's not much of a river anymore. Just a floating mass of watery vegetation." Federico aimed his chin at the image of a large swath the color of jade, bisected by a thin meandering paler line. "The lake is too polluted to drink from. The only souls tough enough to live down there are a few Yěxìng, and lots of alligators, snakes, and mosquitoes."

"And Water Skipper One will be our escort?" Sharon asked.

"Yes," Woody answered. "She's capable of skimming and diving. She'll bring us over the lake and down the river to the containers of rare earths near the harbor. That's where we'll wait for the Strelitzia to rear his head."

Federico pressed the audio-comm button. "Dale, we're prepared to load and launch Water Skipper One. Is she ready?"

"Affirmative," Dale answered. "Once you've launched, I'll bring Belosto-One to hover in the mesosphere over the Milwaukee Deep. If I don't hear from you in twenty-four hours, what should I do?"

"Try to reach JJ, and then do whatever you think is best to save

223

the Qaunik." Woody gave Federico's hand a swift squeeze. "JJ will be okay."

"I pray it's so." Federico turned his hand over and interlaced his fingers with Woody's. "Let's go find home."

"We'll fly like the snow," Woody said.

"Exquisite as one. Inexorable together," Dale finished the Qaunik refrain.

"Dale," Sharon said. "One last thing. Please ask Inu to take good care of Annie and Erik." She pushed back the desire to have Dale tell him she'd be back. But it wouldn't be fair for her to say it, and not be able to keep her word, especially after leaving him in Gaia's Wrath.

"You got it," Dale responded.

"Prepare Water Skipper One for launch. We're on our way." Woody let go of Federico's hand and slipped through the shuttle launch port. Sharon and Federico followed.

Inside the shuttle bay, insect- and bird-like vehicles sat cabled to the floor in rows. Several Qaunik bustled in and out of a shuttle with a long, narrow fuselage the size of a hydro-lorry.

"Water Skipper One?" Sharon asked.

"Yes." Woody motioned for Sharon to follow. "Let me explain how she works."

"I'll do the preflight check." Federico waved and climbed inside Water Skipper One's open hatch.

"The shuttle, much like a submarine, has ballast and trim tanks." Woody pointed to the underbelly of Water Skipper One. "This allows us to adjust her weight so that she's able to walk on water or swampy vegetation."

"That'll come in handy," Sharon said. "The place sounds charming."

"Exactly." Woody pointed to the wings tucked at the shuttle's back. "She's not a great flyer. But the shorter wings allow us to get through rough winds, if necessary, without destroying them." She walked to the other side of the shuttle. "There are six legs. Two shorter ones in the front. A long pair in the middle, and another pair at the aft section of the fuselage." She touched a bent leg. "The long legs bend and tuck beneath her when she's at rest. The two antennae in front are equipped with cameras."

"And those?" Sharon pointed at a menacing steel claw halfway down the right front leg.

"There's one on the other side as well. In nature, a water skipper insect uses the claws to crush prey. Water Skipper One uses them to crush enemies."

"She's one of the most genius and ugly things I've ever seen." Sharon smiled.

Woody laughed. "Ah, beauty is in the eye of the beholder."

Federico popped his head out the open hatch. "We're ready to fly."

"After you." Woody ushered Sharon aboard.

The petite cockpit contained four seats, a command console, a STELA and an OVA. Sharon stowed the backpack containing the box of seeds that Elliot had retrieved, then sat and secured her torso-restraint.

Woody sketched on STELA, and spoke into the audio-comm. "Equalize pressure."

"Pressure equalizing," a woman's voice responded. "Stand by. Pressure equalized."

"Open the Belosto-One launch hatch."

"Hatch opening."

As the hatch opened, the OVA powered up, revealing a view in front of Water Skipper One and its selfie. Her wings lifted as the under-fuselage thrusters lifted her up and forward. The shuttle eased through Belosto-One's hatch into the mesosphere. White clouds swirled below the sapphire sky.

"The flight might get bumpy as we drop through the clouds." Woody tapped out commands. "The outer bands of the hurricane are north of us, but there's still likely to be heavy wind shear. Put her into a dive. Level out once we get below the clouds."

Federico pressed the "D" icon. "Diving now."

Water Skipper One's selfie camera relayed the ship's movements onto the OVA. The antennae on the shuttle swiveled below the nose as it rotated downward.

Sharon's body thrust forward against the torso-restraint before being shoved backward by g-force. Her hands gripped the torso-restraint as the shuttle shook hard.

"Leaving the stratosphere and entering troposphere," Federico said.

Water Skipper One dived into the clouds, vibrating and jerking for several long minutes. Rain pelted the capsule as the craft dipped below the cottony ceiling into a lush green landscape.

"Leveling off." Woody tapped buttons on STELA. "Prepare to land."

Whitecaps rushed up to meet them. Sharon braced herself.

Water Skipper One splashed down onto Lake Moultrie, sank, then popped to the surface and bobbed.

"Extending legs." Woody sketched and tapped commands.

Water Skipper One drifted in the heavy winds until her six legs extended from her fuselage. Whitecaps submerged the extended legs, tugging her farther below the surface.

"We've got to get to the still water." Woody continued to draw commands.

The legs resurfaced and engaged, whisking the shuttle south according to STELA's compass. A wave sloshed over Water Skipper One, shoving it hard to port.

"Increasing speed." Federico traced out commands. "It's still a little gusty from the hurricane's tailwinds. Things will settle down once we get onto the river."

The shuttle righted itself and walked on the murky water that lolled into the remnants of a concrete chute. A lime-green carpet of vegetation lay on the surface.

"What is this?" Sharon asked.

"It's the old Tailrace Canal. It blew out during Lolly." Woody swiped through satellite images on the OVA. "It used to link the lake to Cooper River. Now this whole area is a swamp bigger than the Everglades used to be. The plant that the shuttle is maneuvering over is called duckweed."

"And those trees?" Sharon tried to identify them through the fuzzy green plant that drooped from their branches. "They look like soldiers forming a saber arch for the river to meander through."

"Nice analogy. Cypress and tupelo," Federico answered. "The stuff hanging off is Spanish moss."

"We've got company." Woody cocked her head to port side.

Sharon looked, but all she could make out was a large log parallel to shore. Then the log rose on four stubby legs and slid into the water, its long snout aimed at them. An enormous tail splashed water and propelled the beast closer. "Holy cow, that thing must be almost six meters."

"The American alligator. A massive specimen." Woody tapped a command. Water Skipper One's portside claw opened. "I don't want to hurt you, big guy. You leave my shuttle alone, and I'll leave you alone."

The back of the alligator carved a path through duckweed before diving below the surface.

Federico turned toward starboard. "Guess we didn't look tasty enough to bite." He nodded his head. "There it goes."

With a splash and a mighty thrust of its tail, the gator reached the opposite shore. It lumbered up the fern-covered bank and disappeared into the weeds.

Woody pressed an icon that brought up a topographic map with a blinking white dot. "That's us. The mouth of Charleston Harbor is up ahead. We'll land here and take this high ground the rest of the way." Her finger went to a series of tight lines on the map.

"The same high road the alligator just took?" Federico asked.

"Unfortunately, yes," Woody answered. She sketched an anchor.

Sharon felt the vibration of the anchor unhitching and dropping from the shuttle's belly. She released her torso-restraint and unstrapped the backpack.

Woody pressed the audio-comm button. "Dale, Dale, Dale, Woody here. Do you read?"

"Dale here." A voice came from the audio-comm. "Good to hear from you. How are things going down there?"

"All is good so far," Woody answered. "We're disembarking here. You have our GPS coordinates?"

"Yes," said Dale. "You're blinking white."

"Good. Send a team down to retrieve Water Skipper One. Make sure they stay invisible. We're going the rest of the way on foot. Any word from JJ?"

"Not yet," Dale answered.

"Okay." Woody released her torso-restraint. "The next time we talk it'll be to rendezvous with the Bird of Paradise."

"I sure hope so. Over," Dale's voice cut out.

Federico released his torso-restraint. "*Vamonos.*"

Sharon got up and heaved the pack onto her shoulders. She unbuttoned her jacket, making her hammer, at her side, accessible.

Woody opened a locker. "We'll need the essentials for swamp travel. First, swamp-gaiters. They attach to the top of your boot and up your leg to the knee. Keeps you dry and avoids snake bites." She lifted a pair of tightly woven nylon gloves and a hat with a scarcely visible veil from the locker. "Mosquito netting is a must. The bugs down here carry all kinds of nasty diseases, including malaria." She handed the accoutrements to Sharon. "While I'm guessing you and your hammer could keep most alligators and pythons at bay, let's take extra precaution. We'll each carry a handheld spectraletto." She tipped her head to a row of machetes. "Can't move through a swamp without one of those too."

"If you get into a bind, you can always fall back on the jujitsu JJ taught you." Federico pulled on a pair of swamp-gaiters. "Have I mentioned how much I loathe snakes?"

Woody tightened her swamp-gaiters. "Ah, the underappreciated reptile." She slipped the hat with head-net on over her hijab. "Stick with me. I'll keep you safe."

"You haven't let me down yet." Federico snapped his left swamp-gaiter closed.

Sharon suited up in the offered gear. "I'm more afraid of Yěxíng and their damn prey pits." She pulled the spectraletto holster over her head, adjusted it so that the weapon was in easy reach at her chest, and checked the energy gauge. "Gun's in the green."

"Good." Woody secured a holster at her chest and checked the weapon. "Ready?" She tapped a command on the STELA. Water Skipper One's hatch opened. "It's just a short jump to shore." She grabbed a machete and hopped out.

Sharon and Federico followed her into the juicy, pungent air that swathed them in humidity.

A sweet and lush scent filled Sharon's nose. She couldn't tell whether the moisture on her face came from the heavy, wet air or perspiration. A whirring sound came from behind. She slipped on the slimy bank as she turned to see Water Skipper One's hatch closing them off to the outside. As she planted her palms on the ground to lift herself, a fat mosquito landed on her gloved hand. "Geeze." On instinct, she swatted it.

Federico offered a hand up. "I know, these bastards will take half a liter if you let them." He hoisted her to her feet. "But they can't bite through the gloves."

She brushed mud from her jacket. "That's fortunate. With the size of that thing, I'd probably need a transfusion."

Federico laughed. "Indeed."

With Woody in the lead, they traversed through fern, burweed, and skunk cabbage.

"Careful where you step." Woody scrutinized the ground. "You can't miss the big snakes. But the little ones will take you down." Using the tip of her machete, she pushed the vegetation aside before taking each step.

A rare and lovely sound caught Sharon's attention. "Is that?" She cupped her ear and listened. "Ha! Birds."

Woody and Federico stopped.

"Whitt-whitt-whitt-whitt," the bird called in quick doublets. "Chee-beck."

"There it is." Federico pointed to a branch drooping with Spanish moss. A small olive-colored bird with a yellowish belly perched on the moss.

"A least flycatcher," Woody said.

"I didn't think any birds were left, besides the few that eat carrion." Sharon savored the sight and sound of the tiny feathered wonder.

"There aren't many." Woody pulled an acupalmtell from her pocket and took a picture of the bird. "But in places like this, the smaller insect-eating ones that managed to survive are holding their own. They have plenty of food and water, and they can breed. It's the toxins in what they eat, drink, and breathe that prevent them from thriving, though."

Federico's eyes widened. "Sharon. Very slowly, look to your right. Don't freak out."

She gripped the machete tighter and rotated at the waist. An enormous, thick snake lay curled at the base of a tree within striking distance. Its eyes and mouth were trained on her thigh. "I'm freaking out," she said under her breath. The snake was so close she could smell its foul musk.

"Remember, the swamp-gaiters will protect you from its teeth." Woody's voice was low and calm. "But if it gets hold of you, it'll wrap around you, and cut off the blood to your heart in seconds."

The snake's tongue darted from its mouth.

Frozen, Sharon asked, "Ideas?"

"I hope you're good with that machete," Woody answered. "Because it's a much better option than the spectraletto. You won't get a second chance if you miss. Back away slowly. If it strikes, be ready to take its head off. Just like you did to the mamba in the prey pit."

A drop of sweat slid between Sharon's shoulder blades. Her heart pounded as she held her breath. Out of the corner of her eye, she saw Woody and Federico close in on the snake. She waited until they got close enough to be of some help. Her foot lifted slightly, and the snake lunged. Swinging backhanded, her machete dug into its underside, pushing it away. She leaped to its left.

The snake recoiled.

Woody swung her machete, severing its head.

The body writhed as it bled out.

Sharon shot to her feet. "Fuck." She yanked her machete from the still-thrashing body.

"You okay?" Federico brushed leaves and dirt from her sleeve.

"If I don't drop dead of a heart attack in the next few minutes." Sharon tried to catch her breath. "Thanks, guys."

"No worries," Woody said. "Let's keep a better lookout. Their stealth is their greatest weapon."

Federico shivered. "God, I hate those things."

"We've all got our phobias and weaknesses." Woody wiped the bloody blade of her machete across a mossy tree trunk. "We do our best not to let them get the better of us."

Sharon looked behind, left, right, and forward. "Good eye, Federico. Thanks."

They continued on their way.

The only sounds Sharon heard were her breathing, the flycatchers' singing, and the swish of her gaiters. Her eyes darted around for sneaky predators.

After about ten minutes, Woody halted. "Stay low. The harbor is up ahead." She got to her hands and knees and crawled up a fern-covered hill.

Sharon sank to her belly and crept through the vegetation with Woody and Federico.

At the crest of the rise, Woody peered through the curtain of brush. "There are the containers of rare earths." She pointed at several large boxcars lined along the sandy shore. "You see anyone?"

Federico lifted a pair of OALI to his eyes and scanned the harbor. "Nope." He moved his head. "Wait." He passed the OALI to Woody. "Looks like a black sea devil headed our way. Just one."

Woody looked through the OALI. "Yeah, I see it. Probably a scout making sure all is clear before sending the loading shuttles." She handed the glasses to Sharon. "Have a look. The black sea devil antennae are above the surface by about five meters."

"What kind of vessel is it?" Sharon put the glasses to her eyes.

Four hundred meters from shore, a black rod protruded from the water, making its way toward them at a fast clip. She lowered the glasses.

Federico took the OALI from her and held them to his eyes. "The black sea devil is the Bird of Paradise's deep-sea shuttle. It's modeled after a fish called the humpback anglerfish."

"Better known as the black sea devil," Woody added. "When the Bird of Paradise is deep under water, the shuttle can be launched without being crushed by the pressure. She's essentially a mini-submarine."

"A submarine ready to surface." Federico folded the OALI and tucked it into his breast pocket. "Look."

A bulbous black hull broke the surface and propelled toward land. Its protruding antennae rotated back and forth. Stopping at shore near the containers, its hatch yawned wide like a giant mouth. Four armed soldiers exited and fanned out toward the containers.

"The black sea devil holds more than four people," Woody whispered. "We can count on at least one staying with the shuttle. We'll have to take these four out with as little noise as possible."

Federico lifted his machete. "We'll use these and our hands. Remember your jujitsu. The gun is strictly a backup."

Sharon pulled her hammer from its baldric with her right hand. Her left gripped the machete. The spectraletto sat snug in the holster at her chest.

"Let's spread out between the containers." Woody got to her feet and crouched. "I'll go left, Federico take the center, and Sharon you're on the right. On the count of three."

Federico nodded.

"One," Woody said. "Two, three. *Go.*"

Staying low, Sharon raced toward the containers at her right. A soldier halted and looked in her direction.

She threw herself onto her belly and held her breath.

He started toward her, searching.

Be like the snake.

His footsteps slowed as he neared. Each footfall in the thick vegetation heightened Sharon's heart rate.

Her hands were hot and wet inside the mosquito gloves. She squeezed her hammer and exhaled as she exploded upward.

Throwing his arm in front of his face, the soldier deflected the hammer and lunged.

His large body slammed onto hers. She stumbled onto her back. The head-net tipped to the side, obstructing her vision. The soldier pinned her beneath him. His breath was hot and rancid.

He yanked the spectraletto from her holster and tossed it aside. Then tugged away her head-net. "What do we have here?"

The unobstructed air cooled her face. She grunted and made a futile attempt to fill her lungs. But the soldier's heft compressed her chest. The hard box inside the pack on her back dug into her spine.

Straddling her, he squeezed her wrists. "Drop them."

She gritted her teeth and held tight to her hammer in one hand, the machete in the other. *Think.* Taking stock of his weapons, a holstered knife on his belt caught her eye. It was in reach if she could free her hands. But she'd have to aim for a spot on his body not covered in Kevlar. "Fuck you."

His thumbs dug into her pressure points. "Drop them!"

She growled and her hands popped open.

"Good girl," he snarled. Pressing his pelvis into her, he put his face close to hers. "Good, good girl."

She snapped her forehead into his long, fat nose, feeling a satisfying crunch of fracturing cartilage. Blood splattered her face.

"Fucking bitch!" Wide-eyed, he grabbed his nose.

She swiped his knife and sank it deep into his vulnerable right shoulder.

He rolled off of her and scrambled to his knees. Slobber and blood smeared his face.

As he reached for his spectraletto, Sharon slammed her right boot between his legs.

He howled and doubled over, grabbing his crotch. Blood poured from his nose.

She got to her feet and aimed a punch at his neck. But before she could make contact, he landed a counterpunch hard to her stomach. She gasped and crumpled to her knees.

He yanked the knife out of his shoulder and wobbled to his feet. A sinister, bloody smile spread across his face as he stood over her. "I'm going to get a fucking hard-on when I kill you. The kick to the nuts will be worth it, bitch."

On a half-full lung of air, Sharon scooted on her elbows into the thick brush. It occurred to her that what lurked in the tall, green, musty weeds was more dangerous than the soldier. She scanned the thick vegetation that concealed her for creepy-crawly things.

"Where are you?" He stomped after her.

Shots rang out. The sound came from the opposite direction of the harassing soldier.

Scanning for a better place to hide, she spotted, at the edge of a pool of black water, a gator. Heavy lids blinked over bulbous eyes with slits staring back at her. *Fuck.* The alligator watched from three meters away. It rose on stubby legs and slowly tracked toward her. While she watched the oncoming gator, something grabbed her ankle and yanked hard.

"There you are." The soldier grinned.

With the soldier holding her left ankle against his waist, Sharon felt a moment of déjà vu. JJ's last jujitsu lesson replayed in her head. She lifted her other foot to his waist and pushed against him.

He laughed and pushed back, bending her knees.

Perfect. She jerked her right knee toward her shoulders, causing him to stumble forward. Reversing the momentum of her leg, she rammed the bottom of her boot into the middle of his face. Bone crunched.

His eyelids fluttered and he collapsed, out cold.

Sharon glanced over her shoulder at the oncoming alligator.

More spectraletto shots cut the air, but they disappeared harmlessly into the forest canopy.

She scrambled around the soldier's limp body and dragged his bloodied torso to point in the direction of the advancing reptile. She inhaled a deep breath to calm her nerves. "Come get lunch, you ugly beast. I'm sure you're plenty hungry."

The alligator snapped forward and Sharon scooted back. It sank its teeth into the soldier's shoulder that had already been laid open by the knife. It shook him side to side. The strength of the beast made the big man look like a rag doll.

Pain awakened him. Horror spread across his face and he screamed. He pissed himself.

So much for a silent operation.

The soldier flailed against the beast as it twisted its head back and forth. A crunching, ripping sound preceded his arm being torn from the socket. The gator let go of the detached limb and clamped sharp teeth into its prey's torso, eviscerating and silencing the soldier.

Sharon turned her eyes from the gore. She listened as the alligator dragged the corpse through brush toward the black pool. She lifted Eve's scarf to cover her nose to block out the heavy metallic scent of blood and urine.

Sharon heard Federico yell, "Woody! Watch out." She got to her feet and saw Woody and Federico standing over the bodies of two soldiers near one of the containers about thirty meters downhill from her. They had no cover from another soldier who was standing between them and his vessel on shore, aiming at them. Sharon searched frantically in the weeds for her spectraletto.

At last she spotted her weapon.

Federico put his hands up and side-stepped closer to Woody.

Carefully, Sharon aimed at the side of the soldier's head, which momentarily was still as he assessed the situation with Federico and Woody. She fired.

The soldier was dead before he hit the ground.

Woody turned and mouthed, *thank you.*

Sharon waved an acknowledgment, then located her hammer in the brush. The machete lay nearby. She holstered the spectraletto, picked up her weapons and crouch-walked quickly down the hill, scanning for any other soldiers.

"Stop!" A man yelled.

A laser shot zipped an inch from Sharon's nose. She halted.

"All three of you." A soldier wearing sergeant's insignia covered them with his spectraletto. "Stand right there. Don't move. Let me see your hands."

Sharon recognized him instantly. The sergeant from Boston with black hair, white skin, and a large birthmark on his left cheek, the man who took her wife. Thanks to his badge, now she knew his name too. Sergeant Limmy. Inside, Sharon shook with rage. Outwardly, she kept cool. She lowered her eyes and her weapons, and prayed he hadn't recognized her too.

A blunt force hit her in the back. She stumbled forward and spun around.

A sixth soldier aimed a spectraletto at her chest. His name tag bore the name Rucker. "Drop your weapons."

She opened her hands, letting the hammer and machete fall to the ground.

Rucker yanked the spectraletto from the holster on her chest. "Turn around and go stand next to your friends." He picked up her hammer and the machete.

With the spectraletto barrel at her back, she inched to where Woody and Federico stood. She kept her eyes down, avoiding the sergeant's.

"Any of you three see Maximilian?" Rucker asked. He held a hand above his head. "Real big guy."

Sharon, Federico, and Woody kept silent.

Rucker pointed his weapon at Woody's head. "Somebody better fucking answer my question."

"He's dead," Sharon snapped, and swallowed back the knot of panic in her throat that the soldier might shoot Woody. "An alligator got him."

Sergeant Limmy's mouth twitched and he looked away. "Get them loaded onto the black sea devil."

"What about Maximilian?" Rucker lifted his arm toward the hill. "We can't just leave him up there."

"He's gone. Like these two." Sergeant Limmy glanced at the two bodies lying at their feet. "The gators can have them too. At least their deaths won't be in vain." He placed the machetes and spectralettos that Woody and Federico had carried into a bag. "There's nothing we can do for them." He held out the bag. "Put the other weapons in this and let's go."

"That's fucked up," Rucker protested.

"I gave you an order." Sergeant Limmy looked from the soldier to Sharon and back. "I don't have time for emotion. We have a job to do. Now, move your ass."

Rucker swiveled the spectraletto held by a strap to his back. He yanked Sharon by her jacket collar and slammed her against the container of rare earths.

Sharon bounced off and fell to her knees.

"This will not end well for you." Rucker kicked her in the stomach.

Sharon grunted at the pain.

"Is that really necessary?" Woody put an arm under Sharon's. "It's okay. Let's get you up." She smoothed Sharon's head.

Federico helped Woody lift her. "We got you, *amiga*."

Rucker reached for Sharon again.

"Stop!" Sergeant Limmy pointed his weapon at Rucker's chest. "If you touch that woman one more time, she'll be the last woman you touch. Get the weapons loaded and these prisoners on the shuttle." To Woody, Sharon and Federico, he said, "Hold your hands together." He reached into his shirt pocket and retrieved barbed wrist-ties. "Help me put these on them."

Rucker took one and yanked the pack from Sharon's back. He smiled and cinched her wrists together.

She winced as the barbs dug in.

"I'm hoping the Strelitzia won't go quite as easy on you as

237

Sergeant Limmy." He held up her backpack. "Wonder what kind of loot is in here."

"Give me the pack." Sergeant Limmy held out a gloved hand. "Everything in that backpack belongs to the Strelitzia."

Sharon's hope evaporated. *But I'll find a way, Eve.*

Chapter 18

"This is Black Sea Devil Twelve reporting." Sergeant Limmy sat rigid in the command seat. Through the cockpit-observation mirror, he eyed Woody, Sharon, and Federico, shackled by their feet to the bench seat behind him.

Rucker sat next to him in the tight space, swiping commands onto the STELA. As he pecked at the controls, his right arm occasionally brushed the locked handle on the small, round door labeled EMERGENCY EXIT STARBOARD.

Sharon glowered. If she could free her hands, maybe she could reach one of their spectralettos. She waited for the sergeant to look away before twisting her wrists experimentally. The barbs on the ties carved at her skin. She noticed blood on Woody's and Federico's wrists as well. *No way.*

"The Strelitzia here." His electronically manipulated voice oozed through the audio-comm. "What is your report?"

"We were met by intruders." Sergeant Limmy spoke in flat precision. "A fight ensued. Four men are dead. Rucker and I survived."

"And what of the intruders?" the Strelitzia asked.

"We found three. We captured them and ensured that the containers are secure." The sergeant rubbed at a bloodstain on his uniform. "The intruders are aboard Black Sea Devil Twelve."

"Good work. Your three prisoners, let me guess." The electronic voice bore a sinister gleefulness. "A tall, angry woman with a buzz cut. A short, pudgy one in a hijab. And a lanky Argentinian guy."

"That sums them up," Rucker interrupted. "We also took their weapons and a backpack."

"Is it secure?" The Strelitzia bit back.

"Roger that," Rucker answered.

"Keep it that way. I'll take off the hands of any person who opens that pack before I do. Am I understood?" the Strelitzia asked.

"I'll see to it." Sergeant Limmy fired Rucker an icy look. "The pack and weapons are secured in the shuttle's lockbox. I have the code."

"You're by the book, Sergeant Limmy," the Strelitzia said. "I like that. No drama, just the rules. Your orders are to proceed directly to the Bird of Paradise. We'll surface in thirty minutes. At that time, I'll order that an army of black sea devils escort the container-carriers to retrieve the rare earths. Inform me immediately upon your arrival."

"Yes, sir." Sergeant Limmy glanced up at the cockpit-observation mirror.

"Do tell our guests that I look forward to their company." The Strelitzia sighed. "Over."

Sergeant Limmy sketched a command. "Proceeding now. Over and out." He powered down the audio-comm.

Rucker twisted in his seat. "You're that farmer." He grinned. "The one with the apples. Damn. Catching you will get us a promotion. That's extra food for me and my family."

For the first time since being caught, Sharon noticed the resemblance between Rucker and the man she offered to the monster gator. Same ruddy skin, big nose, round face and wide-set brown eyes. "I'm not a farmer anymore." She stared past him.

"Watching the Strelitzia cut you in half will be revenge for you killing my brother and the other three soldiers."

Ah, that's it, brothers.

"Shut up," Sergeant Limmy ordered. "Pull yourself together."

"An eye for an eye." Rucker faced forward. "Maybe he'll let me be the one to do it."

"Are you Wilhelmina Woodhouse?" Sergeant Limmy asked.

"I am."

"Well, Dr. Woodhouse." The sergeant sketched something indecipherable on the STELA. "I've been hoping to get the chance to meet you." He pressed a finger to the sketch.

Fluid, haunting music of stringed instruments filled the cockpit.

Sharon felt Federico's body tense. She glanced left at him. His expression remained stone cold. She looked right to Woody. *Was that a hint of smile?*

"What the fuck is that?" Rucker stared at Sergeant Limmy as if he had eight heads.

The sergeant lifted his eyes to the mirror and almost imperceptibly nodded.

"One of my favorites," Federico said. "It's the 'Méditation' from the *Thaïs* by Jules Massenet."

"It's on the playlist I made for the day we christened the Bird of Paradise." Woody nudged Sharon with her elbow.

"Hey." Rucker got up. "What the fuck is going on?"

Sharon wondered the same.

"Sit down, Rucker," Sergeant Limmy ordered. "Don't provoke me."

"I'll sit, once you turn this bullshit music off." He put his hands to his hips. Swirling tattoos decorated his forearms. "We're not even supposed to be listening to this crap. Are you out of your mind?"

Sergeant Limmy released his torso-restraint and exploded out of his seat. He slammed his fist into Rucker's abdomen.

Rucker grunted, but pounced in response, shoving the sergeant onto the STELA.

The shuttle lurched and rolled. The port windows dipped below the foaming waterline.

"I built this shuttle!" Woody yelled. "If you fools don't ensure the ballast and trim are maintained, you'll sink us."

241

Sergeant Limmy pushed Rucker off. He ran a hand through his messed hair, sat, and sketched commands.

The shuttle righted and surged forward.

"You've been acting fucking weird ever since your wife died." Rucker flopped into his seat. "You got to get over that shit, man. Don't think the Colonel isn't going to hear about this. Maybe you need a little time in the brig to cool your jets."

"How?" Sergeant Limmy asked. "How do we keep hurting people?"

Sharon closed her eyes and bit her lip. She exhaled and focused on the back of Limmy's head. How dare he ask such a question when he was the one who had taken Eve from her.

"How?" Rucker mocked. "What a stupid fucking question."

Sergeant Limmy scowled at Rucker. "If it's so stupid, why don't you answer for me?"

"To eat. To drink." Rucker jabbed his finger at the window. "To survive the fucking world out there." He pivoted and scowled at Sharon. "To get revenge on those who take the ones we love."

Sergeant Limmy pulled his spectraletto from its holster and put it to Rucker's head. "You have no idea how long I've been waiting to do this." Rucker looked at him incredulously.

Limmy pulled the trigger.

"Pft!"

Rucker slumped forward onto the STELA. A singed hole in his temple oozed gore.

Sharon recoiled in shock, the same as Woody and Federico.

"Yeah, well, I'm done doing just surviving." Sergeant Limmy holstered his weapon, stood, and yanked Rucker's body to the floor. "I owe that much to my dead wife." He turned to Sharon. "And to you for taking yours. I know you know who I am. I saw it in your eyes back on shore." The sergeant grabbed Rucker's ankles and dragged his body to the rear of the cockpit. Stumbling back around to Sharon, he cut her wrist-ties as sweat streaked his temples.

She grabbed her bloodied wrists and tried to rub circulation back into them.

The sergeant cut the ties off Woody and Federico, fished in his pocket for the keys to their shackles, and tossed them to Woody.

"How did you know about that song?" Woody unlocked the shackles at her feet and handed the keys to Sharon.

"I know that you programmed opera into all of the vessels and aircraft you built. The Strelitzia hates opera. That song in particular. He said it reminds him of you. I saw him behead a person just for listening to it. I hoped if I played it, you might guess that I want to help."

"Why would you help us?" Sharon unlocked her shackles and handed the keys to Federico. "You're the man who took my wife."

"And I was cursed for it." He sighed. "The day I took your wife, my wife died from an infection." He unholstered his spectraletto and handed it to Sharon. "Karma, as they say, had the last word. I got the message loud and clear."

She yanked the weapon away and pointed it at him. "Why should we believe you? You could've let us go free on the beach. Instead, you captured us and told the Strelitzia we're on the way. That doesn't seem like help to me."

"You can go ahead and kill me. Without my wife, I'm already dead. Just let me explain myself first." Sergeant Limmy moistened his lips. "I did the things I did because I wanted food and water for Lauren, my wife. I wanted to keep her safe. But while I was out hurting other people for the sake of feeding us, I lost the only person that matters to me. Maybe if you kill me, we'll both feel better. But if you let me live, I can get you onto that ship undetected. The Strelitzia's guard is down now that he thinks he has you under his control. That's why I didn't release you on the beach."

The memory of the soldiers dragging Eve from her replayed in Sharon's mind. She kept the barrel pointed at his chest. How could she trust the man who took Eve in the first place? He put all of this awfulness into motion.

"What are you going to do, Sharon?" Woody asked.

Her insides shook with chaotic feelings. She moved her finger off the trigger. "What do I do?"

243

"Whatever makes you more whole." Woody touched Sharon's forearm.

Instinct in her gut waged war against her heart. All those years of holding the anger and hurt caused by Elliot had made an ugly, festering hole in her spirit. It smoothed over in the instant she'd forgiven him. "You took my Eve. How can I forgive that? And why can't I picture her face?" Her outstretched hand gripping the weapon trembled. "Why can't I see Eve in my mind?"

"Because the people we love"—Federico put his hands to his heart—"are here. That's where you'll find your answer."

"I'll make you suffer if this is a double-cross." Sharon exhaled and lowered the weapon. "We need your help. Eve needs your help." She handed the spectraletto, butt end first, to Woody.

"Thank you," Limmy said, "for the chance at redemption I've been waiting for."

Woody got up and took the command seat. "Federico, I'm bleeding all over the controls here. Please get the medical kit to bandage our wounds. You remember where it's stored?"

"*Sí.*" He headed aft.

"Sergeant Limmy," Woody said.

"Please, call me Limmy. I'm no longer in the Strelitzia's army."

"Very well." She gestured to the first officer's seat at her right. Eagerly, Limmy joined her. "I'm here to help."

"How big is the Strelitzia's army?"

"Not large. Maybe one hundred."

"And civilians?"

"Triple that." Limmy swiped the screen, bringing up a schematic of the Bird of Paradise on the OVA. "As you know, the ship's control center can be cut off from the rest of the ship."

"Yes." Woody pointed at a location in the belly of the fuselage. "The control center was my version of a panic room."

Federico sat at Woody's left and unlatched the medical kit. "A room where no one gets in or out."

"The Strelitzia is seriously claustrophobic, though." Limmy tapped the STELA. "He only goes there when he senses some dire threat."

"So who operates the ship?" Federico dabbed gauze at the cuts on his wrists, then tended to Woody's.

"His five most trusted soldiers." Limmy aimed a finger at an aft section on the fourth deck. "This is the Strelitzia's quarters. Near the black sea devil launch bay."

"Here, Sharon." Federico offered her a bandage roll.

"Thanks. And where is holding cell 6B?" Sharon asked. "That's where Woody said Eve is."

"No." Limmy shook his head. "Not anymore. The Strelitzia moved her."

Federico passed the kit to his left.

"Where is she, then?" Woody took the kit and set it aside.

"He's keeping her under tight security in his personal quarters. He says she's one of his most valuable acquisitions. His plan"— he turned to Sharon—"was to kill you at the Bay of Fundy and take whatever it was you were to exchange for your wife."

"What a surprise that would have been," Sharon commented drily.

"Now he knows we're onto him." Woody studied the schematic. "Our best bet is to take control of the ship. Then go after him. Should be straightforward given that the Qaunik far outnumber his soldiers."

"What about Eve?" Sharon asked.

"If we control the ship and what's in your backpack, we've got the edge. The new exchange becomes his life for Eve's." Woody helped Federico finish his bandaging job by tearing a strip of gauze with her teeth. "Just tie that off. Any ideas for how to get past his trusted five?"

Limmy pointed at a hallway on the schematic. "When we arrive, my guess is that he'll want three of the five to escort you to him, while the other two operate the control room. We'll need some kind of diversion to move the other soldiers from their guard positions."

"How about Belosto-One?" Federico asked. "What better diversion than a family of one thousand and twenty-nine committed souls threatening to storm the ship?" He looked to Limmy. "You said that there are only a hundred soldiers."

"And three hundred civilians," Sharon added. "Won't they help fight to keep the ship?"

"Some, yes," Limmy answered. "But there are many, like your wife, who aren't there by choice. They happened to have some skill or knowledge that suited the Strelitzia. So he took them. They're captives; they have no allegiance to him. Only fear."

Woody tucked the gauze into the kit's biohazard bag. "It's a good idea. We just have to time things right. I don't want to put the Qaunik into unnecessary jeopardy. Hopefully, we can convince the civilians taken by the Strelitzia to help us."

Limmy pressed the clock icon. "The Bird of Paradise is surfacing now. By the time we get there, she'll be above water."

"What about using the Bird of Paradise's emergency entrance hatch for black sea devils?" Federico asked. "Maybe we can get aboard undetected."

"No." Limmy touched a red blinking dot on STELA's small digital screen. "That's the Bird of Paradise. If we can see her, she can see us. They know where we are. What they don't know is that Rucker is dead and I'm helping you. The thing to do is create the diversion in the moments before we enter the ship's main hatch."

"We'll contact Belosto-One and have her send down twenty water skippers," Woody said. "The ocean is calm, which means the ice sheet hasn't fallen. Water skippers can move fast. That'll keep a significant number of the Strelitzia's soldiers busy figuring out what the hell's going on."

"And then we fight our way to the command room," Sharon said.

Limmy traced a line from the entry hatch through a hallway to their target. "If we move fast to take out the three escort soldiers, we might be able to get to the command room before the Strelitzia."

"That makes four of us against three of them, plus surprise on our side." Federico latched the medical kit. "I like our odds." He got up and stored the kit.

"All right. Let's call Dale on a secure frequency and fill her in on the plan." Woody drew frequency numbers onto the STELA and pressed the audio-comm. "Dale, Dale, Dale. Woody here."

"Good to hear your voice," Dale answered. "You still okay down there?"

"Better than okay." Woody smiled. "We've got a new ally and a workable plan. But first, any word from JJ?"

"None," Dale said. "It's been radio silence on all frequencies."

"Dammit." Woody sighed. "Keep listening. The kid's got to be out there somewhere."

"We will. What's our plan?" Dale asked.

Woody scanned STELA's digital screen. "The Bird of Paradise has surfaced at $19^0 55' 5.39"$ N, $66^0 45' 9.5"$ W. Hover in the mesosphere at those coordinates. Prepare to launch twenty water skippers on my command."

"Roger that," Dale confirmed. "Then what?"

"Use the skippers to draw attention away from us while we make our way to the command room. Tell the pilots to fire if fired upon. But their goal should be to create confusion, not engage in a fight. Just yet. Once we take control of the ship. I'll order you to land Belosto-One inside the Bird of Paradise. Then, if necessary, we fight for our ship."

"We're at the ready," Dale said. "Waiting to finally be home."

Woody smiled. "Yeah, me too. Over."

The audio-comm cut out.

"Where the hell could JJ be?" Federico asked. "I'm really worried."

"Remember Pigeon Pam?" Woody asked.

"How could I forget?" Federico scratched his goatee. "JJ eluded not only us, but the Banditti and a tribe of Yēxìng for months in order to keep that silly pigeon alive. And he was only six years old."

"Is that how you met him?" Sharon asked.

"Yeah, his blood family is Banditti," Woody answered. "When he found a pigeon with a broken wing, his family wanted to eat it. So he ran away with the bird. He'd figured out how to sneak into our hideout at the Goldfinch bar in Chicago."

"The kid was stealing from our food stores every night," Federico added. "Took us forever to catch the little thief. Fortunately for him, and Pam, we caught him before the Banditti or Yěxìng. That pigeon lived another five blissful years, perched on JJ's shoulder the whole time."

"Now JJ's part of our family." Woody squeezed Federico's hand. "If anyone can stay on the run, it's him. We'll find him."

"Look!" Limmy jutted his chin at the bow window. "There she is, the Bird of Paradise."

At the horizon, an enormous fifty-story iron flower floated on the ocean. Her oblong hull supported a tall mast with solar panels that flared off of what looked like a secondary hull. She was painted in bright red, orange, yellow, and green.

"She looks like a floating diva." Sharon marveled at the magnificent ship.

"A queen," Federico agreed.

"We have to dive." Woody tapped out commands. "It's time to rescue Eve and our ship."

Black Sea Devil Twelve slipped below the surface.

From the black sea devil's port window, Sharon saw a long, stem-like structure drop from the flower's main hull, reaching deep under water. It widened at the bottom, she assumed for ballast. Thread-like structures spread out, rooting the flower's base.

"How does the ship work?" Sharon asked.

"We're headed toward the stem." Woody studied the ship's schematic displayed on the OVA. "The main body of the ship is connected to it. That's where all of the controls and ballast tanks are located. It's also the main living quarters that can be used whether she's above or below the surface. The mast has sails, or petals, that double as solar panels."

Federico pointed at the secondary hull. "That's the flower's main petal. It's community space where we gather together when the ship is above the surface."

"How does she dive?" Sharon asked. "With such a surprising shape?"

"The flower closes and the ballast tanks adjust to allow the entire ship to drop deep below the surface."

"It's incredible." Sharon shook her head. "I've never seen or read about such a massive ship."

"She's a floating city with plenty of open space. I can't wait to introduce you to her once we free her and Eve." Woody looked at Limmy. "Call in our arrival. After that, I'll give Dale the order to launch the skippers."

Limmy tapped in a frequency and pressed the audio-comm. "This is Black Sea Devil Twelve, ready to come aboard."

"Roger that," a voice answered. "Opening the port hatch now and sending an escort. I'll inform the Strelitzia of your arrival. You are to report at once to the command room."

"Understood. Over," Limmy said.

Nodding, Woody tapped in a different frequency and pressed the audio-comm. "Dale, Dale, Dale. This is Woody."

"Go Woody," Dale answered.

"Drop the skippers." Woody's voice was strong and steady. "Be ready to board."

"On your command. Over," Dale said.

"Let's get ready." Federico got up and strapped on a holster and checked the energy level of the spectraletto. "She's in the green." He grabbed another weapon, checked it, and tossed it to Woody.

To Limmy, Sharon said, "I need my hammer and pack."

Limmy got up and unlocked the cabinet. "All yours." He moved aside.

Sharon fished out her hammer and the backpack. She tucked her hammer into its baldric, and slung the pack onto her shoulders. The adrenaline surging in her veins masked the pain from the many injuries inflicted on her over the past several days. She'd rest and heal when Eve was safely in her arms.

Federico handed her a spectraletto and holster. "You're going to need one of these too."

She took it from him, used her pack strap to secure the holster at her chest, and double-checked the energy level in the weapon. "Let's do this."

Gripping a spectraletto, Woody swiped commands with her free hand.

As they got closer, a section of the giant stem large enough for Black Sea Devil 12 to glide through opened. Light illuminated the murky water. Woody guided the craft inside. The hatch closed. An electronic beeping sound surrounded them.

"What does the signal mean?" Sharon steadied herself as the shuttle sloshed inside the hatch compartment.

"Water is about to be flushed," Federico answered. "So the compartment can repressurize."

"Be ready," Limmy warned. "They'll come in at once. We've got to let them get inside before we attack. Pull their asses into this shuttle, if you have to. Know that they're ruthless men."

Water dropped past the windows. The compartment whooshed and clinked. A buzzer sound replaced the beeping.

"Here they come." Limmy planted himself in front of the door as it slid open.

Sharon, Woody, and Federico hid to the side, spectralettos at the ready.

"Soldiers, I'll need your help," Limmy said. "The prisoners are not cooperative." He moved aside.

Three soldiers stormed into the shuttle.

Limmy fired on the one closest to him.

The other two raised their weapons, but were dropped by Woody's and Federico's lasers before getting off a shot.

Woody holstered her spectraletto and pulled her jacket closed over it. "Limmy, make a good show for the ship's cameras. Keep your weapon pointed at our backs. We'll keep ours concealed. Let's go!"

As they raced along a labyrinth of empty corridors, a siren started to wail. Red lights in the ceiling flashed.

Limmy halted at a doorway. "That's the 'all hands on deck' emergency signal. Be ready."

"Our Dale, right on time to cause a much-needed diversion," Federico said.

Frenzied shouting and the firing of spectralettos joined the cacophony of sirens.

"Get us in there." Woody banged a fist on the command room door. "I'm guessing my fingerprint's been scrubbed from the system. Listen to me, all three of you. Take clean shots. I prefer that you take out the two soldiers without destroying my command room in the process."

Boom, boom!

"Dammit!" Woody yelled. "They're firing the ship's laser cannons at our water skippers. Get me in that room, now!"

"I'll draw them close to the door." Limmy's words spilled out quickly. "Here we go." He pressed the audio-comm at the door. "Major White, this is Sergeant Limmy. I have the prisoners. I need your help securing them, though. They killed Rucker and the escorts."

"We're on our way!" a voice responded. "The ship's under attack."

Woody nodded to Sharon and Federico.

Sharon slipped to the left side of the door. Federico went to the right.

Woody turned to Limmy, "Make it look like you're struggling to hold me. It'll draw their attention away from Federico and Sharon."

Limmy put his arm around Woody, pulled her to him, and held his weapon to her head.

The door hissed open.

The two soldiers poured from the door. Sharon shot the first in the back. As he fell, Federico wheeled around, shooting the second in the chest.

Woody pulled free from Limmy. "Get them out of the way, and let's go."

Limmy and Federico each dragged a body from the doorway.

Woody motioned for her crew to follow her inside the command room.

Sharon, Federico and Limmy trailed her into the spacious room with OVAs on every wall. An enormous command desk and STELA were lit up with screens showing satellite images; pictures of the inside and outside of the ship; GPS coordinates;

weather; biometrics; and a slew of other measurements Sharon didn't understand.

"Get that door locked." Woody pointed at Limmy. "And scrub the fingerprints from it. I don't want anyone else in this room." She rushed to the command seat and ran her palms over one of the STELA's digital screens. "How I've missed you, my ship."

"What do we do next?" Sharon's heart raced. She was so close to finding Eve. "I'm ready."

Woody patted the seat next to hers. "Sit." She pressed the audio-comm button. "This is Dr. Wilhelmina Woodhouse. I command the Bird of Paradise. In a few minutes, you will be surrounded by my army. I invite you to surrender and join us. If you're willing to live by our Qaunik code, you will be spared. Should you decide otherwise, you'll be allowed to leave the ship unharmed. If you fight us, we will fight back to the death." Woody flipped a series of switches.

Cameras relayed images from the inside of the ship. The screens monitoring the hallways showed weary men, women, and children spilling from their rooms.

"They look scared," Federico said.

Woody nodded and hit the audio-comm button again. "I repeat, you will not be harmed if you surrender. You'll no doubt be better off in every way." She tapped in a frequency. "Dale, Dale, Dale, Woody here."

"This is Dale, go." Her voice sounded strained.

"What's happening out there?" Woody asked.

"Our water-skipper pilots and crew seem to have overwhelmed the Strelitzia's soldiers. No one's firing anymore. Unfortunately, we lost two vessels."

Woody bowed her head at the news. "Go on."

Dale continued. "The majority of the Strelitzia's soldiers are either dead, in custody, or hiding."

"Okay." Woody lifted her head. "Bring Belosto-One down to the surface of the ocean. You did great work." Woody held up five fingers. "The Bird of Paradise's main deck hatch will open in five minutes. Come aboard. Do not fire unless fired upon. Those civil-

252

ians who surrender should be collected in the holding bay. Give them food and water. Fight any resistance at all costs."

Federico sketched a command on the STELA. "Main deck hatch opening in five."

"How will you feed all those people?" Sharon asked.

"I don't know." Woody's jaw clenched. "That's a worry for another day."

The OVA on the left wall flashed on, and the Strelitzia gazed out from it. The bird-like mask hid his face, but accented his evil. "Call off your dogs, Wilhelmina." Bound at their wrists, Eve and JJ knelt in front of him.

"No," Federico gasped. "Not my boy."

The Strelitzia smirked. "Guess Sharon isn't the only one with someone to lose." He grabbed a handful of JJ's hair and yanked his head up.

One of JJ's eyes was swollen shut, and the hair on the left side of his face was caked with blood. "I'm okay," his voice rasped.

"He'll be the first to go if you don't exit that command room and get the fuck off my ship." The Strelitzia shook JJ's head by the hair.

Eve twisted and pressed a shoulder to JJ's as if trying to comfort him.

The Strelitzia shoved them apart and stepped forward between them.

"It's not your command room," Woody said. "And it sure as hell isn't your ship."

"Why don't you ask your father about that?" the Strelitzia asked. "Oh wait, he's a fraud like you. And dead." His eyes flicked to Sharon. "Why don't you ask your new fucking guru where she got the idea to build the Bird of Paradise?"

"It was always my father's idea." Woody's voice was calm.

"The rewriting of history." The Strelitzia crossed his arms over his chest. "According to Wilhelmina Woodhouse. A fraud in a bleeding heart's clothing."

"Stop!" Federico yelled. "You're not getting this ship."

"No?" The Strelitzia cocked his head. "Opera man." He turned and kicked JJ in the stomach. "Well, then some people are going to die with me."

"Leave him alone!" Sharon shot back.

Eve lifted her head. Her eyes betrayed exhaustion and something Sharon had never seen in them before. Defeat.

The Strelitzia yanked Eve from her knees onto her back.

With his wrists bound, JJ bent and tried to help Eve into a sitting position.

"No one else has to die today." The Strelitzia's voice softened. "To make that happen, all you have to do is give me my ship and the secret to the apples. I'll even make you a deal. You, Sharon, and Eve can stay on. We'll do great things together."

Sharon let the image of Eve wash over her. She was why Sharon's heart still beat after so much loss. She glanced at Limmy, remembering what he'd confessed about his wife. Now he wanted redemption. So did Sharon. Maybe in order to be redeemed, her inevitable end must come. But she couldn't let it be the end for Eve, Woody, Federico, JJ, Inu, Annie, or Erik. They all had to go on.

But Sharon had a question for Woody. "Why didn't you take what's in my backpack? You had plenty of opportunities."

Woody locked eyes with Sharon. "What belongs to you isn't mine to take."

"Silence!" The Strelitzia stormed forward. "You arrogant hypocrite. You're no different from me. We bulk up in groups and take sides. Humans can't escape their tribal instincts." He directed a long, bony finger at Woody. "Not me, and not you."

"We can evolve," Federico said. "If we hope to survive, we have to."

"Oh, god." The Strelitzia laughed. "The preachy opera guy speaks. Stick to singing. You're much better at it." He regarded Sharon. "And you. You and me, we are as alike as two humans can be."

"No!" Sharon shook her head. "I'm nothing like you."

"Oh really?" The Strelitzia snickered. "Every day, people all around you starved to death. Yet!" He poked a finger skyward.

"You and Eve squirreled away the secret to your apple tree. Not once did you think of sharing it with a starving and desperate world. No. You looked after you and yours. I actually admire that. How many people have you killed or maimed along the way to keeping your secret?"

"Too many to count." Sharon gazed on the image of Eve, trying to remember every touch and sweet moment.

An alarm sounded on STELA. Woody pressed the "A" icon. Words scrolled across the OVA on the far wall. THE WEST ANTARCTIC ICE SHEET HAS FALLEN. THE EXTINCTION WAVE WARNING HAS BEEN ISSUED FOR ALL COASTLINES ON EARTH.

"Time is wasting!" The Strelitzia backed up even with Eve and JJ. He pulled a spectraletto from his flowery robe. "I need to be inside that command room. We've got to dive the ship into the deep if she's to survive the coming monster wave." He pointed the weapon at JJ. "Now! Or I'll kill him."

"No!" Woody yelled.

"That got through to the ice queen." He reared forward and slammed the butt of the gun into JJ's head.

JJ crumpled.

Eve threw herself protectively over him.

The Strelitzia holstered the spectraletto. "Don't doubt for a second the things I'm capable of doing. Remember poor lovely Areva? I will do what needs to be done." He reached behind the bird mask and lifted it from his face.

Sharon stumbled backward. Shock sliced her in two. "You bastard! That's how—" She groped for her voice.

"How I knew everything," Dr. Ryan said as he pressed the audio-com button on the wall behind him. "Except your secret." Without the mask, his voice was no longer electronically modified. "Your underground growing room is quite impressive. But even with the tracking chip in your shoulder, one planted in the medicine case, a pack of Banditti, and kidnapping your wife, I still could not get my hands on it. Now is the day you give your secret to me. Open the box." He bent, grabbed Eve's hair and yanked. "Or I'm going to kill Eve and JJ. Just like I did Areva."

"Don't do it, Sharon," Eve whimpered. "I'm begging you. I'd rather die than see such evil have what we created."

Sharon fumbled in the backpack for the box. She yanked it free and broke the lock with her hammer.

Tears filled Eve's eyes. "I love you. But please, don't give it to him."

Dr. Ryan pulled Eve's hair. "Shut up."

Sharon turned the box around and lifted the lid. Her eyes moistened, but she steadied herself. "There's so much more than the secret to the apple tree in this box." She lifted a vial. "The apple tree's genetic material." She riffled through hundreds of tiny packets. "And heirloom seeds collected over the decades by my family. Everything from vegetables, to herbs and fruits from all over the world. Most aren't viable. But what Eve discovered is that the apple's genetic material can revive them. Given a little time, what's in this box will feed every person on this ship, and then some."

She removed her satchel from the pack, fished out her last apple and placed it on the command desk. "Lots more genetic material can be extracted from this one perfect apple." She closed the lid and slid the box across the command desk to Woody. "I want you and the Qaunik to have it, in exchange for a black sea devil. I'm going home with my wife."

"Of course." Woody's eyes bore into Sharon's as if trying to read her mind.

Sharon turned to Eve's image on the OVA. "Tell me I did the right thing."

"Yes, you did." Eve closed her eyes and smiled. "Thank you, my love."

"You just signed your wife's death sentence," Dr. Ryan growled. "You might make it back to your charred farm, but she won't."

"If you kill Eve, you'll have signed yours too," Sharon said. "But I have another option for you—my so-called friend."

"I'm listening." Dr. Ryan put a foot to Eve's back and pushed her onto JJ.

Seeing him shove Eve filled her body with pain and rage. *Keep your head.* "Spare JJ, and the three of us will escape. Eve, you, and me." The words tasted like acid. "It's either that, or I kill you. Awful and slow."

"Do I look stupid?" Dr. Ryan spit out his words. "If I go with you, you'll kill me the first chance you get. I'd have to sleep with one eye open for the rest of my life."

"Have you forgotten why we shared our apples with you in the first place?" Sharon asked. "Neither Eve nor I know how to make her cancer treatment from the Sprucanidone when her supplies run out. As much as I'd like to kill you, I need you alive to keep Eve alive."

Dr. Ryan straightened his spine, and did not speak for several long seconds. "All right. Have your guru ready a black sea devil for launch from the surface deck in five minutes. That's how long it will take me to drag your wife there. Plus, we don't have time to finagle with an underwater launch. You keep remembering for the both of us, Sharon, that if I die, she dies." He tugged Eve to her feet and drew his spectraletto. Pressing the muzzle to her temple, he shuffled Eve out of the room.

Woody wrapped her arms around Sharon, and whispered quickly into her ear, "Take what you need. But I hope this is a trick. Because I vouch you and Eve in. You're one of us. But you've got to hurry. I've got eighteen minutes, tops, before I have to submerge the Bird of Paradise. The Extinction Wave is coming. We need to be deep in the abyss when it gets here."

Sharon held Woody tight. "Tell me you can synthesize a leukemia treatment from Sprucanidone."

"In my sleep." Woody pulled back and gripped Sharon by the arms. "What are you planning?"

"To give that bastard, Ryan, something to think about other than Eve long enough for us to escape. How do I sink a black sea devil?"

"Blow the ballasts, trim to port, and haul ass out of the starboard-side emergency exit hatch. Look for the applicable icons on STELA. Once the ballasts start to fill with water, the shuttle will sink low enough for water to start spilling into the cockpit from the open emergency hatch. Get out of there before it fills completely. If you don't, you're down with the ship when it sinks like a rock. You'll have maybe two minutes to escape. We'll be waiting on the surface to fish you out." Woody glanced at the clock. "We're down to sixteen minutes. With or without you, I have to dive this ship. Otherwise, everyone on board will die. Now go." She bumped her forehead to Sharon's. "Thank you, for everything."

Sharon wheeled around and raced toward the upper deck.

Sharon stood in front of the open hatch of a lone black sea devil. An ominous breeze ruffled the collar of her jacket, foretelling things to come. Somewhere, out on the vast stretch of ocean, a fiendish wave grew more colossal with each second, hell-bent on swallowing the world whole.

Dr. Ryan emerged from a door to the deck. He held Eve close, keeping the muzzle of a spectraletto pressed to her temple. "Show me your hands."

Sharon lifted her empty palms. It took every ounce of willpower not to run to Eve. If things went wrong, she might never get to touch her again. No matter what, though, if they did go wrong, only one, maybe two more people would die today. She wouldn't let Eve be one of them. Because with Eve and Woody, the Qaunik would survive. They both understood that nature held the answers to humanity's endurance. Eve had to go on. But today was Sharon's day of redemption. She'd leave nothing to chance. Whatever move she made needed to ensure, with finality, that Eve would live and Ryan would die. If that meant giving her own life, so be it. It surprised her, not to be scared. Only sad.

"Get in." Dr. Ryan gestured to the open shuttle.

Sharon smiled at Eve and ached to hold and kiss her. She turned and went inside, taking a quick glance at the STELA to identify the locations of the ballast and trim icons. *There.* She noted the direction of the handle on the starboard emergency exit. She sat in the seat closest to starboard.

Dr. Ryan pushed Eve into the seat next to Sharon, then seated himself in the command seat.

"I've missed you so much," Eve murmured. "I knew you'd come for me."

Sharon breathed in Eve's scent. Their shoulders touched. It felt like heaven to be so close to her again. She heard Eve's breathing. *Soon, soon.*

"Shall we?" Keeping the weapon pointed into Eve's torso, Dr. Ryan tapped out commands. The black sea devil's thrusters whirred to life, lifting the shuttle enough to clear the deck railing.

With his left hand, Dr. Ryan moved the throttle forward and eased the shuttle away from the ship and into the water.

The shuttle bobbed and righted.

Sharon lunged toward the STELA and jammed a finger at the ballast icon, then the portside trim. She yanked the emergency hatch handle upward as the shuttle rolled ninety degrees to port and dropped lower into the water.

"What the fuck are you doing?" Dr. Ryan dropped the spectraletto and fumbled at the STELA. "Goddammit, you're sinking us."

Sharon seized Eve's waist and hoisted her upright.

Water poured in through the open hatch.

Dr. Ryan splashed through the water, groping for the weapon he'd dropped.

"We've got to go." Sharon kissed Eve's neck and hugged her tight. "Swim hard. I'll be right behind you." She helped Eve clamber over the STELA toward the opening.

The black sea devil sank lower as water filled in up to their waists.

"I love you. Now go!" Sharon shouted.

Eve touched her cheek. "My Sharon." She turned and with Sharon's help hoisted herself through the opening where a sliver of clear sky beckoned.

Sharon reached for the rim of the opening to pull herself through. A searing pain tore into her left arm. She fell and splashed into the quickly rising water. Blood from her arm clouded the water. She glanced at it, relieved that the spectraletto had only grazed her bicep.

Dr. Ryan climbed onto her, shoving her face underwater.

She wrapped her arms around him and rolled. As he strained against her, she dug her fingers into a pressure point on his neck.

He thrashed, and went limp.

Sharon shot to the surface. The water was up to her shoulders. She kicked hard toward the hatch. Something snagged the back of her jacket. She thrashed about to free herself. The water rose to her chin. She took a deep breath and twisted around, trying to find what held her in place. Her chest ached to inhale. She straightened to catch another breath. But the water was too high now. She couldn't reach what little breathing space was left in the shuttle. She shook her head, trying to stay conscious.

Small bubbles slipped from her lips. An urge to inhale threatened her resolve to keep her head. She reached again behind her, flailing. Her ears popped. She noticed her peripheral vision blackening. *Too tired.* More bubbles of air escaped her mouth.

Time seemed to slow with the shutting down of her oxygen-deprived body. She watched daylight continue to disappear as seawater snuffed out the cockpit's remaining airspace. The water of the Atlantic Ocean was so much clearer compared to the algae-clogged Pacific. She'd ask Woody about that someday. *Someday isn't coming.* She stopped struggling in order to take in the last fragments of consciousness before dying.

A smile spread across her face. Her mom was there with arms held open wide. Elliot and her father laughed together in a lush field of summer corn. Jon and Mark beckoned for her to follow them in a game of hide-and-seek through the orchard.

Eve. A million memories played out in a medley of images in her head. Some beautiful, some terrible. But every one of them, every single one, had been worth it. Sharon closed her eyes and let peace usher her to the end.

But that fucking gorilla. It pounded on her chest, not letting her go to sleep. It danced and hopped on top of her, relentlessly. Her chest burned and ached.

Please. She heard Inu's voice in her head. Something tugged at her. *Come back to us.* Lips touched her cheek. She breathed in the scent of Eve. A dog barked. *Erik.* Nausea bubbled in her belly. She bolted upright, throwing up sea water in between gasps.

"Welcome back, *amiga.*" Federico smiled. His wet hair and clothing clung to him. "We got you and Eve in the nick of time."

"I'm not dead." Sharon wiped her mouth with her sleeve and let her eyes adjust. She lay inside a closed launch room aboard the Bird of Paradise. Eve, Limmy, and Federico knelt at her side.

"No." Federico grinned. "You most certainly are not. We only had forty-five seconds to spare. But we got you, *amiga.* We're all safe now. Woody put the ship into a deep dive. Down here in the Milwaukee Depth, the Extinction Wave can't touch us." He nodded at Limmy. "He brought you back with CPR."

"You were the gorilla on my chest." She laughed at the irony. "Thank you."

"It's the least I could do." Limmy moved aside, making room for Eve.

Eve bent and put her lips to Sharon's. "I love you."

Sharon felt reborn with her wife's perfect kiss. "And I love you." She wrapped her arms tight around Eve.

"Woody, Woody, Woody," Federico spoke into an acupalmtell. "We got them both. Safe and sound."

"Great news!" Woody's voice beamed through the acupalmtell. "Tell Sharon and Eve their family can't wait to see them. JJ, Inu, Annie, Erik, and me, especially."

Sharon inhaled the scent of Eve. Such a subtle, unmistakable fragrance: like sassafras, clean and slightly resinous.

Epilogue

Sharon maneuvered the black sea devil through the narrow, craggy passage of Neptune's Bellows into Port Foster. The watery caldera of Deception Island was calm. With summer temperatures on the Antarctic Peninsula and the South Shetland Islands averaging 20⁰ C, only a tuft of snow remained atop Mount Pond.

"This was the perfect place to try to grow an apple tree outside of the Bird of Paradise." Eve put a hand to Sharon's back. "Assuming the nutrient compound I put together works. Even if it doesn't, I love our time in this little hideaway."

"Me too. Hell, I love all of Antarctica. The last unspoiled place on Earth." Sharon smiled and drove the vessel up onto the sandy shore below the rise of Mount Kirkwood. "I think our little tree will too. It's the most protected place near the peninsula." She powered down the black sea devil and opened its hatch. Sunlight poured in.

Inu flipped up his seat restraint. "Come, Erik." He scrambled through the open hatch.

The dog barked and chased after him, his tail wagging in circles.

Sharon stood and held out her hands to Eve, pulling her up. "They've only been in each other's lives for less than a year. Now our son and dog are inseparable." She wrapped her arms around her wife. "You were right all along."

"About what?" Eve put her hands to Sharon's face. "That I have impeccable taste in wives?"

"Besides that." Sharon smiled.

"Tell me."

"Just before the Strelitzia took you from me that day in Boston." Sharon pressed her hands to Eve's. "You told me we'd be okay. Deep down I didn't believe it. But here we are in this safe and beautiful place with a family of our own. We belong to a group of people who are the best hope for humanity's survival. We're more than okay."

"Yes, we are, my darling. Because we're in this together." Eve kissed Sharon. "All of us."

About the Author

Bev's road to the place she calls home has been long and winding. Born in the mountains of the West, raised in the Midwest, and educated in the South, she's been a sergeant in the United States Air Force, a scientist, and an environmental lawyer. She's traveled to the Arctic, Antarctica, and lots of places in between. But home is writing stories at the edge of a meadow in Maine where she shares her life with her spouse of twenty-seven years, a clever calico cat, and a couple of honeybee colonies.

Acknowledgments

I started the research for 2^0 while on a trip to Antarctica in December, 2013. Dirty Bird is the name we gave to a scrappy little chinstrap penguin hell-bent on building its nest in a terrible location. Instead of a dry spot free from snow or ice in springtime, Dirty Bird was relegated to the muddy outer edges of the nesting colony. The penguin's otherwise white belly was covered in brown muck. The ornithologist on our expedition explained that rising temperatures on the Antarctic Peninsula were bringing more snowfall, thereby decreasing suitable nesting locations for a variety of penguins. Dirty Bird was undeterred. Like that gutsy penguin, those of us who care about making a difference in the fight to protect Earth as we know it should also be undeterred. 2^0 is for Dirty Bird and all of Earth's wild ones. Thanks for inspiring me to write this story, and to be a better human.

Much thanks also goes to those friends and family who encourage and support my writing journeys. Thanks to Martha for teaching me about submarines. Thanks to Elizabeth Sims for making me a better writer. For Amy, Tracy, Claudia and Phil, thanks for always being interested in whatever is my latest writing project. Thanks to Quark Expeditions for the awesome trip to Antarctica. I'm grateful to those readers who spare me their time and resources to take a chance on my stories. It humbles me. A huge thanks to Bywater Books for giving 2^0 a home. I'm honored to join the family.

Finally, to KC and Lilliput, you bring me the greatest joy—thanks for loving me.

COMPASS **ROSE**

**In the year 2513, the only thing higher than the seas
is what's at stake for those who sail them.**

Rose was born facing due north, with an inherent perception of cardinal points flowing through her veins. Her uncanny sense of direction earns her a coveted job within the Archipelago Fleet, but it also attracts the attention of Admiral Comita, who sends her on a secret mission deep into pirate territory.

Aboard the mercenary ship, Man o' War, Rose joins a ragtag crew under the command of Miranda, a captain as alluring as she is bloodthirsty. Rose quickly learns that trusting the wrong person could get her killed—and Miranda's crew have no desire to make anything easy for her. If Rose is going to survive the mission, she's going to have to learn to navigate more than ruthless pirates, jealous crewmates, swarms of deadly jellyfish, and a host of other underwater perils. Above all, she's going to need a strategy to resist Miranda's magnetic pull.

Compass Rose
Paperback   978-1-61294-119-6
eBook   978-1-61294-120-2

Bywater
BOOKS

www.bywaterbooks.com

Bywater BOOKS

At Bywater Books we love good books about lesbians just like you do, and we're committed to bringing the best of contemporary lesbian writing to our avid readers. Our editorial team is dedicated to finding and developing outstanding writers who create books you won't want to put down.

We sponsor the Bywater Prize for Fiction to help with this quest. Each prize winner receives $1,000 and publication of their novel. We have already discovered amazing writers like Jill Malone, Sally Bellerose, and Hilary Sloin through the Bywater Prize. Which exciting new writer will we find next?

For more information about Bywater Books and the annual Bywater Prize for Fiction, please visit our website.

www.bywaterbooks.com